BLOOD REUNION

Blood Destiny Series, Book 10

Connie Suttle

SubtleDemon Publishing, LLC

To Walter, Joe, Larry, Lee, Dianne, Sarah and Mark.
Thank you.

Acknowledgements

As always, this book is the result of collaboration. If it weren't for the support of my editor, my cover artist and my beta readers, it would be less than it is. All mistakes, as usual, are mine and no other's.

About the Author:

Connie Suttle lives in Oklahoma with her husband and a conglomerate of cats. They have finally banded together to make their demands, which has proven disconcerting to all humans involved.

You may find Connie in the following ways:
Facebook: Connie Suttle Author
Twitter: @subtledemon
Website and Blog: subtledemon.com

Other books by Connie Suttle:

Blood Destiny Series:
Blood Wager
Blood Passage
Blood Sense
Blood Domination
Blood Royal
Blood Queen
Blood Rebellion
Blood War
Blood Redemption

Blood Reunion
* * *

Legend of the Ir'Indicti Series:
Bumble
Shadowed
Target
Vendetta
Destroyer
* * *

High Demon Series:
Demon Lost
Demon Revealed
Demon's King
Demon's Quest
Demon's Revenge
Demon's Dream
* * *

God Wars Series:
Blood Double
Blood Trouble
Blood Revolution
Blood Love
Blood Finale
* * *

Saa Thalarr Series:
Hope and Vengeance
Wyvern and Company
Observe and Protect*
* * *

First Ordinance Series:

Finder
Keeper
BlackWing
SpellBreaker
WhiteWing
* * *

R-D Series:
Cloud Dust
Cloud Invasion
Cloud Rebel
* * *

Latter Day Demons Series:
Hot Demon in the City
A Demon's Work is Never Done
A Demon's Due
* * *

Seattle Elementals Series:
Your Money's Worth
Worth Your While*
* * *

BlackWing Pirates Series
MindSighted
MindMage
MindRogue*
* * *

Black Rose Sorceress Series
The Rose Mark
Rose and Thorn*

Other Titles from SubtleDemon Publishing:

Malefactor
Transgressor*
by Joe Scholes

*Forthcoming

*T*off was seventeen and his life was in ruins. He didn't look seventeen or anywhere near that age. Twelve was closer to the mark; his height and face worked against him. The others teased him mercilessly about it, although he kept up easily in his work and lessons.

Today was one of the bad days. Toff jumped into the chilly pond with the others after a long day of harvesting grapes, throwing off his clothing just as the others did. The boys he swam with were all proud of what they had between their legs.

Toff didn't have that. Had never had that. The word *eunuch* had been whispered around him since he was old enough to work in the fields during the summer and early fall. At first, he hadn't known what the word meant. Toff had learned, however, and the revelation embarrassed him. He was less than the others.

"It's nothing," his mother, Redbird, told him when he came home in tears at age nine. At the time, it hadn't mattered so much. Now it did. The boys his age would pair up at times with one of the girls, and they'd go off together, down by the pond or into one of the orchards. Toff saw their smiles as they returned.

The older boys didn't hold back their sneers or taunts either, whenever they caught Toff looking their way. Of course, they never did it around the elders—they knew better. Toff's persecution was always done away from anyone who might intervene.

"Mother, tell me again what I am," Toff sat dejectedly at the kitchen table while his mother worked to finish dinner.

"You're Vionnu—from Vionn. That's where I adopted you, my son," Redbird smiled at him. She was beautiful— most of her race was. Redbird had hair the color of maple leaves in the fall. Her hair color had given her the name—she was of the Briar Clan and Tiearan, her father, was Head of the Green Fae settlement.

Redbird's skin was clear and youthful in appearance, her eyes a vibrant green. She had power, just as the other Green Fae and their Half-Fae children did, and that was something else Toff would never have.

Redbird's race was a small one—they called themselves Green Birth, a branch of Fae that ate no meat and didn't engage in any form of physical violence. They often married into the mortal races, though, and now lived alongside many Half-Fae and their all-humanoid relations. Their small village had grown during Toff's short life and now held nearly two thousand members, most of them humanoid.

Chapter 1

"Are all Vionnu like me?" Toff had asked this question before, but Redbird always said she didn't know.

"My son, you know I do not have an answer to that question," she tousled his straight, dark hair before setting plates on the square table in their tidy kitchen.

Lengths of tied garlic hung beside the stove, and tightly sealed jars of herbs and spices stood in neat rows upon the counters. Toff's adoptive father, Corent River, often set Toff to sanding and polishing the wood countertops. Corent was Half-Fae, but he had power, just as the other Half-Fae did. Toff only had the strength of his hands, which was another reason he was often teased and humiliated.

Toff's first memories of Corent had been of the Half-Fae's hands—they were large and gentle when he showed Toff how to sand the wood or smooth the stones set in the floor of Toff's bedroom. Corent had built the addition to the house that became Toff's bedroom when Toff turned thirteen.

"Old enough to have a room to himself," Corent had smiled at Redbird and took Toff to select trees to cut for the wood.

"What were the Vionnu like?" Toff was still attempting to obtain information about the planet of his birth as he took a seat at the table. Idly he traced the edge of the blue plate Redbird set before him.

"Like many other races. No more questions; I must finish dinner. Your father will be home soon." Redbird turned her back on him and busied herself at the stove.

Corent came in moments later, his hair a dark blue, which meant the sun was still shining in a clear sky outside. Corent's hair, like that of a handful of Green Fae, changed with the weather. It became a light blue-green if the skies were overcast or gloomy. Deep blue meant a sunny sky outside. Toff had learned to look to his adoptive father's hair as the barometer for the outside climate.

"Son, how was the grape harvest?" Corent smiled at Toff.

"Good, Father." Toff wanted to smile back, but he was too depressed to make the attempt.

"Child, what's wrong?" Corent always knew, even if Redbird brushed it off.

"Nothing, Father." Toff looked down at his plate.

"Have you washed your hands yet?"

"No."

"Then come with me."

Corent didn't scold Toff for not washing his hands before sitting at the table, as he normally would. "Son," he said, dipping his hands into the wash pan filled with clean water, "Don't compare yourself to the others. They know you're not what they are and they do this anyway. They won't grow sense for another ten years, if they grow any at all. I'm beginning to have my doubts about some of them. Tiearan says he may speak with the Queen."

Toff looked sharply at Corent. The Queen. Just the mention of her sent Redbird into hysterics. Redbird was afraid of the Queen. Toff had only seen the Queen from a distance—Redbird had taught him to stay away.

"She'll drink your blood!" Redbird hissed at him once, outside Corent's hearing. Toff had no idea what his foster-mother meant when she'd given him that warning.

"What will the Queen do?" Toff asked as he moved to take Corent's place at the wash pan. Corent dried his hands as Toff reached for the soap and dipped his fingers in the

Chapter 1

water. He'd almost whispered his words; Toff didn't want his foster-mother to hear him say anything about the Queen.

"She'll come and take a look for herself. If they're not suitable to stay, she'll send them away. The Queen gave this land to us to settle on, since we were forced away from Vionn. We're here through her generosity. If those young ones with no power fail to follow the laws, they won't be allowed to remain on Le-Ath Veronis." Toff watched as the deep blue of Corent's hair turned a lighter shade. Clouds must be coming in.

"Where will they go, Father, if the Queen sends them away?" Toff asked as he accepted the towel from Corent to dry his hands.

"No idea. That will be the Queen's worry, not ours. My concern will be their parents—they don't watch them as closely as they should." Corent's eyebrows dipped in a frown.

"Gren's always been a bully," Toff muttered. Corent was lost in thought as he took the towel from Toff and hung it on its peg. He'd failed to hear Toff's words and Toff didn't repeat them. Silent now, they walked to the kitchen for dinner.

* * *

Toff combed his short, dark hair after a bath and readied himself for bed later. Honey-brown eyes examined his face in the mirror, searching for any sign of maturity. He still bore the full, rosy cheeks of a youngling instead of the more adult features Gren and the others wore so proudly.

Gren, Haldis and Sark teased him constantly, calling him baby cheeks and taunting him, then asking if he wanted to run crying to his mother when Toff became angry. Toff was helpless against them—Gren was Half-Fae and had power. Haldis and Sark were humanoid and didn't, but they stuck by Gren no matter what, laughing and encouraging the bully. Toff sighed and went to bed.

* * *

"Baby cheeks gets to crush grapes," Gren laughed the following morning as they made their way to the long, log building where Tiearan and some of the other adults instructed the young ones and made wine. "With the other babies," Gren couldn't help adding, although Tiearan and Rain had walked into the building.

Autumn sunlight shone through the wide doorway, but Toff stood back from the square of light, watching dust motes dance in the early morning sun. Corent was off with another crew, harvesting apples.

Trees were Corent's strength—he could make a tree grow in a tenth of the normal time and the fruit that grew on his trees was the best quality. He sent bushels of apples every year to the Queen's palace. Corent selected those himself and made sure they arrived in good condition.

Toff found himself wishing he could work with Corent. He didn't mind crushing grapes and wanted more than anything to do the other chores for winemaking, but he was always relegated to the crush. Gren constantly made Toff ashamed of his work, though Tiearan always said that any job well done was a credit to the worker.

Tiearan's long, gold hair was tied back that morning, and Rain's dark hair was tucked in a bun on top of her head. Rain was Corent's mother and always looked lovely. She seldom came to dinner at the house, though, and Toff often caught her throwing dark looks at Redbird. Toff had no idea why.

Chapter 1

"Young ones, follow me, we will get the crush underway immediately," Tiearan smiled. He enjoyed making wine and had done it for years uncounted. He put power into the making and the result was a heady mix, according to some. Toff was still too young to be allowed to drink it, although Gren always bragged that his parents let him have a glass now and then.

Gren and the other, taller boys hauled the stems away after the grapes had been gently crushed by the younger children. Toff liked dipping his hands into the grapes, feeling the smooth, round skins in his fingers, squeezing them lightly as Tiearan had taught him. Tiearan said that leaving the pulp in at this stage left more of the fruit taste for later.

Eventually, the crushed grapes would be run through a press that some of the older ones would crank by hand. Toff would miss that stage—he would be sent to the fields to help gather hay and straw for the animals and the barns.

School would also start in two or three weeks, depending upon the harvest. Redbird taught the younger ones—Toff had been in one of her classes when he was very small.

"I get to help Tiearan with the yeast," Gren sneered during lunch break. Tiearan employed power when he worked with the natural grape yeast, adjusting it here and there for consistent results. Tiearan was teaching Gren how to manipulate the natural yeast so the wine would turn out well.

Gren and the others who held Fae power attended additional classes that Toff would never experience. Toff and the others without power were sent off to help with this or that around the village, while the children with power were taught how to use what they had. It frustrated Toff greatly to be surrounded by something he could never do or lay claim to.

"Toff, ease up just a little, the grapes are not your enemy," Tiearan looked over Toff's shoulder as he squeezed the grapes harder than he'd intended. Toff's fingers were already stained and Redbird would have to use power later to clear it from his hands.

"Sorry, Father Tiearan." All the male Fae were called father, whether they were your father or not, while the female Fae were called mother. Toff had grown up with that and it was natural for him to address the Fae in that manner.

"We got these harvested just in time; frost is coming tomorrow," Rain came to stand beside Tiearan. Rain knew the weather in ways that none of the others could.

Toff had learned early on why Corent's hair predicted things—he'd gotten that from his Green Fae mother. Toff, on the other hand, couldn't predict anything. He felt that absence with a painful sharpness he couldn't describe.

Laral looked up at Toff as Tiearan and Rain moved away to supervise some of the younger ones. Laral had been Toff's friend, once—the best one he'd had—but nowadays, Laral stayed away from Toff.

Associating with Toff brought on Gren's brutality, in one way or another. As a Half-Fae, Laral held a bit of power, but he had nothing compared to that which Gren possessed. Gren often preened in front of the others, because he received more of Tiearan's attention than anyone else.

"I will be a winemaker one day, or help grow the trees," Gren had crowed to all of them on many occasions. The first time Gren bragged about growing the trees, Toff had snorted. It cost him a black eye and a bloody nose at the hands of Haldis and Sark.

Chapter 1

Gren wouldn't break the rule of nonviolence the Fae held—he just sent his humanoid bully buddies to do it for him. The humanoids didn't always adhere to the Fae edict, and occasional fights broke out. Usually, Tiearan settled things—he was their leader, too.

The humanoids in their village also ate meat, while the Fae didn't. Redbird didn't cook it, so Toff ate vegetables and grains with his foster family. He often smelled meat cooking on the human side of the village, however, and it smelled good. He just knew not to attempt to get any—Redbird would be offended and place another mind restraint. Toff hated those. His head would bother him for days afterward. She was always the one who did it, too. Corent never tried.

"It's for your own good," she always told him. "You have to follow the rules, just as everyone else does." Toff wanted to ask her at times why Gren, Haldis and Sark weren't held to those rules, but bit the words back before they could leave his mouth.

His foster parents cared for him, kept him clean, comfortable and well fed, even if they couldn't save him from Gren or his followers. Redbird told him too, that he was loved. She said she'd loved him from the moment Tiearan had placed him in her arms as a tiny babe. Toff knew he should be grateful that they'd taken him in. His parents must have been awful, to abandon him like that.

Nobody ever said he'd been abandoned, but what else might have happened? Toff had been deserted as a baby and Tiearan had picked him up and handed him to his daughter. Yes, Tiearan, Head of the Green Fae village was Redbird's father. Toff couldn't even speculate what might have happened to him if Tiearan hadn't come along.

* * *

Blood Reunion

"Mother Rain says it will frost in the morning," Toff announced after coming in from helping Father Willow mend a fence around the cattle barn. The Fae didn't eat meat, but they kept cows for the cheese and other things that could be made from the milk. Father Willow treated his cows better than he treated most people in Toff's opinion, but he didn't have much respect for many of those people, either.

"Then it'll frost." Corent had beaten Toff home by only a few moments. "Come on, let's clean up," Corent motioned for Toff to follow him to the porch where the wash pan was.

* * *

Father Willow was at the door early the next morning, knocking. Corent answered. Toff heard Father Willow's voice inside the house as he was dressing for work. Today, he was to help with the maple syrup making.

"Son, Father Willow's Lily got out again, and he needs your help to find her." Corent stood inside the door to Toff's room. Lily was Father Willow's best cow and had birthed twin calves many times. Father Willow fussed over her constantly. Toff sighed. This wasn't the first time he'd gone hunting Lily with Father Willow.

"I'm almost dressed, father," Toff replied, sitting on the edge of his bed to slip on his boots.

* * *

Toff waded through tall grass as he followed Father Willow toward the higher pastures. The cows grazed there through the summer, because the grasses grew thick and sweet. With cooler temperatures coming, the cows had all been corralled.

Chapter 1

Had the Green Fae settled farther south, they would have been at the equator and spent the entire year in warmer temperatures. Tiearan and the elders wished to raise trees that thrived in a more temperate zone. The maples were among those; therefore, the village had never been moved.

Part of the trade-off came in the hemisphere's extended daylight hours; Le-Ath Veronis spun on its side instead of its axis. The Green Fae used sunlight to enhance their power, so the constant sunlight enabled them to use power at any time. It also filled the precious crystals they employed to help accomplish their work.

An entire half of the planet lived in darkness, too, because of the planet's rotation. The Queen's palace was near the edge of that half and was in constant twilight—Toff had learned that in his geography lessons. He'd only seen a few of Le-Ath Veronis' inhabitants and he was very curious about them.

Redbird had forbidden him from speaking with any of the traders who came to the village. Toff couldn't imagine why speaking with the traders might be wrong—he'd watched them from a distance and they were always polite and accommodating.

"You think Lily headed in this direction?" Toff trotted through frost-covered pastures to keep up with Father Willow's longer legs.

"I think so. Lily didn't like the hay she got last night, so she's looking for green grass. She doesn't realize she won't find any by going in this direction." Father Willow tossed his answer over a shoulder and kept going.

The summer pasture was a good hour's walk from the village. Toff didn't mind the walk—it kept him away from Gren and the others.

Blood Reunion

They followed a well-worn trail to the summer field, hollowed into the dirt from years of cows passing back and forth over the same ground. The morning frost had turned the tall grass brown, Toff noticed, as they made their way past fields that now lay fallow, waiting for winter to pass and spring to come. Then plowing and planting would commence, just as it did every year.

Lily wasn't visible in the field when they arrived. Father Willow stood in the midmorning sunlight while mist rose from the ground around him. Warmer air had arrived after the brief frost, causing the frozen moisture to turn to mist. Father Willow shaded his eyes against the sun's glare as he searched for Lily.

"Toff, go east and check that stand of trees. I'll head in the other direction and see if I can find her." Father Willow began walking before he heard Toff's reply. Toff knew Father Willow was worried; he just didn't want to say that to Toff. Toff walked toward the designated stand of trees.

"Lily," Toff called, once he stepped under the branches of the first trees. Walking farther beneath the canopy, he called out again. A rustling noise came from a crowded stand of trees, deeper in the forest.

The small stand of trees Toff searched was only the beginning of a larger forest that stretched into the northern reaches of the planet, where it became so cold that only evergreens survived. Past that, it became too cold for anything to live.

Toff had heard tales of white foxes and snowy hares that lived in the evergreen forests, but he'd never had the opportunity to go and see these things for himself. He was kept busy for the most part and had never visited the capital

Chapter 1

city of Lissia or any of the other cities that dotted Le-Ath Veronis.

Redbird would likely prevent his going, even if he voiced his desires aloud. Toff caught the rustling noise again, so he called for the missing cow once more.

Father Willow was nearly half a mile away from Toff when he heard him scream, and then scream again. Willow turned and raced in Toff's direction.

Chapter 2

off was only half-conscious when he heard an unfamiliar voice—a woman's voice—saying strange things. "Don't let him die, please," she begged. "He's too young for the turn. You have to keep him alive." That voice was pleading with someone.

Toff was sliding back into unconsciousness when he felt cool hands on his face and even more hands on his badly beaten body. Toff knew he was hallucinating—he imagined that the hands he saw through eyes nearly swollen shut, were large and blue.

* * *

"You've had your chance, I think." The same woman's voice came again.

Blood Reunion

"But we had no idea this might happen. You act as if we planned this." That was Redbird's voice. Toff's foster-mother was nearby and arguing with someone.

"Your father admitted that he'd been watching those two boys and thought they might cause trouble. Yet you failed to call me to deal with the situation. Why is that?"

The unknown voice was accusing. It frightened Toff. Brought back a partial memory of the beating he'd received from Haldis and Sark. They'd been waiting for him in the trees, luring him farther away from Father Willow.

Toff had no memories after the first few punches. Had they meant to kill him? Toff didn't know and his head hurt too much to attempt to piece it together. None of it made any sense to him.

"You cannot take him from me—he isn't fully grown yet. That was the deal—to wait until he was an adult." Redbird argued with the unknown visitor.

"What deal? Who made that deal? You know as well as I that your mindbond has a hold on him, but I will not sit still while you allow this to happen." The voice was angry, now. Toff moved restlessly—he found this upsetting.

"We will take steps to ensure that it doesn't happen again."

"You should have taken steps to make sure it didn't happen to begin with."

"Sleep, little one." Cool fingers were laid on Toff's forehead, and he was asleep in seconds, shutting out the argument that upset him so much.

* * *

"Toff, this is Karzac. He is a healer and one of the Queen's Inner Circle mates." Toff blinked up at his foster-father, who stood beside another man. The man had light-brown hair, green-gold eyes and an easy smile. He was taller than Corent, too, Toff noticed.

"Young one, I am only here to make sure you recover fully," Karzac sat on the side of the bed and lifted Toff's wrist in his fingers. He also placed fingers on Toff's chest, as if he were listening through them for Toff's heartbeat instead of putting an ear against Toff's chest.

Toff had never been sick before, although some of the others—the humanoids—sometimes were ill. The Green Fae had healers, but they'd brought someone else in after Toff was attacked.

"What do you remember of your attack, young one?" Karzac the healer asked after checking Toff over carefully. He seemed satisfied with his findings as far as health was concerned.

"I was looking for Lily, Father Willow's best cow," Toff blinked at Karzac as he dredged up the painful memory. "Father Willow sent me toward a stand of trees, when we didn't find her in the pasture."

Toff lowered his eyes and picked at the quilt that covered him. "I heard rustling somewhere inside the edge of the forest, so I went to check on that. I thought Lily might have gone in there, thinking it to be warmer since it frosted overnight." Toff shuddered.

He hadn't expected the two larger boys to jump him from overhead—they'd been waiting for him to pass beneath the trees. They'd dropped on his shoulders, knocking him to the ground. Then, Sark held him while Haldis punched and hit. Toff only managed to scream twice before he was knocked unconscious. Toff explained that to Karzac as best he could.

Blood Reunion

While he told that particular part of his tale, he gripped the handmade quilt that covered him tightly in his hands. The memories were disturbing. He'd been punched and knocked about before, but never like this. The other attacks hadn't been planned. This one had been carefully thought out.

"Those two are sitting in the Queen's dungeon, although their parents are having fits," Karzac patted one of Toff's hands while a grim expression marred his features. "Did anything precipitate this attack? I ask that you not lie—I will know if you do."

"I don't know what I did." Toff lifted a hand and rubbed his forehead. "They acted as they always did when I saw them last. Nothing was different that I could tell."

"Then we will attempt to find an explanation for this, young one," Karzac stood and stretched. "If you have need, you can always get a message to the Queen. She will respond. Send it through your foster-father, here. He will bring it to our attention." Karzac nodded to Corent who'd stood by, listening to the exchange with little expression on his face.

"What will happen to Sark and Haldis?" Toff asked before Karzac left his tiny bedroom.

"The Queen and the Council will pass judgment on them sometime soon. I cannot say exactly when that might be—they are very busy these days." Karzac walked through Toff's doorway and disappeared from view.

"Father, what do you think will happen?" Toff lifted his eyes to Corent.

"I do not know," Corent sighed and sat in the spot previously occupied by the healer. "While we would merely banish them from our village and place them outside our boundary which they cannot cross, this world belongs to the

Chapter 2

Queen of Le-Ath Veronis and her justice is more severe at times. Do not worry yourself over this, son. They will not touch you again."

Toff didn't tell Corent what he'd been thinking—that Gren had likely ordered Sark and Haldis to do what they did. While they willingly did Gren's bidding on any occasion, they wouldn't have done this except at his direction. With their arrests, Toff had cost Gren his small army. Gren would certainly find a way to retaliate. He wanted to tell Corent about that. "When can I get up, father?" Toff asked instead.

"Probably tomorrow—the healer had help from a Larentii when you were attacked three days ago. They are mighty healers, child." Corent didn't add that without the Larentii's help, Toff would have died after being beaten so badly.

"Larentii?" Toff hadn't heard that word before.

"A race of blue giants, son. They feed on sunlight and are the most powerful of the light races. There are two of them in the Queen's Inner Circle."

"Oh." He realized that he hadn't dreamed those large, blue hands after all. "How many are in the Queen's Inner Circle, father?" Toff was naturally curious, and there was no one to ask about the Queen and her capital city.

"Seventeen, I think," Corent brushed Toff's hair off his forehead. "Your mother has been cooking. Are you hungry?"

* * *

"Here, Tory." Rylend Morphis handed the polish to his brother, Torevik Rath. Whenever Uncle Drake and Uncle Drew came to inspect their practice blades, they expected them to be treated as if they were the finest blades made by

Blood Reunion

Grey House. Tory and Ry had to clean, sharpen and polish before presenting the weapons to their uncles for inspection.

"Do you think Mom will ever let us get tattoos?" Fourteen-year-old Ry looked over at his brother. Tory was younger than Ry—by six days. Both boys were envious of their uncles' extensive tattoos.

Uncle Drake and Uncle Drew had tattoos on their chests, backs and arms. Drake had black dragons tattooed everywhere, Drew had silver dragons. They were twins and half Falchani, although they looked to be all Falchani.

Falchani men wore their black hair in long braids down their backs and the more experienced they were in battle, the more extensive the tattoos. Drake and Drew had full sets, in addition to the claw crown tattooed at the base of their left thumbs.

"You know Mom won't agree to it, even if our dads will," Tory grumped. They'd admired their uncle's tattoos for a very long time.

Ry and Tory worked inside a small room within the palace guards' barracks, finishing their chores for the day before going to afternoon lessons at the palace. The barracks were clean and serviceable, but with few comforts provided. Ry and Tory seldom saw the inside of the lengthy bunk area where the guards actually slept.

The guards had small rooms there while they worked at the palace, with homes elsewhere when they were off duty. Uncle Gavin and Uncle Tony were in charge of the Palace Guard; Uncle Drake and Uncle Drew had command of the army.

Uncle Gavin always made sure that the palace guards had plenty of time off and didn't get burned out on their job.

Chapter 2

Ry and Tory had helped Uncle Tony guard the palace at night upon occasion. They knew how wearing it could be.

"The tourists are coming through to see the palace," Ry remarked casually as he wiped his practice blade carefully with a soft cloth. Tory's blade was already gleaming in the light cast by the fluorescent globes overhead.

Power for those lights was carried through buried lines from the light half of the planet to keep the capital city of Lissia lit in the constant twilight. Tourists visiting nearby Casino City had need of the artificial lighting. Ry and Tory had learned to deal with the planet's unusual rotation, which kept Lissia in semi-darkness.

"Do you think we would be missed from class for a few minutes if I skipped us to the Green Fae village?" A slow grin spread across Tory's face. Tory was tall already—more than six feet—and looked older than his fourteen years. Ry was around five and a half feet tall and envied his brother's height at times.

"You'll have to skip us; if I use any ability, I'll get knocked back at the boundary. Dad limited my power on that sort of thing." Ry sometimes hated the limits his father placed on him. Tory, whose father was Gardevik Rath of the race of High Demons, had inherited his father's ability to deflect power.

Garde and Ry's father, Erland, had experimented with the ability and determined it was only malicious spells or power meant to harm that didn't have any effect on High Demons. Neutral or helpful spells seemed to work just fine. That's how Tory could be healed or transported by others, but Ry couldn't place a mischievous spell on Tory, even if he wanted to.

"I'm just worried we'll get caught," Tory pointed out.

"We didn't get caught when we went to see those two in the dungeon." Ry nudged his brother as he stood to place his practice blade on the rack.

"But if we get caught, we'll end up washing dishes at Niff's or helping Cheedas in the kitchen or polishing the floor." Tory hated polishing the marble floors of the palace; there were miles of them and Web, the comesula in charge of palace housekeeping, was a hard taskmaster.

"Yeah. You think Web truly hates us?"

"He made us redo that stretch in the vestibule last time," Tory grumbled.

"He hates us," Ry heaved a self-pitying sigh. He ran fingers through his black hair for effect, too, but his dark eyes were laughing.

"We know those two in the dungeon are lying," Tory was still thinking about this.

"You got that from your Uncle Jayd," Ry nodded. "Who knew that you'd be a guli? When are you planning to tell your dad?"

"I don't know. Right now, it's more useful when nobody knows or suspects." Tory stood and stretched before hanging his practice blade beside Ry's.

"Yeah. Might come in handy sometime, if nobody else knows."

"Is Sissy coming for dinner?"

"If Uncle Shadow comes, he'll bring her."

"Mom's still mad, and that was six years ago."

"I don't think I'd want to be hauled off to Grey House to be trained at six." Tory still remembered the argument between his mother, Uncle Shadow and Uncle Shadow's father and grandfather. Only their mother had enough courage to argue with those three at the same time. It ended

Chapter 2

up not making any difference—six was the age when all Grey House Wizards went through the rite and started training.

Uncle Shadow had insisted that Sissy would have one parent around her at all times. Their mother had then pointed out (rather loudly) that the parent in question was going to be Uncle Shadow most of the time. Uncle Shadow didn't have an argument for that. Sissy and Mom had both cried and Uncle Shadow had his hands full for a while trying to calm the women in his life.

"Sissy will be twelve in a few weeks. Do you think Mom will let us go offworld to get something for her birthday?" Ry examined a thumbnail—he'd bashed it earlier, practicing bladework with Tory. A half-moon of purple edged the bottom of the nail.

"Maybe. Dad might take us, if he's not busy." Ry looked up at Tory's words.

"You think your cousins might come?" Ry had such hope in his voice. Tory wasn't sure how to answer.

Ry almost drooled every time he saw Tory's cousins, Princess Jhase and Princess Jheri, King Jaydevik's twin daughters and heirs to the throne on Kifirin. The girls were nearly sixteen and identical, with long, platinum blonde hair they'd inherited from their mother. Tory didn't have the heart to tell Ry that they'd already been promised since birth to High Demons from the houses of Weth and Greth. Yurevik Greth and Wendevik Weth were lucky and didn't mind telling anyone about it.

"Come on, let's go see if we can talk to that boy—the one who was beaten," Ry saw the look on Tory's face and decided not to ask questions. As long as Tory didn't say, then Ry's hopes concerning the Princesses remained intact.

* * *

Blood Reunion

"I told you this was a bad idea," Tory hissed later as the two boys made their way through rows of dried cornstalks. Tory's head could be seen over the tops of tall stalks if he stood up straight. With his height and dark hair, he would be easily seen amid dry, pale-brown cornstalks. Therefore, he was forced to bend over as they made their way through the maze of long, rustling leaves.

"You never said that," Ry huffed right behind Tory. "I've done my scry; he's here, somewhere."

"He's hiding, but then we're making enough noise to wake the dead," Tory muttered, angry now with his half-brother.

"Look for where the open field is; that's where he's finished cutting down the dry stalks," Ry whispered.

"What do they do with this stuff anyway?" Tory whispered back.

"Cut it up and mix it with the grain they feed the milk cows through the winter," Ry hissed.

"How did you find that out?" Tory almost straightened up to his full height to turn and look at Ry.

"I read up on organic farming, that's how. Dad made me do a report after I got in trouble the last time."

"Why farming?" Tory was ducking down and tracking through the rows of cornstalks again.

"Dad says it's a good idea to learn everything you can about the planet beneath your feet," Ry grumped. Ry had used a spell that Erland Morphis, his father, had forbidden. He'd paid for that with a twenty-page report.

"What did you do?" Tory wanted to hear this.

"I spelled the ice cream at Niff's. We ran out of strawberries. I improvised."

Chapter 2

Both of them worked at Niff's occasionally, waiting on customers. Niff's was their mother's business, although her ownership had been well hidden. She was partners with two others—her assistants, Heathe and Grant.

The first and largest of Niff's Sweets and Goodies was located in Casino City, and Heathe and Grant often took Ry and Tory with them to help when tourist traffic was especially heavy.

"What were people really eating?" Tory turned around again.

"Spelled blueberries, and they didn't eat any," Ry ducked his head. "Dad said you should never spell food unless it's to put it in stasis. He says it can damage the body if it's done often. He felt the spell from wherever he was and came right away, giving me what for before we could sell the ice cream."

"Good thing, huh?" Tory started walking again.

"Yeah."

"If you're looking for me, leave now or I'll hit you." The boy they'd searched for was suddenly in front of Tory, brandishing a hoe.

"Whoa, wait a minute," Ry held up a hand. "We're not here to attack. We want to talk to you."

"Who are you?" The dark-haired boy shook his hoe in a threatening manner at Ry and Tory.

"We're not here to hurt you, please put that thing down." Tory was much taller than the boy, and with his training, he could disarm him quickly. Tory had no desire to frighten the boy any more than he already had.

"Then tell me who you are and why you want to talk to me. Nobody wants to talk to me." Suspicion, as well as a bit of fear, lay in the boy's honey-brown eyes—Ry and Tory could see it.

"We saw those two who beat you up," Ry offered. "We talked to them. They lied to us. We just wanted to know what really happened."

"You talked to Haldis and Sark?" The boy lowered his hoe to the ground and leaned on it. "What were they saying?" His curiosity had won out, in Ry's estimation.

"That you jumped them and they had to defend themselves."

"That's a lie," the boy insisted.

"We know it's a lie. Everybody else does too—that's why they're still in the dungeons," Tory grinned. "I'm Torevik Rath." He held out his hand.

"Toff. Just—Toff," Toff held his out. Tory grasped Toff's hand in the customary gesture before releasing it.

"Rylend Morphis," Ry had to lean around Tory to take Toff's hand. "We had to sneak into the dungeon to see them—we don't get excitement like that very often," Ry smiled at Toff after letting his hand go. "So we had to come and see this for ourselves."

Ry took in Toff's appearance—only the faintest spots remained of the bruises Toff received from the two in the dungeons, but then a Larentii and a healer had come to make things right. Ry expected nothing less.

"And after they lied to us," Tory was grinning, now, "we really wanted to hear your side of things."

"I can't talk long, I'm expected to get a certain amount done today," Toff looked around. None of the fathers were nearby and he was thankful for that.

"We'll take whatever you give us," Ry said encouragingly.

"All right," Toff dropped to the ground in a sitting position, his hand sliding down the hoe handle as he sat. "What do you want to know?"

"Why do you think they attacked you?" Tory asked right off, after he and Ry sat cross-legged in the dusty row.

"Gren," Toff's face went sullen for a moment.

"Gren?" Ry was puzzled.

"A Half-Fae."

"Oh."

"What did Gren do?" Tory went on.

"He hates me. I don't know why, but he does," Toff laid the hoe down beside him and linked his fingers. Dust covered his clothing and dirt lined the underside of his fingernails, Ry noticed, watching the dark-haired, brown-eyed boy carefully. Ry knew Toff was older than he looked; it was a talent inherited from his mother. Tory wasn't the only one holding things back.

"What does Gren do?" Tory asked carefully, not wanting Toff to shy away from the important questions. So far, Toff had been truthful, as far as his perspective went, anyway.

"He taunts me when the elders are out of sight. Calls me names." Toff swallowed. Some of those names he didn't want to tell and hoped Tory wouldn't ask.

"I thought the Fulls and the Halves didn't engage in violence," Ry said during the silence that followed Toff's last statement.

"They don't, or they're not supposed to," Toff agreed, lifting his eyes to stare at Ry. Ry was handsome, no doubt about it; he'd inherited his good looks from his father.

"But Gren—well, he's all fine and good around the elders," Toff continued. "Tiearan thinks he's the most wonderful thing in the village." Toff turned his head, embarrassed by the admission.

"What do you think of Gren?" Ry asked.

"I think he's the biggest bully. I don't think Haldis and Sark would have attacked me if Gren hadn't told them to." Toff was back to worrying his fingernails, trying to get the dirt from under a thumbnail. Toff hadn't failed to notice the fine clothing his visitors wore, comparing it to the stained and patched hand-woven tunic and pants that he'd put on that morning.

"You know, I think I'd like to meet Gren sometime," Tory muttered, clenching his hands. Toff was honest with him. Completely.

"You don't want to meet Gren. Not without the elders around," Toff shivered visibly. Gren had given Toff nasty looks only that morning. Toff was grateful that Gren had gone to train with Tiearan while he'd been sent to chop and bundle cornstalks. A breeze whispered through the dry leaves surrounding them, bringing Toff back to his task.

"I need to go or I won't get my work done," he murmured, standing and brushing dust from the back of his trousers. The trousers were an oatmeal color—the Green Fae seldom used dyes for work clothing.

"Thanks for talking with us. Do you think we might visit you again? There aren't many our age in the city," Tory said, unfolding his long legs and standing as well. Ry was right behind him, preparing to leave.

"Sure. But not while the others are around. I could get in trouble." Toff lifted his hoe.

"Yeah. Us too," Tory nodded. "Um, good-bye." Toff gave a half-wave and walked away to take up where he'd finished chopping cornstalks.

Chapter 2

Ry thought to help Toff with a spell that would bring down all the stalks, then thought better of it. His power signature would be felt—no doubt about that—and he had no desire for anyone to know that he and Tory had come to visit without asking permission. Ry nodded to Tory, who skipped them back to the palace.

* * *

"He was a little bitter, don't you think?" Ry asked quietly as they walked down the long hall toward their schoolroom.

"Can you blame him?" Tory asked, a thoughtful expression in his blue eyes. "He's getting bullied. Too bad he isn't here with us. Mom wouldn't stand for that."

"What's he doing there anyway? If that's not a fish out of water, then I don't know what it is," Ry snorted.

"There you are, and late on top of everything else." Morwin, Ry and Tory's tutor, glared at the two boys as they walked toward their classroom.

Master Morwin's school lay at the back of the palace, far away from the rooms and hallways the tourists visited. Morwin was an Amtearean Dwarf, knew more things than most people ever wanted to know and was over four hundred years old.

Morwin was shorter than Ry by more than a foot, with thick, red hair and bushy red eyebrows that Ry imagined would look infinitely better if Morwin would only trim them now and then. Ry knew not to suggest it—the one time he'd made the hint, he and Tory had gotten extra homework for a week.

"We are very sorry—the tourists, you know," Tory ducked his head. Ry wanted to snicker—there hadn't been a single lie in Tory's words.

"Hmmph," Morwin grumped and stepped aside so the two boys could enter the classroom.

"Today we will cover the destruction of Trell," Morwin said after both boys were seated at their desks. "Not the official version being taught in other classrooms around the Alliance, but the truth of what happened. We may only discuss the topic inside this classroom, as you know. You may discuss it with your uncles, too, who have firsthand knowledge."

Morwin's bushy eyebrows wiggled while he spoke, and Tory often had to look at the comp-vid on his desk to keep from laughing.

"I warn you, however, that speaking of this topic around your Lady Mother may upset her, so I caution against it." Morwin liked the Queen of Lissia very much and often had dinner with her and the Inner Circle.

"We know," Ry was ducking his head, now. He and Tory both knew. Trell had been destroyed because someone betrayed their mother. Her enemies, thinking she was still upon Trell as their spy reported, had used a terrible weapon to blow the planet to bits.

Their mother found it extremely painful to hear anything concerning Trell.

"I am sending the information to your comp-vids, now. I would like a ten-page paper on the subject, with emphasis on the economic impact Trell's destruction had upon the Alliance. It will be due at this time next week."

* * *

Chapter 2

"Trell had the exclusive rights to manufacture components for the solar collectors," Ry scanned through information on his mini comp-vid while he and Tory walked toward their shared suite of rooms after class.

"Who made them after Trell was destroyed?" Tory glanced over Ry's shoulder at the information.

"The contracts went to Refizan, but only after months of negotiations with the Alliance members. The Grand Alliance Council finally had to intervene—the rest of the Alliance came to a locked decision. Refizan had the factories already in place; they just had to rework the assembly robots," Ry added.

"Then we'll start with that," Tory said. "There has to be something else, though. Morwin expects us to go digging. There's something else he wants out of all this; I just know it."

"Yeah. He always wants us to look deeper than he says to look." Ry didn't mind, actually—he learned new things that way. The boys passed down a long hall leading to the residential wing of the palace, nearly reaching the door to their shared suite when the floor shook beneath their feet and the lights went out.

* * *

"Casino City almost had a five-second meltdown before the backup generators kicked in," Uncle Tony sat down later at Ry's desk inside his bedroom. "We had people trying to loot in two blinks."

"Anybody in the pokey?" Tory grinned—he loved hearing Uncle Tony's descriptions of hauling in prisoners.

Blood Reunion

"Sheriff Trevor hauled in about twenty, but you didn't hear that from me." Uncle Tony had black hair, and gray eyes that twinkled when he smiled. His eyes were twinkling now.

"Okay, we never heard that from you. But I do have a question for you—what do you think was the economic impact of Trell's destruction, as far as the Alliance goes?" Ry asked, flopping onto his bed. They were all on his side of the large suite he shared with Tory.

"You might look into the taxes Trell paid," Uncle Tony said thoughtfully. "And you should look into who was allowed to join the Alliance shortly after Trell's destruction, to fill that slot. Find out what they're paying in taxes instead." Uncle Tony's grin widened.

"Wow, I didn't even think of that," Tory grabbed his handheld comp-vid and started tapping in notes. His hands stilled when his mother walked into the room.

"Are you two all right?" Queen Lissa came over to give Ry a hug and kiss on the cheek before going to offer Tory the same. "I worried about you the whole time we had to sort out that stupid Council meeting after the lights went out."

Tory tossed his comp-vid onto Ry's bed, face down, and draped an arm around his mother's shoulders. "What happened, Mom? An earthquake? Have we ever had one of those before?"

"Not since I've been here," his mother grumbled. "This is a first for all of us." Queen Lissa was five feet tall, with strawberry-blonde hair and blue eyes. She turned heads wherever she went.

"Are we going to check into this?" Uncle Tony asked, rising from Ry's desk chair.

Chapter 2

"We need to; I hope Kifirin comes in soon. If anybody knows whether there are problems with quakes, then he's the one to ask."

"You think Uncle Kifirin might come?" Tory asked.

"He might. He hasn't been here in weeks." Queen Lissa put an arm around Uncle Tony when he came to stand beside her. Tory looked at Ry over their mother's head. Kifirin. He was remote and frightening at times, though neither boy could truly explain why.

"Lissa, are you all right?" Uncle Norian came rushing through the door.

"I'm fine, Nori. I just wanted to check on my boys. I couldn't get away from the Council meeting before now. When did you get in?"

"I heard the news while I was out, so I asked for a ride," Uncle Norian replied. Uncle Norian was another one you didn't want to anger. He wouldn't hurt Tory, Ry or anyone inside the palace, unless they tried to attack the Queen. Then you'd get to see the other side of Norian Keef. He was Director of the ASD—Alliance Security Detail—which was currently stationed on Le-Ath Veronis.

"Can you stay for dinner?" The Queen smiled at him.

"I can stay the night," Uncle Norian replied, smiling in return. The three adults walked out of Ry and Tory's suite, after the Queen hugged both her sons again.

"Something's up," Tory flopped down on Ry's bed.

"Yeah," Ry agreed.

* * *

Something about the quake had the elders worried. Toff could feel it, even if they weren't saying anything. Toff and a few others were finishing up with the cornstalks when the ground shifted beneath his feet. Many of the youngest were frightened and crying afterward. Father Willow, who wasn't very good with the younglings, went to fetch Rain, who eventually calmed them down.

Toff might have tried, but none of them wanted anything to do with him, either. Gren had seen to that. They were all too frightened to befriend Toff. Gren was telling them that they'd be hauled off to the Queen's dungeons, like Haldis and Sark. Gren was already spreading the rumor that Haldis and Sark's arrests were Toff's fault.

Perhaps that was his plan all along. Toff had no way to reason with Gren's warped logic and since he no longer had the bruises to prove he'd been badly beaten, the others were all siding with Gren. At times, he was thankful for the healing he'd received. At other times, he wished that things had been left alone.

* * *

Toff wound string around the last bundle of cornstalks with practiced ease and hefted it onto the wagon Father Willow brought to the field. Mother Rain had taken all the younglings back to the village with her—it was best to take them to their parents when they were so frightened.

"Time to go back," Father Willow said. Toff climbed onto the wagon seat beside Father Willow, who looked as if he wanted to say something else to Toff but ended up holding back.

Toff sat in silence, watching the bare field pass around him as Father Willow flapped long reins against the horse's backs. Together, they drove off toward the village.

* * *

Chapter 2

"Some of the little ones fell." Toff answered Corent's question over dinner. Corent had asked him how strong the quake had felt out in the field. "I staggered, but managed to keep standing. Mother Rain had to come and take the little ones back to the village."

Redbird lifted an eyebrow at Corent when Toff mentioned Rain. Toff pretended not to notice, dipping into his stewed potatoes instead.

"I've talked with Mother Fern; she is willing to teach you how to make pottery, Toff," Redbird said casually. Toff lifted his head and stared at his foster-mother in surprise.

"I don't want to make pottery," he blurted without thinking.

"You're good with your hands," Redbird said stiffly. "Tiearan thinks this might be a suitable fit for you."

"What would Father Tiearan know about anything?" Toff wanted to storm away from the table, but Redbird would only place another mind restraint and that frightened him. Tiearan couldn't see through Gren; how would he know what Toff might be good at doing?

"Son, you are treating your foster-mother disrespectfully," Corent admonished. Corent's hair was going toward purple—a true sign that Corent was angry or upset.

"Father, may I be excused?" Toff was back to staring at his bowl of stewed potatoes.

"You must eat more of your food before you get up. And you will clean the kitchen tonight." Corent was definitely not happy with Toff. Toff chewed his lower lip. Everyone else was treating him badly, why not his own parents?

* * *

"You'll break that if you're not careful." Redbird was getting onto him when Toff banged the crock down harder than he meant to after drying it with the cloth in his hands. The cloth was hand-woven by Mother Berry and her apprentice weavers. Those were girls, mostly, but Toff had more interest in weaving than he did in making pottery, and he didn't have much interest in weaving.

"Wash the cabinets too," Redbird told him before walking out of the kitchen. Toff wanted to grumble, but was too afraid she'd hear.

* * *

Toff heard Corent's voice as he passed his foster parents' bedroom on the way to bed later. He stopped to listen—he couldn't help it.

"What else was I supposed to do? The others won't have anything to do with him and Fern was the only one willing to take him," Redbird snapped at Corent, after Corent's voice rumbled something Toff didn't catch. Corent's voice rumbled a second time. "I know Willow would be happy to take him, but he'd keep him out all night during calving season," Redbird retorted.

Toff wanted to speak up immediately; he didn't mind being out all night during calving season. Father Willow didn't talk much but at least he didn't ignore Toff like so many of the others did. Besides, nights were almost as well-lit as the days, but calling it night meant it was the time designated to sleep. Father Tiearan said it was the only way to keep order in the village.

"Zervias would have counseled us, but he is no longer here. The Queen allowed him to leave." Corent had walked closer to the door and Toff could hear him now.

Chapter 2

"Zervias," Redbird snorted. "He left us when we needed him most."

"I do not blame him—we failed to listen to him when it was important."

"And what would you have done differently? Tell me that." Redbird was angry.

"You know what should have been done differently." Corent was angry as well. Toff tiptoed away.

Chapter 3

ifirin had come for dinner—a rare occurrence. Ry and Tory ignored that for the moment; Uncle Shadow had come and brought Sissy with him. Their mother was nearly in tears when she saw her daughter.

"It's okay, Mom, really," Sissy said, hugging her mother.

"Nissa, honey, your dad needs to bring you more often."

"You could come to Grey House," Shadow muttered. Queen Lissa turned sharply toward Uncle Shadow. "I'm just saying," Uncle Shadow had both hands up; whether in defense or resignation, Ry couldn't tell.

"And you know why I won't," Lissa snapped.

"Lissa, Dad and Grampa want to apologize. Really. But you cut them off every time." Uncle Shadow attempted to defend himself.

Blood Reunion

"I might have thought about it, until they took my Nissy away. At age six, no less." Ry gave Tory a look. They were going over this old ground. Again.

"Lissa," Uncle Shadow sighed and pulled a chair out at the long table in the family dining hall.

"I'll shut up, but I won't forget," Lissa said and pulled her chair out before anyone else could get to it.

"Uncle Roff's here," Tory whispered as he took his seat next to Ry at the table. When the Queen sat, everyone else could sit. Somebody was supposed to pull her chair out for her, though. She was angry and kept everyone from helping her.

Roff had come in late, too—it looked as if he'd rushed through a shower to get to dinner on time. His hair looked slightly damp and his wings weren't held as snugly against his back as they normally were. Ry figured that Roff was letting them dry out before folding them tightly.

Ry and Tory were fascinated with Roff's wings. When he had them fully spread, they measured more than twelve feet across, wingtip to wingtip, and felt like the softest leather. Roff had let them touch when they were younger.

They now knew that Roff was being patient with them—his wings were sensitive, though he often used them as a weapon when he sparred with someone on the practice grounds.

Lissa remarked once that wings like Roff's, which resembled those of a bat, were the basis for the old myths. When Ry asked what myths, his mother had brushed off the question. Ry still didn't have an answer for that.

Roff had also taken them flying a time or two, when their mother wasn't around. Tory and Ry knew their mother would be frightened to death to know her boys were taken up so high without her knowledge.

"Is your mother pissed?" Erland Morphis sat in the empty chair next to Ry.

"A little. With Uncle Shadow." Ry whispered low, though he knew his mother still might hear.

"No surprise." Erland Morphis dropped a napkin on his lap and accepted a glass of wine from one of the comesuli servants. "I heard there was some excitement earlier."

"We had an earthquake. Or what felt like one," Ry grinned at his father. Erland pulled Ry against him and kissed the top of his son's head before letting him go.

"That's for coming in late for your lessons," Erland laughed at Ry's embarrassment.

"Let me guess, you were late, too." Gardevik Rath sat next to Tory.

"I was." Tory didn't lie to his father. For any reason. Both boys knew not to attempt to lie to their mother. Uncle Tony always said she could smell a lie a mile away.

"Did Morwin give you extra work?" Garde sipped his wine.

"No, Dad."

"Then you're getting more inventive with your excuses."

"Maybe." Tory was trying to hide a grin. "Dad, I need to go shopping. Sissy's birthday is almost here."

"I think your Aunt Glindarok wants to go off-planet. Your Uncle Jayd said he'd take her. Do you want to go when she goes?"

"Yeah. That will work out great. Thanks."

"I'll let her know. She'll contact your mother."

"I want to go, too." Ry interrupted.

Blood Reunion

"Why would I ask Glinda to take only one of you, when I know you can't bear to be apart?" Gardevik reached across Tory to tousle Ry's hair. "You're worse than twins."

Ry grinned at Uncle Gardevik. He liked his High Demon uncle quite a bit. The only trouble was, Uncle Garde, with his dark hair and good looks, didn't appear different from any other humanoid, most of the time. You'd never know he was High Demon until he became angry and smoke curled from his nostrils.

Ry hadn't seen Uncle Garde go Thifilathi, but Tory had. Uncle Garde had forced the turn for Tory, so he could see what he might be someday. Tory said that it would be frightening to anyone who didn't know what they were seeing.

Ry had seen all the life-sized sculptures of High Demons in Full Thifilathi inside King Jayd's palace, too. Unlike the smaller Thifilathi that all male High Demons had, only Full Thifilathi likenesses lined the marble halls of the High Demon palace on Kifirin.

Yes, the whole planet was named after Uncle Kifirin. Ry and Tory were still trying to piece that puzzle together. All those statues at the High Demon palace stood around seventeen feet tall and depicted horns, lengthy canines and scale-covered torsos. Ry shuddered at the memory.

"Honey, are you all right?" Ry had drawn his mother's attention.

"My son is fine," Erland rubbed Ry's back before turning to smile at the Queen.

"Erland Morphis, he's my son, too," the Queen grumped.

Chapter 3

"I know that," Erland was still smiling at Lissa. The Queen wrinkled her nose at Ry's father and went back to talking with Sissy.

* * *

"We think something's up, and I'd give anything to be in that Inner Circle meeting right now," Tory informed Sissy. They sat on Tory's long bed—the palace staff had brought in a larger one when Tory hit six feet.

Sissy had light-brown hair—a mix of her father and mother. She had her father's gray eyes, though, and someday she would be a beauty. Anyway, that's what Tory's father said. Sissy kept her long hair in a braid most of the time, otherwise it curled furiously and she hated that.

"What are they talking about?" Nissa asked. "Tory, have you been eating in bed again?" She pointed to a stain on the edge of the coverlet.

"That's grape juice. I was hoping it would blend in," Tory muttered, flushing with embarrassment. He was hungry most of the time. Uncle Tony said it was because he was growing so quickly.

"Purple doesn't go with brown," Nissa teased.

"Could have fooled me," Ry tried to tickle his little sister.

"I think they're talking about the quake and the power outage," Tory wasn't getting in on the rumpus. "Uncle Tony said they hauled twenty tourists off to jail in Casino City. He didn't say, but I think they're worried that those people were expecting something like this. Uncle Tony said that people were trying to loot immediately. I wonder how Niff's managed."

"Niff's is fine; they have backup generators for all the freezers," Ry said, letting his sister go. She stopped giggling and settled into the crook of Ry's arm.

"You want to go see the two in the dungeon?" Tory changed the subject.

"There are two in the dungeon?" Nissa almost squeaked the question.

"Yeah. Both seventeen. Beat up a boy in the Green Fae village. Almost to death, that's what we heard," Ry nodded knowingly. "We went to see the boy yesterday, because we knew those two downstairs were lying when they said the other boy started it. If you saw him, you'd know just by looking that he didn't start anything. He said as much, but he also said that one of the Half-Fae put those two downstairs up to the whole thing. Tory and I think he may be right." Ry squeezed Sissy's shoulders and dropped his arm. "Want to go see? Uncle Drake and Uncle Drew are in the meeting, and Uncle Gavin and Uncle Tony are in there, too."

"But how are we going to get past the guards?" Nissa looked at both her brothers. She wanted to see this for herself, but knew she'd be in trouble if they got caught. Their mother didn't want them to go anywhere near the dungeons.

"I'll skip us in after bro here checks things out," Tory grinned. "That's what we did the last time."

"Let's go." Nissa liked intrigue just as well as anyone.

* * *

"Why do all the vids show dungeons as dark places with water dripping somewhere?" Nissa whispered as she followed her brothers down a well-lit corridor and past cells lining one wall. Each cell had a sink inside, in addition to a narrow bed made of spelled wood. The wood couldn't be torn apart to make any kind of weapon. The sheets and blankets were clean, too, as were the floor and walls.

"Those vids are just to frighten you," Ry whispered back. "People ought to be more afraid of losing their freedom."

"Practicing philosophy again?" Tory elbowed Ry.

"That's what Em-pah Wylend said. He's the philosopher," Ry poked Tory in the ribs. Tory's rubber-soled shoes squeaked on the stone floor as he attempted to get away from his brother.

"Will you two settle down?" Nissa hissed at her brothers. "We could get caught, you know."

"We'll behave," Tory said, slapping Ry on the back of the head.

"Hey," Ry went after Tory again. Nissa stopped still in the middle of the corridor and put her hands on her hips.

"Sissy, that's just scary—I thought you were Mom for a minute," Ry teased.

"Come on, those two are down at the end," Tory came to take his sister's arm.

"Leave us alone." Those sullen words greeted Ry, Tory and Nissa as they reached the proper cell. Nissa stared at the two boys inside.

"They're both seventeen, although the dark-haired one is slightly older than the blond," Ry said, pulling Nissa back from the bars.

"How big is the one they beat up?" Nissa looked up at Tory.

"About your size," Tory answered.

"Didn't your mothers teach you not to hit the smaller ones?" Nissa placed her hands on her hips again.

"Leave our mothers out of this," the dark-haired boy hissed. "Leave us alone or Gren will make you sorry, I promise."

"Now, that's the truth—as he sees it, anyway," Tory nodded.

"How will Gren know to make us sorry?" Ry asked.

"None of your business." The blond boy finally spoke.

"Who is Gren, and how will he make us sorry?" Nissa weighed in on the questioning. Her arms were now tight across her chest and Tory and Ry knew this was upsetting their sister.

"Why should we tell you?" The dark-haired one snapped. "He'll get that little eunuch first, though."

"What did you call him?" Tory took a step closer to the bars.

"He's a eunuch. Don't you know what that means?"

"I know what that means," Tory huffed. "But that's not what he is, or why he's missing—well, certain things."

"I suppose you're going to tell us? You being so smart and all," the blond taunted.

"Tory, the guards are coming," Ry hissed. He'd gotten a hit on his perimeter shield. The two prisoners blinked in surprise as all three children who'd come to visit disappeared suddenly.

* * *

"That boy in the Fae village needs our help." Nissa insisted for perhaps the fourth time. Tory had skipped them to the arboretum, which was located on the top level of the palace.

Huge and mostly circular, the arboretum was built of curved glass walls all around, except for one flat side that

Chapter 3

backed up to the palace at the rear. All three children sat at the front of the glass, cross-legged on the floor and staring out the thick window at the capital city of Lissia. The city had been named for their mother, after all.

"But Sissy, we've already been late to class once this week. Dad found out. He didn't do anything this time, but he might if I'm late again." Ry glumly toyed with a shoelace.

"But I only have tomorrow to do anything," Nissa complained.

"What are you going to do?" Tory looked down at his little sister.

"I have this." She pulled a necklace from beneath her tunic that had a gray jewel strung on it.

"A protection jewel?" Ry sounded surprised.

"I made this myself, when nobody was looking," Nissa whispered. "I can key it to someone else. I think that boy needs this."

"His name is Toff," Ry nodded, getting on board with Nissa's suggestion.

"If we hurry after blade lessons tomorrow morning, we might be able to do this." Tory considered the possibilities. "Meet us in the sword room in the barracks. We'll go from there."

* * *

Toff was digging in the likeliest place he could find for the clay Mother Fern demanded. She'd only given him the barest of instructions on how to find it and left him in a deserted spot just inside the boundary Father Tiearan erected around the village.

Mother Fern had instructed him to go to the old streambed and dig. That was the extent of his teaching. Toff had two large canvas bags to fill with clay—if he could find any.

Toff jerked backward and sat down with a thump on a damp patch of ground when three people appeared before him. The two boys he recognized, but they'd brought a girl with them, this time. She was right at Toff's height, with a slender build. Toff imagined they could wear the same clothing, they were so close in size.

"We didn't mean to scare you," the one named Ry held out a hand to help Toff off the ground. Toff accepted the offered hand and allowed Ry to pull him up and get him steady on his feet. "This is our sister, Nissa," Ry introduced the girl. Toff nodded shyly at her.

"We came to give a warning, and to bring you something," Tory said. "We don't have much time, so we'll make this quick. We went back to the dungeons last night to see those two who hurt you, because Sissy wanted to go." Tory nodded at Nissa, who seemed embarrassed to be called Sissy in front of Toff.

"Those boys said that somebody else wanted to get back at you," Nissa pulled a necklace over her head. "I've already rekeyed this, so all you have to do is put it on and it will tune itself to you." The gold chain with the dark-gray jewel was offered to a gaping Toff.

"It's a protection jewel," Ry said, when Toff continued to blink at them in confusion. Nissa took Toff's hand and dropped the necklace into it.

"Wear this at all times," she said. "Even when you're bathing. You never know when your enemies might strike."

"Keep it inside your shirt—you don't want to let anyone know you have it. Once it keys itself to you, it's worthless to anyone else. It will only protect you from now on." Tory offered Toff an encouraging look.

Toff looked around him—he was hidden well enough in the copse of trees that grew along the old streambed. He'd been sent out alone, too, but he always suspected Gren of having him watched.

"There's nobody close enough to see or hear," Ry reported. He'd already checked. He didn't want tales going back to his parents of how they'd all sneaked away to do this.

The protection jewel that Toff was getting—many kings and monarchs across the Alliance couldn't afford what Nissa handed to Toff. Toff slowly slipped the long chain over his head, trying to comprehend the gift he'd been given. He had no idea of its worth, but if it could protect him, then he might feel a bit safer around the others.

"It won't protect against words or disease," Ry seemed to be reading Toff's mind. "You'll still have to deal with that. And, since this is Sissy's first protection jewel, we don't know how strong it will be. If somebody tries to attack you, do what you'd normally do."

"What I normally do is run, unless they catch me and hold me, like last time." Toff tucked the gray jewel inside his oatmeal-colored tunic and patted it against his chest.

"I put the best spell I could make on it," Nissa said with a modest shrug. "I hope it helps." She reached out and patted Toff's arm. Toff blinked at her in surprise. Nobody touched him. Not because he didn't want them to—it was because they didn't want to touch him. Redbird and Corent hugged him sometimes, but that was all.

"We have to go," Tory insisted. "I'm sorry we can't stay longer and talk." Toff's visitors turned to leave.

"Wait—will you come and see me again?" Toff blinked hopefully at Nissa as he asked the question.

"I train at Grey House so I can't come very often, and Tory has to bring us or we'll be found out," Nissa offered Toff a sad look.

"But when can you come again?" Toff pleaded.

"Toff, I only get to come home once a month, on an off-day," Nissa said. Toff nodded, disappointment showing in his face.

"Thank you for the jewel," he lowered his eyes. When he looked up again after only a moment, the three were gone. Toff turned back to searching for the elusive clay Mother Fern demanded.

* * *

"How did he end up there?" Nissa asked the moment Tory skipped them back to his bedroom. Ry and Tory were busy gathering comp-vids before rushing off to class.

"Don't know. We'll talk later." Tory opened the door and he and Ry raced down the hall, leaving the door open and their sister staring after them.

* * *

"Mom, what will happen to those two boys in the dungeon?" Nissa knew she wasn't supposed to know about those two boys, but the comesuli did tend to gossip inside the palace. She could have come by the information in any number of ways.

"Honey, I'm going to stop trying to figure out how you three know about anything," Queen Lissa gave her daughter a hug. Nissa sat next to her mother at a private lunch inside the arboretum.

Chapter 3

"You're not going to tell me?"

"We don't know yet. Everybody is still discussing this." Nissa's mother sighed and stared out the tall, glass windows overlooking the city of Lissia. A table had been set up and lunch had been served only minutes earlier, just for the two of them.

"You're not going to send them to Evensun, are you?" Nissa worried about that. Sentencing a criminal to Evensun was often a death sentence.

"I don't know, baby." The Queen's blue eyes were worried about that, too, Nissa decided. "With the ones who are already on Evensun, those two boys won't last a day. The final decision on this rests with the Council, and I only have one vote in that. I'm trying to find a place where they can't cause trouble for a while and their parents can go with them, if they want."

"Their parents will still face judgment, when the time comes." Kifirin appeared, blowing smoke from his nostrils.

"Honey, calm down," Lissa stood and took Kifirin's hand. "Nobody's trying to get around that."

"Avilepha, I grow tired of this. They should have turned the boy over to you when he was injured. Yet they did not. How can they think this will improve their lot in my eyes?"

Kifirin was darkly handsome and Nissa watched him closely. She, like her brothers, was wary around Kifirin, though he wore an angel's face. Nissa didn't think Kifirin would harm any of them, but there was a dangerous edge about him that couldn't easily be defined.

"Little one, you should not be frightened." Kifirin turned his nearly-black eyes on Nissa.

Nissa was too frightened to speak, so she nodded at Kifirin instead. She wondered if Kifirin would stand by his statement if he learned she'd given a protection jewel to Toff. She assumed he was the boy Kifirin meant.

"I was thinking about suggesting we send those boys to the southern continent on Harifa Edus," Lissa found another chair for Kifirin and shared her plate with him. There was more than enough food.

"Wolves are there, now," Kifirin remarked as he dipped into the lasagna Cheedas had made for them. "If that is the Council's decision, I will not help them if they are attacked."

"I don't expect you to—I was thinking about placing a boundary around their farm."

"You will build a farm for them?" Kifirin was back to blowing smoke.

"I don't think those two were the only ones involved in the attack." Nissa looked up sharply at her mother's words, and then quickly dropped her eyes. She should have known—not much got past her mother.

"Yet the others have made a vow of nonviolence." Kifirin drank from the Queen's glass. Kifirin liked to eat—when he did eat.

"That's what worries me," the Queen grumped. "It's hard to pinpoint something like this."

"Yes." Kifirin agreed around a mouthful of food.

Kifirin didn't stay long—he ate, discussed the disposition of the two young prisoners a little longer and then left, disappearing just he always did.

Someday, Nissa would be taught to fold space, but that wasn't allowed until a wizard was at least twenty, achieved at least a Fifth-Tier status in their training and been certified by Great-Grampa Glendes, who was Eldest of Grey House.

She felt a twinge of jealousy at times because Tory was allowed to skip. That's how the High Demons got around—it

Chapter 3

was a series of jumps—like skipping rocks on a pond. Tory had been able to skip since he turned twelve. Now, everybody was waiting to see if Tory could turn Thifilathi. Uncle Gardevik was practically holding his breath over it. That ability, or lack of it, would determine much of Tory's future upon the High Demon planet named after Kifirin.

"What do you really want to do with those boys?" Nissa often acted much older than her nearly twelve years, but then she was surrounded by those older than herself most of the time.

Nissa studied under Calebert, Master Wizard of the Weapons Division of Grey House. Nissa was learning to remove rust from old weapons using her power. The work was deadly dull. Her father, Shadow Grey, worked in the K'Shoufa Jewelry Division. Both he and Grampa Raffian were Master Wizards and jewelry makers.

Great-Grampa Glendes had stuck her in the Weapons Division as soon as she'd gone through the rite to manifest her power instead of allowing her to work with her father and grandfather.

Nissa wasn't even supposed to know how to make a protection jewel, yet she'd done it. The one she'd given Toff was the third she'd made—the first two had gone through a testing phase to make sure they were effective. Nobody else knew that—not even her brothers. If Great-Grampa Glendes found out what she'd done, she would certainly be in trouble.

"Hi, Daddy," Nissa smiled brightly at her father. Shadow Grey had folded in and now sat in Kifirin's abandoned chair before Nissa's mother could answer the question about the two boys in the dungeon.

"Shadow, we were having a private lunch." The Queen brushed back strawberry-blonde hair and frowned at Nissa's father.

"Kifirin was here. Am I not welcome too?" Neither Nissa nor her brothers had ever learned what Grampa Raffian and Great-Grampa Glendes had done to alienate her mother, but she refused to visit Grey House and Shadow often grumbled that he was in the doghouse more often than not.

"Honey, let's not go there today." Nissa's mother leaned down and bumped her head on the small table. She was hugging herself tightly with her arms. Nissa was worried that all this talk about the two boys in the dungeon was upsetting her mother more than anyone thought.

"What's wrong?" Nissa's father had a hand on her mother's head immediately. Shadow wasn't qualified as a healer, but he had some skill in that area.

"I just don't feel well," the Queen lifted her head. "I think I'll cancel the Council meeting this afternoon." Lissa rose and quickly walked away from them. Nissa listened as her mother's footsteps softened and then disappeared. The Queen had left the arboretum.

"Daddy, she never cancels meetings." Nissa rose to follow her mother.

"No, she doesn't. Maybe I'll ask Karzac or Selkirk to take a look. She gets headaches, too, though that shouldn't be possible." Shadow looked worried.

"But she'll hold meetings, even if she has a headache," Nissa persisted. Shadow motioned her down again.

"Finish your lunch, sweetheart. Then we'll see if something needs to be done." Shadow breathed a frustrated sigh.

"Daddy, what did Grampa and Great-Grampa do to upset Mom?" Nissa turned her eyes on her father.

"Baby, we want to tell you about this someday soon. Right now, all I'll say is that they almost cost her Le-Ath Veronis as you know it."

Nissa knew from the look on her father's face that she wasn't going to get any information other than that. It didn't matter—this was more than she or her brothers had gotten before. No wonder Mom wouldn't set foot in Grey House.

* * *

"That's what he said—that Grampa and Great-Grampa almost cost Mom Le-Ath Veronis. What could they have done?" Nissa was still turning her father's words over in her mind as she sat with her brothers in the pool area.

The palace had a very nice indoor pool—heated, of course, and there were sunlamps spaced evenly around the perimeter if you wanted to use them. They weren't employed often except by the comesuli, who didn't make it to the light half of the planet once a week as they should.

"Don't know, but we did find out that Grey House was invited into the Alliance after Trell got blown to bits," Ry responded. "And we researched the records—Grey House pays as much in taxes as Trell did. Just think—a single family paying what an entire planet did before. Grey House must be doing very well."

"Daddy says Grey House always does well. People are willing to pay high fees for the work," Nissa said. "And I get stuck removing rust from old daggers."

"Well, there has to be a market for that—loads of royal houses have those old swords and knives hanging on their

walls. All that junk, sitting around collecting dust and rust."
Tory grinned. Nissa realized he was teasing her.

* * *

Toff had to wash his hands twice and he still had dirt under his nails. Mother Fern hadn't been happy with what he'd brought back to her, scolding Toff about the roots and detritus still in the clay. She grumbled that the Halves working with her had been able to get rid of most of that using their power. If Fern intended to make Toff feel small and useless, then she'd hit the mark.

"Father, I can't get this dirt out," Toff washed his hands a third time.

"Clay isn't easy to deal with, son," Corent eyed Toff's hands. "Here." Corent gathered the tiniest bit of light around him and removed the dirt and clay with power. "There. All clean."

Toff sighed at the small amount of effort Corent had expended. Even a tiny amount of power would have been welcome, but he was destined to have none. Toff followed his foster-father to the kitchen, where Redbird had dinner waiting.

* * *

"The baby eunuch is going off to play in the dirt," Gren hissed at Toff as Toff left the small school building after lessons were over the following day. Gren was headed to his other lessons; Toff was going to dig for more clay.

The day was fine and crisp, but Gren ruined it. Toff was thankful that Mother Fern's pottery shed was on the opposite side of the village—he had no desire to walk near Gren and listen to more insults.

Chapter 3

Mother Fern lived very close to the northwestern border of the village—she'd chosen that location so the smoke from her kilns wouldn't bother the other inhabitants when she worked.

Currently, Fern had four apprentices with power and one without. Toff was the one without. He was beginning to have doubts that Mother Fern would ever let him do anything other than gather clay, work out as much of the roots, rocks and other bits as he could and then dry and sift what was left.

After Toff did his work, there would be workable, dry clay that could be added to water so the others could form the plates, bowls and other vessels the village needed.

Toff sighed and shook his head. He had no doubt that Gren would continue his verbal assaults. Toff was waiting, too, for Gren to form a new army—one that would be happy to deliver physical abuse at Gren's direction.

"Good afternoon, Mother Fern," Toff spoke the accepted, polite greeting as he joined the potter and her older apprentices. Mother Fern's apprentices looked up at Toff's entrance. Two were Halves; two were Fulls.

The youngest of the four was twenty-two and had been working with Mother Fern for eight years. Toff was the newest and most unwilling, if he were honest. He was getting a later start than the others, who were all female.

Gren regularly referred to him as a eunuch, so that didn't make him much different from the girls working for Mother Fern. Toff's shoulders slumped at the thought.

"I want you to find more clay. Try to get something cleaner this time," Mother Fern pointed to the shovel and the canvas bags waiting by the door.

Blood Reunion

Toff would have preferred cleaning the dusty pottery shed to going out and digging for clay. Either way, it was a dirty job. Toff hefted the shovel over his shoulder, lifted the two canvas bags and trudged out of the shed toward the old streambed to look for more clay.

Luck was not with Toff that afternoon—everything he found was filled with rootlets and bits of rock and gravel. The grayish, slick clay was the width of a hand or two beneath the topsoil and with the multitude of plants growing above it, it was guaranteed to be filled with roots. Toff tried to pull the roots out of the clay in one piece, but they were small and fragile, breaking off every time.

A large patch of poison leaves grew nearby, too, which he was trying to avoid. As luck would have it, the better clay was beneath those poison leaves. Toff carefully shoved the edge of his square spade beneath the plants and tossed them aside, once he'd scooped them up. He had no desire to get any part of those leaves on exposed skin—the rash could be debilitating.

Once the layer of topsoil with the leaves and vines was cleared away, Toff turned to digging up the clay. Briefly, he worried over touching the roots to get them out of the clay, but he had to put that out of his mind and get to work. Mother Fern would be waiting.

Chapter 4

"**I** know you two have been fretting over this, so I brought you in to hear the decision."

The Queen had invited both her sons to the Inner Circle meeting. Ry and Tory had only gotten to attend a handful of other meetings, none of which dealt with anything as serious as this. The decision on where to send Haldis and Sark would be revealed to them tonight.

Nearly all the Uncles were coming, including Ry and Tory's fathers. Only Uncle Norian, Uncle Thurlow and Kifirin were missing. Tory sat beside Ry on one of the sofas in the Queen's Library.

The library was spacious, with row upon row of books of all kinds, plus the more modern vids and other forms of storage. Rich rugs covered blue-gray marble floors, veined with gold and silver.

Blood Reunion

Artwork was scattered across the library's walls; some by artists long dead and most of it worth fortunes. The library was a good place to spend a rainy afternoon, as long as an Inner Circle meeting wasn't being held there.

Uncle Drake and Uncle Drew had come in with their mother, and the two boys followed. Drew had an arm around the Queen until the others arrived.

"Young ones," Uncle Gavin spared the boys a rare smile as he settled in a chair nearby. Uncle Rigo walked in right behind Gavin and sat in a chair next to him. Uncle Rigo ran a spy network for the Queen. Ry and Tory weren't supposed to know that, but they did.

Uncle Aryn taught history at the University in Lissia and sometimes ran Council meetings with Aurelius. Uncle Winkler gave the boys a wolfish grin as he settled on the opposite side of Gavin and Rigo.

Uncle Tony sat beside Uncle Winkler, Uncle Roff and Uncle Shadow came in and then Uncle Reemagar and Uncle Connegar, the Larentii, folded in.

Uncle Reemagar was short for a Larentii—barely eight feet tall. Uncle Connegar, though, was nine and a half feet tall. His blue skin was a shade lighter than Reemagar's, and his hair was a lighter blond, too—almost the color of wheat. The Larentii stood for the meeting. Uncle Karzac arrived and then Gardevik and Erland, the boys' fathers, arrived last.

"Mom's pacing," Tory jerked his head toward their mother, who was walking back and forth in front of all of them, her arms held tightly around her.

"She doesn't like this," Ry muttered.

"Keep your voice down, son," Erland scooted Ry over so he could sit. Garde sat beside Tory.

"The Council wants to send those boys to Evensun," Queen Lissa didn't preface her statement with any words that might soften the blow.

"I thought you'd have the final say," Tory spoke up. Garde put an arm around his son.

"Honey, this is a capital offense—that means that someone almost died over this. And I'll be honest—that boy would have died if Connegar and Karzac hadn't gone to tend him right away. His internal injuries were too severe. The Council passes judgment in cases like this, not I. The only one who can circumvent this decision is Kifirin, and he agrees with them."

"What about their parents?" Uncle Winkler asked.

"They will give me a decision in the morning," Lissa said. She sounded tired to Ry. Tory was thinking the same thing—he spared a swift glance at his brother.

"How did the vote go?" Uncle Drake asked.

"Ninety-four to send them to Harifa Edus, two hundred sixteen for Evensun. With two abstentions." Ry looked over at Tory. The Council had overridden their mother's suggestion by a very large margin.

"When will they be taken?" Ry asked.

"Tomorrow afternoon. Drake, Drew and Gavin will drop them off." The Queen breathed a troubled sigh. This was likely a death sentence—everyone knew Evensun was populated with criminals and unsavory characters. Once you were placed there, you were never allowed to leave. The planet was heavily shielded as a result.

"My love, the child almost died." Lissa looked up in surprise at Roff's words. His wings rustled after he spoke—he normally didn't involve himself in the politics of Le-Ath Veronis. Not to this extent, anyway.

"I know, honey. Now two other children are likely to die, too. Yes, I know they did this, but I'm not convinced we have all the ones involved in the crime."

Tory stole another look at Ry. They knew the truth of that statement, but saying anything now would only get them in trouble. Ry found himself hoping that Nissa's protection jewel would keep Toff safe from further attacks.

* * *

"Son, what did you do?"

Toff itched all over and blinked in agony at Corent's question. He couldn't stop scratching, and a red rash completely covered his face, hands and arms. Corent quickly pulled Toff's tunic over his head and found the rash spreading to Toff's neck and chest.

"Father, I scooped the poison weed out of the way before I dug for the clay underneath." Toff was still scratching.

"No," Corent whispered before shouting for Redbird.

* * *

Tiearan and Rain had come, bringing Mother Rose, the Fae's best healer, with them. Toff had been soaked head to heels in an oatmeal bath, even as Mother Rose used power to neutralize the poison from the roots of the plant.

Toff was beginning to feel halfway normal when he overheard a conversation between Tiearan and Corent outside the bathing room.

"I eradicated the poison weed myself—there shouldn't be any of it inside the perimeter," Tiearan insisted.

Chapter 4

"He can't go outside the perimeter—not without one of us with him," Corent replied angrily. "Someone holding power placed that plant, unless your power is fading!"

"My power is not fading and I used crystal to assist in the eradication," Tiearan shot back. "There shouldn't be any of it inside our boundary. We will go and see this for ourselves. Bring crystal and come."

"Lie back and let the oatmeal do its work," Mother Rose pushed Toff gently back in the tub. Toff settled in with a sigh.

* * *

"Here are the plants." Corent used power to lift some of the withered, poisonous leaves Toff had dug up that afternoon. It was still light outside, but the natural wobble of the planet tilted it slightly away, giving off a dimmer light than the morning sun.

"There is so much of it," Tiearan breathed. "How did this happen?"

"You're the one in charge; I expect you to find answers to this," Corent grumbled. "If Mother Rose hadn't come, we would have faced a more serious problem. I don't think the Queen would be happy to see this so soon after the attack."

"Then I am thankful this was a problem we could deal with ourselves," Tiearan sighed and focused his power on the crystal globe he held. It took nearly half an hour to get rid of the poison weed, roots and all.

Corent and Tiearan then went to visit Mother Fern and used even more power to eliminate any signs of the plant from the shovel and the clay Toff had brought to her.

* * *

Blood Reunion

"You'll stay home for two days, then Mother Rose will check on your rash before allowing you to go back to school or to Mother Fern's," Redbird set breakfast in front of Toff. Corent was already eating.

"Son, we've always gotten rid of the poison weed wherever we were, so I never thought to teach you everything about it. All of it is poison, not just the leaves and vines. It is dangerous to burn it, too, so never try that. It can make you extremely ill if you breathe any of the smoke."

"I'll remember." Toff would certainly remember. After he'd dropped the clay off with Mother Fern, the itching had become unbearable until he was nearly crazy with it by the time he'd gotten home the day before.

He'd barely had time to slip the jeweled necklace off and shove it in his trouser pocket before his foster-father found him in the washroom, scratching and trying to scrub his skin. Corent recognized the rash and called for help immediately. Toff had been saved from a terrible and worsening rash due to Corent's swift action.

He hadn't forgotten Tiearan's and Corent's words from the evening before, either. Someone had deliberately placed that plant inside the boundary. More than likely, they'd put it right where Toff would come in contact with it. It made Toff angry, but there wasn't anything he could do about it.

Toff had gotten his necklace out of his trousers, too and slipped it under his pillow. He didn't want Redbird finding it when she washed his clothing. Toff wouldn't be able to wear it again until Mother Rose was done checking on him.

The rash had spread to his chest area and she looked at that along with his hands, arms and face. He was glad he didn't have to go out of the house until the necklace was safely around his neck again.

Chapter 4

Toff's thoughts often wandered to the girl who'd given it to him. None of the others his age or close to his age, even, had shown any concern for his welfare. Ever. But three strangers had shown up from nowhere, listened to him and then offered what protection they could.

Toff sighed at the complexities of his life.

* * *

"Your mother didn't want you to see this, but your fathers thought you should come." Drake and Drew weren't having Ry and Tory practice with them, today. They were going to witness the final judgment against the two in the dungeon.

Ry and Tory were never invited inside the Council Chamber, which was large enough to house the three hundred ten members of the Council plus assistants and others necessary to conduct meetings. It could hold six hundred easily, and if you walked into it while it was empty, it echoed.

Ry and Tory followed Drake and Drew, who were dressed in full battle gear—black leathers and two blades crossed over each back. They caught up with Gavin and Tony, who were clothed in the formal palace uniforms of black with silver trim. Their uncles were representing the Queen's Palace Guards and the Queen's army at the proceedings.

"Sit here," Uncle Drake led them to seats in the gallery at the back.

The gallery seats were raised so anyone sitting there could see the entire Council. A set of steps led up to the balcony. Ry turned in his seat to watch the vid crew setting up in a similar gallery on the opposite wall. All the Council meetings were recorded and some were broadcast live, not just to Le-Ath Veronis but to other Alliance worlds as well.

"Look!" Tory hissed in Ry's ear, bringing his brother around quickly. Ry drew in a sharp breath.

Wlodek, Adam and Merrill had come. Neither Tory nor Ry could sufficiently describe the race to which those three belonged. Their mother often said that knowledge of their race protected itself and none could speak of it unless they had permission.

Ry had firsthand experience with that—he'd tried and failed. His mother also said that this particular race was the smallest race—in numbers, anyway—that existed. Uncles Drake, Drew, Winkler, Gavin, Tony and Karzac all had ties to that race.

That still didn't give Ry or Tory permission to speak of it. Not even a little. They could discuss it with each other, but not with outsiders. Their words would be held back by some sort of invisible shield. They'd learned to live with it.

"Why do you think they've come?" Ry whispered. Tory just shook his head. They sat and watched as the Council gathered and took their seats. Their mother came in, flanked by Tory's father and Uncle Rigo. Aurelius and Uncle Aryn, who served as the Queen's personal advisors, were already there and waiting for the Queen to be seated.

Erland slipped in and sat next to the boys before the sentencing began. His father's face looked grim, Ry thought. The prisoners were brought in next and then the palace guards led in the prisoners' parents. Both young offenders looked pale.

"We are here to pass sentence upon Haldis and Sark of the Green Fae village," Aurelius made the announcement

Chapter 4

after the prisoners came to stand before the Queen and the others who stood with her.

Aurelius shook his shoulder-length, dark-gold hair back as he read the charges off the comp-vid in his hand. Those charges included attempted murder, assault and conspiracy.

"You have been sentenced to the prison planet of Evensun. You may make a short statement, if you wish." Aurelius stepped back after announcing their punishment.

"The stupid little eunuch should have died," the one called Haldis snapped. He sounded close to tears. Ry exchanged a glance with Tory.

"He is not a eunuch." Their mother spoke for the first time. "That is how his race is. If you'd bothered to do any research, you could have found this out for yourself."

The Queen was upset and angry, Ry and Tory could tell, as were their fathers and uncles. The Queen's voice was even, though, so only those close to her might be able to tell how upset she really was. "Is that why you did this? You didn't think he was whole?"

Neither of the boys spoke, now. "If there are no other statements?" Aurelius spoke again. "The parents of the accused wish to accompany their children to Evensun. They have signed waivers to this effect, and those are on file for public perusal," Aurelius went on. "This business of the High Council upon Le-Ath Veronis is now concluded. The prisoners will be transported to the space station and taken from there to Evensun. The Queen and the Council's word is law."

Aurelius nodded to the guards, who came forward to take the prisoners from the Council chambers. Ry and Tory watched them go. As soon as they were gone, the Council members rose and began filing out.

Blood Reunion

It took a while for all of them to leave—some spoke to others, holding things up. Erland's arm stole around Ry's shoulders.

"That should not have been, son," Erland hugged Ry tightly before letting him go.

"Yeah. Dad?" Ry looked up at his father's face.

"What, son?"

"I love you."

"I know." Erland stood and waited for Ry and Tory to rise. "You should know how much I love you, too. Come on, I think your mother is about to have a meltdown."

* * *

"Flavio, I don't care whether you think this is justice or not." Queen Lissa was arguing with the only Council member left inside the chamber. He was an old friend of their mother's, Ry knew. Lissa was comfortable telling him exactly what she thought.

"I know you didn't want to send them there because of their age. If you recall, all of us saw the Larentii's images of that child after he was beaten. He would have died without outside help. Even you admit that. This surprises me." Flavio's mouth was set in a grim line, marring his handsome features.

"Flavio, I have a headache and I really don't want to argue about this anymore. I just want to crawl out of my skin and be somebody else for a while. Somebody who doesn't care about any of this." Lissa rubbed her forehead.

"Cara, come." Gavin was at the Queen's side immediately, trying to convince her to come with him. Everybody else was backing away—although Drake and Drew seemed disappointed that Gavin got there first.

Chapter 4

Gavin had his arm around Lissa as they walked out of the Council Chamber. "Cara, do you feel like eating now?" Gavin asked softly. Ry knew his mother had been too upset to have breakfast earlier.

"No, honey." Lissa's words were barely a whisper, and if Gavin hadn't been holding her up, she would have fallen to the floor when she fainted.

As it was, Erland, Drake, Drew and the others were rushing to the Queen's side when she almost went down, and Gavin was shouting for Karzac and the Larentii the moment he lifted her in his arms.

* * *

"I know you want to go to your mother, but right now we all have to stay out of the way." Garde was holding Ry and Tory back. They stood against a wall in the Queen's suite of rooms while Karzac and both Larentii checked on the Queen.

"What's wrong with her, Dad?" Tory sounded scared.

"We think she just fainted, but Karzac and the Larentii are checking to make sure. This has been a harder blow than we thought. She didn't want any part of sending those boys to Evensun, although the crime they committed was one of the worst."

Karzac turned and glared at the gathered crowd. "We need everybody out of here. Now." Tory's father jerked around and stared at Uncle Karzac. Even he knew not to argue with the curmudgeonly physician, however.

"Let's see if Cheedas can get us a snack," Garde gripped Ry and Tory's arms and hauled them out of the Queen's suite.

Blood Reunion

Cheedas ordered his assistants to find food and then sat next to Tory's High Demon father. "Do not think that I won't hear," he grumbled. "What is wrong with my little girl?"

At any other time, Ry might have found that amusing. Cheedas considered the Queen his adopted child, and she called him Papa Cheedas. She often went to him for advice or consolation, if all the uncles and his father were on the outs with her. She'd offered Cheedas other positions—more important positions—in the palace. Cheedas liked to cook and run the kitchens. He stayed right where he was.

Cheedas was comesula. Nearly five hundred fifty years of age, he was slender of build, stood around five feet six inches tall, his dark hair had silver in it and he ruled the palace kitchen with an iron fist wrapped in an oven mitt.

"They didn't tell us anything, either." Garde was close to blowing smoke, Ry knew. He was holding back for Tory's sake—Tory still looked scared. Ry didn't feel good about it, either.

Erland had insisted on staying in the Queen's suite, as did several others—Garde had been the one to get the boys out of the Queen's bedroom. This shouldn't be—their mother wasn't susceptible to illness as a rule.

"There are sixteen Larentii inside the Queen's suite," a comesula servant skidded into the kitchen. He was ready to add to that statement when he caught sight of Garde and the two young Princes. "I'll just go wash the vegetables and cut them up." He recovered quickly and walked swiftly toward the pantry.

"Stay here," Garde ordered and Ry and Tory were left to wonder as Garde skipped away right in front of them.

"Young ones, you should not worry. The Larentii will take care of things." Cheedas sounded worried, too, as he

Chapter 4

attempted to reassure the Princes. "Tell me about your schoolwork."

Tory hesitated for a few seconds. "We're working on a report," he admitted. "On the economic impact that Trell's destruction had on the Alliance."

"Hmmph. Many things happened at that time. That mess upon Cloudsong was the worst. Upset my little girl, it did." Cheedas slid off his stool and went to supervise the cooking. One of Ry's eyebrows lifted as he stared at his brother.

* * *

"How is this possible? It should not be possible." Those were Karzac's words as Tory and Ry were led inside the library by Grant, one of their mother's assistants. Grant had been sent to find them in the kitchen.

Karzac was pacing, too, and raking hands through his light-brown hair, which now looked wild. Ry and Tory stopped dead just inside the wide door into the library.

"Is Mom sick?" Tory almost whispered the words.

"Young ones, come and sit." Karzac pointed to the sofa they'd sat on the night before.

"It is not bad news." Uncle Reemagar came up behind them and herded both boys toward the sofa. Ry and Tory sat as instructed. Even Ry felt cold and shivery—something not normal for him.

"Your mother has managed to get herself pregnant, when we all thought that was impossible. Even she thought it impossible." Karzac sighed and sat across from Ry and Tory. "You had surrogate mothers, as you know—the Larentii manipulated donor eggs with your mother's genetic material, making them her eggs in every way. Your sister was conceived using the same method. And now this."

"The Wise Ones say that since your mother is what she is, that the eggs will only be released in her body after great lengths of time," Reemagar knelt next to Ry's side of the sofa. "They also say they know who the father is, but they will not announce that information at this time. They tell us that it will come later."

"You mean one of us could have a full brother or sister, and not a half?" Tory asked, his eyes wide.

"Yes, that is a possibility," Reemagar smiled, causing the blue skin around his eyes to crinkle just a little. Ry remembered that his mother always said that when a Larentii smiled, it was like watching the sky smile on a sunny day.

"So, when?" Tory didn't finish his question.

"In about seven months," Reemagar was still smiling.

"We will have to be careful with your mother—she is not built for this," Karzac grumbled. Ry looked at Uncle Karzac— he could be the father too, and Ry had only just thought of that.

Kevis, Karzac's only son with another mate, was a year older than Ry and Tory. He came to visit occasionally, when he wasn't in school.

"She is small, with a thin build, and being what she is," Reemagar explained Karzac's statement. Ry and Tory both nodded. Their mother was five feet tall, if that, and both boys towered over her, as did all their uncles.

"It won't hurt her, will it?"

"We will make her as comfortable as possible through this," Reemagar replied. "And we will monitor things with her. These Council meetings and any other business that she tends to may have to be cut back, or others may handle them for her. It will not be the first time."

"It will be the first time in fourteen years," Uncle Drake pointed out. He and Uncle Drew had just walked in. Ry knew that they'd come from their mother's suite.

"Who took the prisoners to Evensun?" Tory asked quietly.

"Aurelius and Aryn escorted them," Drake answered the question. Tory nodded at the reply.

"Will we know if they—you know."

"We'll know." Tory nodded at Drake's reply.

"Can we go see Mom?" Ry wanted to know.

"You can see her, but she is asleep at the moment. She was frightened by the news at first, so a healing sleep was placed. Connegar is with her now, as are Pheligar and Renegar. They will wake her shortly—she does not need to go without eating."

Reemagar rose and motioned for the two boys to rise too. Reemagar didn't ask them to walk down two flights of marble steps and then traverse endless corridors and hallways to get to their mother's suite in the residential wing. Reemagar folded them in.

"Go ahead, she will not wake." Connegar sat in a very large chair next to their mother's bed. He'd brought something in with power—the chair didn't match anything they had inside the palace.

"She always looks so little in this huge bed," Tory whispered.

"Your mother presents a much larger image to those around her—she is powerful, you know," Connegar said gently. "It is only when she sleeps, or on the rare occasions when she relaxes that she shows herself as she truly is."

Blood Reunion

Ry nodded and sat on the side of the bed. He took his mother's left hand in his; there were rings on nearly every finger of both hands—several on some fingers. One for each of her Inner Circle mates. Gavin's ring was the largest, and had a huge diamond in the center, surrounded by swirls of smaller diamonds.

Many people across the Alliance had copied that ring and many wives of important men proudly wore something similar. All the Inner Circle mates had a ring, too—a large gold signet ring with the claw crown engraved upon it. That design was guarded carefully and no one was allowed to copy it. It was the official seal for the Queen of Le-Ath Veronis.

"I will wake her, if you will help us convince her to eat," Connegar smiled. Ry smiled back—it was rare to see two Larentii smiling on the same day.

"How is she?" Thurlow, whom Ry and Tory hadn't seen in nearly a month, walked in with Norian. Thurlow must have gone to get Norian—he'd been on Hraede to handle some business there.

Thurlow sometimes had the same feel about him that Kifirin had, only to a lesser degree. And he didn't blow smoke as Kifirin did at times. Thurlow had dark hair and a slightly crooked nose; otherwise, he would have been quite handsome. As it is, he still drew interest whenever he was off-planet.

"As well as can be expected," Connegar replied to Thurlow's question. "She should eat, though, before she becomes nauseous."

"When will we know who the father is?" Norian asked.

"The Wise Ones do not wish to give out that information for a while," Connegar replied.

Chapter 4

"So they want to leave us in the dark." Norian wasn't happy and Ry and Tory both knew it. "We'll all have our hopes up, and then get disappointed."

"Will this make you treat her any differently?" Reemagar asked.

"You should know better than that," Norian snapped. "We all think of these children as ours in some way."

"Then think of this one as yours as well." Connegar rose from his chair and made it disappear with a thought. "Wake her, young one." Connegar tapped Ry on the shoulder. Ry nodded and leaned down to touch his mother's shoulder.

"Mom, wake up and come eat," Ry said softly. He knew his mother would hear—could have heard from across the room, even.

"Honey, what are you doing?" The Queen's eyes opened slowly.

"Trying to get you up so you can have dinner with us," Tory said over Ry's shoulder.

"I don't know," the Queen sat up with Connegar's assistance. "I feel queasy."

"If you will eat, that will subside," Connegar pointed out.

"Are you going to be like this for the next seven months?" Queen Lissa swung her legs over the side of the bed. She was still dressed in the same clothing she'd worn to the Council meeting. "I need to change."

"Here," Connegar used power to change what the Queen wore. She now had denim pants and a stretchy shirt on. She looked down at her outfit.

"I sure hope the others don't freak when I show up at the table looking like this."

Blood Reunion

"I do not care what you have on, you will come eat. Now." Gavin was there and pulling her off the bed. "Come along, young ones. We will stand over her if necessary and make sure she eats."

Ry grinned at Tory as they followed Gavin and their mother from the royal suite.

* * *

Calebert sat across from Glendes, Eldest of Grey House, in Glendes' private study. "I can't fault her work," Calebert stated. "But Nissa takes so long to accomplish a single task. She should be working much faster than this."

"What do you have her doing?" Glendes had the tips of his fingers together as he watched the Master Wizard of the Weapons Division carefully.

"Cleaning rust from daggers and blades," Calebert replied. Nissa was Glendes' great-granddaughter, and it grieved him to bring this news to Glendes. "It takes her an entire day to clean a single dagger, and it takes two days to do a sword. She should be taking an hour at the most for a smaller blade."

"Have you talked to her about it?"

"Several times." Calebert blew out a sigh. Calebert's short vest was dyed yellow—the color for the Weapons Division of Grey House. Glendes wore the black robes of the Eldest of his clan. Calebert picked at a loose thread on his vest for a moment, before repairing it with power.

"Do you think we shouldn't try to train her?" Glendes asked, tapping his fingers together. Calebert recognized the gesture—Glendes was agitated.

"No, I didn't say that. She has ability. I'm just not sure it's being directed properly."

Chapter 4

"When was the last time you spoke with her?"

"Today."

"Then give it a few more days. If she doesn't improve, I will talk with her." Glendes dropped his hands. That was his way of telling Calebert the interview was over. Calebert rose, dipped his head respectfully and left Glendes' study.

* * *

Nissa sat at a corner table in the family dining hall, away from anyone else. Her father was working late again, as he usually did. Grandfather Raffian was working too, and there wasn't anyone else near her age to have dinner with or talk to.

She picked at her chicken dish. Calebert had gotten onto her again today. He couldn't understand why it took her so long to clean the rust from the daggers and swords. Nissa didn't know, either. He'd said to make them look like new. That command was what she concentrated on when she worked on them.

They gleamed as if newly made when she handed them in for inspection, but quality wasn't what they were looking for, apparently. Nissa wished for her mother in times like these, and wished that her father hadn't limited her mindspeech ability.

She and her brothers all had it, but it had been muted so they couldn't get into trouble by using it at inappropriate times. If Nissa could have, she'd have sent mindspeech to her mother already.

"Don't forget the report that's due tomorrow." Her schoolmaster, Fourth-Tier Wizard Moris said as he passed her table. His words caused Nissa to slump over her dinner—she was only half done with the report and now she'd have to stay up as late as possible and turn in what might be substandard work.

She'd become more and more frustrated in the past few days—she knew Calebert was dissatisfied with the amount of time it took to finish what she was handed and three more daggers waited tomorrow. She was afraid she would only get one done and that wouldn't do.

The royal house on Invardine was set to crown a new king and they'd dragged all the old ceremonial daggers from storage, asking Grey House to clean off the rust so they could be worn at the coronation. The deadline was approaching, Nissa was the one given the assignment and she was falling horribly behind.

* * *

"Look—the baby's made mud pies." Gren took full advantage of the fact that there weren't any adults around when he taunted Toff. Laral, Toff's former friend, stood behind Gren, sneering at Toff. One of the others—another Half with very little power, also stood behind Gren, laughing at his words. Toff was covered in drying mud—he'd dug up more clay for Mother Fern.

Unfortunately, there wasn't a pond or stream near the old streambed so Toff could wash the muck away. Toff's cheeks were pink as he ignored Gren, carrying his two heavy canvas bags of clay past the bully and his two new sidekicks. Who knew that Laral would turn on him this way?

"Hey, we're talking to you, eunuch." Gren reached out and poked Toff on the shoulder. Toff sidestepped and kept walking, although his temper was rising. Gren had never put a hand on him before—he'd always depended on Haldis and Sark to do it for him. He wondered what this meant—and also wondered about Laral and Clover—the other Halves who'd joined forces with Gren.

"Look, he's running away, just like the scared little baby he is." Gren's words and Clover's laugh followed Toff as he made his way toward Mother Fern's pottery shed. Toff's shoulders drooped and he breathed a heavy sigh as he trudged along.

* * *

"Get in here—we need the roots taken out of that and what you brought in last time sifted," Mother Fern grumbled as Toff walked into the pottery shed. "Tiearan is going to force the rain tonight and I want the sifting done before the dampness gets into everything."

"Yes, Mother Fern," Toff muttered and went to do as he was bid.

Chapter 5

*T*ory stared at Ry. Ry handed the comp-vid to him so he could read the account himself. Tory was holding his breath, there at the end. "Cloudsong tried to level a judgment against Le-Ath Veronis, because Glendes wanted Uncle Shadow to marry somebody else to get heirs?"

"This is a huge mess," Ry nodded. "Glendes told Uncle Shadow he had to marry that woman to have heirs, only it turned out that her first husband had committed treason on Cloudsong and Cloudsong demanded compensation from his family. Taking on that woman's debts was part of the marriage agreement, so Cloudsong went after all parties, including Mom, since Shadow was one of her Inner Circle mates. I can't find any records that say the marriage was completed, just that the initial agreement was signed, leaving Grey House obligated for the debts. What I'm trying to figure out is how the crown prince was found alive later, when he was supposed to be dead. Nobody says anything about that—just that he magically appeared when the judge was telling Mom that all the profits from Le-Ath Veronis would be paid out to Cloudsong. And this was after Mom had given Uncle Shadow's ring back before he was supposed to marry the other woman. They passed judgment against Le-Ath Veronis when it wasn't even involved."

"That's why Cloudsong wasn't allowed into the Alliance—did you see that?" Tory turned the comp-vid around so Ry could see for himself.

"I saw," Ry nodded. "So that left the door open for Grey House a little while later, when Trell got blown to bits."

"I wonder what Uncle Shadow had to do to get Mom to take his ring back." Tory wondered aloud. "And then convince her to get a surrogate so Sissy could be born."

"Yeah—that must have taken some convincing, all right."

"Cloudsong still got a lot of gold out of it," Tory pointed out.

"Yeah. I saw that, too. I can't imagine that Cloudsong would be high on Mom's list, can you?" Ry was copying parts of the information into storage for his report.

"They'll never be allowed to join the Alliance—not as long as the Founder and the Twenty have anything to say about it. They denied their application in perpetuity."

"Which allowed Grey House to join the Alliance and replace all the taxes that Trell had been paying," Ry was following his brother's logic.

"At least we know now why Mom is still pissed at Glendes and Raffian Grey and won't set foot in Grey House," Tory sighed. "Should we tell Sissy?"

Chapter 5

"We can let her read this herself—it's not like the information is hidden or anything. We found it, easy enough."

"True. Why can't we use mindspeech?" Tory was grumbling over one of his and Ry's favorite complaints. They wanted communication with their sister. And each other. Life would be so much simpler, that way. Their fathers had muted the ability—afraid it might be used to cheat on tests or get into trouble. Ry and Tory managed to be in trouble often enough, even without mindspeech.

* * *

"I can't tell him this is a fool's errand. I just can't. He's old and it would kill him." Crown Prince Brandelin sat before the fire in his younger brother's bedroom. They were in the King's palace in the capital city of Cloudsong.

The palace was in disrepair, as was most of the planet. Brandelin knew it was shortsightedness on his father's part—he'd kept the wrong advisors around him during his entire reign and now Cloudsong was destitute. Brandelin looked up at Jenderlin, his brother, who stood before the fire, trying to warm his hands. A very cold winter had come to Cloudsong and much of the population was starving.

"He should never have gone near that rogue wizard—father has emptied the treasury trying to get back at Le-Ath Veronis. He believes everything that charlatan tells him, and Zellar blames the Vampire Queen for all our troubles. Zellar keeps assuring father that he has a way to destroy the Queen and her world and exact the funds he needs to keep Cloudsong from dying."

"He should have concentrated on bringing industry to Cloudsong instead of placing his hopes on joining the

Alliance. Being a member of the Alliance brings no guarantee of profitability." Brandelin rubbed his forehead—he'd been getting more and more headaches lately.

"Look at Twylec," Jenderlin agreed. "They failed to diversify and when another Alliance world developed better technology, they almost destroyed themselves. The old Queen there invited Solar Red in when they offered to pay to set up their temples."

Brandelin blew out a breath at his brother's assessment—Solar Red was a brutal religion that engaged in torture and sacrifice. It was outlawed by the Alliance and had been mostly destroyed by the ASD.

"I'm glad they never approached father," Brandelin shuddered. He knew, as did his brother, that their father might have been persuaded to allow Solar Red to set up their temples on Cloudsong—for the right amount of money.

"Brandelin—we have to be careful where we talk and what we discuss," Jenderlin said softly. "Father's mental state is not stable. He would not hesitate to imprison either of us, especially if Hedris brings the information to him."

"Hedris." That word said it all, in Brandelin's opinion. It had been Hedris, acting as the judge in the Le-Ath Veronis matter, who'd brought this fate down on all of them in the beginning.

Hedris hadn't been satisfied with Brandelin's rescue from the fire and explosion. He'd still demanded money from the Queen of Le-Ath Veronis. The money was paid, but Zellar's appearance and Cloudsong's complete downfall followed quickly.

No other worlds wanted to do business with Cloudsong after the trumped up charges were leveled against both Grey

House and Le-Ath Veronis. Hedris had attempted to extort money by manipulating Cloudsong's legal system.

His efforts backfired, and once the money he'd demanded had run out, Cloudsong became a bankrupt world. They had nothing to offer to the non-Alliance planets and King Kenderlin, who still chose to listen to Zellar and Hedris, had embarked on an attempt to exact revenge against Le-Ath Veronis and its Queen.

"Do you think Zellar is being truthful—that he has a contact, now, on Le-Ath Veronis?" Jenderlin was still worrying that bone of information.

"That old liar—you can't sort out his truth from fiction," Brandelin snorted. "Surely even Hedris can see that all Zellar has done is empty father's personal accounts. He hasn't produced a single bit of evidence that he's done anything for father and it's all illegal anyway. If the ASD finds him, he'll be connected to father and to Cloudsong. It will destroy what little is left."

"It's too bad the Alliance doesn't know that Zellar still lives," Jenderlin pointed out. "I think there would be a larger price on his head, otherwise."

"Are you thinking about letting them know?" Brandelin lifted an eyebrow at his brother.

"Not on your life. I'd like to rebuild this planet someday, as your advisor." Jenderlin bowed to his brother, who was destined to be king one day.

"And I would have to lean heavily on you," Brandelin agreed. "If there is anything left to rebuild."

* * *

Zellar? Gren's mindspeech was always tentative when he contacted the god. Zellar had introduced himself that way to Gren—Gren had allowed his mind to wander—something which Father Tiearan had warned him against.

Gren had been rewarded instead of punished—Zellar inserted images into Gren's mind. Images of distant worlds and wondrous things. *I am the god of the dark worlds*, Zellar said and then began instructing Gren.

Zellar had shown Gren how to tap into the core of Le-Ath Veronis and pull energy from there to do all he wanted or needed. The first time he'd caused the ground to shake beneath his feet, but that had subsided quickly. Now that Gren was successfully tapped into that power, it was his to command.

What is it, my favored son? Zellar's reply sounded sleepy, but he never failed to compliment Gren in some way.

The poison weed was discovered, my lord. Tell me what I should do next?

Zellar paused for a moment. *Perhaps I should leave that to you and see how inventive you can be, my child. Bear in mind, your target must be eliminated before he reaches adulthood. Otherwise, the Queen will destroy you and all the others. That promise was made fifteen years ago. You tell me that he is nearing his eighteenth birthday. Destroy him before then or I will not be able to help you.*

Gren wanted to smash things. The god was leaving this to him? He'd made a vow of nonviolence to Father Tiearan. Now, Zellar wanted him to take care of this? Toff's eighteenth birthday was in four months. Gren's followers would balk if Gren told them to do what he'd told Haldis and Sark.

Just the thought of his two best soldiers, sent off to a prison planet to die had Gren cursing. He knew the profane

Chapter 5

words; some humanoids who lived alongside the Halves and Fulls were well-versed in cursing.

Gren had listened carefully and then sought out meanings to words. He wasn't stupid. Perhaps that was what the god was counting on—Gren's intelligence. This was a test. Gren squared his shoulders and swore to come up with a way to rid his village of the baby-faced eunuch.

* * *

"Your reports, please." Morwin didn't waste any time, asking for their reports the moment Ry and Tory sat down at their desks. Ry handed his to Morwin as the Dwarf passed between both desks. Tory handed his in reluctantly.

"Young sir, you seem to be holding back," Morwin admonished Tory.

"I went in the wrong direction, instructor," Tory stared at the top of his desk.

"How did you get pointed down the wrong path?" Morwin looked ready to tap a point-toed boot.

"You asked us to write on the economic impact on the Alliance after Trell was destroyed. I got sidetracked on Cloudsong, and I'm afraid I wrote about the economic impact on that world more than the other." Tory had indeed gotten sidetracked. Cloudsong was now destitute, with none willing to bail it out.

"So, you found the insect in the sugar cake, did you?" Morwin's lengthy eyebrows were wiggling again. "Cloudsong ensured its ruin when it attempted to reinterpret its laws to perform extortion. Does your report include that, young prince?"

"Yes." Tory nodded, still not looking at his tutor. "I listed the laws and how they were bent so Cloudsong could exact retribution from uninvolved parties."

"And how is Cloudsong faring now, young prince?"

"Not well at all, instructor. They are on the verge of destitution and their people are starving. I learned that several factions have attempted to take over, but even they have not been able to oust the existing monarchy."

"And what have you learned from all this?"

"That the laws are in place for a reason and when you bend or break them to suit your purposes at times, it can adversely affect your world." Tory looked up at Morwin, now.

Morwin seemed extremely interested in what Tory had to say, when it was normally Ry who had the better papers and deeper insight. "The Alliance refused their membership application and no other worlds were interested in working with or for Cloudsong after they saw how things went in this case. Cloudsong effectively isolated itself in that way, and as they had no self-sustaining manufacturing or anything else to lure business to their world, their current situation is the result of their shortsightedness and greed."

"I agree with Tory," Ry offered. "It was a lesson to the worlds in the Alliance, too—what happened on Cloudsong. The ones that didn't diversify now looked to do so. Twylec was one of the first, with several others following. I have a list of those in my report." Ry nodded to the comp-vid that Morwin held in his hand.

"Very good," Morwin nodded to Ry. "Did you research the taxes from those worlds—before and after the diversification?"

"No, tutor Morwin. But I can—that sounds interesting."

Chapter 5

"Why don't you both do that—five pages, due next week?" Morwin was almost grinning.

* * *

Toff only picked at his dinner. Gren had given him dark looks during classes all morning, didn't say anything to him as he trudged off to dig more clay afterward and had Laral taunt him as he was coming home after working all afternoon. Corent misinterpreted Toff's gloominess.

"Son, she won't have you digging clay forever—you're the newest and therefore you have to start at the bottom. You've only been digging for a short time."

Toff didn't even spare a glance at Corent. Redbird was eating and watching both Toff and Corent but declined to say anything. Toff decided that a noncommittal nod was the best way to go as he pushed squash and lentils around his plate.

* * *

"Can't you see he's miserable?" Corent asked Redbird later, when he was sure Toff was in bed. "We should have let him go with Willow—at least he might be eating instead of playing with his food. Fern doesn't like him and you know it."

"This is the best thing for him; Father said so." Redbird was adamant as she stood defensively with fists on hips.

Corent couldn't argue with her when she was like this— Tiearan was her father and head of their clan. He couldn't expect either of them to listen when he was worried about Toff.

"Besides," Redbird went on, "even Fern will have to teach him something after a while. She's obligated, since she accepted him as an apprentice."

Blood Reunion

"But what will she teach him?" Corent knew the argument was useless. Toff would likely receive substandard instruction. He knew why none of the others would stand up for the boy. None except Willow, anyway. Willow had taken a liking to Toff, since Toff was good with Willow's animals.

"I suggest you take this up with my father." Mentioning Tiearan was Redbird's way of having the final word more often than not. Corent had learned to dislike that statement very much, indeed.

Even his mother wouldn't speak to him on this matter, although Rain held sway with Tiearan on many things. She wouldn't take any part that meant Toff might benefit. Corent wanted to grab his hair (which was now turning a dark purple) and pull it out by the roots.

"Where are you going?" Redbird called after him as he stalked out of the bedroom.

"Out," was Corent's one-word answer, and Redbird heard the front door to their cottage slam only a moment or two later.

* * *

Toff played with his protection jewel and thought about Nissa—the girl who'd given it to him. He wondered if he'd ever see her again. He was careful, not pulling it out while others might see, including his adoptive parents.

Things had seemed so much better when he was younger—the adults more amenable, the children willing to talk to him. Now, things were so much different. When he'd hit the age of sixteen, things started going downhill—as if the adults were all waiting for something awful to happen, only he didn't know what that might be.

Chapter 5

Nobody ever spoke to him and there wasn't any way he could comfortably ask questions. More than likely, his questions wouldn't be answered and Redbird would place another mind restraint. He'd heard Corent go out the door earlier and wondered where his foster-father was going.

Toff sighed. He wasn't likely to find out, he figured, and tucked the gray jewel inside his loose pajama top.

* * *

"I need all that pounded and finely sifted," Mother Fern pointed to the box filled with dried lumps of clay. Toff watched little puffs of clay dust rise around his boots as he walked across the multicolored, flagstone floor to the shelves where the mallet and the sifting screens were.

He would start out pounding dried clay with a wooden mallet and a folded cloth, then use the largest sifting screen and gradually work his way through to the one with the smallest holes.

The clay dried his hands when he worked with it this way, but he was afraid to ask Redbird or Corent to approach Mother Rose for some of the lotion she made. He imagined that Mother Fern had some somewhere, but it hadn't been offered to him and he couldn't bring himself to ask.

After pounding the lumps of clay and pulling out the largest bits of roots and detritus, Toff placed an empty, wooden box beneath the large screen before dipping out handfuls of dried clay. He then began to shake and rub it back and forth, allowing the clay to fall through while the screen kept tiny rocks, roots and other stray bits out.

Preparing the clay for use was a painstaking process and Toff couldn't decide which he hated more—digging up the clay or sifting it afterward. Once it was sifted through the smallest screen, he would add water to it, allowing any stray bits of organic material to float to the surface.

He could pour that off and begin working the lumps out of what was left. Then he would lay the clay in a thick layer on top of porous stone and allow the excess moisture to dry out of it. The clay would then be wedged by pounding it and rolling it slightly with the heels of his hands to get the lumps and air bubbles out. As a result, Toff went home with sore muscles on most days.

A natural rain was falling outside when Mother Fern let him go and Toff shivered as the cold drops hit him in the face on the way home. Finer weather had greeted him that morning, so he'd only taken his light jacket.

Now, covered in clay dust and muck, Toff didn't want to put the jacket on if he could help it—it would have to be washed, just like his clothing if he did so. Instead, Toff held the jacket over his head in an attempt to keep the rain off. The wind was whipping some of it in his face anyway, making the long walk home a miserable one.

Temperatures were falling, too; Toff could see his breath blowing out before he reached the back door to the cottage. His shoes had to be removed before stepping inside and his shoulders slumped at the amount of mud and bits of clay that clung to them. He'd be forced to give them a thorough cleaning.

Thunder rumbled overhead as he poured water into the wash pan to clean his hands and face. He could clean his shoes after dinner.

* * *

"Laral's uncle suffered a brain hemorrhage," Corent said, taking his seat at the dinner table. He'd come home

Chapter 5

later than usual while Redbird and Toff waited patiently for him to appear.

"Will he be all right?" Toff asked. A brain hemorrhage often meant death; Mother Rose couldn't fix something if it were damaged badly enough.

"I don't think so, son. He hasn't wakened since he collapsed after chasing after one of Willow's heifers." Toff stared at Corent, his eyes wide. He couldn't help thinking that he could have chased after Father Willow's heifers just fine.

"He was old and this is his time—he had no power," Redbird said callously, dipping peas onto her plate. "He was one of the Vionnu and in his fifties when he joined us." Toff jerked his head around to stare at Redbird, but she hadn't realized what she'd allowed to slip out—that there were others of Toff's race right there in the village.

She'd never told him that before—he thought he was the only one. Now, Laral's uncle Barthe was dying and Toff wouldn't be able to ask questions. Then something else hit him. If Barthe was Laral's uncle, then Laral was part Vionnu. Toff knew for sure that Laral wasn't missing any important body parts—he'd seen that for himself.

"Do you think he will wake at all?" Toff turned back to Corent.

"I doubt it, son. When it's this bad, sometimes that's for the best."

* * *

"Nissa, I expected better from you." Nissa hung her head as she sat in one of the chairs that Great-Grampa Glendes had in front of his desk. She hated coming into his study—every time she'd been there she felt as if she were in trouble over something, or was being scrutinized by the Eldest of Grey House.

She was never allowed to talk or laugh with her great-grandfather. Nissa felt, and not for the first time, as if she were under a microscope. Great-Grampa was frowning at her now, as if he were terribly disappointed. She knew why—it took her too long on the daggers. A First-Tier Wizard had been forced to help her finish the last two—she didn't get to them in time.

"I'm sorry, Great-Grampa." Nissa didn't want to look at Glendes of Grey House, so she kept her eyes down, staring at the rug on the floor instead.

Thick and beautifully crafted, the Serendaan carpet was worth much. Nissa had no idea how old it was and couldn't put a true value to it, either. Everything in Great-Grampa's study was expensive, though, and Nissa knew the rug wasn't any different.

"Calebert is upset that he had to pull one of his First-Tiers off another project to help you finish. We could have lost the commission if they'd been returned late."

"I know, Great-Grampa." Nissa toed a pattern in the rug with a rubber-soled shoe.

"We're putting you with Killien for the next month or two. You'll be cleaning paint off brushes," Glendes said. Nissa raised her eyes to her great-grandfather, then. Glendes showed no emotion as Nissa almost broke down in front of him.

Removing old paint from paintbrushes was what they started the six-year-olds on in the Art Department. Killien was a Master Artist and his workshop turned out paintings, sculptures and worked gold leaf for plaster columns and other architectural elements.

Chapter 5

Nissa couldn't speak—knew that she'd weep if she tried. She nodded and lowered her eyes again as Glendes excused her. She was halfway to her father's suite before the sobs came. She began to run as she wept.

* * *

"Nissa?" Shadow called out after hanging his blue vest on the peg just inside the door. There was no answer. "Nissa?" He called louder the second time.

Nissa heard her father, both times. She was huddled on a corner of her bed, wedged as it was against the wall. Her room was windowless—Grey House had been hollowed out of a mountain and only the Master Wizards and a few First-Tiers had windows allowing a view of the mountainside. "Nissa." Her father stood in the doorway to Nissa's room, staring at her. "Why didn't you answer me?" he demanded.

"I don't feel good, Daddy."

"You're not sick—I know your great-grandfather is sending you to Killien until you sharpen your skills and cut down on the time it takes to do simple tasks. This is for your own good, sweetheart. You're better than this." Shadow Grey raked a hand through thick, black hair.

Nissa didn't give her father a reply. "Did you have dinner?" he asked. Nissa didn't answer that question, either.

"I want to see Mom," she muttered instead.

"You cannot run to your mother every time something doesn't go your way," Shadow snapped. Nissa's lower lip trembled.

* * *

"Take this." Gren handed the knife to Laral. Laral's eyes grew wide as the handle was placed in his hand. Clover, standing nearby, gulped as a similar weapon was handed to him.

"Where did you get these?" Clover stuttered.

"I borrowed them from Laral's uncle Barthe—he used them when he butchered his pigs. He doesn't need them anymore. Now, we wait near that old streambed where the eunuch gets the clay, and I'll jump out of the tree to get him running. You're going to wait behind those two trees that are growing close together farther down. One of you should be able to get him." Gren sounded grimly purposeful and Clover and Laral stared at him—they were about to commit murder.

"Come on, you're not about to back out on me now or I'll place a mind restraint." Mind restraints and mind commands were only two of the tricks Zellar the god had given to Gren, in order to accomplish his purposes.

Laral and Clover's faces paled at the threat. They had no desire for a mind restraint—those made their heads hurt for days afterward if their parents placed them.

"Let's go," Gren ordered, when neither of his soldiers said anything. "Remember—get him in the chest if possible, that way we won't have to keep stabbing him." Gren began walking toward the old streambed to put his plan into action.

* * *

Nissa removed the paint from another bristle in the brush she was working on. She wasn't allowed to hold the brush in her hands—it was locked in a vise in front of her and Killien had placed a wizard's barrier between her and the vise. It was impossible for her to touch it with anything other than her mind.

Chapter 5

White rice paper was set out beside the vise holding the brush and each bit of paint had to be carefully laid on the rice paper, ready for Killien's inspection later.

Cleaning brushes was mind-taxing work. At least she'd been able to hold the daggers in her hand to remove the rust and make them like new, as Calebert had asked. This brush was nearly finished—it should take someone with sufficient power an hour to finish it, and she was working at a pace slightly faster than that.

Killien instructed her to get all the paint off the bristles and she was even going below the crimping line in the metal ferrule to remove all the paint. She hoped Killien would be satisfied with that.

Nissa was down to the last three bristles on this particular brush when the replacement protection jewel she'd made for herself tingled against her skin. She'd managed to connect it to the one Toff wore so she'd know if Toff's was preparing to activate. Nissa jumped from her seat in alarm.

* * *

"Run, you pathetic little eunuch!" Gren chased after Toff. Gren's legs were longer, his pace faster. Toff was terrified and breathing hard already as he ran through the drifts of autumn leaves in his attempt to escape the larger boy. "You can't get past the barrier, baby face," Gren continued to taunt Toff as he closed the distance between them, their labored steps crunching through dead, crisp foliage.

"Leave me alone!" Toff shouted the words over his shoulder, but they sounded weak—he was tiring. They were almost at the barrier and Toff was searching for a space among the tightly crowding trees to veer off. He panicked as nothing appeared; there was no safe place to hide.

Toff couldn't outrun Gren forever—Gren's legs were too long and they were too far away from the village for anyone to hear Toff's cries for help.

Was Gren finally going to deliver the beating himself instead of asking someone else to do it? Toff headed straight for the two trees that grew together at the very edge of the barrier. If he could get behind those, maybe he could play cat and mouse for a few moments with Gren, allowing a brief space to catch his breath before he had to start running again.

Almost there, Toff attempted to reassure himself, when the worst thing imaginable happened. Gren hadn't been alone, after all. Laral and Clover leapt from behind the twin trees and Toff barreled right into them.

What was that they were holding? Toff only had a moment to glimpse the long metal blades as they were pulled out; then the brightest of flashes surrounded all of them, accompanied by the smell of ozone.

Power was released from somewhere, knocking his attackers away and throwing Toff straight through the barrier that none of them were able to cross without assistance.

* * *

"No!" Nissa shouted before desperately attempting something she'd never done before—folding space. If she'd had time to think, she might have amazed herself. She transported herself straight to where Toff's protection jewel had fired, landing her amid three unconscious boys in a thick stand of trees.

Chapter 6

"**N**issa?" Toff's voice came to her as if in a dream. Nissa stared at the three unconscious boys for minutes, frightened that they were dead.

"Toff!" She whirled to see where he was. He was standing feet away from her, his hands splayed against an invisible barrier.

"Nissa, I can't get back through." Toff sounded desperate.

"Toff, what happened here?" Nissa turned back to the three boys.

"They tried to kill me. I think your jewel went off or something."

"It went off, all right." Nissa was now seeing the knives in two of the boys' hands. Cautiously kneeling beside the unconscious boys, she heard their breathing as she removed the knives and tossed them aside. "At least they're not dead." Nissa blew a soft sigh of relief.

"How can I get back inside? Maybe somebody will believe me now when I tell them what they tried to do." Toff was near tears and he didn't want Nissa to see that. He liked her and didn't want to appear weak in front of her.

"I believe you and when I tell my mother, she'll believe you, too."

"Your mother? Who is she and why will it matter if she believes me?" Toff didn't sound hopeful and Nissa wondered why that was.

"My mother is the Queen of Le-Ath Veronis," Nissa replied, a tiny bit of haughtiness in her voice. "Of course it will matter to her." Nissa watched as horror spread across Toff's face and before she knew it, he'd turned and began to run away from the barrier.

"Toff!" Nissa shouted. "Toff, you will be safe, I promise! Come back!" Nissa had doubts that Toff had heard her—he was already far away. She looked down at the three boys at her feet; one was moaning and beginning to regain consciousness.

Hastily she snatched up the knives again and threw them, unthinking, toward the barrier. Surprisingly, they sailed right through. "So it only holds people back," she muttered to herself.

Nissa looked around for any other weapons and not finding any, now concentrated on what to do about her current situation.

* * *

Lissa's Journal

Chapter 6

"You're saying that someone managed to get through the barrier you have around Grey House and then kidnapped my daughter." I stared in disbelief at Glendes, Eldest of Grey House, who stood before my desk inside my private study.

My eyes were likely red, while claws and fangs threatened to make an appearance. Somehow, he'd let my daughter be taken and I was not only frightened, I was furious. "What the hell do you plan to do about this, Glendes?" I hissed.

* * *

Glendes felt much like Nissa had days earlier when he'd gotten onto her. He had failed to protect his great-granddaughter and even now, her life could be in danger—if she weren't dead.

Glendes pulled his thoughts away from that possibility. He and Lissa had accumulated a long list of enemies over the years. Lissa's two Falchani mates, Drake and Drew, stood on either side of her as she sat behind her desk, hugging herself tightly at the news Glendes delivered.

"Killien says that all his assistants heard Nissa shouting 'No' just before she disappeared. That's all. The one word and then she was gone."

* * *

Lissa's Journal

"Where is Shadow? Why is it that you seem to pop up whenever there is bad news to be delivered from Grey House, instead of my Inner Circle mate? Does he conveniently forget that we are married and that Nissa is our child—together?" I was shaky and short of breath, so I had to force the words to come.

101

"Shadow is in a healing sleep. Selkirk placed it when Shadow almost took Killien's workshop apart." Glendes looked beaten, ducking his head before me.

"And what about that?" I kept pushing. "I thought she was working in Calebert's workshop. Did my mate forget to tell me about that, too?"

"Lissa, now is not the time. Nissa is missing. We have to find her." Glendes raked a hand through dark hair in an agitated manner.

"I have everyone I can spare out looking for her," I snapped. "Reemagar came to deliver the news shortly before you arrived, Glendes. At least my Larentii keep me informed. You and your grandson certainly don't."

I knew I was close to hyperventilation. Forcing it away for a moment, I glared at Glendes. Somehow, something was blocking me from *Looking* for Nissa. That terrified me more than I could say. In my experience, only one had been able to accomplish that in the past and my imagination was running wild.

"Lissa, calm down, all right?" Drew knelt beside my chair. "We're calling Karzac."

"He'll just put me in a healing sleep while somebody else makes all the decisions," I gasped, standing up and almost falling again. Drew and Drake both had hands on me when Karzac arrived in a flash of light.

"What is this?" my healer mate demanded.

"Nissa's missing," Drake muttered.

"I heard. And who is at fault over this?" Karzac glared at Glendes. "Letting our little one disappear, then upsetting the Queen when she should not be upset. Lissa, Lara'Kayan, don't struggle," Karzac said softly, placing fingers against my forehead. Everything went dark and I was asleep in seconds.

Chapter 6

"Now," Karzac turned angry eyes toward Glendes as Drake and Drew carried Lissa from her study. "What is it you intend to do to get our little girl back?"

Making her hair look like Toff's had been Nissa's biggest challenge, but she looked as much like him now as she possibly could, given her limited memory of him. Even her clothing had been altered with power and she'd scrubbed handfuls of dirt around the knees of loose-fitting pants as she hurriedly dug clay and tossed it into the two canvas bags Toff had dropped in his flight.

The shovel had been harder to find—he'd dropped it first thing. "He should have just used it to whack them," she muttered to herself. She'd had to *Look*—a trick her mother taught her two years earlier, to discover what it was that Toff was supposed to be doing.

Nissa had never dug up clay before or worked it to be used for pottery. She was also removing all extraneous material with power as she worked.

Nissa left the three boys behind, too. *Let them wake on their own and wonder what happened,* she snorted softly. Nissa couldn't get through the barrier a second time—she'd already tried, thinking to go after Toff.

She couldn't get the folding trick to work a second time, either. She'd been desperate before and it had just come— Nissa didn't know how to duplicate the feat. Again, she wished her mindspeech hadn't been deactivated—she would have called for her mother first thing and this would have been sorted out right away, with those three boys hauled off to the Queen's dungeons.

Now, Nissa would be forced to use every bit of talent she had to make sure she stayed alive until someone came looking for her.

* * *

"Sissy's missing?" Tory was stunned. Ry wanted to crumble, but that wouldn't help their sister. Erland and Garde had come to deliver the news to their sons.

"I'm afraid so, and none of us can get a hit on her by *Looking*. Not even the Larentii and that's extremely unusual." Garde didn't want to show the boys how upset he was over this. It would have been devastating at any time, but with Lissa pregnant, it couldn't have been any worse.

"What happened?" Ry demanded.

"Son, settle down. We have to think carefully about this instead of letting our emotions rule our heads," Erland replied. "Grey House thinks she's been abducted, but they can't find any evidence that this is what actually happened. There was no power signature and Glendes swears that his shields weren't breached. We're left with the mystery of how she was transported through Grey House's shields. Your grandfather Wylend has offered to send some of his best, including me, to go take a look, but Grey House doesn't want outside interference if they can help it."

Erland sounded angry over that. The long, unspoken agreement not to tread on each other's toes still held for the moment between the Karathian Warlocks and the Wizards of Grey House.

"I wish we had our mindspeech back; we could contact Sissy that way," Tory muttered angrily.

Chapter 6

"We're going to unlock yours for the time being, in case someone is targeting us," Gardevik Rath sighed. "Misuse it though, and you'll be without it again."

"Dad, don't you think we know better?" Tory looked hurt.

"Son, don't go there, things are bad enough as it is."

* * *

The only thing not working against Toff at the moment was the light. It wasn't dark and wouldn't be getting dark. Not completely—not on this side of the planet. He was tired, hungry, and a light rain was falling, making him cold as well. He couldn't understand why he'd run away like that—he should have stayed and talked with Nissa. Perhaps she was right and the Queen wouldn't harm him, though Redbird had insisted over the years that she would. Toff had no idea where he was and couldn't really say what direction to take to get back to the barrier.

Corent would come looking for him when he didn't show up for dinner, but what would he find? Nothing. Toff couldn't explain how he'd gotten through the barrier—the protection jewel must have done it.

Corent would assume that Toff was still inside the barrier and would exhaust himself, looking for something he couldn't find. Toff kicked miserably through deep piles of soggy red and gold leaves—he was walking through a stand of bare maples, the fallen leaves thick and wet around his feet. He was grateful he had his old boots on; they were made of spelled and weatherproofed canvas and wouldn't allow dampness to reach his feet.

Toff frightened a deer a short while later. The deer had been foraging for acorns in the stand of oaks he now slogged through on his journey to find food and shelter. The misty rain had gotten heavier, Toff had gotten hungrier and he felt as if the world had already forgotten that he'd ever existed.

Mist and fog were now rising from the ground and Toff worried that it would get so thick he wouldn't be able to see after a while. "Must be going through a low spot," Toff mumbled and the sound of his voice in the muted quiet almost made him jump. He only wore a thin jacket, which was well on its way to getting completely soaked.

* * *

"It took you long enough," Mother Fern snapped when Nissa walked in with Toff's two canvas bags filled with clay and the shovel tucked under an arm.

"My apologies, Mother Fern." Nissa had gotten the name by *Looking,* in addition to other information on her trek back from digging clay. Nissa would have to be extremely careful—she'd been thinking about Toff and determined that the farther he was away from these people, the better off he was. She was buying time for him to find a safe place. At least that's what she hoped was happening.

"Dump the clay and start working on the roots and gravel," Mother Fern grumbled, leaving her potter's wheel to examine what Nissa had brought. Nissa was frightened that Mother Fern might discover her disguise, but Mother Fern didn't notice a thing except the clay Nissa dumped on the table.

"Where are the roots?" Mother Fern demanded as she examined the clay.

"I uh, pulled them all out," Nissa felt a flush creeping across her cheeks.

Chapter 6

"It's about time," Mother Fern snapped. "Leave that there to dry and go pound what you brought in two days ago. It's dry enough, now."

Nissa hurried to do as she was bid.

* * *

"Son, did you happen to see Gren, Clover or Laral today?" Corent was seated across the table from Nissa, eating a vegetable stew. Nissa had almost balked at the food—there wasn't any meat in it.

"At school," Nissa told the small lie. Toff would have seen them there and she was taking Toff's place.

"They had to be treated by Mother Rose when they got home today," Corent went on. "They said they fell, but had too many bruises for a mere fall. I was just wondering if you'd seen anything."

"No. I don't think I've ever seen Gren fall."

"Don't worry about it—Rose just wanted information, that's all."

Nissa didn't realize she was holding herself stiffly, waiting for discovery to come. Redbird, Toff's adoptive mother didn't seem to notice anything, either. Nissa had no idea how that could happen—her mother would have sniffed out the disguise in less than a blink. She forced herself to relax.

Toff's closet was tiny and Nissa only found work clothes inside it later—mostly hand-woven items in natural colors. Nissa found three dyed shirts with pants in coordinating colors—certainly nothing compared to what she normally wore—even to work.

Blood Reunion

Sighing, she pulled pajamas from the small chest beside Toff's narrow bed and went off to get a bath before going to sleep.

* * *

Toff's teeth were chattering and he was shivering, his arms held tightly against his thin body. He kept walking—he knew that if he stopped now, his body temperature might drop too low and he could die.

He'd been walking forever, in his estimation, and hadn't come across anything—no people, villages, or even signs of life. Daylight was still with him, however, so he knew he hadn't wandered across to the darker side of the planet. He didn't realize that not only was he headed in the wrong direction now, he might have to walk for days to reach that portion of Le-Ath Veronis.

Hunger was also gnawing at him—supper would have been long ago and he missed it with an intensity that surprised him. He hadn't gone without a meal before— Corent and Redbird always made sure he was fed.

Fear also kept him going—he knew that eventually he'd have to stop and rest, and in the falling temperatures, it could be fatal. Many times over the past few hours, he chastised himself for running away.

He should have stayed. Nissa would have gone to find someone who could bring him back inside the boundary. Now, he wasn't sure which way the boundary might lie. Toff was in alien territory and completely lost.

The leaves he slogged through were so completely soaked with rain that they no longer crunched beneath his feet and he hadn't seen a nut tree anywhere since leaving the boundary line. He knew the deer ate the acorns he'd passed through earlier, but he'd never thought of them as a food source. He might have to rethink that if he found another oak grove.

Toff was nearing exhaustion later, his mind wandering. He realized at times that he was muttering to himself and considered more and more often finding a large tree to huddle beneath and sleep for a while.

His steps were slowing, the cold and dampness were taking over and he was ready to succumb to the temptation when he heard something. Thinking at first he was imagining things, he trudged on for a few more weary steps.

"How in the name of the skies did you get in here?" The voice was right in front of him as a hand reached out and grabbed his arm.

* * *

Toff huddled inside the blanket he'd been given after the woman ordered him to remove his wet clothing. She'd taken him to a small house that was so warm inside compared to what he'd been walking through, it felt like the sun on the hottest of days.

He'd been given soup with small chunks of meat in it and Toff was blowing on the hot broth before sipping it carefully so as not to burn his mouth.

The woman sat at the tiny table inside her kitchen, watching him eat. She looked older to him, with the beginnings of gray in her auburn hair. Her eyes fascinated him, however—they were nearly gold and he'd never seen anything like them before.

The house was cluttered and not very clean—what he could see of it, anyway, but the woman appeared to live there by herself.

Blood Reunion

"Where am I?" Toff ventured to ask, happy that his still-chattering teeth didn't cause him to stutter on the words.

"You are here, inside my little island of solitude," the woman replied. Her tone made Toff blink—she wasn't happy to be on that island, he could tell.

"How big is it?" he asked, sipping more soup.

"About half a day's walk, one end to the other, in every direction."

"Are there any others here?"

That question caused the woman to hmmph and clear her throat. "There's nobody until you get to the Green Fae boundary on the south, the Elemaiya village to the east and the comesuli farms west of us. The comesuli bring me food once a week, but I've had to learn to cook. How's the soup?"

"Good. I like it." Toff nodded and took another bite. It might have been a bit too salty, but he wasn't about to complain.

"How did you get in here?" The woman repeated her first question to Toff.

"I don't know," Toff hedged. "An explosion came and knocked me right through the boundary."

"Probably had some power in it—you wouldn't fly through a boundary any other way," she muttered. "What's your name?"

Toff hesitated for a moment, deciding not to make something up on the spot. "Toff," he replied. "What's yours?"

The woman stared at him for what seemed an eternity to Toff before she came back to herself. "I'm Narissa," she told him. "Do you know how to cook and clean, or do anything else of value?"

"I can clean. I cook a little, but I only know how to prepare vegetable dishes."

Chapter 6

"You would," Narissa breathed, causing Toff to look up from his food. It had cooled enough that he could eat it without blowing on it or burning his mouth. "Go on, eat your food before it gets cold," Narissa pushed her wooden chair back and stood up.

"Tomorrow is laundry day. I hope you know how to wash clothes since it looks like you might be here for a few days. And wash your dishes when you're done." She nodded toward the sink. "I'll see if I have anything you can wear."

Narissa disappeared through the kitchen doorway. Toff heard her walking down a narrow hall into another portion of the house. He ate while he pondered just what it was he'd gotten himself into.

* * *

Do not fail me again. Zellar's words came to Gren as he lay miserably on his bed. Mother Rose had removed the headache, but his body still felt the aches and pains from the blast. How had the little eunuch managed to do that?

Gren was too frightened to say anything about it to Zellar, who'd sent mindspeech, asking if Toff had been eliminated. Gren had been forced to say no, though he and his disciples had made the attempt. Zellar cut off the communication, too, after telling Gren not to fail next time.

Gren had carefully planned this attack, and now the little ground crawler would be looking over his shoulder, watching for the next try. Gren ached and wanted to call for his mother to help but thought better of it.

This should have been accomplished already. Zellar told Gren on several occasions that Gren had more power and ability than anyone else in the village. One day, Gren planned to be the one taking Tiearan's place.

111

Blood Reunion

Gren looked forward to that day with an anticipation bordering on obsession. "I'll get the baby," Gren whispered the promise to himself and painfully rolled over on his bed to sleep.

* * *

Narissa hated doing laundry. That was the only conclusion Toff could come to as he hefted another basket of clothes into the wash water. He'd already done four loads by hand and was now starting on the fifth.

Narissa sat near the fire inside her little laundry shed, sipping hot tea and watching Toff work. He was glad he'd helped Redbird with laundry from the time he was tall enough to bend over the washtub.

He scrubbed the sheets and towels with his hands in the soap Narissa handed to him. Toff hadn't seen anything like it before—the soap was a powder instead of the cut blocks Father Bark made.

The soap was stored in a container Toff hadn't seen before, too. Narissa looked at him as if he were ignorant, called the container plastic and told him to get on with the washing. Toff got on with the washing.

It was a clear day, thankfully, and warmer than the day before as Toff hung the latest load to dry. Every line that Narissa had strung across her backyard was filled with clean laundry.

Redbird didn't have half as many lines up, but then she tended to do laundry more often, Toff figured. Narissa cooked meat later, setting Toff to peeling potatoes for mashing and snapping green beans for cooking.

"What is this?" Toff cut a bite of meat with a knife as he'd seen Narissa do.

112

Chapter 6

"Pork. The chops are good if you broil them," Narissa said, taking a bite of the meat. Toff watched her chew for a moment before putting the bite in his mouth and chewing.

"This is good," Toff said, busily cutting another piece.

"Of course it is. What have you been eating? Don't those humanoids you live around cook meat?" Toff couldn't decide whether Narissa's words were meant to ridicule, but they sounded as if they were.

"I've only been allowed to eat vegetables." Toff's reply caused Narissa to hmmph annoyingly.

"It's a good thing you're the way you are—eating meat after so many years of eating only vegetables would make anyone else sick." Toff jerked his head up at Narissa's words, but she didn't elaborate.

"Tomorrow, you'll clean the house and put some things in the storage shed out back," she said instead. "I haven't been able to do it for myself and you look strong enough." Narissa was already planning his day.

Toff had been thinking about going back toward the boundary to see if he could get through it again. He'd been foolish to run away like that. Unfortunately, Narissa didn't seem to have any plans to let him go and didn't seem concerned that he'd been separated from his family. He missed Corent. He might have missed Redbird a little, but Corent was the one uppermost in his mind.

* * *

Nissa was bored the entire morning. Classes were woefully behind her current level and parts of the geography lesson had been incorrect. She was afraid to offer suggestions—that would only make her stand out, which was the last thing she wanted right then.

Instead, she worked on mindspeech. Her father had muted it, true enough, but then she shouldn't have been able to fold space, either. Nissa practiced mindspeech, sending out messages to her mother and both her brothers with the small hope that she might get through to them. When she received nothing in return, especially from her mother, she knew she'd failed during this attempt. Perhaps, if tomorrow's lesson were just as boring, she'd try it again.

"There's the little eunuch now," Gren had a nasty smile on his face as he blocked her path outside the school building. The other two—Nissa had learned they were called Laral and Clover—stood behind Gren.

They almost looked frightened, though, and that gave Nissa some satisfaction—her protection jewel had made them afraid. Good. The more afraid of her they were, the better off she was.

She didn't want any of them coming after her with a knife again, either. She had permission to protect herself, but she'd taken an oath at Grey House never to use her power to attack anyone except in defense of her life. These three could certainly push that oath to the limits, however.

"And there's the little bully," Nissa retorted at Gren's gibe. "Stay away from me." She marched away from them.

"Better keep looking over your shoulder," Gren taunted as Nissa hurried away.

* * *

"Sweep out the pottery shed," Mother Fern handed Nissa a broom the moment she walked inside the shed. The other apprentices were giggling as they turned plates on potter's wheels.

Chapter 6

The wheels were foot-powered and Nissa wanted to watch how pottery was made, but Mother Fern was keeping a sharp eye on her, so she began sweeping the floor as she'd been told.

"Now, go out and draw water to wash down the flagstones," Mother Fern set Nissa at another task as soon as the floor was thoroughly swept. "Then go out and see if you can get more clay. You can sift tomorrow—that last batch should be dry enough by then."

Nissa didn't say anything; she just grabbed the rope-handled bucket by the door and went toward the well between the shed and Mother Fern's small house.

It took seven buckets of water and plenty of scrubbing with the broom to get the remaining clay dust and clumps off the flagstone floor to Mother Fern's satisfaction.

Nissa's shoulders ached—she wasn't used to this much physical labor—most of her work at Grey House had been accomplished with mental ability. She grabbed the shovel and two canvas bags and headed toward the old streambed.

Warily watching to make sure Gren and his followers weren't anywhere nearby, Nissa began digging not far from the boundary line. She'd gone *Looking* again, and discovered clay there.

Thankful that her mother had taken the time to show her how to focus her mind on a single bit of needed information and locate it with power, Nissa focused on Gren while she dug. She found him at his lessons with Tiearan, Head of the Green Fae village.

Gren was helping adjust the yeast for the winemaking and seemed very happy that he'd been the one chosen to perform that task.

"Showoff," Nissa muttered to herself as she turned up another shovel full of clay.

All the clay inside the canvas bags was cleared of roots and other impurities before she headed toward Mother Fern's shed. It was getting late, too, and Nissa knew she'd be scolded for holding up dinner. That was the feeling she'd gotten from Redbird, anyway.

* * *

"Where have you been?" Sure enough, Redbird was trying to scold the moment Nissa walked through the door.

"Mother Fern gave me extra chores," Nissa muttered, hanging her head.

"And what chores were those?"

"Sweeping and washing down the floor in the pottery shed, and then going after more clay." Nissa didn't look up to meet Redbird's eyes.

"Tell Mother Fern next time that I do not like holding dinner." Redbird stalked off toward the kitchen. "Get cleaned up—you're covered in filth from hair to heel."

Nissa lifted her eyes to follow Redbird's retreating back. She wanted to stick out her tongue but thought better of it. She headed toward the washroom instead.

Using a bit of power to clean the clay from beneath fingernails and then a bit more to clean off most of the muck from her clothing, Nissa arrived at the dinner table a few moments later.

"You can do the dishes after dinner," Redbird announced. Nissa jerked her head toward Toff's foster-mother, biting back a retort. Corent came in, then, sitting down in his usual seat.

Chapter 6

"Finally got all the maple trees tapped today," Corent sighed and dipped into the sliced turnips and greens that Redbird set on the table. "The syrup making is going well this year. The early frosts helped with that."

"Are we going to trade some of it for wine corks and the metal nails we need?" Redbird asked as she ate. Nissa watched Redbird as she dipped into her own meal.

Redbird was always dressed better than either Corent or Toff, gauging by the clothing she'd found inside Toff's closet. Today, Redbird wore a red blouse and tan pants with red shoes.

Redbird was beautiful, with her hair gathered back and tied with a scarlet ribbon. Something bothered Nissa about Redbird, however, and Nissa couldn't quite put her finger on it. She kept eating as Toff's foster parents talked over dinner.

Nissa wiped the countertops down after all the dishes were washed and dried and then put a hand to her right shoulder—it ached. She wished she could have taken a class or two with Selkirk at Grey House—Selkirk was the best healer they had. Now she had no idea how to go about using power to eliminate the aches in her body.

"Go to bed, son, this looks good enough." Corent had a hand on the shoulder that Nissa had just rubbed. Power passed from his hand, too, and Nissa's shoulder felt better.

"Thank you." Nissa ducked her head and walked toward the narrow hallway that led to her bedroom.

* * *

"What is Belen doing here?" Tory whispered to Ry as he pulled his brother toward his side of their shared suite. Neither of them could properly describe Belen or name what he was. Belen was an enigma.

"He asked to meet with Mom and the others—the Inner Circle," Ry whispered back. That's why Ry had come to see Tory after they were both supposed to be in bed. Ry had gone on a secret raid of the kitchen and had caught sight of Belen walking through the halls with his mother. Belen sometimes had a light around him and Ry couldn't explain that.

"Do you think he knows anything about Sissy?" Tory asked.

No word had come to them for two days regarding their sister, and Grey House was still doing an investigation. At least that's what Uncle Shadow said. He'd come in earlier that day, and Ry's father had pulled the boys out of the dining hall as Shadow dropped to his knees in front of their mother and laid his head in her lap.

Ry thought he heard a sob as Erland hauled them toward the kitchen to finish their meals there. Whether it was their mother or Uncle Shadow who wept, Ry couldn't say for sure.

"Do you think Belen might be looking for her, too?" Ry hoped that was the case. He felt power whenever Belen was around—power with a capital P.

"Now is when we need invisibility," Tory muttered. "We could hide in a corner of the library and listen in."

"Like Mom wouldn't know," Ry did a little muttering of his own. "Dad swears she can see through walls, sometimes."

"And sniff out anything from a mile away," Tory agreed. "Of course we don't know what effect being pregnant is going to have on all that."

"You're pregnant?" Ry grinned and poked at his brother.

"I've got a headlock right here, bubba." Tory went after Ry.

Chapter 6

"Hey, did you see the vids earlier on Cloudsong?" Ry and Tory were both flat on their backs on Tory's bed—they'd pummeled each other for minutes before tiring.

"Yeah. It's worse than we thought. Those kids are starving." Tory sat up and lifted a pillow off the floor—he and Ry had knocked everything off his bed while they wrestled.

"I know it might not be a good thing to bring up with Mom—Cloudsong, you know, but those kids." Ry didn't finish his statement. He'd seen the thin, emaciated bodies that the documentary crew had recorded.

"Yeah, but she's always done things for kids," Tory nodded. "Maybe we can get her interested in this."

"It won't bring Sissy back." Ry rubbed his eyes. He was scared witless, if he were honest with himself. Nobody had come forward demanding a ransom or anything. "Why would somebody break through the Grey House barriers, just to take Sissy? There are multiple fortunes in spelled jewelry, weapons and artwork. If they wanted money, all they'd have to take was a little of that."

"I know. I heard Uncle Tony and Uncle Rigo say the same thing earlier." Tory slumped on the bed. "What are we going to do, Ry? We have to get Sissy back. Next week is her birthday."

* * *

"Be sure you get the corners." Toff wondered what Narissa had done before she'd acquired him as her personal slave. He had no idea what to do to get away from her—she watched him every waking moment.

He was wearing some of her old clothing, too—old tops and pants that hung loosely about his small frame. He was using a ragged cloth to clean the corners of the floor while he wondered what she'd set him to doing next.

"Tomorrow is food day—we'll pick it up at the western boundary," Narissa was smiling. "You can handle the wheelbarrow, I think." Toff looked up at her briefly—she sat at the tiny kitchen table sipping tea. She hadn't offered him any, he noticed.

"The western boundary?" he asked casually. Toff didn't want to express too much interest in case Narissa decided to withhold the information. He'd made the mistake earlier of asking her why she was alone inside the boundary.

She'd cursed and then ordered him to clean the corners of the stone floor in the kitchen. The stones were fitted tightly against one another—whoever laid them had been a master at building. They were sealed and watertight, too. Toff discovered that when he'd mopped the floor before starting on the corners.

"The one between me and the comesuli farms, of course. You think those Fae would share anything without payment?" Narissa hmmphed again. Toff was beginning to dislike that sound intensely.

"What about those others—what did you call them—to the east?"

"Elemaiya. They don't share either, as a rule. They'll talk if I find one of them down on that side, but they don't often come in this direction. They stay farther south; it's warmer there."

"I've never heard of that race—what do they look like?" Toff asked.

"Just like most other humanoids. They used to have power." Narissa sniffed at the admission.

"What happened?"

Chapter 6

"The Queen of Le-Ath Veronis happened. No more questions." Narissa got up and walked out of the kitchen, leaving Toff alone with his questions and his task.

* * *

"We're going to have to use power." Gren's statement made Laral and Clover cringe. Who knew what kind of trouble they might be in if their parents learned of this? Laral and Clover had very little power, though they were Halves, just as Gren was. Gren had increased his power lately and his two disciples were at a loss to explain it.

"But what are we going to do?" Laral felt helpless—he'd thought that cozying up with Gren would allow him access to Tiearan and better lessons. It didn't. Tiearan would take Gren and two of the older ones and teach them apart from the others.

Rain would take the ones with lesser ability and work with them during their lessons. Neither Laral nor Clover had ever gotten to work with the sun crystal and that was Laral's chief desire. Now he found himself trapped in Gren's plot to do away with the baby-faced worm.

Yes, they all called him that; even Laral's parents, for some reason. Toff was generally despised across the village and Laral had no idea why. None of the adults spoke about it and Gren refused to explain why he thought Toff should die.

"We lost the knives—that's why we have to use power. I'll try to sneak away with some sun crystal—we can use that to focus," Gren replied. "We can use the nut breaking chant, only we aim it at his head instead of the thick-shelled nuts that Father Oak grows."

"But his head will explode." Even Clover wanted to back away from this idea.

"This is what we're going to do, and you'll help or I'll tell the entire village that it was you who tried to jump him with Barthe's missing knives," Gren hissed. "You know Tiearan wanted to know where they went, don't you?" Gren gave both boys a threatening look.

Laral swallowed hard. Theft would get them banished outside the barrier. Theft and attempted violence would see their power removed and they would still be banished. It wasn't an attractive prospect. Clover and Laral paid attention while Gren outlined his plan.

Chapter 7

"These are not our ceremonial daggers." The Prime Minister for the newly-crowned King of Invardine bade his two escorts dump two large boxes on the reception desk. The Second-Tier Wizard who manned the desk in the antechamber of Grey House's sales office stared at the Invardinian Prime Minister in shock.

"But those were never out of our possession until you came to take them four days ago," the Second-Tier Wizard blustered. "We cannot be responsible for anything that has been outside our control for several days."

"These are the daggers we were given, and they are new. These have been checked carefully—the jewels are the same but the metal is not ancient. We have had our experts examine them carefully. The ancient method used to create the metal for these ceremonial daggers was not as sophisticated as it is now and there were impurities in the steel that are no longer present. I suggest you get someone here who can explain what has happened to our original daggers. I am at a loss as to why you would keep the old knives yet return the jewels—the knives have no value except to us—as heirlooms of our kingdom." The Prime Minister had white hair, piercing green eyes and wrinkles everywhere—he was ancient but determined.

"Let me see who I can find to speak with you," the Second-Tier Wizard muttered and sent out mindspeech. Calebert and Glendes both appeared moments later.

"What is this?" Calebert lifted one of the daggers from the box. "These are what we sent back—I detect the residual power around them. Are all the daggers like this?" He looked across the tall desk at the ancient Prime Minister.

"No, two were as they should be. All the others have been replaced with new blades."

"Let me take a look." Glendes reached out for the blade Calebert held in his hand. His eyes unfocused for several moments while the Prime Minister waited impatiently.

"Calebert, did you do anything other than a visual inspection on these when Nissa finished with them?" One of Glendes' dark eyebrows was raised quite high.

"No, Eldest. She was so far behind that the visual was all I had time to do. What have you found?" Calebert was beginning to worry.

"What did you tell Nissa to do, exactly, when you handed this assignment to her?"

"I told her that I wanted them like new," Calebert had to go back in his mind to the day he'd handed out the assignment.

Chapter 7

"And that's exactly what you got—like new daggers. All of these have been altered at a molecular level. They are new, Master Wizard Calebert. My great-granddaughter achieved something that some of the First-Tiers might have problems with. Take these back and rework them. Surely you remember the time in which they were made?" Glendes handed the dagger back to Calebert and folded away.

"What did he just say?" The Prime Minister was attempting to sort it all out, and still failing to understand.

"That the one who was given this assignment took the assignment too literally," Calebert grumbled. "Do not fear; you will have your daggers back in their original condition, minus the rust, of course. They'll be ready in two weeks. I trust you won't need them until then?"

"No, just as long as we get them back. With a partial refund for the trouble."

"I'll see to it," Calebert nodded to the Prime Minister before he and the boxes of daggers disappeared.

* * *

"She did what?" Shadow didn't understand. Glendes was having trouble with it as well. Nissa was stronger than any of them realized. Already at the level of a First-Tier? Unheard of. And the fact that there had only been a handful of female First-Tiers over the years hadn't gone past them, either.

"We've never had a female Master Wizard," Glendes sighed. "And if we don't find her, we may not have one still. What is the latest on the search?"

"Nothing, Grampa." Shadow sat heavily in one of the chairs before Glendes' desk. "The Larentii are tighter than clams, saying they can't interfere, Belen came to Le-Ath

Veronis two days ago and spoke to Lissa and Thurlow but I don't know what that involved, and everyone else is out looking, including the Karathian and some of Wylend's handpicked warlocks. So far, they haven't found anything."

Neither one was saying what had gone through their minds repeatedly the past few days—that their last words to Nissa hadn't been kind ones.

* * *

"They'll be along shortly." Narissa settled herself on the dry, brown grass next to a sliding wooden platform. It sat half in and half out of the boundary.

"What is this for?" Toff pushed the wheeled platform with a hand—it slid forward easily.

"They place the food on that side and slide it toward me. That's how I get my supplies. They can't enter here," Narissa sniffed angrily at that bit of information. "I'm sure they'll be quite surprised when they find you here with me." Narissa unsuccessfully attempted to hide a smile.

"Will I be in trouble?" Toff worried about that. Would he be found out and sent back to Corent and Redbird, only to be bullied and threatened by Gren and his followers again?

"Oh, I don't think so," Narissa didn't try to hide her smile this time. "See, there they come."

Toff squinted in the direction Narissa pointed and saw a cart with two people on board in the distance. He stared— there was no horse or ox pulling the cart; it was moving on its own. "Not seen one of those before?" Narissa laughed and the laugh didn't sound kind. Toff whirled to look at her.

"How did this one come to be inside your boundary, Narissa?" One of their visitors spoke. Toff forcibly shut his mouth—these two looked familiar to him, but he couldn't say exactly how.

One was only a few inches taller than Toff, with black hair like Toff's. The other was slightly taller, with dark-brown hair. Both had slight builds, but hefted the boxes of food and provisions easily onto the platform.

"You know as much as I," Narissa retorted. "Please inform the palace that I will be willing to negotiate a trade."

Toff reached out to lift the first of two boxes when he set it down again with a thump on the wooden planks. "What?" His voice was sharper than he intended.

"You don't think I was just going to put up with you forever, do you?" Narissa's voice sounded gleeful. "I think I can negotiate a little to trade you back to the Queen, you know. Don't look so shocked, young one. This boundary wasn't set because I wanted it. This is my prison and I intend to use you to make it more comfortable, if not gain my freedom back. Now—you'll do what I say, just like you have been, and you won't be harmed."

She was threatening him? Toff backed up in alarm. Narissa was no different from Gren and the others—he'd just been too blind to see through her intentions.

"Don't worry, young one. We'll have you out of there before you know it," the dark-haired visitor declared, climbing back onto the cart with his companion. "If she lays a hand on you, the Queen may kill her herself." The cart backed away and turned to drive off in the opposite direction quite fast indeed, leaving Toff facing Narissa.

"You—you're no different from the others," Toff snarled sullenly. He was weary of being bullied, used and constantly threatened.

Blood Reunion

"This is the way life is—get used to it," Narissa snarled back. "Do you think I plan to live the rest of my life inside a shielded boundary, with nobody to talk to who has any sense at all? Do you? Load those boxes in the wheelbarrow and come along. It's nearly time for dinner." Narissa took off toward her cottage. Toff watched her walk away for a while before piling boxes in the wheelbarrow and following Narissa in resignation.

* * *

"Tory," Ry whispered as he jerked his head at the comesula guard who bowed as he walked into the dining hall. At a nod from Lissa, the comesula approached her place at the table.

"Veris, I haven't seen you in a while," Queen Lissa stopped him from kneeling at the side of her chair.

"My Queen, I bring urgent news," Veris couldn't keep himself from bowing again as he spoke.

"What is it?" Lissa asked, lines of worry appearing on her forehead.

Drake and Drew, who sat on either side of the Queen, also seemed interested.

"Somehow, a young one has gotten inside Narissa's boundary and she is offering to bargain for him. We know not how he made his way inside, only that he is there and quite shaken. Narissa is forcing him to fetch and carry for her, if my reports are accurate."

The Queen stood abruptly at Veris' words, and Drake and Drew were standing with her, with one other of her Inner Circle mates. Most were out looking for Nissa, however, so it was only Drake, Drew and Rigo to go with the

Chapter 7

Queen. "Mom," Tory shouted, just as Lissa was about to fold away with help from her two Falchani.

"You want to come?" Tory and Ry's mother looked as if she were about to take something—or someone—apart.

"Yes," Ry answered the question first. They were all folded away.

"Lissa, remember your pregnancy," Rigo cautioned as Lissa strode quickly toward Narissa's cottage. They'd folded directly inside Narissa's boundary—It couldn't hold the Queen or the Falchani back—they were too powerful.

"Narissa," Lissa shouted. "Come out now before I turn your house into matchsticks!"

* * *

Toff jerked at the shout—it sounded very close. He'd been sitting at the table, having dinner with Narissa after cooking most of it for her.

"Well," Narissa wore a nasty smile, "that didn't take long, did it? Come on, boy." Narissa jerked Toff from his chair, had a knife held to his throat quickly and hauled him toward the door.

Toff was terrified—the protection jewel had turned black after it thwarted the attack from Gren and the others. Toff figured it was made to work once, but he couldn't bear to part with it—it was all he had of Nissa, though she most likely would never speak to him again after he'd run away like that.

Now, someone he barely knew was threatening his life again. Narissa pushed the front door to her cottage open and forced Toff out in front of her, the knife still at his throat. Toff, terrified as he was, still was surprised by the people who stood outside, waiting.

Blood Reunion

* * *

Ry dug an elbow into Tory's ribs to keep him from calling out to Toff. Both boys recognized him, all right, and Ry was quickly piecing together just how Toff might have come to be inside Narissa's boundary.

"Narissa, harm that child and I'll kill you." Those were the Queen's words, and Tory and Ry both knew their mother wouldn't bluff about something like that.

"What are you going to do, Lissa?" Narissa sounded unhinged in Ry's estimation. Toff must have realized it too—his eyes were wild with fright as Narissa tightened her grip on him, bringing the knife just under his chin.

"Surely you know as well as anyone just what I might do," Lissa snarled.

Drake and Drew flanked her, which meant that Narissa's eyes were on the Queen and the twin Falchani instead of Rigo. Narissa should have watched him, but Ry imagined this may have been the plan all along.

Rigo could move as swiftly as any vampire and he was behind Narissa, had the knife in his hand and Narissa flung to the ground in the space of a heartbeat. Toff was left standing and holding his throat, which had the barest of bloody scrapes on it.

"Toff, honey, are you all right?" The Queen went straight to him.

Toff wanted to shrink away from her. "How—how do you know my name?" he sputtered, still gripping his throat. Tory and Ry were beside their mother in two blinks, doing their best to check on Toff.

Chapter 7

"Honey, I've known your name since you were tiny," Lissa murmured, holding a hand out to Toff. Toff was too afraid of her to take it.

"Mom won't hurt you," Tory tried to reassure Toff. Toff blinked at Tory and Ry before extending a shaking hand to the Queen. Her hand gripped his and he was pulled against her in a tight hug. She may have kissed him on the cheek, too, but Toff was too dazed to know for sure.

"Honey, I can't believe that Redbird and Corent haven't been camped out on my doorstep, wondering where you were," Lissa held Toff away from her and brushed hair back from his forehead. "And I have to say, I don't think I'm willing to let you go back unless you just can't stand to be parted from them."

"What?" Toff didn't understand any of this. "Where's Nissa?" He turned toward Tory and Ry, who both hung their heads. They were just about to get in trouble with their mother.

"Nissa's missing, honey. Has been for several days, now. How do you know about her?" The Queen held Toff's face in her hands. Toff was surprised—the Queen's hands were gentle as she held him.

"Redbird always said you'd drink my blood," Toff blurted without thinking. That caused the Queen to go still.

"Did she?" Toff didn't realize how angry the Queen had become in less than a blink. "Well, let's go have a talk with your foster-mother."

Toff didn't know what happened. One moment he was outside Narissa's cottage, the next he was standing at the door to his home inside the Green Fae village. One of the tall men with a long black braid down his back was knocking on the door. Redbird answered with Corent right behind her.

"Would you care to tell my why Toff has been missing for six days now and you failed to report it?" The Queen was asking as nicely as she could under the circumstances. Ry and Tory stepped up to flank Toff, each holding onto an arm. Toff was glad they were there—he felt safer, somehow.

"But Toff has not been missing," Redbird insisted. "He has been here all along, hasn't he, Corent?" Redbird turned to look at her mate.

"Toff has been inside Narissa's boundary for the last six days; we just went to get him when we found out Narissa was threatening him," the Queen insisted, sounding quite angry.

"He has been here the entire time," Redbird said, "and now you show up with some trumped up lie, when Toff is supposed to be out gathering clay for Mother Fern."

"You say he's been here all along, and is out working right now?" The Queen's eyes narrowed at Redbird.

"But you have him right there," Redbird pointed at Toff.

"This Toff has been inside Narissa's boundary, trust me on this," Lissa stated. "Now, would you like to go with me and find the Toff you've been harboring, or will you stay here and cower while I go do it?"

"We'll come," Corent stepped around Redbird and out the door. Toff was transported again just as before, but the scene that greeted them at the old streambed had Corent shouting, Redbird screaming and Drake and Drew running.

* * *

Nissa wanted to grumble as she shoveled clay and then used her power to remove roots and bits of rock before dumping it in the canvas bag. More than once, the sides of the canvas bag had collapsed inward, causing the clay to

Chapter 7

slide down the outside instead of dropping inside the bag as it should.

Nissa was so busy concentrating on her work that she failed to notice the sounds of leaves rustling. She didn't miss Gren's taunt, however.

"Look, it's the baby worm, digging through the dirt. Going to eat that dirt like the other worms, baby eunuch?" Gren laughed at her.

"At least you're smart enough to know what worms eat," Nissa snapped, shoving the edge of her shovel into the dirt and watching Gren warily. "Where are your spies, Gren? You normally don't go anywhere without them."

"Why are you worried about my friends?" Gren still had a smile on his face.

"Because you're just the distraction," Nissa said. She was doing her best to go *Looking* for anyone else in the area, even as she kept a close eye on Gren.

"Now!" Gren shouted and Nissa's head felt as if it were about to explode as her protection jewel activated, blowing her and Gren away from one another.

* * *

Lissa's Journal

"My daughter is in your household for six days, and you don't even notice?" I paced in front of Corent and Redbird. Tiearan and Rain had come, too, but Tiearan knew better than to say anything at this point.

"The disguise was very good," Redbird muttered, hanging her head and refusing to meet my eyes.

"But surely you must have noticed some differences," I insisted. I certainly would have, even if I didn't have the

133

scents. I would have known my daughter and my sons anywhere.

I was waiting to hear from Karzac—he'd come to check on Nissa, who was still unconscious. He was also treating Gren and two others, both of whom Toff identified as the three who'd had attacked him six days earlier.

"And you also failed to notice that Toff was getting bullied and marked for death. As was my daughter. Those three boys will be held in my dungeons, I can guarantee that. I intend to find the reason for all this, I assure you. Toff is also coming with me. You've worn out your chances on this." Even my hair was crackling with energy, I was so angry.

"But the mindbond," Redbird whined.

"How about that?" I snapped. "Do you know what he said to me when we found him? Do you? He said that you told him I'd drink his blood. You've been filling his head with lies. What else have you been telling him, Redbird?"

Redbird was lucky I settled for merely saying her name with contempt. I wanted to do so many other things, and most of them involved a great deal of pain.

For her.

"Is that what you've been telling him?" Corent was now looking at his mate in alarm.

"I wanted to keep him with me," Redbird was back to whining again.

"You'd have done better to protect him from those bullies," I shouted. Yes, I wasn't behaving in the most rational way possible, but then I'd never been faced with this much idiocy while I was pregnant.

"Avilepha, you cannot reason with her—there is not much there to reason with," Kifirin appeared in a burst of light. "Come home with me now. We will take care of your

Chapter 7

two young ones and watch the others in the dungeons. Had their parents been more vigilant, this might have been avoided."

"But you cannot just take them," Tiearan was now standing and disagreeing with Kifirin.

"We will take them. You depended too heavily on that boundary you placed around your village, Tiearan, and failed to notice the blight within. Now you will pay the price. We will advise you on the final disposition of those three miscreants." Kifirin blew a curl of smoke from his nostrils and Tiearan backed away.

* * *

"Toff, we have enough space in our suite if you'd like to stay there," Ry offered. Toff blinked at Ry and Tory, shocked by what was offered. He now realized that they were both Princes—sons of the Queen, just as Nissa was the Queen's daughter and a Princess.

Nissa was being treated inside her suite and the Queen, a healer and a tall, blue Larentii were in attendance. Ry and Tory had led Toff away, though he wanted to go to Nissa's bedside to see how she was.

"We'll check on Sissy tomorrow—she got a blast to the head. Anyway, that's what Uncle Drake says. Uncle Drew said that those three were doing a chant normally used to crack nuts open. He says that if Sissy hadn't had her protection jewel, she'd have died."

Tory shivered as he made his statement. Both boys were leading Toff down endless corridors toward their suite of rooms. "Are you hungry?" Tory stopped in his tracks. "I am. We didn't finish dinner earlier."

"Let's go to the kitchens. Tory, can you skip us in?" Ry grinned. They had Sissy back, Karzac would make her well again and Toff wasn't being bullied anymore. Things were looking up at the moment.

"What is skipping?" Toff managed to ask before he disappeared from one place and appeared in another. The other place turned out to be the largest kitchen Toff had ever seen. It had things in it that he didn't recognize, too. Three people were inside the kitchen, cleaning up.

"Young ones, I am not surprised to see you, since you failed to finish your dinner earlier," one of the three came forward to eye Tory, Ry and Toff. "And who is this? He looks quite familiar to me."

"This is Cheedas, who runs the palace kitchens," Tory nudged Toff. Toff was gaping at Cheedas, who looked familiar to him, too. Cheedas had silver in his hair, an indication to Toff that he might be old.

"Would you like something to eat?" Cheedas reached out and ruffled Toff's hair. Toff was surprised by the gentle gesture.

"I am hungry," Toff nodded.

"Then you'll eat. Sit. All of you," Cheedas commanded, and Toff sat while Cheedas and the other two found food for him and the Princes.

"What is this?" Toff had never had anything he liked so well. It was a tender steak that had been breaded and fried. The main course was served with mashed potatoes, gravy and tiny peas. Toff hadn't realized how hungry he was.

"Mom calls this chicken-fried steak and we make fun of her because it isn't chicken at all," Tory grinned, cutting into his steak and placing a bite in his mouth.

"I like this very much," Toff was busy eating.

"How old are you, young one?" Cheedas leaned on the kitchen island across from the three boys. "My guess would be around eighteen."

"Really?" Toff couldn't believe it. He would turn eighteen in less than three months. "Everybody else says I look twelve."

"But your kind matures slowly," Cheedas replied. "Did they not tell you that? You will not reach full growth until age twenty-nine. Do not be discouraged—it is just what you are."

"Redbird always said I was Vionnu—from Vionn." Toff swallowed his bite of food before speaking—it was polite. Tory snorted at Toff's statement. "Is that not true? I'm not from Vionn?" Toff glanced from Cheedas to Tory in confusion.

"I know not the reason why she might say that to you," Cheedas straightened. "You are most certainly not Vionnu. How did this Redbird explain your lack of genitalia?"

Toff stared openmouthed at Cheedas. The cook had just revealed Toff's most shameful secret. How had he known? How?

"I see that it was not explained to you," Cheedas said. "It is not a deformity, young one. All your kind are born this way. You are what I am, young Toff. Comesula. That is singular. Comesuli is plural. We are native to Le-Ath Veronis and your foster parents should have told you of this long ago. From Vionn, they said." Cheedas walked away, shaking his head.

"We knew the minute we saw you," Ry said. "Is that what they did—make you ashamed because you weren't like them? That's awful. This is how you're supposed to be."

Toff was now staring at Ry. "Don't worry," Ry continued. "I think Mom will send someone in the next few days to explain things to you. You're a whole person, Toff. Don't let anybody tell you otherwise."

"But what about girls and coupling and things like that?" Toff was almost afraid to voice those fears. He liked Nissa very much, but according to Gren and the others, he had nothing to offer her. That upset him.

"As I said, Mom will send somebody to explain that to you. Don't worry. You have options." Tory patted Toff's shoulder. "Finish your food. Maybe we can sneak into the pool, too, before somebody finds out we're not in bed."

* * *

"This is all you use this for?" Toff was astounded that there was a pool of warm, clear water used only for swimming and nothing else. All three boys had jumped into the water without clothing, and Ry was busy trying to splash Tory.

Toff was also shocked that neither of the others had said a word about what he lacked. Cheedas had told him it was natural—he was supposed to be this way. Why had the Fae and the Halves told him otherwise? Toff couldn't fathom a reason.

They'd been in the water for perhaps an hour when someone walked in that Toff hadn't seen before.

"Hi, Dad, we just wanted to have a swim," Ry grinned sheepishly at Erland Morphis.

"That's Ry's father, Uncle Erland," Tory whispered to Toff, who nodded. He was afraid they were all about to be in trouble.

"Time for bed, all of you," Erland had fists on his hips. They reluctantly climbed out of the pool and Tory headed for the pile of towels on a nearby table. He tossed towels to Ry and Toff, then dried himself with another and wrapped it around his waist afterward. Toff watched closely and followed Tory's example. Erland led the way and took all three of them toward Ry and Tory's suite.

"We brought in another bed—there's room in between with an extra closet," Erland pointed Toff toward the largest bed he'd ever seen. "We'll see about getting clothing for you in the next day or so. Welcome to the palace, young Toff." Erland smiled at Toff and closed the door to Toff's new bedroom behind him when he left. Since Toff didn't have pajamas with him, he slid naked between smooth sheets for the first time in his memory.

* * *

"Nissa, baby, Daddy's not mad." Shadow had Nissa pulled onto his lap as soon as she woke. "How's your head, sweetheart?" Shadow stroked Nissa's hair. Nissa wrapped arms around her father's neck and wept.

"Baby bird, it's all right." Uncle Karzac was there in a moment, rubbing her back gently and using power to clear away any residual headache. Nissa pulled her head away from her father's shoulder and blinked tearfully at Karzac.

"They tried to kill me, didn't they?"

"Baby, don't think about that now," Shadow attempted to calm his daughter. "You need to eat something, I think. You missed your dinner last night and breakfast this morning. Your mother is about to have one of her conniptions, I think."

Nissa gave a trembling smile. Conniption wasn't a word used in any of the languages recognized by the Alliance. It was something that her mother used, however, and Uncle Tony said that it was a legitimate word. Somewhere.

Blood Reunion

"Come on, young one," Karzac smiled. "We'll have lunch with your mother and your brothers."

"What happened to Toff?" Nissa looked into her father's gray eyes.

"He's here, too. Your mother refused to leave him behind this time. Good thing, too—they were filling his head with all sorts of lies." Karzac huffed angrily over that fact.

"They were calling him a eunuch. When they thought I was Toff, they called me that, too. And worm, baby face and a bunch of other ugly names," Nissa wiped a stray tear off her face.

"Neither you nor Toff are any of those things," Karzac declared. "Come, I think Cheedas has made chicken and dumplings for you."

"Really? They never make it at Grey House." Nissa was ready to eat.

"Because they don't know how," Shadow let Nissa slide off his lap. He rose and draped an arm around his daughter's shoulders as they made their way out of Nissa's suite and down marble halls toward the dining room.

* * *

"Nissa?" Toff stood the moment she entered the room, accompanied by Karzac and another man.

"Toff." Nissa went straight to him and wrapped her arms around his neck. "I was so worried about you." She even kissed his cheek before letting him go. Toff stared after her as she went to sit next to her mother at the head of the table. Toff was sitting between Ry and Tory only a little farther down.

Ry tugged on Toff's borrowed tunic and Toff remembered to sit down again.

"Uncle Roff," Tory nudged Toff and Toff turned swiftly in his seat, his breath catching in his throat for a moment as Roff walked into the dining hall. Tory's Uncle Roff had wings. They were held tightly against his back for the moment, but Toff could only imagine what they might look like if they were spread out.

"Ask him to fly you around, sometime," Ry whispered as they watched Roff glance briefly in their direction before finding a chair next to Tony. Several servants came to serve the meal and Toff knew they were of the same race as he—he recognized it now, thanks to Cheedas. One of them winked slyly at Toff as he served a soup. Toff smiled at the servant before he hurried away.

"Toff, we want you to take a day or two off to recover. We'll set you up with Morwin after that—he'll tutor you in the mornings while Ry and Tory are practicing with Drake and Drew," Queen Lissa smiled at him.

Toff felt a bit of shock—the Queen had been so kind to him. She'd hugged him last night, and may have kissed him, even. Now she was offering lessons. "Do you want to stay in the same bedroom you had last night, or do you want one to yourself?" The Queen asked.

"I can stay with Tory and Ry?"

"We want you to," Tory nodded. "If you want to, that is."

"I want to." Toff stared at his hands for a moment. He wanted to ask why he was in the palace and why everybody was being so nice to him. He was nothing to them, yet they were treating him as if he were a member of the family. "I would like that very much, thank you," he remembered his manners, albeit a little late.

"Good. We have someone coming in who will bring some clothing for you. You can pick out what you like," the

Queen went on. "Is there anything you want brought from home? Corent has already offered to send whatever you need."

Toff was embarrassed to ask for the small wooden box of bits and pieces he kept beneath his bed. "We'll just have him send everything, and you can pick and choose," the Queen told him. "Let's eat, I'm starved."

Everybody started eating, then, and Ry and Tory quickly had Toff smiling as they teased one another, and then Nissa was getting onto her brothers and soon they were all laughing. For Toff, that hadn't happened in a very long time.

* * *

"Careful, she spits." Tory snickered at Ry's words after Tory sneaked Toff, Ry and Nissa into the dungeon to see the prisoners. They were coming up on Narissa's cell. She did try to spit at them, but her efforts fell short.

Narissa called them unkind names as they stared at her. "Mom says she's not right," Nissa told Toff softly as they walked away from the cell. Next on the list was Clover's cell. Toff stared at his would be murderer and shook his head. Clover looked lost and dejected.

"Gren's a pig," Toff whispered as they walked from Clover's cell to Laral's. Laral looked to be in much the same state as Clover. Gren, whose cell was next to Laral's, began shouting and forced Tory to skip them all away from the dungeons before the guards came running.

* * *

Lissa's Journal

Chapter 7

"Roff, why don't you offer to let him help out at the winery in the afternoons? Corent said Toff has helped with that before. Mostly the crush, but he understands the basics."

I took Roff's hand and pulled him down to the sofa beside me. Roff allowed his wings to loosen—his way of resting them, before he allowed the one nearest me to unfold completely and wrap around my shoulders.

"Raona," Roff breathed as he leaned down and kissed me.

* * *

"He has not had sufficient teaching in geography or history, and nothing at all in Alliance Studies." Morwin gave his report to me later. "He is very bright and is good with basic mathematics, as far as his instruction has gone, anyway."

"Can you bring him up to the proper levels?" I looked across my desk at the best private tutor in the Alliance. I felt lucky to have Morwin—many couldn't see past his race, all of whom thought that the bushier and lengthier your eyebrows, the more knowledgeable you were.

Knowledge was highly prized by the Amterean race, and information often brought more riches than gold or jewels. As curiosity went, they were nearly on a level with the Larentii. Morwin's eyebrows wiggled as he considered my question. I'd learned not to snicker when he did that.

"I think he will come along quickly, as long as he applies himself. I worry about the stress that such a move will cost him, however." Morwin was pointing out one of my own fears.

Toff's background with the Green Fae was vastly different from life in the palace or any other place on Le-Ath

Veronis. That would affect anyone, I think. We would all be watching Toff closely, to make sure he was adjusting to his new environment.

"I'm hoping that spending afternoons at Roff's winery will help with that," I sighed. "Please keep me informed if he needs help in adapting. I want him to be as comfortable and happy as we can make him."

* * *

"We still make the oxberry wine by hand." Roff was showing Toff through the winery. "It's the most expensive wine we sell."

Much of the winery was automated, but Toff was amazed at the number of comesuli there, all busy as ants at one task or another to get barrels and barrels of wine made.

"More than likely we did the crush at the same time you were doing it at the village," Roff went on. "The fermentation is going on with this year's crop and we'll be bottling and corking some of last year's press soon." Roff led Toff past stacked wine barrels.

"This is overwhelming," Toff stared up at the tall racks that held several barrels, one on top of another.

"I don't want you to feel that way," Roff placed a hand on Toff's shoulder. "We can start you out on the floor and allow you to work your way up if you want. And if you decide that this isn't for you, just let us know. We'll find something else. Something that you want to do."

"No, I want this," Toff breathed. "It's just so different from what I'm used to."

"I know. When I started out, we did it all by hand—my father, brother and I. My oldest child came along and helped after a while."

Chapter 7

"Where is he now?"

"My oldest child is dead." Toff knew by the tone of Roff's voice that this was a painful subject. Toff nodded and didn't ask any more questions.

"All our power is from the sun—the collectors are on the light half of the planet," Roff showed Toff the control room where all the power lines were monitored. "The workers are paid a very good salary and receive four weeks' vacation every year. When you work, you will be paid for your work. It won't be much in the beginning, but your salary will increase as you gain experience."

"I've never had money. Someone will have to teach me about that." Toff hunched his shoulders. There was so much to learn, and the weight of it troubled him at times.

"Morwin will show you that, and you can ask anyone if you don't know about something. We realize this is a large step for you, and we want you to be comfortable." Roff patted Toff's shoulder to offer comfort and encouragement.

Toff wanted to ask Roff why he was being offered a new home, an education and work that he liked, but held back. What if the answer was something that frightened him? Redbird's words came into his mind more often than not, although he hadn't seen anything that might make him think she'd been correct on any of it.

Toff resolved to wait and see. Meanwhile, he enjoyed spending time with Ry and Tory, and if Nissa were there, he liked it even better.

Chapter 8

"Toff, I have to go back to Grey House tomorrow." Nissa sounded depressed. Toff sat beside her in the arboretum. Nissa had grabbed his hand after dinner and led him up several flights of broad marble steps until they'd reached the top level of the palace.

There, Toff found the most wondrous garden—it was lit with solar lamps and multitudes of plants and foliage grew inside, all of it lush and full. Small waterfalls and fountains placed here and there provided soothing sounds while visitors enjoyed the garden.

"I don't want you to go." Toff took a chance and put his arms around Nissa. Surprisingly, she leaned her head against his shoulder as they stared through the windows at the capital city of Lissia. Toff had learned about Lissia from Morwin only that morning.

"Daddy won't let me stay, and since they know I made two working protection jewels, they'll step up my training."

"Don't they ever let you take a break? Roff told me that his workers get four weeks of vacation time."

Vacation time was a new term for Toff, and he'd asked Morwin about it during one of his lessons. Morwin had explained it completely. There was so much that Toff didn't know and he was determined to learn as much as he could as quickly as possible.

He missed Corent, but was surprised to discover that he didn't miss Redbird very much. He certainly didn't miss any of the others, except for Father Willow.

"I'll be back in four days—it's my birthday," Nissa said softly. Toff tightened his arms around her.

"How old?" Toff thought about kissing Nissa's cheek but held back.

"I'll be twelve."

"You look more grown up than that."

"Thanks." Nissa smiled at Toff. "And we do get summers off, but that's when Ry goes to train with his dad on Karathia. Tory spends a lot of time on Kifirin, too, which means we still don't get to see a lot of each other."

"I'll be here." Toff surprised himself by saying it.

"I know. We'll have to see if Mom will let us spend time at the beach house, or go work at Niff's in Casino City."

"The beach house?"

"It's on the light side, right on the ocean."

"I've never seen an ocean." Toff had learned about them—there were three on Le-Ath Veronis. One stretched so far into the dark side of the planet that most of it was covered in ice.

Chapter 8

"Hey, you two," Ry and Tory skidded into the arboretum. It looked as if they'd run up all the stairs to get there. "We want to ask Mom if we can go to Niff's for ice cream."

Nissa pulled Toff off the bench immediately. "Come on," she grinned at him. "I want ice cream."

"Mom's in her office signing papers," Tory said as they all clattered down the endless steps to the first level of the palace. Toff was running to keep up with Tory's long-legged strides.

Ry and Nissa were nearly trotting, so Toff didn't feel so bad. Eventually they made their way to an elaborately carved door that stood open on the first floor.

"Mom," Tory said first thing as they made their way inside a spacious room that Toff could only stare at in amazement. It was furnished in beautiful fabrics with rich paintings hanging on the walls. The Queen sat behind an ornate desk that looked as if it had gold trim around it.

"What is it, honey?" The Queen looked up from a paper she held in her hand.

"We were just wondering," Ry managed to get out before Toff clapped his hands over his mouth to keep the shriek from escaping. A huge snake lifted his head over the top of the desk and stared at them.

"Don't worry," Nissa's hand rubbed Toff's back as he stared at the snake in fright. He'd never seen a snake that large and this one had to be poisonous—its head was a triangular shape and lengthy fangs were visible when it opened its mouth. The creature was rising higher, now, right beside the Queen. Toff was terrified she'd be bitten.

"It's the full moon tonight, I forgot," Tory turned to Toff. "That's Uncle Norian. He's a shapeshifter, and that's his lion snake. He won't hurt you unless you decide to attack one of us."

Toff was still staring in shock. He'd seen Norian earlier at dinner. Now he was a snake? "Nori," the Queen said, reaching out to run a gentle hand down the snake's neck and body. "You're scaring Toff." Toff watched in amazement as the snake turned his head and looked at the Queen, his slitted eyes blinking at her.

"He understands everything, just as he does in his humanoid form," the Queen reassured Toff. "Do you know about the ASD?"

"What does that mean?" Toff asked. He recognized the letters, but there appeared to be another meaning to them.

"Alliance Security Detail," Nissa supplied the information. "They keep the Alliance safe from criminals and other factions that are unlawful inside the Alliance. Uncle Norian is the Director of the ASD."

"I've never seen a shapeshifter before," Toff breathed, lowering his hands.

"Too bad Uncle Winkler isn't here," Nissa hugged Toff. Toff wasn't sure about Uncle Winkler but he was sure about the hug he got from Nissa.

"We wanted to go to Niff's for ice cream," Tory was back to their original mission.

"Let me find someone to go with you," the Queen said, standing up and stretching. Norian slid his body onto the top of the desk, showing Toff his full length, which was twelve feet. Black and gray patterns ran the length of the scaled body. "Bring some back for Norian and me, too," the Queen smiled at the snake.

* * *

Chapter 8

"Uncle Norian loves ice cream," Tory said as they followed Drake and Drew toward the entrance to the palace. "We get to ride tonight. I love riding to Casino City."

A tall man waited outside a metal carriage at the bottom of the palace steps. "This is Radomir, an old friend of Mom's," Nissa whispered to Toff as they climbed inside the vehicle. The seats were soft and comfortable; Tory rode in the front seat with Radomir and Drake and Drew rode in the back, facing Ry, Nissa and Toff.

"What is this called?" Toff asked as Radomir did something to start the carriage and then steered it away from the palace steps.

"A limousine, young one," Radomir said over his shoulder.

"Radomir hears everything, just like Mom does," Nissa patted Toff's hand. "And Uncle Gavin, Uncle Tony, Uncle Winkler, Uncle Aryn and Uncle Rigo. Don't say anything anywhere around them that you don't want them to hear."

"We're going fast," Toff marveled as the vehicle picked up speed along a smooth road.

"We'll have to stop at the checkpoint at the walls, but we'll be at Niff's pretty quick after that," Ry said. "Have you had ice cream before?"

"I didn't know what you were talking about, but I wanted to go with you anyway," Toff admitted shyly.

"You'll like it," Nissa assured him and sat back in her seat to enjoy the ride.

* * *

Zellar, I'm in the Queen's dungeon. Gren's mental voice couldn't hold back the whine. He'd never been imprisoned before and there was something surrounding the dungeon itself that prevented him from using any of his power. A dampening field had been placed around his cell. Gren's connection to the planet's core had also been cut off and he felt that absence like an addict kept away from his drug of choice.

Energy from the core had kept Gren confident and feeling powerful. Now he had no control over his power and he hated the Queen for doing this to him. Hated Toff for forcing the issue. The baby should be dead and Gren should be basking in Zellar's compliments. Instead, he was inside a bare cell with few comforts.

What have you done, you foolish imbecile? Zellar's mindspeech was scathing. *You will not breathe a word of your connection to me when they come to question you, do you hear me? Not one word! Idiot. Pathetically hopeless.* Zellar went off on a rant, speaking in several languages that Gren didn't understand. Zellar finally spoke again in one that Gren understood. *I will kill you myself if you tell anyone about me. Do you hear? And your death will be a slow and painful one.* Zellar cut off the communication. Gren slid down the whitewashed wall of his cell and wept.

* * *

"Zellar, where are you going?" King Kenderlin of Cloudsong stood in the doorway to Zellar's suite. He'd come to confer with the warlock, but he found the warlock packing instead. Zellar turned his face toward the King, showing Cloudsong's monarch the scarred and sightless side of his face.

"I am going to someone who may be able to help us," Zellar replied. He failed to interrupt his packing, as he should have done out of respect for the King. "I am

152

Chapter 8

prevented from going to Le-Ath Veronis, but someone I know may be able to travel there. If we find a way, then things will go much smoother for Cloudsong," Zellar closed the lid of his packed trunk and locked it with power.

"Get everything you can from that witch," King Kenderlin snapped, his voice wavering slightly. Kenderlin was nearing the end of his years and his reason was not what it once was. He was soft clay in Zellar's hands, and Zellar had his own agenda to pursue with the Queen of Le-Ath Veronis.

Zellar was draining every bit of what remained of Cloudsong's wealth as well as the power from its core in order to exact his revenge. Cloudsong was expendable. Zellar's vengeance was not.

* * *

Toff was speechless. Casino City was brightly lit and people were everywhere. All kinds of people. All colors of people. Dressed in ways he might never have imagined, too, and all of them laughing, talking and patronizing seemingly endless streets of shops and restaurants. There was a line to get into Niff's when they arrived. Chasing lights outlined a Niff's Sweets and Goodies sign over the shop's door. Inside, the store was huge, with glass-walled counters through which you could see tubs of frozen treats in many colors. There were also plates and plates of pies, cakes and something called brownies.

"I can't decide whether I want strawberry ice cream or a brownie sundae," Nissa stood on tiptoe to see everything from her place in line.

"I'll get whatever you do," Toff decided. If Nissa liked it, it had to be good.

Blood Reunion

Radomir stood beside Tory at the head of their little group, Drake was beside Toff and Nissa while Drew stood behind them with Ry. The desserts were worth the wait when they finally got to the counter and ordered; Toff moaned in pleasure the minute he tasted his brownie sundae.

"If Uncle Roff brings us, he's always swamped by people admiring his wings," Ry said. "He likes to come here, but not when there's so many people around."

Three giggling girls passed their table as they ate. "Did you see? I asked him to bite me and he smiled!" One of the girls was nearly breathless as she held an ice-cream dish in her hand.

Toff stared at the girls as they rushed out the door.

"Fangers." Ry said the word with disgust. Toff didn't understand the term and was about to ask but Nissa offered him a paper napkin, so Toff ignored it for the moment.

* * *

"Mom, there was a big crowd at Niff's," Tory handed the box of ice cream to his mother inside her study. Norian was still there in snake form and Queen Lissa pulled out a dish of ice cream and set it in front of him. Toff stared as the snake dipped into the ice cream, eating it with seeming pleasure.

"He really loves ice cream," Lissa smiled at Toff. "I hope this doesn't frighten you. I know you're not used to this." Toff found himself smiling shyly back at the Queen.

"I'll get used to it," he said. Nissa reached over and took his hand. Toff would get used to shapeshifters and anything else if he could see Nissa now and then.

"Now, young ones, it's off to bed. Off-day tomorrow and the day after. If you have reports, off-days are good for that," Drake shooed them out of the Queen's study.

Chapter 8

"We have to finish an assignment for Morwin," Ry grumbled as they walked down the hall toward the residential wing.

"He gave me a report to do, too," Toff agreed. "I've never written one, so he showed me some samples and gave me a comp-vid to look things up."

"What did he ask you to do?" Nissa was still holding Toff's hand and he didn't want to let her go.

"He assigned a report on a Faldaran battle six hundred years ago that involved a branch of Fae and the humanoids who lived there. He wants me to write what the impact of the battle had on the current conditions of the planet."

"Sounds interesting," Ry grinned.

"Or not," Tory was grinning, too. Ry gave Tory a sideways kick. Tory retaliated with a shove.

"They always do that," Nissa whispered beside Toff.

"Looks like fun," Toff murmured back.

* * *

Toff felt depressed. Nissa had been whisked away right after lunch. Tory and Ry weren't happy either.

"She'll be back in three days for her birthday," the Queen came to hug Toff's shoulders. Toff knew the Queen was misty-eyed, too.

"At least Uncle Shadow released her mindspeech so we can talk," Tory said.

"You have mindspeech?" Toff stared at Tory.

"We do, but it was muted until Sissy came up missing."

"And it will be muted again if you misuse it," Queen Lissa gave her tallest son a hug around the waist.

"But what if I want to send a message to Nissa?" Toff blurted.

Blood Reunion

"We'll let you use more conventional methods," Queen Lissa squeezed Toff's shoulders after letting Tory go. "Write her notes and I'll see they get delivered."

"You can do that?" Toff allowed his hopes to rise a little.

"Of course. Ry can even send them, if you ask," Tory swatted Ry on the back of the head.

"In the meantime," the Queen glared an admonishment at the two Princes, "I'd like to go with Tory's Uncle Jayd and Aunt Glinda offworld to shop for Nissa's birthday. Want to come along, Toff?"

Toff stood rooted to the floor, he was so stunned. He nearly stuttered when he found his voice again. "Roff said he'd pay me for my work at the winery. Can I borrow against that so I can buy something for Nissa too?"

"Honey, you'll receive an allowance for a few chores in the palace, plus whatever Roff pays you," Lissa reached out to touch his cheek. "Just pick out what you want to give Nissa and I'll take it out of that."

"Come on, dude, let's go get dressed for shopping." Toff was hauled away between Tory and Ry, shock on his face at being called dude, among a multitude of other things.

* * *

"I like this." Toff pointed at a comb that held a jeweled flower. It reminded him of the magnolia tree that stood outside Father Willow's cottage. Willow had the only magnolia tree inside the Fae village and Toff loved the velvety petals of the huge flowers when they bloomed. "It will look good in the top of her braid, don't you think?"

They stood inside a jewelry shop on Hraede. Uncle Rigo had come with them—this was his home planet, according to Ry and Tory. It was also the safest world in the Alliance. King

Jayd and Queen Glinda of Kifirin had come too, with their twin daughters Jhase and Jheri. Ry couldn't take his eyes off them, Toff noticed.

"I think it will look good in her braid," Ry agreed. Toff had gotten a credit chip from Grant, one of the Queen's assistants before they'd set out, and Queen Glinda had folded space to get them all to Hraede.

"Here," Toff handed his wrist over—the credit chip was on a bracelet and the clerk scanned it before boxing up the comb. Toff kept looking around him as they made their way through a crowded shopping district in the capital city of Hraede.

Tory and Ry bought a bracelet and matching necklace for their sister before they were done for the day.

"Want to see the High Demon palace on Kifirin?" Tory whispered to Toff when the shopping was over.

"Can we?" Toff was extremely curious. Only one thing might have made this day better—if Nissa had been there with him.

"We can go for a little while," Lissa agreed—she'd heard what Tory said to Toff. Toff realized that Ry hadn't been lying when he'd said his mother could hear anything said nearby.

"So, how are you feeling?" Glinda asked Queen Lissa later when they landed inside the palace vestibule on Kifirin. Toff noticed it was very much like the palace on Le-Ath Veronis.

"Both palaces designed by the same person," King Jayd leaned down to inform Toff before he could ask.

"Tybus was an amazing architect, don't you think?" Tory's father, Gardevik Rath walked up while packages were sorted. Garde was King Jayd's brother and Prime Minister on

Kifirin, in addition to being one of Queen Lissa's Inner Circle mates.

"Is that his name?" Toff stared at the vaulted ceiling made of marble veined in blue, silver and gold.

"Was his name. He died long ago when Le-Ath Veronis was destroyed," Garde replied, tousling Toff's hair. "How are you, Toff? Are you doing well? You must tell us if there is anything amiss."

"Le-Ath Veronis was destroyed?" Toff hadn't heard that before.

"Around one hundred fifty thousand years ago," Tory answered Toff's question. "Mom is still rebuilding it."

"How long have you been rebuilding it?" Toff asked Lissa.

"Nearly eighteen years," Lissa was smiling at Toff. "Did you enjoy the trip to Hraede?"

"Yes. Can we go again, sometime?"

"You will be welcome on Hraede anytime," Rigo nodded.

They had a light snack with Glinda, Jayd and the others, and Tory showed Toff through the hall of ancestors. Toff stared at the huge sculptures.

"What are those?" Toff didn't know what to think—the images seemed frightening.

"High Demons in Full Thifilathi," Ry replied. "That's what King Jayd and Uncle Garde are—High Demon. Tory here is half."

"You turn into that?" Toff now stared at Tory in disbelief.

"Not yet." Tory sounded embarrassed.

"Plenty of time, young one—don't rush it," King Jayd draped an arm around Tory's shoulders, although Tory was as tall as his uncle.

Chapter 8

Toff's head was spinning. What else might he see? Tory, a High Demon? He hadn't heard of that before. Norian Keef, the Director of the ASD, a shapeshifter lion snake? Ry and Tory had hinted that their Uncle Winkler was a shapeshifter, too. What did he become? Toff was afraid to ask.

"Do you do that often?" Toff nodded to the nearest huge sculpture. The sixteen-foot statue depicted something between humanoid and animal, Toff thought, with widely spaced fangs in the open mouth, horns that bent back above the ears and claws on fingers and toes. The scaled skin, carved in marble, appeared tough and impenetrable.

"Once a month," Jayd nodded. "Or if we are attacked, the Thifilathi will come. That is how we fight our enemies."

* * *

Roff sat next to Toff at dinner later. "Would you like to come with me tomorrow to Kifirin and cut back the oxberry vines?"

Toff hadn't seen natural sunlight on Le-Ath Veronis since coming to the palace. "I think I would like to come," Toff nodded. "I just need some time tomorrow evening to finish a report for Master Morwin."

"We'll have you back in plenty of time for that," Roff smiled, showing even, white teeth. "Wear something you won't mind getting dusty or scratched up. The oxberries have thorns."

"Wear denim pants and leather boots," Ry suggested. "I've cut oxberry vines back before. You'll be covered in dust and leaf bits when you're done."

"Can't be much different from cutting and binding cornstalks," Toff smiled back at Roff.

Blood Reunion

"Much the same, except for the thorns," Roff agreed, accepting a glass of wine from a servant.

* * *

"This is my favorite place to sit." Toff sat beside the Queen, listening to her as he stared over the capital city from the uppermost dome of the palace. Toff was glad he wasn't afraid of heights—he might have been screaming if he were, they were up so high. "I had to bring you now, because Karzac tells me that in two weeks I can't use my power until after the baby comes."

Toff jerked his head around to look at the Queen. "You're pregnant?"

"Yes, honey. It came as quite a shock, let me tell you. I thought it was impossible, but that, like many other things, has changed."

"But Ry and Tory." Toff didn't finish. He meant Nissa, too, he just couldn't say it. How was Lissa their mother, if she hadn't been pregnant before?

"Ask Master Morwin to explain genetics to you," the Queen hugged Toff before letting go. "My Larentii manipulated donor eggs with something of me, and my three children were born to surrogate mothers. They're still mine in every sense of the word, just as they belong to their fathers. Now, we're all waiting to see who this one belongs to." Lissa patted her almost-flat stomach.

"It is much the same in the Fae village," Toff agreed. "At times, they have to wait until the baby is born and see what color his hair is."

"The Fae don't reproduce very often, so they are anxious to get children any way they can," Queen Lissa agreed. "Kifirin says it is because they are an immortal race. If they

160 "

reproduced as often as the mortal races, they would quickly overpopulate, unintentionally."

"Cheedas says that my race lives to be around six hundred or so," Toff sighed.

"That is a very long life. I hope yours is as happy as you could wish it," Lissa said softly.

"It has been miserable until recently," Toff replied.

"Do you miss your foster parents?"

"I miss Corent. And Father Willow. I don't think I miss the others much at all. I certainly don't miss Gren. He tried to kill me, even though he took the vow of nonviolence. And then he tried to kill Nissa." Toff found that unforgiveable.

"Yes. I can't tell you how thankful I am that she flaunted her great-grandfather's instructions and made protection jewels."

"I still have mine, though it isn't good anymore." Toff lifted the blackened jewel from under his shirt.

"Shadow says it was fine work and performed flawlessly," Lissa fingered the jewel before giving it back to Toff. "And she did it without any instruction." Toff knew that Queen Lissa was proud of her daughter.

"We'll see her in three days," Toff sighed.

"We will. Cheedas has something special planned in the kitchen. We'll eat well for sure," Lissa said.

* * *

"Wear these," Roff handed leather gloves to Toff. Toff had been quite shocked when they arrived at the farms on Kifirin. They went on forever in his estimation, and comesuli were everywhere, some with young ones. Even a few of the very young, barely old enough to walk, followed a parent around. All had been transported to Kifirin to work on the oxberry vines.

"Roff, where are the women and girls?" Toff asked softly.

"Child, they are all as you are—born without genitalia. See that one over there with the sling over his shoulder?" Toff looked where Roff indicated.

"What is inside the sling?" Toff saw that there was something carried inside the sling on the comesula's left side. The strap holding it up was slung across the comesula's right shoulder.

"That is a baby pouch—it is how the comesuli reproduce. Generally, they have one or two children during their long life. When it is time, the pouch drops off and the child makes his way out, much like a turtle hatching from an egg."

Toff had stopped still, staring now at the pregnant comesula. This was completely foreign to Toff, although it was his race. "But what about mating and such?"

"That is a question best left for later, young one. Come, we will take care of the vines today, and we will tend to your education later. Comesuli will not reproduce until the age of sixty or so, with most occurring around the age of one to two hundred years. The second one, if it comes, will happen sometime after that. Do not fear, you are not about to drop a child next week." Roff patted Toff's shoulder. Toff had to tear his eyes away from the pregnant comesula. If they had no genitalia, how did they get pregnant to start with? Toff was beginning to get worried.

He did get extremely dusty, cutting back oxberry vines right alongside Roff. He kept up with him, too, leaving many of the others behind. Toff had experience with this—he'd been doing it for as long as he could remember. The thick, leather gloves protected his hands as he cut the thorny vines back, tossing what he'd cut to the side as Roff instructed, allowing others to gather the cuttings and haul them away for burning. The cutting kept the vines from growing too tall and thick; thick and tangled vines always made it more difficult to harvest the berries the following spring.

They stopped for lunch at midday, and Toff enjoyed eating with the comesuli, including the little ones. One or two climbed onto his lap, and he was shocked that they ate mostly meat, with only a few vegetables.

"They eat protein straight from the birthing sac—they're born with a full set of teeth," Roff explained as Toff helped a tiny one eat. He could barely get himself around by walking, though his parent said he was nearly two. Toff recalled Cheedas' words—that comesuli matured slowly and wouldn't reach their full growth until age twenty-nine. This brought it home to him—he hadn't thought it over before.

"Your life with the Fae has caused you to grow up faster emotionally," Roff told him later when they were back to cutting vines. "Your body hasn't caught up yet, but it will. You should not worry over this, child. All things will come in time."

Toff wanted to ask if Nissa would come to him in time, although he wasn't destined to have genitalia. What could he offer her, indeed?

"Go have a bath, young one," Roff placed a hand on Toff's head affectionately after they'd arrived at the palace on Le-Ath Veronis. "Then come straight to dinner. We ran late finishing up, but we got it all done today. You are good with your hands, child. You did well."

Blood Reunion

Toff grinned at Roff before trotting down the hall toward the suite he shared with Ry and Tory.

* * *

"Why should I help you? Fifteen years you've been at this, and all you have to show for it is a destitute world, empty pockets and less sense." Zellar blinked at the old warlock's words. He'd been so sure that Vardon would help him. Vardon had no love for the King of Karathia or his granddaughter, the Queen of Le-Ath Veronis.

"I know what you're thinking, Zellar. Vengeance is a fine dream, but after a while, the smart warlock learns to channel his efforts in other directions. There is no satisfaction in killing them—you'll be left empty afterward, make no mistake. Find something else to occupy your time. Feed those starving children on Cloudsong—that is a task worthy of your ability."

Vardon didn't point out that Zellar was likely responsible for much of the hunger upon Cloudsong. He'd probably tapped into the core of the planet, removing the energy the planet needed to sustain itself. Tapping was forbidden sorcery and would warrant a death sentence if Wylend Arden, King of Karathia, learned of it.

Any being with power knew what tapping into the core meant. Famine and death would come quickly if it were done over an extended period of time. Zellar had been on Cloudsong nearly fifteen years. Long enough to destroy that world, and nothing short of a vast replacement of power could save it now.

"Then I will have to look elsewhere," Zellar sniffed and turned to go. He might have considered killing Vardon— thought about it, even, but Vardon wasn't a fool. He would be

Chapter 8

ready and held more natural talent than Zellar. Zellar relied on Vardon's outlaw status to keep him from going to Wylend or to the Alliance—both of whom had a price on Zellar's head.

There was one other that Zellar could approach, though it might prove extremely dangerous. Zellar hoped he could offer something to this one before he allowed his appetite to overcome his sense, making a meal of Zellar instead of an alliance.

Chapter 9

"*T*his is what we're going to do." Lissa smiled at Ry and Tory—they'd brought the problem to her and in her usual way she'd devised a workable solution. Toff sat on the sofa with Ry and Tory; he was invited to the Inner Circle meeting with everyone else.

Only a few members were missing, so Toff was getting to see new ones tonight. He hadn't met Gavin or Tony, although he'd heard of them from the Princes. Both Larentii were also present, and they made Toff marvel with their height and blue skin. Toff now knew they fed off sunlight—Morwin had explained that—and all of it amazed him.

Toff turned back to the Queen as she flipped on the vid screen. What he saw shocked him—there were starving children on a planet called Cloudsong. He liked the planet's name—it sounded beautiful to him. Only now, the ugliness of poverty and starvation were everywhere upon that world.

"We're going to take away the poorest of the population," Lissa smiled happily. "They'll be relocated on Morningsun, the sister planet to Evensun. They are opposite each other and are hidden from view by the sun between them," Lissa went on, "although they have the same temperate climate for the most part. We received help from friends to put up housing and gathered food from many worlds that had a surplus. We were able to buy at bargain prices and several Alliance worlds helped with funds and supplies. Le-Ath Veronis helped out, too, in addition to securing the planet."

"But what does Cloudsong think about all this?" Tony asked.

"They don't know about it, and won't know about it until it's done. Don't worry; I've already talked to Ildevar Wyyld. He says that there is precedence—that the Alliance has assisted outside its boundaries if the population of a world is dying. There is no doubt that Cloudsong is dying. The Larentii have confirmed it."

"And how are we getting them from Cloudsong to Morningsun?" Rigo asked.

"Need you ask?" Toff drew in a breath—a woman appeared who looked very much like Narissa, down to the auburn hair and gold of her eyes.

"Young Toff, you are correct—Narissa is my homicidal great-grandmother," the woman smiled at him. She'd read his mind, Toff realized. Tiearan had done it a few times, but normally he didn't bother. This one had taken the thoughts straight from him without any trouble. "I am Kyler," Kyler came forward, leaned down and kissed Toff's cheek. "Welcome to the real Le-Ath Veronis."

"Um, thank you," Toff said, feeling bewildered. Kyler gave him a lovely smile before turning toward Lissa. "Aunt Lissa, Youon and the others are ready."

"That's how they're doing it," Tory breathed beside him. "The Black Ra'Ak."

"Who are they?" Toff asked, but the situation quickly became controlled chaos as people began to disappear all around him.

"Darn it," Tory muttered. "I wanted to see this."

* * *

"Here it is!" Ry waved a hand and the sound came up on the vid screen inside their bedroom. Toff was still attempting to get used to technology and marveled at the newsfeeds they received from across the Alliance. Someone was standing on the deserted streets of a city that had been reduced to poverty.

"It is official, coming from the offices of the ASD. Many destitute and starving citizens of Cloudsong have been relocated, although we do not know where that is at the moment," the man reported.

Toff watched in complete fascination as other cities on Cloudsong were shown in insets—all of them deserted. "With a few exceptions, the only population that remains is that inside the capital city, and even many of those are now gone. We have received reports that the crown prince and his younger brother have also disappeared. If we had not received this information from the ASD, many would have termed this a religious event."

The reporter's image disappeared, replaced with one of people lining up to receive food and water in a meadow somewhere. Temporary hospital tents stood in long rows and children and the elderly were receiving medical attention. The images were limited and soon were exchanged for that of the reporter.

"They did that so people wouldn't figure out where they'd been taken. I'll bet that old geezer on Cloudsong is having a conniption." Tory grinned at Ry's use of their mother's word.

* * *

Brandelin didn't recognize any of the rescuers, with the exception of one. He recognized her easily. Grabbing Jenderlin by the arm, Brandelin hauled him along until they came to the woman with strawberry-blonde hair. Brandelin dropped to his knees before her.

"I thank you for these lives," Brandelin wept at Lissa's feet.

"Get up from there," Lissa pulled him to his feet. "I've done what I could to save them. Now, you do what you can to keep them alive. You'll still lose a few—some of them are too far gone. This world is yours, now, and I'll be watching to see what you do with it. Don't make the mistakes your father made."

Jenderlin stared at the Queen of Le-Ath Veronis—the last person who should have come to their aid. "There's something you should know," he blurted. Lissa stared at him in surprise.

* * *

"I say we raid the kitchen in celebration," Tory headed for the bedroom door.

"Come on," Ry pulled Toff along with him. They'd almost reached the wide portal into the kitchen when the

Chapter 9

palace shook beneath their feet, throwing all three of them to the floor.

Pots and pans fell from hooks in the kitchen and Toff heard shouts and screams all around as heavier things began to fall—the ground was shaking harder. Toff curled into a ball and wrapped his arms around his head, just as Ry and Tory did the same.

* * *

Kifirin strode through the palace in Full Thifilathi—nearly twenty feet of dark, angry god. Someone had attacked Lissa's planet and he was furious. A few of the inhabitants of the palace had been injured in the quake, but Kifirin was searching for the cause. His senses sent him skipping to the dungeons, where he stared at the cell assigned to the Half-Fae called Gren. It was empty. Kifirin caused the palace to shake again with his deafening roar.

* * *

"Who's on the list?" Queen Lissa was shouting and weeping as she held a dying Cheedas in her arms. Ry and Tory were in tears as they hugged one another while staring down at the comesula cook. Toff was frightened; he was watching one of his newest friends die right in front of him.

"Oluwa is coming, my love," Gavin knelt next to the Queen.

"Child, we will do our best to save him," Roff's arms came around Toff and held him tightly.

"But what can you do?" Toff only then realized he was weeping—the tears in his eyes kept him from seeing Roff clearly as he looked up at him.

"It is what is done when one of the worthy is dying," Roff whispered. "Hush now, everything will be done that can be done." Toff watched as a tall, dark-skinned man was led into the kitchen. He knelt next to Cheedas and the Queen.

"Lissa, pretty girl, back up and give me some room," the one called Oluwa said gently. "He's still with us. I'll save him if I can." Lissa nodded and allowed Gavin to pull her away.

"Young one, this will be frightening and unpleasant to watch, so I will take you away if that is your desire," Roff said.

"What is going to happen?" Toff whimpered.

"We will attempt the turn," Roff replied. "Usually we have more time than this. Oluwa will have to hurry."

Toff watched in horror as a very sharp claw emerged from one of Oluwa's fingers, and he used it to slice into Cheedas' wrists—three lengthwise slits on both. Blood began pumping from Cheedas' veins. Toff's mouth worked but he couldn't force a moan past his lips. Ry and Tory were now hugging their mother, who'd come to stand beside them. Gavin was kneeling next to Cheedas' head, keeping him from moving as Oluwa lifted one of Cheedas' wrists to his lips and began to drink.

Toff couldn't say later how he'd managed to keep his feet—perhaps it was Roff, standing there with him, hushing him and reassuring him, telling him that this was the way things were.

Toff watched as Oluwa stopped drinking from Cheedas' wrist, laying it down gently beside the cook's body. Oluwa held a wrist out to Gavin, who formed a claw on a finger and opened Oluwa's veins. Dark red blood welled up immediately.

Chapter 9

Oluwa then held his wrist to Cheedas' mouth as Gavin raised the old cook up, and Oluwa's command to drink had Cheedas swallowing the vampire's blood. Radomir came in from somewhere and began counting the time aloud. At some prearranged moment, Radomir called time, Oluwa removed his wrist from Cheedas' blood-covered mouth and Cheedas' heart stopped beating.

"That is the way of it, my child," Roff crooned softly, lifting Toff and carrying him from the room.

* * *

"We should know something soon," Oluwa sighed as Gavin lifted Cheedas from the floor.

"Oluwa," Lissa went to him and wrapped her arms around his waist, allowing her head to droop against his chest.

"It will go as it will, little Queen," Oluwa soothed. "We should take him to the waiting rooms and clean him up a bit."

"You can't leave him here?"

"It is better this way," Oluwa assured her. "Come now; let me do my duty as a sire." Oluwa allowed Gavin to carry Cheedas away.

"Mom?" Tory's voice was shaky as he reached out toward Lissa.

"Honey, I'm so sorry you had to see that," Lissa went to her boys.

"Mom, Uncle Tony explained it to us two years ago. We just weren't prepared for the reality, and we weren't ready for it to be Cheedas," Ry wanted to weep or scream—he couldn't decide which.

Blood Reunion

"It's always that way, honey. You're not prepared for it to be the one it is. Cheedas had a heart attack, I think. I didn't see any wounds on his body."

"I can confirm that," Karzac appeared in a brief flash of light.

"What happened to Toff? Where is he?" Lissa looked around her.

"Uncle Roff took him."

"Did he see this?"

"Yeah, Mom. He did."

"Oh, no." Lissa raked a hand through her hair.

"We will explain to him, little firefly. We will do our best to make him understand," Karzac had hands on Lissa's forehead. They eventually wandered down to her abdomen. "The baby is fine and strong," Karzac allayed any fears in that direction.

"Avilepha, the Half-Fae difik has escaped." Kifirin was back to himself when he appeared in the kitchen. "With help, but he escaped, nonetheless."

"Let me guess—Zellar?" Lissa sighed as she looked up at Kifirin. His eyes still appeared completely black; otherwise, he was back to normal.

"Zellar and another," Kifirin confirmed. "We must hunt all three of them, now. If Tiearan had spoken his fears earlier, this might have been avoided. I grow weary of waiting for Toff to reach adulthood."

"Eleven more years," Lissa muttered.

* * *

"Toff?" Lissa came into Toff's bedroom, followed by Ry and Tory. Roff was still there, Toff held tightly against him as they sat on Toff's bed.

174

Chapter 9

Toff looked up as the Queen and the two Princes walked in. "Honey, I'm so sorry you had to see that. We wanted to wait to tell you about this. You have to believe me when I say that this is what Cheedas wanted. This is what he and many others hope for at the end of their lives." Lissa came to sit on Toff's bed. Ry and Tory stood behind her.

"What is it? What did he hope for? I saw that man drinking his blood." Toff's voice sounded sullen. Roff's wings rustled in agitation.

"Honey, I know they never taught you what Le-Ath Veronis means. I wanted to wait awhile before we told you, so you could get used to all this. That's not an option any longer."

"What does it mean? What are you talking about?" Toff wasn't sure now what he should do. He didn't want to go back to the Fae village and he was nearly too frightened to stay at the palace.

"Honey, Le-Ath Veronis is from an ancient language. You remember that Le-Ath Veronis was destroyed all those years ago? Nobody speaks that language anymore, except Kifirin, perhaps. Toff, Le-Ath Veronis means Heart of the Vampire."

Toff struggled in Roff's grip, but Roff wasn't letting him go. "Sit still, little one and let us explain," Roff said softly.

"I have to explain what the comesuli truly are—what they were created to be," Lissa began. "You know how some insects have a nymph stage—they look much like an adult, only smaller?"

"Y-yes," Toff couldn't keep the stutter from his voice.

"That's what the comesuli are. Young vampires. Vampire children, you might say. If you decide to stay with us after we explain things to you, then I will show you the laws that govern Le-Ath Veronis. The first of those laws levies a death sentence against any vampire who drinks from a child. And, as Cheedas told you, you are not considered an adult until you reach the age of twenty-nine. That means no comesula under the age of twenty-nine can be considered for the turn. That is what Oluwa did for Cheedas—he has attempted the turn. We should know in three days if Cheedas survived the turning to become a vampire. Sometimes it takes longer than that, but if the body survives intact for three days, that is a very good sign that the turn will be successful. If Oluwa hadn't done what he did, Cheedas would now be dead. That is another of our laws—that the candidate must be dying and of good character before the turn may be attempted. Vampires are strong when they wake. We do not make criminals into vampires; their penchant for disobeying laws follows them into their next life."

"That's when the comesuli become whole, child. While you have no genitalia now, if you are turned one day, you will wake with what you did not have before." Roff's voice was gentle and even.

"But what if I don't believe you?" Toff shuddered at the images he'd seen before—Cheedas' blood, drank by another.

"You should believe me," Roff turned Toff around so he could look into Toff's eyes. "I was comesula, once. Only a few of us—honored among the comesuli—will become Winged Vampires, however. Child, you will be a Winged Vampire one day, if that is your choice."

Toff's shock was now complete. Roff—a vampire? But he'd walked in daylight earlier. Toff's memory was dim, but he thought that vampires were kept in darkness because the sun would kill them.

Chapter 9

"I know what you're thinking. There are a few of us who are not just vampire now. We have been changed somewhat, so we can walk in the sun," Roff nodded. "Most vampires still have to live on this half of the planet because the sun burns their skin. I can assure you that one day, if this is your choice and the Queen finds you worthy, you will be as I am—able to walk in daylight as a vampire. Not many receive this gift, child. And it is a gift, make no mistake about that. Someday, I will introduce you to the vampire who is my sire. His name is Flavio and he is a patient parent."

"As is Oluwa," the Queen added. "Oluwa and I have known each other for a while and I trust him. I cannot say that about many people—vampires included."

"Are all your Inner Circle mates vampires?" Toff ventured to ask.

"No, honey. Only Gavin, Tony, Rigo, Aryn and Roff are vampires. Drake and Drew are Falchani, but they are also Spawn Hunters for the Saa Thalarr. Winkler is a werewolf and a Spawn Hunter. Ry's father, Erland, is called Lord Erland Morphis and is high in the court for my grandfather, King Wylend Arden of Karathia. Garde, Tory's father, is Gardevik Rath, Prime Minister and brother to Jaydevik Rath, King of the High Demons on Kifirin. You know what Norian is—you've seen that. What you don't know about him is that he is heir to Ildevar Wyyld, the founding member of the Alliance. Karzac was Refizani, once, but is now a Healer for the Saa Thalarr. Nissa's father, Shadow Grey, is a Master Wizard of Grey House and Grandson of Glendes, Eldest of Grey House. Rigo was once Rigovarnus the First, a High King on Hraede. The Larentii—Connegar and Reemagar—are the most powerful race among those from the light side of the universes. Thurlow and Kifirin, well, let's just say that both of them are minor gods. Kifirin outranking Thurlow, of course."

"Why are you telling me all this?" Toff wiped dampness from his cheeks. "Why are you being so nice to me? Surely it isn't because I might be a Winged Vampire someday."

"No, honey, that isn't the reason." Lissa looked carefully at Roff before she answered Toff's question. "I knew your father when you were tiny, Toff. In fact, I was going to adopt you after your father was in an accident. That's when the Green Fae came along. They thought they were kidnapping King Wylend's grandson and heir to the Karathian throne. They picked the wrong baby. They wanted to force the Karathian warlocks to help them when they came under attack by the Vionnu and one of their renegade religions. The Full Fae can do what they call flashing to take themselves from one world to another. The Half-Fae can't do it—it causes their bodies to disintegrate. They would have to leave their Half-Fae children behind to be slaughtered by the Vionn army, or they were going to have to force a Karathian to help them. They kidnapped the baby they thought was Wylend's heir to make things come out in their favor. They got you instead. You, who were about to be adopted by the Queen of Le-Ath Veronis. I went to Vionn to keep the Fae— Full, Half and otherwise—from being destroyed, expecting to get you back afterward. I was very wrong."

"Mom, you never told us this," Ry sounded lost.

"Honey, there wasn't any point, was there?" The Queen reached out to take his hand and squeezed it gently. "I thought Toff was lost to me when Tiearan came and told me afterward that Redbird placed a mindbond on Toff. He would think of her as his mother. He didn't even recognize me when I tried to take him. He was screaming and holding onto Redbird. She stole him away from us in a way that couldn't be reversed. Toff was around two when that happened, and the Larentii said that if we tried to reverse the mindbond it could damage his brain, he was so little. I was forced to leave Toff with the Green Fae. Eventually they were attacked again, and in order to make sure Toff remained safe, I had to bring all of them here. Kifirin and Thurlow have promised judgment against them when Toff comes of age. That's eleven years from now."

"Is that why they all despised me?" Toff's cheeks were getting wetter.

"Hush, child, none of this is your fault." Roff rocked Toff carefully. "They should know not to shift blame for their mistakes onto an innocent child. Nearly all of them chose to do the kidnapping, even when they knew it was wrong. And then Redbird thought to keep you for herself, because she could not have children with her Half-Fae mate."

"It's true," Lissa said. "Did you not notice that the Fulls can become parents, but the Halves can't—not with the Fae. They might with a humanoid, but that's it, and their children will be born without power. It's just the way things are with the Fae."

"That was you, then, arguing with Redbird after I was attacked by Haldis and Sark." Toff looked at the Queen, unsure what to feel.

"Yes. Sadly, I sometimes let my temper run away with me. You can believe me when I say, though, that I never stopped loving you, Toff. Never gave up hope that you'd come home to us, where you belonged. I realize that Redbird's mindbond may still have a hold on you, but I can't leave you there when they mistreat you. After they tried to kill you—twice—I had to get you out of there. Corent may come and visit anytime he wants. As can Father Willow. Redbird is not welcome in my home. Tiearan and Rain will never be welcome, either. Rain came up with the idea to do the kidnapping, Tiearan stole you away and then Redbird placed the mindbond. I will not forgive that willingly."

"There is one other who is on that list as well," Roff said quietly, tightening his arms around Toff.

"Yes. I know." Lissa stood and sighed. "Toff, please stay. You will break my heart if you don't, and Nissa will be heartbroken as well."

"I will stay." Toff couldn't look at the Queen when he said the words. He cared for her in some way and he couldn't explain it. And Nissa? Toff would walk through fire for her.

"Then you should sleep now, young one. You have had a terrible day, and I hope your dreams are sweet." Roff gave Toff one last hug before letting him go. "Come to me or any of the others; we will help you if we can, and if you cannot sleep, Karzac will remedy that." Roff rose. "Come, Raona, we will leave the young ones alone." Roff took the Queen's arm and led her from the suite.

"Oh, my gosh." Tory used one of his mother's favorite phrases. It wasn't cursing—she always did that in a language they didn't understand.

"Toff, do you know what this means?" Ry sat in the spot his mother had previously occupied.

"What does it mean?" Toff picked at his coverlet.

"That we're practically brothers." Ry reached over and swatted Toff on the arm. Toff looked up at Ry in surprise and then slowly—very, very slowly—Toff began to smile.

* * *

Chapter 9

"I want to see Cheedas." Nissa looked as if she were about to cry and Toff couldn't stand it. She'd arrived for her birthday party, but that was the last thing on her mind. She worried for the old cook, who'd watched over her and her brothers all their lives.

"Honey, right now he'll just look like he's dead," Lissa held her daughter against her side and stroked her hair.

"But I need to see him, mama."

"Baby, are you sure?" Lissa held Nissa and kissed her temple.

"Mom, please."

"All right, honey. Do the rest of you want to go, too?" Nobody felt like eating right then, though the kitchen was still operating. Some of the cooks had been brought from Niff's in Casino City—the regular kitchen staff had been given time off.

Toff was nodding right along with Ry and Tory.

"Come on, we'll go, then." Lissa stood, lifting Nissa with her. Gavin, Tony and Roff went with them and they didn't drive this time, someone folded them straight to the hospital.

"These are called the waiting rooms," Lissa led them down a quiet corridor. "There are five turns in progress now. We must be quiet—not for the ones who are going through the turn, but for the sires who are waiting and watching over them," Lissa said softly.

She rounded a corner and walked through a door that led to another corridor. This one was lined with windows made of one-way glass. They could look down into the waiting rooms but the turning sires could not see the visitors. That's why they had to keep quiet—noise might upset the vampire waiting for his newest child to wake.

Blood Reunion

"See, there is Oluwa," Lissa whispered as they peered through the darkened glass at the scene below. Cheedas was lying on a narrow bed, covered by a blanket while Oluwa was sitting in a comfortable chair nearby, watching over the old cook.

"It is good that his body is whole, still," Gavin knelt next to Nissa and placed an arm around her waist. "If he were not making at least a partial turn, his body would be gray and already turning to ash. This is a very good sign, little one."

"This is what happened to you?" Nissa turned to look into Gavin's deep-brown eyes.

"Yes. Long ago. Aurelius was my sire, pretty girl, and you may ask him all the questions you like about my turning. Aurelius was a better parent than my natural parents, even."

"I like him," Nissa agreed. "I just didn't know that he made you vampire."

"Gavin's Cousin René, who was also turned by Aurelius, was my sire," Tony said softly, kneeling on Nissa's other side.

"What happened to him?" Nissa put an arm around Tony's neck.

"He died saving my life," Tony replied. "Your mother and Gavin were both there when he died."

"So many people believe that vampires are evil, because they drink blood to live," Ry said softly next to Toff. "But just like any other race, they can be loving or brave."

"With vampires, the odds are better for those qualities, since their sire chooses them carefully," Gavin said. "There have been bad vampires, but the race has always weeded those out as quickly as possible."

"They drink blood from people all the time?" Toff asked.

"No, honey," Lissa explained. "We've developed a very good blood substitute, and it tastes almost the same. A

Chapter 9

vampire on Le-Ath Veronis drinks from the comesuli perhaps twice a month, and the comesuli ask for the bite. They find it pleasurable. Feel free to ask any of the adults inside the palace—they will tell you that they like it."

"They don't ask—they beg," Roff snorted. "I have been on both ends of that bite, and I can verify that it is intensely pleasurable. It does not matter that you do not have those parts we spoke of—the bite negates the need for them," he added.

"Toff, honey, the vampires are taught to be gentle with the bite by their sires. They have no desire to harm the ones from whom they take blood. In fact, many of the comesuli love the vampires who bite them—they have their favorites. Someday, those vampires may be their sires." The Queen was asking him to understand.

"I am trying to understand, it just may take some time getting used to this," Toff sighed.

"Many of us had no idea that vampires existed when we were turned," Gavin said. "Lissa most certainly had no idea, and her story is more tragic than any others that I know."

"Honey, don't go into that," Lissa said, turning back to the window to look down at Cheedas. "Cheedas, make the turn for me," she said softly.

"He will if it is at all possible," Gavin rose to put an arm around the Queen. "He will not want to disappoint you, cara."

"Nissy, this is the worst birthday for you," Lissa said, looking at her daughter.

"Mom, right now all I want is for Cheedas to turn into an amazing vampire."

"Me, too," Lissa agreed. "And if he makes the turn, he will be an amazing vampire."

Blood Reunion

They went back to the palace shortly after that and had a quiet dinner, followed by a nice cake for Nissa's birthday. Shadow came for that and Nissa opened gifts. She hugged Toff when she opened the comb from him and Toff turned pink when she gave him a kiss on the cheek, too.

"We'll let you decide what you want to do tonight," Queen Lissa told Nissa after the gifts had been opened and admired.

"Can we play in the pool for a while?"

"Of course. With or without adults?"

"Can we do without adults?" Nissa looked hopeful.

"Yes. But I'll keep an ear open anyway," Lissa smiled at her daughter.

"That's fine, Mom—you can save us if we're drowning."

"I'll be there in no time," Lissa promised.

* * *

What Nissa really wanted to do was hear the story from Toff, Tory and Ry about Toff's kidnapping by the Green Fae. They barely got into the water after dressing in swimsuits before she asked.

"Really? They tried to kidnap Wyatt?" Wyatt was King Wylend's heir and the child originally targeted by the Green Fae.

"And somehow they got Toff instead. I'm not sure how they managed to mess that up, but they did," Ry said. "I'm going to ask Em-pah Wylend about it when I see him again, if Dad won't tell me anything."

"Why didn't they tell us about this?" Tory was still trying to figure that out.

"Mom said it wouldn't do any good—she didn't know whether Toff was going to come back to us or not."

Chapter 9

"At least I know now that my parent is dead instead of abandoning me, as I always thought," Toff muttered. "All that time I thought my parents were awful for just leaving me for the Fae to take."

"The Fae took you, all right; they just didn't have permission. Things might have turned out different for you if that Redbird person hadn't done the mindbond."

"Yes, that was the turning point in all of this," a tall, brown-haired man appeared at the edge of the pool and sat on a chaise.

"Who are you?" Nissa was ready to call for her mother.

"I'm your grandfather," the man replied.

Chapter 10

"You're Wyatt's father." Ry had pieced the mystery together, somehow. He hadn't met Wyatt's father, but he knew that Wyatt had a father. "Why aren't you the heir instead of Wyatt?"

"Because I am the Oracle," the brown-haired man replied, smiling indulgently. "I would have to give that up to become King of Karathia. My warlock's skills were never awakened and I have no desires in that direction. Therefore, my son was named heir. If he hadn't come along, Lissa would have been named Wylend's heir instead."

"You're Mom's father, too." Nissa stared at the man. He didn't look like their mother.

"I am. You may call me Griffin. Most people do."

"Why are you here? Why haven't we met you before?" Tory asked.

"Because Lissa doesn't like for me to come here. She doesn't know I'm here, now. I just wanted to come and set a few things straight, now that Toff has been told why he spent fifteen years of his life with the Green Fae."

"What things are you setting straight? Are you saying Mom didn't tell us the truth?"

"No, your mother has been completely truthful. She just left some things out to protect someone."

"Who is she protecting?" Nissa huffed, crossing arms over her chest and glaring at Griffin. Toff moved to her side and placed an arm around her shoulders.

"Me," Griffin replied.

"But you just said you weren't welcome here—why would she protect you?" Ry demanded.

"Because Lissa knows how to love. Sometimes I think I'm still learning. The Fae didn't mistake the babies—they all wore identification bracelets when Toff was taken. I switched Wyatt's bracelet for Toff's, so they'd take the wrong child. My talent is foresight, that's why they call me the Oracle. I just didn't look far enough to see that Redbird would place the mindbond. I thought Toff would be brought home as soon as Lissa took care of the army and the religious order who were about to attack the Green Fae on Vionn. It was a very large mistake on my part. I came to apologize to Toff for that. I am afraid to apologize to my daughter. It will cause me pain when she throws it back in my face."

"What was she like, growing up? Mom, I mean?" Tory asked shyly.

"I do not know," Griffin answered. "I was kept from her and she was raised by her mother and stepfather. He wasn't a good man. He killed her mother and almost killed my baby." Griffin looked genuinely sad about that.

"Is that what Uncle Gavin was talking about when he said that Mom's turning was more tragic than any other?"

"Her childhood, her turning and even what happened after that—all tragic," Griffin nodded. "She will never tell you, and it is not my tale to tell, either. I know that she used to keep journals, but I do not know if they still exist anywhere. I warn you, if you ask her about any of this, it will only aggravate old wounds and I do not wish to do that. Toff, you have my apologies. You are not obligated to forgive me. All I can say is that if you ever have need, I will do what I can." Griffin rose, nodded to the four children and disappeared.

"Holy cow," Ry used another of his mother's favorite phrases, even if it made no sense at all.

"Does he know about the baby?" Tory breathed.

"Maybe it's better if he doesn't—look what happened to Toff," Ry muttered.

* * *

Nissa was leaning against Toff on Tory's bed as they talked later. They discussed Toff's life with the Green Fae, rehashed what they knew of the kidnapping, end to end and went over Griffin's visit, too, sifting through his words and wondering what had happened with their mother.

"At least we know about the whole Grey House thing and how Cloudsong got involved with that," Ry said. He was lying on his stomach making notes in his comp-vid.

"I wish I knew what that woman's name was—the one who Great-Grampa Glendes wanted Daddy to marry," Nissa said.

"We can try to find that out," Ry seemed ready to accept the challenge. "If we can get our hands on those legal records from Cloudsong."

"Do you think she's still out there?" Tory was curious.

"If she was from a wizard family, then there's a good chance of that," Nissa replied. "Most wizards have long life spans, if not nearly immortal ones."

"Yeah. There's that," Ry nodded and made more notes.

Toff put his arms around Nissa and watched as Ry tapped away on his comp-vid.

"What do you think happened to Gren?" Nissa brought up the subject they'd avoided all night.

"I overheard Kifirin say that he had help to escape." Tory had sneaked a slice of cake and a glass of milk from the kitchen. He was eating and trying to keep crumbs off his coverlet at the same time.

"Do you think he's still on Le-Ath Veronis?" Ry glanced at his brother.

"No—if he were, I think Kifirin would have hauled him right back to the dungeons. Did you hear what Mom said? Kifirin and Thurlow are minor gods? I didn't even know they existed. Now I know why I always felt uncomfortable around Kifirin."

"How did they get involved with Mom? People just don't end up with gods for mates." Nissa relaxed against Toff. Toff played with her hair.

"Don't know," Tory mumbled around a mouthful of cake.

"I'm not about to ask," Ry shivered at the thought.

"But Griffin said Mom used to keep journals. Do you think those are around here somewhere?" Nissa asked.

<h1 align="center">Chapter 10</h1>

"If they are, they're locked up. Can you imagine if those journalists got hold of something like that?" Toff blinked in surprise at Tory's words. He'd been recently initiated into the world of newsfeeds and vid-screens. He had no idea how things could turn out if sensitive information fell into the wrong hands.

"Toff, there are always unscrupulous reporters out there who can take even the most innocent material and make someone look like a criminal instead of who they really are," Nissa twisted in his arms to look up at his face. "Even we don't know the circumstances around Mom's turning. We don't need a stranger getting that information and then manipulating it for their own gain."

"They would lie?"

"Toff, there are universes of liars everywhere," Ry sniffed. "Thank goodness Tory can tell the liars from the ones who tell the truth." Ry smacked his taller sibling on the arm, knocking the half-eaten plate of cake onto the bed.

"Here we go," Nissa muttered, sliding out of Toff's lap and pulling him off the bed with her as her two brothers went after one another. Toff watched in alarm until he discovered they weren't really hurting each other. Then he started chuckling.

* * *

"Where are we?" Gren turned in a circle, his head craning back as he stared up at the high walls of an abandoned stone building. He stood in the basement, but the floors overhead and everything else had been stripped away, leaving a gutted shell behind. Fire had claimed it at one time, and anything left of value had been taken afterward until only the stone walls and a tile roof remained.

Blood Reunion

"On Mazareal. Know where that is, boy?" Zellar flung the insult at Gren. Gren stared at Zellar's face. Half of it was scarred and wrinkled from severe burns, the skin thin and red. One eye—the left one—was puckered and closed forever.

Gren knew Zellar to be nothing more than an angry and vengeful warlock now, but that didn't keep him from worshipping at Zellar's altar. Zellar had knowledge and abilities that Gren longed for. Power that Gren hoped to obtain. Zellar would show him those things if Gren followed Zellar's instructions.

The other—well, Gren knew to stay away from that one. He appeared benign until he struck, becoming a monster that Gren could not have imagined in his worst dreamings. He devoured people in his other form—swallowing them whole, even while they screamed.

Gren had no desire to disappear down that wide and scaly throat. Zellar called him Tandias and even he was wary around him. Tandias held power that neither Zellar nor Gren could ever understand or suspect. Zellar had made a deal with a devil even he failed to see clearly.

"No need to go outside, boy," Zellar went on. "There's nothing left on Mazareal. If we eat, we'll travel away from here to do it. This is a safe place to sleep and nothing more. Get used to being wanted by the ASD."

Zellar's laugh sounded unhinged, but Gren didn't care as long as his ambitions were eventually satisfied.

* * *

"This is fun." Toff enjoyed operating the label machine. All he had to do was set the bottles on a conveyor belt wide enough to hold them and they were moved along automatically until they were spun around, coming out with a label beyond that point.

Two other comesuli were taking the labeled bottles off and stacking then onto racks. Some would be packed for shipping; others would be hauled to the local casinos—it was a specialty to have oxberry wine at their best restaurants.

"Each bottle sells for six hundred Alliance credits here on Le-Ath Veronis," Roff smiled at Toff as he watched Toff operate the machine. "If it ships off-world, it sells for a thousand Alliance credits or more, depending on the year it was pressed."

"Is that a lot?" Toff still had difficulty wrapping his mind around the concept of wealth.

"Here, let someone else do this for a moment and we will take a trip to a local wine shop," Roff grinned mischievously. Roff motioned for another comesula—he'd been introduced as Dariff—to come over and run the rest of the bottles. Roff and Toff walked away from the bottling and labeling room and out of Roff's winery.

A little while later, Toff stared at racks and racks of wine bottles inside a wine shop in Casino City. All kinds of wines were sold there, holding Toff spellbound as he read label after label, printed in the common language of the Alliance.

"This is a good red," Roff lifted a bottle from an upper shelf and handing it to Toff. Toff read the label. This wine had come from Refizan. "Refizan is famous for its vineyards," Roff explained. "Their wines are among the best in the Alliance. They have good soil and good vintners there. This bottle sells for one hundred Alliance credits."

"Ah, Roff." The proprietor had come from the back as soon as his clerk informed him that the Winged Vampire winemaker was in his shop.

Blood Reunion

"Whilton, may we trouble you to see your exclusive stock? I am teaching my apprentice about the value of wine." Roff smiled at Whilton, who'd been selling wine for a very long time.

He'd come to Le-Ath Veronis to retire and run a small shop in Casino City. He owned chains of wine shops across the Alliance, and Whilton appeared to be a round person to Toff, who'd never seen a Veridiali before. Veridiali were all rotund in shape, although their height, hair and eye colors varied. Whilton had graying red hair, kind brown eyes and an infectious smile. He was also afflicted with a skin condition, which was aggravated by sunlight. Le-Ath Veronis with its constant twilight was the perfect place for him.

"Of course you may see my private stock," Whilton gestured for Roff and Toff to follow him. Toff was close behind Roff as they were ushered down a flight of stairs and into a dimly lit, climate-controlled room. Toff stared in wonder at the racks of bottles lining the walls, floor to ceiling, inside the small cellar.

"See, this one is worth fifteen thousand Alliance credits." Toff peered at the dusty bottle Roff pointed out on a rack. Toff's eyes widened in surprise as he stared at the bottle and then at Roff.

"I have other bottles worth more, but they are in storage elsewhere," Whilton said. "I keep telling Roff that I can get better prices for some of his, but he ignores me."

"I still have some from the pressing eleven years ago," Roff grinned.

"And I will trade you this bottle for two of those," Whilton pointed to the bottle Roff had shown to Toff.

"Even you know that you can sell it for twice as much," Roff chuckled.

Chapter 10

"Yes, you can certainly do that," Whilton laughed.

* * *

"What did you learn, child?" Roff asked Toff as they walked out of Whilton's shop later.

"That some rare wines are worth a lot of Alliance credits." Toff smiled up at Roff. Roff laughed and hugged Toff briefly as they walked along the padded sidewalk. Toff didn't fail to notice that every person they passed stopped to stare at Roff's wings.

"Want to truly give them something to whisper about?" Roff was still smiling.

"What would that be?"

"This." Roff lifted Toff easily, as if he were light as a leaf, leapt into the sky and unfurled his wings with a snap, beating them in a steady rhythm as they flew over Casino City.

* * *

"Roff, did you frighten that child?" Lissa stood on a balcony attached to her suite, her hands on her hips as Roff and Toff landed there moments later.

"No, Queen Lissa, it was fun," Toff was completely out of breath—he'd laughed while Roff flew them along, shouting out questions as to what this or that was as they passed overhead. Roff had answered all his questions.

"Come inside—it's nearly time for dinner," Lissa gave Toff a quick hug and then offered a longer embrace to Roff.

* * *

"So, how was it," Tory whispered as he sat down beside Toff at the table. Ry took the seat on Toff's other side.

"How was what?"

"Flying. With Uncle Roff."

"Incredible." Toff still got chills, thinking about it. He'd never thought to travel that way.

"I have an announcement to make," a man walked into the room, dressed quite finely, Toff thought. He was handsome, too, with dark hair and eyes.

"That's Flavio, Roff's vampire sire," Ry hissed next to Toff's ear. Toff stared.

"Flavio, please say it is good news." Lissa was now standing at the head of the table.

"Cheedas has just wakened and accepted his first meal from his sire. He is well, my Queen, and has asked about you already."

"Thank goodness," Lissa dropped into her chair with a sigh.

"Will we see him soon?" Toff asked.

"Perhaps in a few weeks, young one," Karzac came in late to the table. He'd overheard Toff's question.

"Yes, the sire-child bond must be strengthened," Flavio replied, turning in Toff's direction. Being vampire, he'd heard the question clearly, even from a distance. "That will take a month or two. After that, you may visit if you like."

* * *

"My Gren did this?" Gren's mother asked in disbelief. Tiearan had to be lying. He was trying to implicate her son in an act that defied their race and its values. Bren, Gren's father, a humanoid from Vionn, was just as stunned. "I think you are lying to me—that filthy Queen has somehow managed to put this lie in your mind, Tiearan."

"Dalla!" Rain hissed at Gren's mother. "You know to be respectful!"

Chapter 10

"But they say that my Gren invited an evil in and now that evil has stolen him away. I say they killed my son and are making up lies to cover their crime!"

"Dalla, you are the one making up lies," Tiearan breathed a tortured sigh. Gren had been before him all along and Tiearan had never gone looking for the root of the boy's unexpected surge in power. He'd thought Gren had suddenly chosen to apply himself. He couldn't have been more wrong. "I have checked this myself. I believe that the Queen does not realize the damage as yet, so we will attempt to set it right. Gren tapped into the core somehow. Most likely, at the insistence and with the instruction of the one who spirited him away from here. I was remiss in not looking for the reason behind his increased power. Yes, he displayed ability that I previously thought he did not possess. I admit I was hoping that he was one of the multitalented—we have none of those remaining, now."

"Except for you," Rain dipped her head respectfully to Tiearan.

"He did not get this from the sun crystal?" Gren's father was bewildered. "He told me you were allowing him to use it."

"Not until there at the last, and then only a tiny amount. Nothing that would have enabled him to do as he did," Tiearan muttered.

"So, what will you have us do, since you are so sure my son is at fault?" Dalla wasn't giving up on her son's innocence.

"Your Gren allowed his mind to wander and it was ensnared by an evil. Do not think I have my head in the pastures all the time," Father Willow snapped. "All of you—I am ashamed to call you Fae. You betrayed yourselves the moment you chose to take that child. We all know of the mistake made after that. Then, when judgment was promised to all of us, we began to grumble and place the blame on the boy when it was our fault. Those words of blame were spoken in front of your children, were they not? What did your child do as a result, Dalla? Redbird, you should have sent that boy home long ago. Yet you remained selfish, and here we are. Tiearan, when you are ready to form the Circle, call me. I will be with my animals until then. They do not deceive." Father Willow stalked out of Tiearan's home.

"We still have two of ours in the Queen's dungeons," Clover's mother wept. "What will become of them?"

"It was your son who got my Laral in this trouble," Laral's mother pointed an accusing finger at Dalla. "If he dies, his blood will be on your hands."

"Stop this! Stop now!" Tiearan tried to calm the chaos erupting inside his home.

* * *

"Yes, good," Master Morwin nodded in approval as he looked over Toff's report. "See, the Fae thought to protect themselves by placing one of their own upon the throne. Tell me what happened after that, young one."

Toff had never had lessons such as these. In the Fae village, he'd memorized his lessons and did his sums and such. Morwin was forcing him to think things through.

"Well, the Fae were peaceful and did not engage in violence," Toff was well acquainted with that concept, having lived among the Green Fae all that time. "King Corle, being Fae and not human as he appeared to the others, did not know how to lead his people into battle when he was

Chapter 10

attacked from the other side. The enemy overran his kingdom and then attacked the Fae forests, killing most of the Fae and destroying their forests and fields. The Fae should have left things as they were and tried to approach the real King Corle instead of taking him and placing a changeling in his stead. Master Morwin, did you hand me this assignment because it closely parallels my own situation?"

Morwin grinned, wiggling his bushy red eyebrows. "Yes, young one. You see, this isn't the first time the Fae have made a mistake."

"I know that now," Toff sighed.

* * *

"I have information." Ry said the words in a singsong voice as he waved his comp-vid at Toff and Tory. Toff was slipping into clean clothing after working at the winery all afternoon. Dinner was fast approaching and he had to get ready.

"What's that?" Tory swiped at Ry's comp-vid, almost taking it from his brother's hand.

"I have information on the woman Shadow was supposed to marry and have children with." Ry's smile was wide. He was proud of himself for tracking this down.

"Who was she? Is she still around?" Tory flopped onto Toff's bed—his space was in the center of their shared suite so it was easier just to meet there.

"Melida of Belancour," Ry said.

"Get out," Tory laughed. "The Belancour Clan? Ry, sometimes your looks make me forget you have brain cells."

"Dad says that's the objective," Ry laughed.

"What? Belancour? Who are they?" Toff asked, confused. He'd never heard that name, but being sheltered inside the Fae village had kept him from many things.

"They turn out midlevel wizardry," Ry replied, making himself comfortable against Toff's thick pillows. "Nothing near what Grey House can do or a couple of other houses. Their big thing is spelled jewelry. It protects against minor attacks, but if you want the good stuff, you go to Grey House."

"And it's ugly," Tory added. "Everybody knows you went to Belancour if you get a look at the jewelry."

"Sissy says it's overpriced, too. For what it does." Ry agreed. "They charge about three-quarters the price of a Grey House piece, for half the protection." Toff drew his blackened jewel from beneath his tunic—he refused to take it off. It had turned an even darker black, resembling obsidian.

"Toff, have we ever told you how lucky you were that Sissy made that and was able to rekey it to you?" Tory grinned at Toff.

"I'd be dead now," Toff nodded solemnly, tucking the jewel back inside his shirt.

"Worth the price," Ry sighed.

"So, Melida of Belancour," Tory whispered as they walked down the lengthy, marble-floored corridors to reach the dining hall.

"The records don't give much," Ry hissed while Toff and Tory listened. "Grey House forced a writ of detachment, when they found out Melida was pregnant with somebody else's whelp when she got to Grey House. Melida's lying about the Cloudsong stuff didn't do her any good, either."

Chapter 10

"Don't say any of this around Mom," Tory whispered to Toff as they made a turn into the dining hall. Toff nodded. He knew how the information might be hurtful.

* * *

"Ry?" Toff, already dressed in pajamas, slipped inside Ry's bedroom.

"What, bro?" Ry looked up from a game he was playing on his handheld.

"While ago, you said that Grey House got a writ of detachment for that woman. I didn't know what that meant, so I looked it up on my comp-vid."

"Yeah? Did you find what you wanted?"

"Yes." Toff sat on the edge of Ry's bed. "But I'm confused. You only need a writ of detachment if you are already married." Ry's fingers stilled on his game keys.

"Holy crap," Ry muttered and sent a shouted mental message to his brother.

* * *

"I have no use for him." Marid of Belancour paced in front of the magistrate. "He's, well, he's not right. We've not even bothered to teach him, because of this. Now that he's orphaned after his mother's accident, I want to turn him over to the state."

"I don't like this—the state can't arbitrarily accept children just because a family doesn't want them. What about his father?"

"Melida wouldn't say who the father was. Never gave that information."

"She was never married?"

"Twice. Her first mate was killed; the second one forced a writ of detachment."

"Who was the second one? Was she pregnant while married to either of her mates?"

"She was pregnant while married to both, although her second mate wasn't the child's father."

The magistrate stared at Marid of Belancour. He remembered all too well the legal debacle on Cloudsong. He huffed out a sigh and pulled up the legal records for their home planet of Shaaliveer.

* * *

Lissa's Journal

"A letter from the judicial system on Shaaliveer," My assistant, Grant, dropped the envelope on my desk. "How are you feeling?" he added. With a worried frown and an eyebrow lifted, he asked the logical question. Likely it was because my face was turning a pale shade of green.

"Queasy," I muttered, holding a hand against my belly.

"Do I need to get someone?" Grant was backing up. He was vampire, just as Heathe, my other assistant was. His nose, like any vampire's, was quite sensitive. "Lissa, are you going to hurl?" he asked in alarm.

I didn't answer; I was too busy losing my breakfast in the wastebasket. Grant was out the door and shouting for a healer in less time than it took to blink.

* * *

"Nissa?" Shadow stood in the doorway of Nissa's tiny workshop—Calebert had given it to her to learn alongside Frimus, a Second-Tier Wizard who taught some of Calebert's more promising students.

Chapter 10

"Daddy?" Nissa looked up from her work—she'd been imprinting a spelled design into a gold-washed sword pommel.

"Nissa, come with me, baby, your Great-Grampa wants to see us." Shadow held out his hand. Nissa finished off the spell she'd just done on a whorl design before setting the heavy sword aside. Nissa felt her stomach tighten. Was Great-Grampa going to send her down to her former level? She was working as quickly as she could.

"Baby, this doesn't have anything to do with your work. Calebert says you're doing fine—he just has to make sure you understand exactly what he wants from you, otherwise you tend to do too much. He has to reel in your talent so it's suitable for the job at hand." Shadow actually smiled at Nissa.

"Good," Nissa sighed with relief. "Do you know what Great-Grampa wants?"

"Not much of it. We need to hear it from him, I think."

Nissa walked beside her father as they traversed the endless halls and corridors of Grey House. Protected by wizardry and enlarged too many times to count, Grey House filled nearly the whole side of a huge mountain.

Grey Planet was small—as small as a planet might be and still be considered a planet. Surrounded by spells and wizardry of Greys uncounted, it appeared to anyone without talent as a burned-out asteroid circling its sun.

Nissa had seen the beauty of the mountain range surrounding them since she'd first been taken outside Grey House as a small child. Nissa reached over and slipped her hand inside her father's much larger one as they walked along. Shadow Grey squeezed her fingers lightly and held on.

* * *

Blood Reunion

Lissa's Journal

"Lissa, are you well?" Gavin was there in moments, but Karzac had already arrived and removed the offending smell (along with the wastebasket) from my study with power.

I leaned back in my chair, a cool cloth draped over my forehead. Karzac was kneeling next to the chair and stroking my belly while light formed around his fingers.

"Better now," I mumbled.

"Sometimes we just have to deal with this," Karzac said softly, making slow circles over my skin.

"Gavin?"

"Cara mia?"

"Open that envelope on my desk—the one from the courts on Shaaliveer."

Gavin lifted the envelope—it was heavy and bore the crest of the Shaaliveeran judicial system on the front. Forming a vampire claw on a single finger, he slit it open carefully and drew out the contents.

* * *

"Daddy, we already found out about it—Tory and Ry had to do an assignment over the economic impact that Trell's destruction had on the Alliance. One thing led to another." Nissa toed a carved leg of Great-Grampa Glendes' desk. The leg resembled the head of a sea serpent.

She wasn't looking at her father, her grandfather Raffian, who'd also come, or her great-grandfather. She was worried she'd be in trouble for the information she held.

"Nissa, they are offering Melida's child to us. And to your mother, since she was Shadow's other mate at the time.

Chapter 10

Melida was married to your father for a short period of time, although they were never close."

Glendes looked across his desk at his great-granddaughter. He should be holding her on his lap or next to him to deliver this news. Why had he held back all this time? The poor child looked completely lost. Nissa held so much of her mother in her. Glendes sighed.

"Are you going to take him? Or her?" Nissa amended her first supposition.

"Nissa, this child will be turned over to the courts on Shaaliveer if someone doesn't come forward."

"Does he have talent? Why won't his other family keep him?" Nissa didn't understand this. The mindspeech she'd gotten from Tory indicated that the Belancours were doing fine.

"We don't know what he has—they haven't bothered to send him through the rite." Glendes slid a photograph across the desk toward his granddaughter. Nissa glanced briefly at Glendes before lifting the photo. She gasped at the image.

* * *

Lissa's Journal

"Lissa, do not hyperventilate—I only got your stomach calmed down," Karzac was attempting to get my head pointed toward my knees.

"What," I wheezed, "did those idiots," another wheeze, "think they were doing?" I was breathing with difficulty and trying to straighten up at the same time. Karzac shoved me down again.

"Lissa, you should have waited to go *Looking*," Karzac scolded gently.

"She," I huffed, "took," another wheeze this time, "drugs." I started coughing.

"Love, do not distress yourself," Connegar appeared, causing Gavin and Karzac to step aside. Connegar knelt beside my chair and placed one hand on my forehead, the other on my abdomen. "There, that's right," Connegar soothed as a calming light formed around me. "Take this one as yours, Lissa, and Reemagar and I may be able to set some things right."

"But he's fifteen," I wailed in distress.

"Does that mean he needs love less?"

"No." I reached up to wipe away the tear that insisted on falling. "Connegar, what are we to do?"

"Hush, now, the Wizards of Grey House are here. With your daughter."

Chapter 11

*T*rikleer Belancour stared at his shoes. One was larger than the other. It didn't matter—he couldn't walk anyway—the smaller foot was attached to a shorter, withered leg. One of his hands, too, looked the same—withered and nearly useless.

Trik had learned to feed and dress himself one-handed over the years. He ghosted about the Belancour Manor—the lower level of it anyway, in a motorized chair.

Since his mother's death, none of the family bothered to speak to him. Even Melida had gone for days without speaking to her only child. Marid, Trik's grandfather, refused outright to test Trik for talent. Trik had overheard too many conversations during his fifteen years. Conversations that always began with *"He's useless without both his hands."*

Trik had come to hate those words. His right hand wasn't completely useless. He used it to brace things, or he

207

could grasp lightly, if it were clothing to be slipped on. Trik used every bit of what he had to the best of his ability. He'd taught himself, too—thankfully, someone had shown him his letters early and he'd picked up reading quickly. They wouldn't have bothered, otherwise.

Now, he often sneaked into his grandfather's library at night, pulling down books that wouldn't be missed with a pole he'd devised himself, with a little help from two younger cousins. It would reach up and grasp things that were too high for him to get any other way. Family members usually grumbled if he asked them to do it for him.

On this day, he'd been asked to dress nicely for visitors. For Trik, it was his nicest outfit, handed down from one of his cousins. Seev had outgrown just about everything, and this particular tunic and pair of pants hadn't seen much wear before Seev needed something larger.

Trik hadn't asked why he needed to dress nicely—he'd heard the whispers. If these people didn't take him, he'd be sent off to one of the state-run homes and spend the rest of his natural life there, an oddity that nobody wanted.

* * *

Toff had seen the photographs, just as Ry and Tory had. Tory swallowed hard at the image; Ry's expression had been grim. Toff's heart thumped painfully in his chest—here was likely another who'd been bullied and ignored because he didn't have what the others did. Toff now stood between Queen Lissa and Roff, while Tory and Ry waited with their fathers. Karzac had come, too, with Connegar and Reemagar.

Toff learned how easy it was for the Larentii to disguise themselves. They looked like any other humanoid, now. He and the others waited in a reception area of Belancour

Chapter 11

Manor until the contingent from Grey House arrived. A Belancour Wizard—an old woman, stood near the door, waiting for all of them to gather before taking them to see Trikleer Belancour.

"Toff?" Nissa's voice was almost breathless when she tapped him on the shoulder. Toff's grin was wide with relief as he hugged Nissa, lifting her off the floor the moment he turned around. He'd been afraid she wouldn't be allowed to come.

"I missed you," Nissa whispered in Toff's ear as he set her down again. Nissa stepped back and adjusted her finely woven tunic; the fabric was dyed a beautiful shade of green. Toff thought Nissa looked very pretty in it.

"Come with me," the female wizard snapped, bringing Toff's attention back to their mission. He thought he heard a slight snicker from Lissa before they all moved forward.

* * *

"Straighten up, Trikleer," Marid ordered sternly as Trik leaned over a bit to catch a first glimpse of the people walking toward Marid's private study. Trik stared, his mouth open. The woman was stunning. And the man standing near her, did he have wings?

Marid hadn't given him any information regarding the identities of these people—he'd only said that his mother had ties to them somehow, and since Marid could no longer keep him in his home, he would either go to these people or to the state facility.

After getting a good look at these, however, Trik knew what his fate would be. All these people were whole and pleasing to look upon. Trik had none of that. They would turn him away without even speaking to him. That's why he was shocked throughout when the woman walked up to him, took his withered hand in hers and said, "Hello, Trikleer. Are you well today?"

* * *

"Call me Trik," Trik had no idea how he'd come to be seated between the woman who'd introduced herself as Lissa, and a man who said his name was Connegar. Trik thought that slightly humorous—someone had named his son in the Larentii fashion. Everyone knew Larentii names always ended in "gar." They were having luncheon at Marid's formal table today—Marid ordered an appropriate meal for his guests, at least.

"How far have you advanced in your studies?" Lissa asked, watching Trik work his way around the veal on his plate by cutting it with the edge of a fork. Trik had given up years ago on any hope of holding a knife and fork at the same moment.

"I have read all of grandfather's history books—he doesn't have anything newer than sixty turns ago," Trik said, nibbling the piece of veal. He waited until he'd chewed his bite and swallowed before continuing. "The mathematics books are probably outdated as well, but likely are still good unless there have been new advances. If so, I would certainly like to see the new materials. I wish I had a comp-vid, but grandfather doesn't allow them in the house."

"Do you ever want to practice wizardry?" Another male—dark-haired and gray-eyed, asked from farther down the table.

Wizardry. Trik longed for that more than he longed for anything. Yet his hand—his grandfather had refused to consider wizardry for Trik because of his hand. Trik sighed.

Chapter 11

"Don't tell us what others think," Lissa said quietly beside him. "Tell us what you think. What you want."

"I've always wanted it," Trik dropped his fork and lowered his good hand to his lap. "But I don't have two good hands."

"How do you feel about coming to live with strangers?" Lissa asked.

"I think it might be worth a try." Trik found almost anything more appealing than a sterile existence at a state-run facility.

"Trik, if you agree to do your best, I will agree to do my best in this matter." Lissa's blue eyes met his.

"Then I will do my best. If you wish for me to work to help earn my keep, then I will do what I can."

"Then we may put you to work," Lissa nodded. "Don't worry, everything we put in front of you will be within your ability and hopefully to your liking." Lissa patted Trik's shoulder.

"But what about your children?" Trik hadn't failed to notice those four. He hoped they wouldn't tease him or take his things away the moment the adults' backs were turned.

"Ask them."

Trik jerked his head up. "Now? Here?"

"Of course." Lissa smiled. Trik drowned in that smile.

"Don't worry, I think everybody wants you to come," Nissa leaned her head over her plate so Trik could see here easily.

"If you don't like it," Trik lowered his eyes again, "you can always take me to the home."

Trik, the voice came into his mind, shocking him speechless, *I don't think that will be necessary.*

* * *

"Don't worry, I'm new, too." Toff came to sit on the sofa next to Trik's motorized chair. "I've only been with them a few weeks. I—I love all of them already. Just be prepared for some of them to be, well, different."

"I know about different," Trik blew out a breath. "I've dealt with it all my life." He stared at his withered, useless leg.

"I think you have a better education than I do, and you've taught yourself," Toff went on. "I'm trying to catch up with my studies. Master Morwin is very patient."

"Master Morwin?"

"Our tutor," Ry came to sit next to Toff. Trik watched as the tallest of the males, Tory, sat beside Ry. Nissa was talking quietly with the black-haired, gray-eyed man in the corner.

"We'll have the same tutor?"

"I think so," Tory said. "I think they'll put you in our class," Tory pointed to himself and Ry.

"He won't be—is he—will he?" Trik couldn't think of a way to ask if Morwin would mistreat him because he wasn't whole.

"Hmmph. Wait until you meet him," Ry grinned. "He has bushy red eyebrows that wiggle when he talks. Don't ever point that out or you'll get extra homework for a week."

"What's taking so long?" Toff asked Nissa as she wiggled her way onto the sofa beside him. Toff put his arm around her shoulders and hugged her.

"Legal stuff—Marid wants to sign all rights over. Mom keeps asking him if he's sure he wants to give up the rights to his grandson. She's telling him that once he does it, he can't ever come back for any reason, even if he wants to. She's

Chapter 11

offering to let Trik keep the Belancour name if Marid still wants to consider him family."

"Let him sign it," Trik grumbled. He wasn't surprised that Marid wanted to get rid of him completely. Marid always considered Trik to be a useless mouth to feed.

* * *

"Ready?" Lissa looked tired but still she smiled at Trik. They gathered in the reception room again, Trik with them. Trik had only been transported this way twice in his life.

His mother and grandfather could fold space; they just seldom had seen fit to take him anywhere. Not that he didn't want to go; he did. They just hadn't wanted to take him along.

Everything went dark for a moment, and then he found himself in a brightly lit space.

"Where are we?" Trik's heart stuttered and he stared in surprise. He'd landed in the rotunda of what looked to be—it couldn't be. He was inside an enormous library. They'd just looked for a place large enough to land all of them safely, he surmised. After all, there were at least twenty around him.

"Greetings, young one, this is the Palace of the Queen of Le-Ath Veronis," someone stepped forward to greet them. "Lissa, the Council meeting was a little bumpy today."

"That's Aurelius. Gavin's sire," Ry bent down to whisper to Trik as Trik stared at the golden-haired bear of a man who stood before him.

"What's the problem now?" Lissa really did sound tired.

"Lissa, I suggest you get something to eat and sit down to discuss this with Aurelius," Karzac said. "Connegar and Reemagar can go with the young ones."

Blood Reunion

"Why is Lissa discussing a Council meeting?" Trik looked up at Ry.

"He doesn't know," Ry grinned and elbowed Tory, who'd come to stand next to Trik's chair.

"Mom's the Queen," Nissa said. She and Toff had come to stand on Trik's other side. "And my Dad is Shadow Grey of Grey House," Nissa continued when Trik stared at her in shock. "Dad says you have talent, but until you go through the rite, he can't say how much for sure."

"But before that takes place, young one," Connegar grew before Trik's eyes and his skin turned blue, "Reemagar and I will see about healing as much of this as we can."

Trik couldn't speak for minutes as Connegar, a real, blue-skinned Larentii, lifted him from his motorized chair and folded him and the other teens into a spacious suite.

* * *

"It'll take a while to do all of it, and the muscles will have to be exercised," Ry said as he and the others admired what the Larentii had done with Trik's hand.

"Mom says that there are hospitals and clinics all over the Alliance that could have done this easier when you were a baby, but since Shaaliveer isn't an Alliance world, then your family would have had to pay for the medical care. It can be expensive," Nissa said.

Trik couldn't believe it, either. Right away, they'd done this—his right hand looked normal. Connegar said that he and Reemagar would come back in a week, when Trik had time to get used to it and exercise his hand every day, before they attempted to do more.

After about a month, his right hand and arm would look exactly like the left. Then they would start on his leg. He'd always heard the Larentii were powerful beings, but until today, he'd imagined that they might not be quite real.

"Want your chair or do you want Tory to skip us to dinner?" Nissa asked. Toff had both arms around Nissa as she leaned against him.

"I think I'll do the chair, but only because I want to see the palace," Trik breathed.

"And you don't have to room with us unless you want to," Tory said. "But we like having Toff with us. If you're here, we can plot and plan without having to sneak into your bedroom."

"And after the Larentii are done with you, you'll come to train at Grey House," Nissa said. "It'll be so nice to have someone there who's a friend and close to my age."

"They'll train me?" Trik's voice was almost a squeak.

"Yes. Like I said, Daddy told me they'd check your ability when you go through the rite. Great-Grampa Glendes will probably do it himself."

"Glendes of Grey House is your great-grandfather." Trik's voice held awe tinged with a bit of alarm.

"Yeah, why?"

"Marid complains about him constantly. Says he takes away Belancour business."

"We have all the business we can handle. We send the excess out to other houses," Nissa sniffed.

"No, no, I didn't mean it that way. Grandfather just gets grumpy at times," Trik said. He was still in shock at the sudden change in fortunes for him. Finally, the wind seemed to be blowing in the proper direction.

"Young ones, are you ready to come to dinner?" A tall, dark-haired man appeared in the doorway.

Blood Reunion

"Uncle Rigo, this is Trikleer," Nissa made the introduction.

"Most pleased to meet you, young sir," Rigo nodded to Trik.

"Uncle Rigo used to be King of Hraede," Nissa said conversationally as Trik steered his chair through the suite he now shared with Tory, Ry and Toff.

"Am I missing something here?" Trik was completely confused.

"Do you know about Le-Ath Veronis?" Ry turned and smiled over his shoulder.

"My history books didn't cover it," Trik replied.

"Then we'll bring you up to date," Tory laughed, reaching over to flick Ry's ear.

"Here we go," Nissa grumbled, rolling her eyes. Toff burst out laughing when Ry wet a finger in his mouth and stuck it in Tory's ear before running down the lengthy marble corridor.

* * *

"Toff, you have a visitor." Toff couldn't fathom why he'd been called to Lissa's study after dinner, but now he knew. Corent sat in one of Lissa's chairs, waiting for him.

"Father!" Toff rushed toward Corent and Corent lifted him up, hugging him hard.

"I missed you, son," Corent smiled at Toff as he set him down again. Corent's hair was a blue-green—clouds must be moving in, Toff thought as he smiled up at his foster-father.

"I missed you, too."

"Toff, why don't you take Corent to the arboretum upstairs," Lissa suggested.

"All right." The arboretum would be perfect—it held all kinds of plants and trees. Toff hadn't ever seen the gardeners that tended it, but they had to be good—the plants were all thriving.

"Do you like it here?" Corent asked as they walked up the last flight of stairs to get to the arboretum.

"Father, I do. I mean no disrespect to you or my foster-mother, but I feel at home here. Nobody bullies me or calls me names. And I learned that my lack of, well, that my lack is normal for what I am. I jump in the pool here with Tory and Ry and they don't even look."

"Child, I should have told you that long ago, but Redbird thought it would confuse you. I see now that it was a mistake. Those children in the village were being taught to ridicule by their parents, who had less understanding than they should." Toff merely hunched his shoulders at Corent's words. Nothing could take away the emotional bruising he'd received at the hands of his peers in the Fae village.

"Father, what can you tell me about these trees?" Toff decided to break away from the subject of his past once they walked into the arboretum.

The enormous, indoor garden was beautiful, with sunlamps hanging everywhere inside the glass enclosure. From the outside, Toff thought the arboretum looked like something from an old tale of castles and such, sitting atop the palace as it did and always lit from within.

"These trees I haven't seen before," Corent went to touch the first of many. "I was born on Vionn, you know."

"Then you would have been left behind, if the Fulls had gone on when the threat came."

"Yes. My mother didn't want to leave me to whatever fate awaited, so they devised an alternate plan. That turned out to be a mistake. I could have melted into the forests with the others—the Vionnu army would have had a difficult time tracking us."

"Then why was Mother Rain worried?"

"She was afraid that Tiearan would move on to another world and not go back. She did not want to leave me on Vionn. So here we are, son, our lives changed forever because of decisions others made."

"But why did Mother Rain think it wouldn't bring harm to someone else?"

"She knew it would, but she thought it was only temporary harm. Redbird decided to make it permanent."

"I can't understand that, father."

"I don't understand it either, child. Father Willow says to tell you hello and that he misses your hard work. He is having difficulties getting the others interested in throwing hay to his cows."

Toff and Corent spent about an hour going from tree to tree and plant to plant, talking while Corent put his hands on this tree or that, closing his eyes to give it a bit of his power.

Toff always liked watching Corent work—the Half-Fae loved the living things he touched. Toff walked with Corent to the palace gate later, a guard following discreetly behind. Toff hadn't realized until then that he was guarded just as closely as the Queen's natural children.

"Toff, take care and enjoy your life," Corent squeezed Toff's shoulders before walking through the gate and away from Toff. Toff felt a sadness he couldn't describe as Corent walked away from him. As if Corent were saying good-bye for all time.

* * *

Chapter 11

Lissa's Journal

"No, I will never tell that child who his father is," I grumped. I wasn't feeling very well right then and Norian was irritating me. I considered barfing on his shoes.

"Even if he asks you someday? As an adult?" Norian was Director of the ASD at the moment, not my mate. Hence the annoyance.

He'd been shocked by the information I gave him, but didn't doubt its veracity. I could smell parentage in the blood. My nose was better than any DNA test Norian had ever seen, and he employed it as often as he could. Some days—actually most days—being Liaison to the ASD was aggravating in the extreme.

"Norian, let him grow up without that taint, all right? If he's stable and happy as an adult one day, then sure, we can tell him. But as long as I have my doubts about his mental state if we pass that information along, then no, it stays with us."

"Do you think the ASD's new most wanted even realizes he has a child?"

"I find that highly unlikely," I retorted. "But if he did, and if there was the slightest chance he'd try to get him back, well, you see how that could go wrong in a hurry."

"How do you think it happened?" Norian settled onto my sofa and patted the seat next to him. I frowned at my lion snake shapeshifter mate for a moment before settling beside him. Norian ran gentle fingers over my forehead. I considered punching him, while wondering if pregnancy affected every woman the same way.

"I don't know what you have in your files on all this, Norian, but Melida supposedly was pregnant with her husband's child before he was killed on Cloudsong."

"I have that information," Norian nodded. "I also have records that say she miscarried."

"Except she didn't."

"What?"

"Oh, she probably wanted to miscarry, but she didn't. We all assumed that Findal, Melida's husband, approached Black Mist. I don't think he did. I think Zellar may have approached Melida on Black Mist's behalf, offering all sorts of promises to her and Findal if they'd get Black Mist what they wanted, which was Brandelin's death."

"Sounds as though he offered her something else, too."

"Yep. Maybe she did that whole miscarriage thing just to throw Zellar off the track in case he got suspicious. Either way, we both know she showed up at Grey House already pregnant and she wouldn't let Cleo touch her when she didn't feel well. Cleo would have known. Heck, Selkirk probably would have too, just by putting his hands on her. She had a really good illusion spell going, I think, to fool them. I saw the records—Trik was born two months after Grey House sent her packing."

"You think Marid knows? Who the father is?"

"I hope not. I don't want Trik hurt or upset by any of this. I think he's had a hard enough life so far. He doesn't need any more trouble."

"When are you going to tell Toff that his father is still alive?"

"When I think he's ready," I sighed.

"Just lean back, breah-mul, and close your eyes. You've had a long day." I settled into the crook of Norian's arm and did just that.

* * *

Chapter 11

Tory had gone to the kitchen for a snack. And then, deciding to sneak past his mother's study just to see why the light was shining underneath the door so late, he'd skipped close to her door so she wouldn't hear his footsteps. Tory only caught the last bit of conversation between his mother and Norian. Tory couldn't wait to tell Ry and Sissy what he'd heard.

* * *

"Why did you haul me out of bed, you lumbering ox?" Ry would have hit Tory with a pillow if he still had one within reach. He didn't—Tory had skipped Ry right to the top of their mother's palace.

"I have to tell you what I heard, and I can't let anyone else hear," Tory hissed.

"All right, what did you hear? And this better be good, I was asleep."

"I skipped right beside Mom's study, and she was talking to Uncle Norian," Tory whispered. "Mom said Toff's father is still alive."

"What?" Ry's shocked reply had Tory clapping a hand over his brother's mouth.

"You heard me—she said she was waiting to tell him when he's ready."

"Holy cow," Ry's voice was now a whisper, too. "Who do you think it is?"

"Well, do you think there are any records or anything? Mom said Toff was two or so when the Fae took him, so his dad's accident, whatever that was, had to happen before then. You think we can get into Uncle Gavin and Uncle Tony's records? They keep everything that happens in the palace."

Blood Reunion

"We'll have to get Uncle Drake and Uncle Drew's, too—they have everything that happened outside the palace."

"Come on, let's get back inside—it's freezing up here." Tory skipped them back inside their bedroom.

* * *

I'm not kidding, Sissy. That's what I heard. Tory's mindspoken admission to his sister the next day shocked Nissa just as much as it had her brothers. *Do you think your dad will tell you anything?*

I don't know. Besides, he's likely to tell Mom if I ask. I don't want to get in trouble and I don't want to upset Toff. What if his father is a bad person? Maybe that's why we haven't been told.

Wow, Sissy, I didn't think about that.

Well, we don't know, do we? If you and Ry start digging, don't get caught.

I heard they're going to start the discussions in the Council on those two in the dungeon.

What are they going to do? Those two wouldn't have done anything without Gren pushing them. I just know it.

But they tried to kill you. I know they thought you were Toff, but that's no excuse.

I know. Nissa's mental sigh came through plainly to her brother. *Tory, I have to go, Calebert wants me.* Nissa cut off the mindspeech.

* * *

Trik was amazed at Master Morwin's appearance. He'd not seen any vids of Amterean dwarves before and did his best to hide his surprise. Ry and Tory were correct, however; Master Morwin's eyebrows were indeed long and bushy,

222

Chapter 11

wiggling animatedly when he talked at length on any subject. Trik hadn't had much to smile about in all his fifteen years. He wanted to smile now and couldn't.

"Young one, I would like twenty pages on the history of the Alliance in the past sixty years—just hit the high points and hand it in three weeks from today. I think that will catch you up nicely with Ry and Tory. Then you will receive the same assignments they do," Master Morwin gave Trik his first homework.

"Thank you, Master Morwin," Trik nodded. He already liked having lessons. Plus, it was nice to have an opportunity to discuss what he'd read or learned with others.

"How's the hand today?" Tory asked after lessons were over.

"Not bad—someone named Rik came to work the muscles with me this morning while you were out practicing—is that right? You're learning how to fight with blades?"

"Ask Rik about that when he comes back—he's Falchani too and can fight with the best of them," Tory grinned. Rik was taller than Tory, but there was a chance he'd catch up to the tall warrior before he was grown.

"Just the ones I wanted to see," Uncle Aryn found them going down the hall toward their shared suite.

"Uncle Aryn?" Ry said. They didn't often have dealings with Uncle Aryn. Their mother always said that Aryn didn't have a lot of experience around young ones. Aryn was very old as a vampire—more than ten thousand years.

"Your mother is giving permission for all of you, Toff included, to attend the Council meeting tomorrow afternoon. We will be discussing the two in the dungeon. The Council will decide whether they should be charged with a capital crime or a lesser charge. You will be seated in the back and you must remain silent through the proceedings, of course. If you cannot do so, then say now and you will be excused."

"Oh, no. I want to come," Ry said immediately.

"Me, too," Tory agreed.

"The Council?" Trik was new and hadn't gotten all the information yet.

"It is the Council of Vampires on Le-Ath Veronis. Do not fear, child, you will be quite safe, I assure you." Aryn actually smiled at Trik—something Ry and Tory had seldom seen.

"Then I want to see it," Trik breathed. "I will certainly come."

"Then we will see you there. The Falchani will bring you in and get you seated beforehand." Aryn walked away from them.

* * *

"I'll be there with you—your mother says that some Council members may want to ask questions," Shadow told Nissa when she came from Calebert's workshop. She wanted to change before going to the dining hall for dinner. Shadow met her inside their suite so he could tell her that she'd been summoned to Le-Ath Veronis.

"Daddy, that's scary," Nissa shivered in alarm at the thought of being questioned.

"Your mother will remove livers if anyone harms or upsets you," Shadow smiled at his daughter.

"Can't vampires get along without their livers?" Nissa looked up at her father's face.

"Sweetheart, I'm not sure what they can or can't live without. Go get dressed, baby—we'll have dinner together. I think your great-grandmother wants to dine with us."

Chapter 11

"Gramma Lira is coming to the dining hall?" Nissa was surprised. Grampa Glendes' wife usually had her meals in her and Glendes' suite.

"Yes. She says she hasn't paid as much attention to her youngest grandchild as she should."

"I thought Great-Grampa and Great-Gramma didn't want to play favorites." Nissa's lower lip trembled slightly.

"Baby, we forget sometimes what it's like to be young," Shadow pulled his daughter to the sofa. "Come on, sit here with Daddy for a while, all right?"

"Mom didn't forget," Nissa bit her lip to keep it steady.

"I know. But your mom is somebody really special. Just like her baby girl." Shadow hugged Nissa—hard. "I know you miss her while you're here. We have to work to get her to come back."

"You and Grampa and Great-Grampa messed up," Nissa mumbled.

"Yes, baby. We messed up. Now we have to get your mother to forgive that."

Chapter 12

*D*rake and Drew brought Ry, Tory, Trik and Toff into the Council chambers, and Toff and Trik were doing their best to stare around them unobtrusively while they walked through the cavernous hall.

Floors and walls were formed of rare marble, while many rows of comfortable seats surrounded a dais where a podium, several chairs and a desk were placed.

"One of the news crews will set up elsewhere," Drew grinned at the four teens as he and Drake hauled them to a balcony on a lift. They were getting one of the best spots in the chamber, and could see everything from their elevated perch.

Trik's motorized chair was settled behind a sturdy barricade so he wouldn't be in any danger; Toff, Ry and Tory had seats next to that. All of them could watch the Council meeting from the balcony usually reserved for a vid crew.

Blood Reunion

Three extra chairs were lined up behind them, making Toff wonder if others were coming. "Remember, Toff, someone will come for you and for Nissa if your testimony is required," Drake tousled Toff's hair. "Don't worry about anything, just speak the truth. Roff will be here with you soon, and Shadow Grey will bring Nissa shortly."

The Falchani twins left them alone and went to tend to other business, but Toff's question had been answered; Roff, Nissa and Shadow Grey would occupy the extra seats.

"We've only been here once before, when Haldis and Sark were sentenced," Ry whispered to Toff and Trik. "Normally we're not allowed, and we don't get to attend the Inner Circle meetings either, unless Mom says it's all right."

"What did they do with Haldis and Sark?" Toff asked, shivering slightly. He'd only known that both boys, along with their parents, hadn't returned to the Fae village.

"Sent to Evensun," Tory answered. "Their parents signed waivers so they could go, too."

"Evensun? The penal colony planet?" Trik had heard of it, although Toff hadn't.

"Yeah. Mom was dead set against sending them there—she said they were too young for that sort of punishment. She wanted to send them to Harifa Edus, but the Council voted for Evensun." Ry answered Trik's question.

"Harifa Edus?" It was Toff's turn to ask.

"It means Hunter's Eyes," Tory whispered. "It's the werewolf planet."

They were forced to curtail the conversation; Council members began to file inside and none of them wanted to be sent away.

Nissa and Shadow Grey folded in shortly after the Council began to arrive. Nissa sat next to Toff while Shadow took the seat behind her. Roff came in last, choosing to fly up to the balcony instead of taking the lift. He sat behind Toff and reached up to pat the young comesula's shoulder. Toff turned and smiled nervously at the Winged Vampire. Roff smiled and nodded encouragingly at Toff.

Toff and his companions recognized Aurelius and Aryn as they came forward first and opened the meeting. "All rise for the Queen," Aryn spoke clearly and solemnly and everyone in the Chamber except Trik rose from their seats.

Shadow placed a hand on Trik's shoulder in a comforting gesture as Lissa walked into the chamber, taking a seat behind the ornate desk. Ry and Tory knew she'd normally stand behind the podium, but Karzac insisted that she sit. Therefore, the desk had been brought, allowing her to rest. Her children and the Inner Circle all knew it was to keep her from tiring during her pregnancy.

"Be seated," Aryn said, as soon as Lissa sat down. "Bring forth the prisoners," Aryn added after the Council took their seats.

Laral and Clover were led inside by Gavin and Tony. Both wore cuffs, Toff saw, and figured those were to subdue them if it became necessary. Toff didn't expect both boys' mothers to come, but Drake and Drew brought them in as well.

Hyacinth, Clover's mother and Storm, Laral's mother—both Full Fae, appeared angry as they walked in with the Falchani. Seats were provided for them near the dais. Laral and Clover sat at the edge of the dais, closely guarded by Gavin and Tony.

Several members of the Council questioned Laral and Clover, after Aryn instructed both prisoners to speak the truth inside the Council Chamber. Toff was shocked by the revealed information. Both said that their parents had spoken of Toff in derogatory terms, and when Gren came along and whispered to them that Toff had to die, they thought it was only right. Roff placed his hand on Toff's shoulder and didn't remove it while Nissa clasped Toff's hand in hers and didn't let go.

"So, you, not fully understanding what or who Toff was, or why he was there in your village, took it upon yourselves to get rid of him, is that correct?" Flavio, senior member of the Council, was now questioning Clover.

"Yes, but Gren threatened us there at the end, saying he'd see that we were stripped of our power and banished if we didn't do what he said. We didn't want to stab Toff with the knives or perform the nut-cracking chant. Gren forced us." Clover was nearly in tears. He'd never thought that breaking the laws would have him standing before an old vampire with more than banishment and a stripping of his power at stake.

Clover knew he'd attempted murder, and his life hung in the balance. He should have paid more attention to the whisperings regarding Haldis and Sark's punishments.

Laral's questioning went much the same. His story echoed that of Clover.

Toff was called after that. Roff flew him to the dais, and Toff sat in the chair vacated by Clover and Laral.

"Young one, you will only speak the truth inside the Council Chamber," Aryn's words held power of some sort—Toff could feel it. He nodded to the old vampire.

Toff did his best not to be frightened, but he was questioned long by several members of the Council. At one point, water was brought to him before the questions began again.

Muted growling came when he described how he was bullied by the other children. He didn't want to tell the names he'd been called, but was compelled to do so. He wanted to weep and couldn't—he could only sit there, answer questions and tremble.

Toff honey, it's all right. Somehow, the Queen's words came into his mind and he didn't know how that could be. He swallowed hard and went on. Finally, they were done with him and Roff appeared to return him to his seat. Nissa was brought down by her father. She squeezed Toff's hand before Shadow Grey folded her out of their box and down to the lower floor for questioning.

Roff now sat next to Toff and had a comforting arm around his shoulders while Toff watched Nissa answer questions. She talked about her treatment, not just by Gren, Laral and Clover, but by Mother Fern and the others. Toff was surprised at Nissa's indignation at her treatment on his behalf.

"So, you were chastised for coming late to dinner, after this Fern woman forced you to perform extra duties?" Flavio asked.

"Yes. I could tell that none of them liked Toff or appreciated what he did for them. Corent was kind, as was Father Willow when he asked me to help feed hay to his milk cows. None of the others were—I felt as if they thought I— he—was much less than they."

"Yet the female—Redbird—wanted him for her own when the kidnapping initially occurred," Flavio now addressed the Council.

"Flavio, the ones answerable to those charges are not present." The Queen was now standing. Toff thought she didn't look comfortable.

"My apologies, my Queen," Flavio said quietly. "I have no further questions." Flavio returned to his seat.

"We will now take a vote regarding guilt or innocence of the charges," Aurelius stood and made the announcement. "Place your vote on the comp-vids located beside your seats. The votes will be tallied during a brief recess. A disposition will be discussed after that. Please return in half an hour."

"Young ones, we must see to your Lady Mother," Roff lifted Toff in his arms quickly and swooped down to the floor below. Drake and Drew appeared to bring Ry, Tory and Trik down, while Shadow brought Nissa.

"That's Uncle Winkler," Tory said softly to Trik as they watched the tall, dark-haired man help Queen Lissa from her seat.

"This way," Drake and Drew cleared a path through the wide chamber door. The moment they turned a corner to go down a lengthy hall, someone folded all of them to Lissa's library.

Trik watched as Karzac, Lissa's Refizani healer mate, had his hands on the Queen as soon as Winkler set her on a comfortable sofa. "What's happening?" He was concerned for the Queen as well, and it was only beginning to sink in that he was one of her children, now. Morwin had given him a copy of the papers, naming Lissa as his adoptive mother and Shadow Grey his adoptive father.

"Mom's pregnant," Ry said quietly at Trik's side. "She shouldn't have been in there that long without somebody seeing to her."

"Don't worry, Trikleer, the Queen loves you already, I think." One of the tall, blue Larentii knelt beside Trik's chair. "When she was human, she was unable to bear children, so you and the others are like gifts to her."

Chapter 12

Trik stared at the Larentii in shock. No one had ever thought of his existence as anything other than an annoyance. Yet the Queen thought of him as a gift? "Young one, we will come soon and work on your leg and foot," the Larentii went on. "How is the hand? Is it becoming easier to work?"

"Yes," Trik almost stuttered his answer. He flexed the hand and moved the fingers for the Larentii to see. He could hold things now and he didn't lose his grip if those things weighed more than a few ounces.

"Very good. You will be standing and running with these others in no time." The Larentii patted Trik's shoulder and stood, moving toward the Queen.

"Toff, I was so scared," Nissa put her arms around Toff's neck and hugged him—hard. Toff's arms were about Nissa's waist and he was hugging her back.

"You sounded so calm and clear," Toff whispered. "I was the mess."

"No," Nissa murmured. "Ry and Tory were nodding at all your words. And I think Mom is really proud of you."

"I will be coming to the rest of the meeting, I do not care how awkward it looks," Karzac snapped. "These young ones do not have to return unless they wish to. In the meantime, feed them something—they are all hungry as birds," Karzac added.

That's how they were all served a quick meal inside the Queen's Library. Tory was happy, his stomach had been growling for an hour.

"Do you want to go back?" Nissa nudged Toff's elbow.

"I do and I don't," he sighed.

"Come on, you know you'll be asking us what happened afterward if you don't," Ry coaxed.

"But what if something awful happens?" Nissa frowned.

"Nissa, those two could have gone to an adult and said what was happening. Yet they didn't," Trik was happy to hold half a sandwich in a hand that couldn't, only a few weeks before. "What might they have done if Gren had been successful? Now, Gren has associated himself with something even worse."

"What? How do you know that?" Ry hissed.

"I listen," Trik replied. "I've always listened. I knew things at Belancour Manor, even when I wasn't included in conversations. People said things, thinking I wasn't within hearing distance or wouldn't understand."

"They'll send them to Evensun," Tory sounded positive as they were settled into their box seats later, when the Council reconvened. The half hour had been stretched to an hour so Karzac could see to the Queen. The healer now had a seat not far from the dais in case Lissa needed assistance.

"I agree—their crime wasn't that different from Haldis and Sark's," Ry nodded. Toff and Nissa hadn't stopped holding hands, once they'd arrived inside the Council chamber. Trik, too, was quite shocked when Nissa took his hand as well. Shadow and Roff claimed the seats behind the children, just as before.

"All rise for the Queen," Aryn said once more, and Lissa walked in and sat behind her desk. The Council members reclaimed their seats.

"The tally of the votes is thus," Aurelius read from his handheld comp-vid, "Guilty, by a unanimous vote, of attempted murder upon Toff the comesula and upon Princess Nissa Beth Grey. Now, we will decide the punishment."

Chapter 12

"If these two were adults, the punishment would be death," Casimir, a vampire from old Earth rose and spoke. "But as they are not adults and were easily led astray, I suggest they be sent to Evensun."

"I realize that I was outvoted last time, but I would like to offer a sentence to Harifa Edus instead," Queen Lissa spoke firmly from her seat on the dais.

"Lady Queen, we know of your feelings in this matter, and we would like to spare you if we could. But I cannot in good conscience vote for a lighter sentence than Evensun," another vampire named Montrose rose and spoke. "Let us take the vote now, as we did the last time. When the vote goes one way or the other, then this will be settled and we can turn to other matters. The parents will have the option of going with their children if that is their desire."

"Very well," the Queen sounded exhausted to Trik's ears.

Nissa squeezed Trik and Toff's hands tightly as the votes were submitted by comp-vid. Aurelius announced the results.

"Three hundred two votes for Evensun, eight for Harifa Edus and two abstentions," Aurelius pronounced the sentence. Clover shouted, even as his mother stood and attempted to cast Fae magic at the Queen.

* * *

"You should know that the Council chamber is spelled against any kind of magic," Erland Morphis, Ry's father, hissed at Hyacinth, Clover's mother. The meeting had been extended due to Hyacinth's attempt to hurl a spell at the Queen. She would now face charges of her own.

Blood Reunion

"Erland, she was only thinking of her child," Lissa said weakly. Karzac was out of his seat immediately and kneeling beside the Queen's chair.

"Then let us take all prisoners to the dungeons," Erland was still glaring at Hyacinth, who shrank back in her seat. Storm, Laral's mother, was sent away earlier.

Drake and Drew escorted Laral, Clover and Hyacinth away before the Council was officially ended for the day. Ry and Tory stood to help Toff, Nissa and Trik, who were all stunned at Hyacinth's outburst.

* * *

"Hyacinth attempted to cast the ripening spell at the Queen," Storm reported to Tiearan, Rain and a few other elders at the Green Fae village. "And this was after the Queen had argued for a lighter sentence for our children. Tiearan, I think the core's draining is affecting all of us in terrible ways. Hyacinth would not have done that, otherwise. We all feel the imbalance of things, as we are closer to the planet itself. How quickly will this affect the others, so they will come looking for a cause? We need to form the Circle soon."

"You are correct, I fear, and I weep for Laral, Clover and Hyacinth," Tiearan said. "And we owe a debt to the Queen—we all know that." He turned his gaze on those gathered, daring any to argue. The Queen had saved them, their Half-Fae children and the peaceful Vionnu. Twice. They were all indebted to Lissa and they'd done little to discharge that debt. "Charge your crystal. We will do this soon."

* * *

"Ry, could that woman hurt Mom?" Nissa whispered as they walked down the corridor leading to the family wing.

Chapter 12

"Sissy, you didn't see Aurelius and Uncle Gavin, did you?" Tory asked.

"It happened too quickly," Roff came up behind them silently. "Many inside the chamber held power. Gavin and Aurelius would have killed that woman if she'd managed to harm a hair on your mother's head. Are you all well enough? Shall I send for another healer?" Roff added.

"We're just shaken up," Ry offered with a shrug.

"Then call if you need assistance," Roff replied. "Go now, and dress for dinner. It is scheduled for the usual time." Roff strode away.

"I wish we could see Cheedas," Nissa muttered.

"Sissy?" Tory looked down at his younger sister. He wasn't surprised when she burst into tears.

* * *

"Better now?" Nissa nodded at Toff's words—she was embarrassed that she'd cried in front of her brothers.

"It's nothing to be ashamed of," Toff whispered gently. Nissa clung to him while she wept, even as Ry offered a cool, damp cloth for her eyes. Trik watched in surprise; at Belancour Manor, the older ones would have ridiculed the younger ones for weeping instead of offering support.

"Come on, Sissy, we'll be late for dinner," Ry pulled Nissa toward her suite. "Get changed; we'll meet outside the dining hall."

* * *

"Mom doesn't look good," Ry muttered when they entered the dining room later.

Karzac was seated beside the Queen, watching her carefully. Dinner was a quiet affair, with hardly anyone speaking. Toff glanced at the Queen often, but her eyes were on her plate and Karzac continued to watch, silently urging her to eat more.

We'll talk when we get back to our room, drifted into Toff's head—it was Ry's mental voice. Toff almost jumped at the nonverbal contact. Instead, he nodded discreetly and went back to his dessert.

* * *

"What can we do?" Tory paced inside their shared suite later. Toff sat on the floor next to Trik's power chair, while Nissa settled beside Toff. Ry had his back to the headboard of his bed, listening while his brother spoke.

"There's a shield around Evensun," Tory went on. "As a High Demon, I might be able to get through, but anybody else might get fried on the grid. That means if I take anybody with me, they could die. And once I get there, I don't have the ability to set up any kind of perimeter for them."

They'd been talking nonstop ever since they'd shut the suite door behind them. All knew that Clover and Laral deserved punishment, but being sentenced to life on Evensun was practically a death sentence. It was no secret that terrible people had been sent there—older people who wouldn't hesitate to kill the convicted teens quickly.

"This is Gren's fault," Toff muttered angrily. "If he hadn't convinced them," Toff didn't finish.

"Yeah. We know that for sure," Nissa agreed. Gren's name had come up many times in all the testimony. He was at the bottom of everything.

All of them jumped when a light knock sounded on the door. Lissa walked in, followed by Drake, Drew and Erland. "Mom, what's going on?" Nissa asked.

Chapter 12

"Dad?" Ry stared at Erland.

"We're going on a covert mission," Erland's grin was blinding.

"Where?" Tory asked. "Mom, I thought you didn't feel good."

"I'll feel better when we get this done," she sighed. "We know you're upset about this too, so you're all going with us. You, too, Trik." She came to him and smoothed hair back from his forehead.

"But where?" Tory repeated his question.

"We're going to Evensun," the Queen whispered.

* * *

"Wow," Ry breathed, turning in a circle. "Why isn't anybody here? This is nice."

A field of tall grass and wildflowers lay about them, with a stand of trees on one side.

"We've shielded this area, that's why," Erland placed an arm around Ry's shoulders. "Now all we have to do is find Haldis, Sark and their parents. They get a thousand acres to do with as they like, and none of the others will be able to get through. Clover, Laral and their parents will be brought here tomorrow—Drake and Drew will see that they're dropped off in the proper place."

"I will find them." The teens blinked when a strange Larentii arrived with Connegar and Reemagar.

"Hi, Ren, how are you?" Lissa smiled up at the eight-and-a-half-foot Larentii. "I haven't seen you in a while."

"I have been quite busy. I see that you have, as well." He smiled at Lissa and placed a large blue hand on her abdomen.

"It wasn't planned. I'm not complaining, either," she patted his arm.

"The child is quite fine," Ren proclaimed before taking his hand away. "I will return shortly." He disappeared.

"Mom, who is that?" Nissa asked.

"An old friend," Lissa said.

"Are we breaking the law?" Trik asked.

"Sort of," the Queen nodded. "Nobody is supposed to get preferential treatment on Evensun."

"I can see why the laws might say that. I can also see why the law needs to be bent in this case," Trik sighed.

"Then you see more than most," Connegar knelt beside Trik's chair. Trik blinked at the tall Larentii, whose face was not far from his. Had he ever thought to see a Larentii, or even more wondrous, to receive a compliment from one?

"Your observational skills are quite sharp, young one," Connegar smiled at Trik. "They serve you well."

"I expect all of you to keep this secret," Lissa said. "I only brought you because I knew you were upset about this, too. Toff," she turned her gaze to the young comesula, "You don't mind this?"

"I don't mind. This is better, I think," he nodded his dark head toward the Queen. "Gren is the one who deserved the worst punishment, and he managed to get away."

"I feel the same way." Lissa came to stand next to Toff, pulling him into a warm embrace. "I wanted to make sure this is what you want, too, because you're the one they wanted to harm."

"This is what I want," Toff said when Lissa let him go. He noticed that the Queen was brushing away tears, but chose to ignore it. He liked it, too, when the Queen hugged him. He'd gotten more affection since coming to the palace than he'd received in a very long time.

Redbird had tended him often when he was small, but when he became older, she'd pulled away. There at the end, she felt like a stranger to him, and he didn't understand it at all. Her treatment of him, too, had bordered on mistreatment. No surprise, considering all the lies she'd told. Toff shook himself to dispel the memories.

"What about Narissa?" Tory asked quietly.

"Well. That—well," Lissa shook her head and walked away.

"Mom, we know she's our great-grandmother. Dad told me," Tory offered.

"She's done a lot of bad things in her life," Lissa lifted blue eyes to her tallest son. "She won't be given special treatment when she gets here. She was here before, but she was given clemency and a comfortable place to live on Le-Ath Veronis because she gave me information I needed once. She just negated all of that. If she'd contacted me right away when Toff showed up inside her perimeter, she might be getting better treatment still. Instead, she threatened Toff." Lissa tossed up a hand in resignation and turned away.

"She's been the same for thousands of years. Her willingness to cooperate in the past seems a temporary anomaly," Erland moved toward Lissa and pulled her against him. "Love, you can never predict what those with a predilection for betrayal might do."

"Seems to run in the family, doesn't it?" Lissa said.

"It does indeed, my love," Erland whispered.

"They're kissing again," Tory muttered. Tory wore a smile, though, when Toff turned in his direction.

Blood Reunion

"Here we are," Renegar the Larentii announced, as he appeared with Haldis, Sark and both sets of parents. All were dirty and much thinner than they'd been when Toff had seen them last.

"Will we really be shielded?" Sark's mother begged, dropping to her knees. "We have been hiding for days, and have been forced to hunt for food at night."

"You will be shielded," Lissa moved away from Erland and came to stand before them. "This land is yours, to farm or do with as you please. The others will not be able to cross the boundary. I warn you, though, step outside that boundary and you are on your own." Lissa gazed, unblinking, at Haldis and Sark. Her words were meant for them. They'd crossed another line already, when they'd beaten Toff.

"Clover and Laral are coming with their parents, tomorrow," Toff offered, though his voice trembled. It was difficult, after all, seeing Haldis and Sark again. His last memory of the two had been of them punching him in the face.

"Gren got to them, too, didn't he?" Sark blinked at Toff.

"Yes." Toff wasn't willing to offer more of an explanation.

"Don't make me sorry I've bent the rules for you," Lissa's voice was hard as she gazed at Sark. "If you'd killed Toff when you beat him, I wouldn't have made the attempt."

"We understand that, Lady," Sark's father dipped his head respectfully. "We have had a talk with our children, who were unaware of all the facts. They now understand things better."

"Good. Erland," Lissa turned to her Karathian warlock mate.

Chapter 12

"Here is a supply of sun crystal." Erland employed power to bring in twenty pounds of what the Green Fae called Indis-Banuu—holder of the sun. "This should enable those coming tomorrow to help grow plants and such. And this," he gestured a second time, "is enough seed and cuttings to grow a garden." A large, wooden crate appeared. Toff blinked—the crate was nearly as tall as Erland, and twice as long. "There are gardening tools inside, plus a few other necessities. Sheep for wool, cows for milk and chickens for laying will be brought in a day or two. You will not starve unless you choose to do so."

"We thank you for these gifts," Sark's father bowed. "We cannot repay them."

"I don't expect you to," Lissa huffed. "Just teach your children better."

"I promise to do that."

"Good. We're done, here. The others will be brought tomorrow."

"We will welcome them. Thank you."

"Are you ready to go?" Lissa turned to Toff and the others.

"We're ready, Mom." Nissa hadn't spoken before that, but she went to her mother and put an arm around her.

"Good. Connegar, will you take us back?" Lissa asked her tallest Larentii mate.

"I will." All of them disappeared.

* * *

Lissa's Journal

"Lissa, don't fret, my love. I know those young ones should have apologized to Toff, yet they did not. I do not understand what it is their parents are teaching them."

Erland attempted to stop me from pacing inside my suite. "Come to bed. You need rest, Renegar says so."

"Those Green Fae and their humanoid neighbors blame Toff for their troubles, still. I could see it in their eyes. It's their fault, plain and simple. They decided to take Toff in the beginning, and then Redbird decided to perform the mindbond. Honestly, Redbird ought to be cooling her heels on Evensun, too, for her part in this. If Kifirin hadn't promised to level judgment against them when Toff turns twenty-nine, I'd have put her there right after Toff came back to us." I was still angry that Toff hadn't received an apology.

"Lissa, they did not decide to take Toff in the beginning. They desired to take Wyatt. We know who is responsible for switching bracelets so the children would be confused."

"Do not say that name to me, Erland Morphis, or you'll be sleeping alone tonight."

"I know that, love. I am merely stating fact."

"How is my brother, by the way?"

"He is well. Wylend is teaching him many things, and he is making good progress in his lessons. I must say the few lessons he received in healing were his best—he is outstanding in that area."

"His mother is a healer. I'm not surprised," I tossed up a hand in resignation. "Do you see him often?"

"Wyatt?"

"No. Wyatt's father."

"He is often at breakfast with Wylend, your grandfather."

"Yeah, I suspected as much."

"Lissa, please don't force Wylend to choose."

"I won't."

"But it upsets you."

Chapter 12

"How can it not?"

"Come here. Lie down beside me." Erland motioned for me to join him in bed.

"Erland, where is this going to end? Does my grandfather have warlocks searching for Zellar?" I climbed onto the bed and settled beside my Karathian warlock.

"Yes. They have already gone to Cloudsong, but Zellar has left that world with a drained core and used the last of its power to hide his power signature. We are back where we started, love." Erland pulled me next to him and tucked my head against his shoulder.

"What if he's draining other worlds? That's a death sentence, Erland. Zellar hides himself with the power he gains from draining cores, and I couldn't go after him right now, even if I could find him." I touched my belly.

"I know this. Stop worrying. It can't be good for the baby."

"Of all the times to get pregnant," I grumped. "I can't even use any power now, or Karzac will have a conniption."

"It could harm the child. You know this."

"Yeah, don't remind me."

Chapter 13

"**M**aster Morwin, what are you doing?"

"Writing a history, young one." Morwin's bushy, red eyebrows wiggled as he smiled at Trik. Trik had arrived early for lessons, only to find his new tutor tapping away on a comp-vid.

"A history?"

"Yes. I have published many during my long life."

"Really? Have I read any of them?"

"I do not know what books may be in your grandfather's library, so I cannot say. If you are interested, I can copy something onto your comp-vid."

"I'd like that. I like to read," Trik replied.

"I know that about you already," Morwin nodded. "This history concerns the Green Fae after they came to live on Le-Ath Veronis. Very little is known and less is written about them prior to that event. I fear that the race may be dwindling, and had they been allowed, they might have mingled with and offered their gifts to the Vionnu while they were still there. As it is," Morwin tapped the end of a sentence and dropped his comp-vid in a drawer, "they were chased from Vionn by a terrible, renegade religion. Vionn will suffer as a result, I think."

"So you believe that every action sends out ripples and affects everything it touches? I read that in a philosophy book," Trik said.

"Yes. I am more than four hundred years old and have already seen much of this during my life. It seems that the more lives the initial action affects, the more ripples are sent out. Now, have you a report for me?" Morwin lifted a long, thick, reddish eyebrow, making Trik want to snicker.

* * *

Lissa's Journal
"Cheedas?" Oluwa had brought his newest turn to the palace, because Cheedas insisted on seeing me. I'd been reading reports at my desk that morning, but I lifted my head as Heathe ushered visitors into my study.

"Raona, what do you think?" Cheedas smiled and held out his arms. He was taller, now, his skin a shade or two darker than it was before and the silver had disappeared from straight, dark hair.

"Cheedas, I missed you," I rose and walked toward him quickly, wrapping my arms about his waist.

"Oluwa tells me that a child is on the way," Cheedas murmured against my hair as he embraced me. "I feel like a grandfather."

Chapter 13

"You will be a grandfather," I pulled away and smiled at him. He was happy; Oluwa was obviously treating him very well.

"Oluwa says I may visit with your young ones soon—I hear they were asking about me."

"Every day," I nodded. "Have you fed already?"

"My sire has seen to that. We are on our way to visit Casimir—I will learn the bite today."

"Thank you Oluwa, for this," I grasped one of Oluwa's large hands and squeezed.

"My Queen, it was my pleasure, and I could not ask for a better child." Oluwa smiled broadly, his white teeth a contrast against very dark skin.

"I am sorry to leave the kitchen, but I cannot countenance regular food, now," Cheedas sighed.

"Honey, we'll fix that someday, after Oluwa has taught you everything he knows."

"Will you? Will I be able to walk in sunlight again, Raona?"

"If that's what you want," I nodded.

"I do. I promise to do my best for my sire, so I may deserve this."

"I believe," Oluwa grinned, "that the Queen's love for you might have something to do with it."

"Papa Cheedas, you've always been there for me," I hugged him again. "I'll be there for you, when the time comes."

* * *

"He's at the winery with Roff," Tory whispered as he, Ry and Trik shut the door to their suite after lessons. "We know you're really smart, Trik, so we want you to help with this."

"Help with what?" Trik allowed the compliment to wash over him—nobody had bothered to compliment him before he'd come to Le-Ath Veronis. Coming from Tory, the compliment meant a lot.

"Toff. Well, actually, Toff's father." Ry flopped onto Tory's bed. "Tory overheard Mom saying that Toff's father is still alive. Toff thinks he's dead. We want to find out who Toff's father is and if he's a big criminal or something, and that's why they won't tell him." Ry drew his knees up and stared at Tory's ceiling. "Bro, how did you get chocolate sauce on your chandelier?"

"It was your fault," Tory grumped. "You left that rubber lizard under my pillow."

"You tossed perfectly good chocolate sauce at the ceiling over a rubber lizard?" Trik snickered. He was having fun—a foreign concept to him until recently.

"He squealed like a little girl, too," Ry chuckled.

"I can make you squeal," Tory went after Ry.

After several minutes of unproductive wrestling, during which neither Ry nor Tory emerged as the winner while Trik laughed, both boys settled on the floor in front of Trik's motorized chair to discuss the topic of Toff's father.

"What do we have, information-wise?" Trik asked.

"Well, I heard Mom say she'd tell Toff his father was still alive when she thought he was ready," Tory offered.

"And she told Toff already that she knew him and his father when Toff was two, but his father was in an accident. She didn't explain the accident, so Toff thinks his dad is dead," Ry added.

"Uncle Roff said Toff would be a Winged Vampire someday," Tory turned to Ry, his eyes wide. "Remember? On the day Cheedas was turned? Roff was trying to calm Toff down and he told him that."

"Oh, yeah. I forgot all about that," Ry whispered. "Good job, bro." Ry punched his brother's shoulder affectionately.

"How many Winged Vampires are there? Does it run in families or just show up randomly?" Trik asked, his green eyes curious as his gaze wandered from Tory to Ry.

"Winged Vampires are rare, and it only runs in families," Ry breathed, searching pockets for his mini comp-vid. "Look—the stuff is right here," he showed the comp-vid screen to his brother. "Only two comesuli families are Infilathi."

"Infilathi?" Trik accepted the comp-vid from Tory and studied the screen.

"Look—he's using his hand!" Ry crowed. Trik lifted his eyes triumphantly and grinned. His right hand, once withered and useless, now appeared normal and was growing stronger every day. He held the comp-vid easily while he tapped the information he wanted with his left index finger. "Oh, here it is—it means winged ones in the High Demon language. And it does say that there are only two families who are Infilathi." He turned the comp-vid around for Tory and Ry to see. Trik loved using comp-vids— he had a universe of information at his command, without having to struggle to lift heavy books or take them from shelves too high for him to reach.

"So, Toff's father has to belong to one of those two families," Ry chewed his lower lip thoughtfully as he stared at the comp-vid screen. "That really narrows it down."

"You're forgetting something, too," Trik grinned.

"What's that?"

"Roff is a Winged Vampire, and his family is one of the two listed."

"Holy cow," Tory muttered.

"Is there any information on Roff's turning?" Ry was standing quickly and taking the comp-vid from Trik's hand. Ry's fingers flew over his comp-vid, searching for the required information.

"Holy cow," Ry repeated Tory's phrase as he dropped awkwardly to the floor. He stared at the multitude of entries that popped up on the screen regarding Roff.

All three boys blinked in shock as the records, including the Council meeting entries, were read.

"Roff was staked," Tory breathed. "By somebody trying to murder Mom."

"Roff is Toff's father," Trik nodded. "It makes sense—the dates match and a comesuli child's name tends to reflect something from his parent."

"This could be awkward," Tory observed. "I mean, Roff probably wants to tell Toff, but he's not sure how Toff might react. Really, I'm not sure how Toff might react, either."

"Yeah." Ry flopped onto his back on the floor. "What a conundrum."

"Should we send mindspeech to Sissy?" Tory asked.

"I think she'd want to know," Trik said.

* * *

"Nissa, this is fine work," Calebert complimented Nissa on the sword she'd completed, running his fingers over the spelled designs she'd imprinted in the worked gold alloy.

"Thank you, Master Wizard Calebert," Nissa ducked her head, her cheeks going pink. She'd never received such a compliment from Calebert before.

Chapter 13

"I think it won't be long until you're elevated from apprentice to Fifth-Tier." Calebert actually smiled. A smile from the autocratic Master Wizard was certainly a first. He was meticulous in his work and expected only the best from those who toiled in the Weapons Division of Grey House.

Nissa stared at Calebert. A twelve-year-old being elevated to Fifth-Tier was unprecedented. She swallowed with difficulty. *Sissy?* Ry's voice sounded in her head. *We found out who Toff's father is.*

* * *

"His birthday is in six weeks?" Lissa stared at Roff in surprise.

"My second child was born nearly eighteen years ago," Roff sat on the edge of Lissa's desk.

"What are we going to do? Roff, we really need to tell him. I want to give him a nice birthday party, too—with your permission."

"I want to tell him too, but I don't want him to be upset or disappointed." Roff rose and raked a hand through his hair in agitation. "He seems to love working at the winery, and Dariff and Markoff have to bite back their words at times, they want to include him in family matters so badly." Roff's honey-brown eyes were troubled as he glanced at Lissa. "I love my son. Have always loved him. What if he doesn't love me?"

"Roff," Lissa sighed. "I can only hope that if he doesn't love you already, that he'll come to love you. Redbird has so much to answer for. All the Green Fae do. And my father," she held up a hand to keep the words from escaping Roff's mouth.

* * *

Blood Reunion

"Well, Narissa, you've managed to get yourself into trouble you won't be able to wiggle out of this time." Griffin appeared and sat on a bench outside his mother's cell. "You're looking old, too."

"Shut up," Narissa snarled, pressing herself against the bars of her cage. "You always were the worst of my whelps."

"Hello, Mother." Jeral appeared and sat beside Griffin.

"Well, well. You're still alive," Narissa sneered at Jeral. "Both my sons, turned vampire."

"All three of your sons were turned vampire," Griffin pointed out. "Davan died a few years ago. Want to know why Jeral and Davan never wanted to see you, mother?"

"You're the one I dumped on your father, aren't you?" Narissa ignored Griffin and stared at Jeral.

"Yes. My father died long ago. He was barely sixteen when you took advantage of him."

"Have you come to gloat now?" Narissa turned away from her sons.

"Merely to see you before it's too late," Jeral sighed. "Griffin sent mindspeech—you won't survive the return to Evensun."

"You lie," Narissa turned swiftly and shook a fist at Griffin.

"I can't lie, mother. I might stretch or manipulate at times, but I can't lie outright. You know that. You know what I am."

"I curse Rabis. He surely saw what you'd become and didn't tell me."

"I have no idea whether Rabis saw that. He didn't tell me either, mother, if he did see it."

Chapter 13

"Quarter bloods. The root of all our troubles can be found with the quarter bloods," Narissa pounded her hand against a thick cell bar.

"The root of all your troubles can be placed on the Elemaiya's treatment of their quarter blood children," Griffin pointed out. "Had they not mistreated them, all this might have been avoided."

"Had they heeded the H'Morr, many other things might have been avoided. Hello, Narissa." Rabis appeared beside Griffin's bench.

"Traitor!" Narissa threw herself against the bars of her cell.

"Go ahead and scream as loud as you want," Griffin scooted over to give Rabis room to sit. "I have this area shielded. Nobody will hear a thing."

* * *

Tandias looked just as human as the others crowding about him, waiting on the high-speed train to arrive. He'd chosen Gloesse as a target—he hadn't fed there yet and the population was enormous. Who would miss a few if they disappeared? Besides, he needed his strength. Zellar wanted to launch an attack on Le-Ath Veronis soon and Tandias also had vengeance to exact against the Queen.

He'd enjoyed a soft life with Viregruz and Black Mist—Viregruz made sure that Tandias was always fed and kept others from hunting him. He'd been away on an assassination mission for Viregruz on that fateful night, when the Queen and the ASD had taken Viregruz and Black Mist down.

Tandias, like anyone else who could work a vid-screen, had seen Viregruz's horrible death. Zellar knew of Tandias' secretive efforts on Viregruz's behalf, although they'd never met. When Zellar came to him with his plan to destroy Queen Lissa, Tandias only pretended to consider it.

After all, he could devour Zellar and his acolyte with little thought after the Queen's death. No trail would be left behind, just as Viregruz taught him. Without a word, Tandias followed three prime humanoids as they climbed aboard the train and walked a short distance toward a private car.

Tandias didn't mind devouring the wealthy—they generally furnished a more nourishing meal than the poor or homeless. These three would provide adequately for him. "This car is reserved and off-limits," one of the men snapped as Tandias stepped inside the luxury compartment.

"Excellent," Tandias smiled hungrily, revealing many, pointed teeth.

* * *

Tory, Calebert says I might be elevated to Fifth-Tier soon, Nissa's mental voice was breathless when she replied. *I'm sorry I blew you off earlier, but I was talking to Calebert. What's this about Toff's father?*

Sissy, Trik helped us, and we found out that Roff is Toff's father.

Nissa, who was curled up on her bed with a comp-vid doing lessons, sat upright swiftly. *What?* she sent. *Are you sure?*

Yeah. There are only two comesuli families who are Infilathi—you know, the ones who will become Winged Vampires? Well, we did research, and Roff got staked by somebody who was trying to kill Mom around fifteen years ago. The dates match, Sissy. Toff's father is Roff. What we can't figure out is what else happened around that time. Ry

Chapter 13

and I are trying to figure everything out, and Trik is helping as much as he can, but he's with the Larentii right now. They're already working on his leg. Sissy, he gets better every day with his right hand and thanks to the Larentii, he'll be up and walking soon.

That's great. About Trik, I mean. What are we going to do about Toff? I don't want to keep the information from him, but what if it upsets him when we tell? And if we don't tell him, will he be mad at us because we knew and didn't tell him?

We've been trying to figure that out, too. I don't know what to do. Tory's mental moan was almost audible. *He still thinks his father is dead. I think Toff needs to know that he's alive, at least. I'd want to know, if I thought my dad was dead.*

Yeah, Nissa agreed. *I'd want to know for sure. What do you think we should do? How should we tell him?*

No idea.

* * *

Lissa's Journal

"Lissa, I need your help. Actually, I need your nose."

I stared at Norian in exasperation. "Norian," I gave him a sigh and a shake of my head. "If you think Gavin, Karzac, the twins or Winkler will let me go offworld, then you'd better think again."

"I don't need your power, just your nose," Norian whined.

"Why?" I lifted an eyebrow at him. I could *Look* for the information, but truthfully, I wasn't feeling well. Breakfast was two hours earlier and looked to make its reappearance at any moment.

Blood Reunion

I had a Council meeting in the afternoon, too, to determine the fate of my homicidal grandmother. Evensun was likely in her future and I didn't plan to stop it. I might abstain, but that's it. She'd threatened Toff. Roff got upset every time he thought about it. Hell, I got upset every time I thought about it.

"I have three disappearances on Gloesse. Simultaneous disappearances. All three of them high-level scientists who worked for Schuul Enterprises. I have records where they boarded the train, and vids show them entering their private compartment, but not exiting it. Those private compartments don't have vid-cameras inside—for obvious reasons."

"They just vanished?" My queasiness was ramping up as I moved my foot around to locate the wastebasket beneath my desk. Hooking an ankle around it, I pulled it forward, positioning it for an easy catch.

"Yes. Dantel Schuul is crying foul and demanding the ASD get involved. You're still my Liaison. Even if you are pregnant."

"Call Winkler, he's the one least likely to remove your head when I ask him to transport us," I said, before bending over and heaving into my designer trash can.

* * *

"Lissa, are you sure?" Winkler's dark eyes raked my face. Even after cleaning myself up and convincing Norian to get rid of the wastebasket, Winkler still knew I'd been sick. Werewolves and their freaking sensitive noses.

"Just get us to Gloesse, Winkler. Norian won't shut up about this until I sniff around." I ruined my tough-girl stance by leaning my forehead against Winkler's shoulder.

Chapter 13

I can't say for sure, but I imagine he was glaring at Norian across the top of my head. Winkler's arms went around me while he kissed my hair. He ruined the tender moment by growling at Norian Keef, who'd taken a step toward us.

"Just get us there, werewolf. The sooner we go, the faster we return," Norian hissed. I considered kicking his snaky ass the next time I wasn't pregnant. Winkler growled again and folded space.

* * *

"Ra'Ak," I snapped two seconds after Norian led us onto the detached private compartment. If Winkler had been wolf, I imagine his hackles would be bristling. Norian settled for staring at me.

"Look, there's room enough for a Ra'Ak to turn here, if he coiled himself up," I pointed out. The compartment was a luxury compartment, and larger than an old Pullman car. "Schuul Enterprises must be doing well if they can afford this kind of transportation for their scientists."

"They are," Norian grumped. "What are we supposed to do now?" He raked fingers through his hair in frustration. "We have a rogue Ra'Ak eating important Alliance researchers and my weapon against them is pregnant and helpless."

"Say that again, Keef, and I'll put you through that window over there," Winkler said. The growl that came with his words told both of us the werewolf was prepared to show up.

"Norian, what the hell would you do if you didn't have me as your weapon, as you so romantically put it?" I wasn't happy with him either, and he was just getting that idea.

"Honestly, you put your fucking job ahead of people. Every. Single. Time." Yeah, the pregnancy hormones were showing up. Big time.

"Keef, I think I'll take Lissa back to Le-Ath Veronis. You can find your own way back," Winkler muttered.

"No, wait. I didn't mean it like that," Norian was suddenly apologetic. I imagine it was because he didn't look forward to finding traditional passage back to headquarters, which was on Le-Ath Veronis.

Sometimes, I wanted to show up at Ildevar Wyyld's palace and ask him what the fuck he thought he was doing, dumping the entire ASD in my lap. Of course, he probably didn't think I'd ever end up pregnant either, so I might consider yelling at him only half as long as I originally intended.

"Norian, if this is your baby, I swear I'll punch you in the face," I snapped.

"Breah-mul, you can't mean that," he whined. Winkler didn't waste any time, and he was gracious enough to haul me (and Norian) back to Le-Ath Veronis.

* * *

"Mom's glaring at Uncle Norian," Ry nudged Tory with his elbow.

Hey, she can probably hear you. I've been studying vampires on my comp-vid, Trik sent.

You got mindspeech? Ry sent as he stared at Trik in wonder.

I'm Belancour—or was. My mother and my grandfather both had mindspeech, and it only makes sense that I might have it. Besides, I practiced for the first time with Connegar and Reemagar when they worked on my right leg this afternoon. They smiled and sent mindspeech back, explaining what they were doing. It was amazing. Trik's smile came through in his mental voice.

All three boys sat in their usual seats at the dinner table, grinning like fools. *Man, we can cause havoc now,* Tory snickered.

Roff and Toff are here, Ry interrupted. Roff and Toff had clearly just arrived from working at the winery all afternoon. All three watched as Roff gave Toff a smile and steered him toward the three boys at the table before walking to his usual place near the Queen's chair.

"Hey, we're having pot roast," Tory nudged Ry. Tory loved pot roast, but the kitchen staff seldom prepared it.

"This is great—I can cut my own meat," Trik announced.

"All right!" The Queen clapped and laughed.

"Way to go, bro," Tory slapped Trik on the back.

* * *

"See, they look the same," Trik pointed at his right leg and foot. "It doesn't hurt, either, when the Larentii work on it." He, Ry, Tory and Toff had gathered in Ry's section of their shared suite. The suite had been enlarged to include space for Trik. Trik suspected the Larentii had a hand in that, too, but didn't voice his suspicions aloud.

"Toff, do you ever wonder about your dad?" Ry asked quietly while drawing a pattern on his comforter.

"Corent?" Toff asked, turning to Ry.

"No, not your adopted dad, your real one," Tory said, ducking his head to hide the unwanted flush that crept up his neck.

"He's dead," Toff shrugged.

"But what if he wasn't?" Trik asked. "If your father were still alive, would you wonder about him?"

"Of course. But Queen Lissa says there was an accident."

"To put it mildly," Ry muttered.

"And what if," Trik continued, "your real father, assuming he's alive, was afraid to tell you who he was, because he was worried you might be upset about it or reject him when you found out?"

"That's silly," Toff murmured. "Why would I be living in the palace if my father were still alive? Why would the Queen want to adopt me if my father were still alive? Wouldn't she just hand me back to him?"

"I think the Queen—Mom, sort of loves you, Toff. I think she's loved you for a long time," Ry said. "Since she met you, in fact, when you were a baby. You've been inside her office. That painting she has behind her desk? The one with the little boy under the tree?"

"I saw it. That has to be one of you," Toff blinked at Ry and Tory.

"Nope. Look at the date next to the signature, dude. That was painted before Ry and I were born. That painting is you, when you were little."

Toff stared at the brothers. "That can't be," he whispered.

"We've been working on this from the back end," Trik sighed. "Toff, if you want to know about your father, I have the information on my comp-vid. Your father was in a terrible accident, except it wasn't really an accident. Somebody tried to kill Queen Lissa, and he stepped in front of her to save her life. He got staked instead of her."

"He died, saving the Queen?" Toff stared at Trik.

"Well," Ry sounded embarrassed.

Chapter 13

"You saw what was done for Cheedas," Tory said. Toff jerked his head in Tory's direction.

"My father's a vampire?"

"Yeah."

"Is that why I can't go to him—they're afraid he'll hurt me?" Toff's mind was whirling with dread.

"No. No, man, nothing like that," Ry held out a hand toward Toff. "I think he's just worried that you won't want him after all this time. I don't think he ever stopped loving you, either."

"The mindbond got in the way, and you didn't remember Mom or your dad," Tory sighed. "I think they're both worried about you and how you might feel about all this."

"But where is he? You seem to know all about this and I don't know anything." Toff was suddenly close to tears, and he didn't want to reveal the weakness to Tory, Ry and Trik.

"Just remember he loves you, and is trying to bring you back into his life the best way he knows how," Ry said, floating Trik's offered comp-vid toward Toff. "We can leave you alone while you read if that's what you want."

"Yes." Toff brushed away moisture from his face and didn't look up as Tory skipped the others away.

* * *

Toff had washed his face to remove the streaks, but his eyes still looked red and swollen. No surprise—he'd scrubbed them often as he read Roff's records. Markoff and Dariff, from the winery, were his uncle and cousin. They were always nice to him. Roff had been careful and thorough whenever he explained anything to Toff or taught him to use any of the equipment at the winery. Roff had taken him flying, too, holding him securely against his chest while he'd sailed across Casino City and Lissia.

Roff—his father? It didn't seem real. If Toff could have picked his father from all those he knew, he realized that Roff would have been his choice. Now, he wandered through the residential wing, searching for Roff's suite.

He'd been brought into the palace, not just because the Queen wanted to adopt him, but because his father lived there. His father was one of the Queen's mates. Toff hesitated as the realization hit him. Wiping his eyes again, he continued his search.

* * *

"This is bad," Ry turned in a circle, taking in his empty bedroom. "Mom is going to kill us, because we let the cat out of the bag and now Toff has run away."

"Come on, bro, let's find Uncle Drake and Uncle Drew," Tory muttered, raking a hand through dark hair in confusion. "I thought he'd want to know. I would."

"Contact your uncles, but we should probably let Roff know first," Trik sighed. "This is our fault, and Roff deserves to be the first to know."

"Yeah, I guess you're right," Ry agreed reluctantly.

Uncle Drew? Ry sent mindspeech as all three made their way into the hall and turned, going as quickly as Trik's motorized chair would allow toward Roff's suite of rooms.

* * *

Toff raised his hand to knock. Roff's name was on the outside of his suite, just as all the other names were. He hesitated. How was he going to tell Roff that he knew? Should he ask? Could he do that, without breaking down?

264

Chapter 13

Thoughts leapt and whirled inside his mind, none of them staying for more than a moment, keeping him from latching onto any of them for careful examination. Redbird's face appeared, replaced by that of Corent. Rain. Father Tiearan. Willow. Gren. Toff sobbed as the images appeared and disappeared. They'd taken him away from his parent.

"Child?" Roff flung the door open and knelt next to Toff. "What is wrong? Are you hurt? What has happened?" His hands went to Toff's face, which was wet with tears.

"Papu?" Toff broke down completely.

* * *

Once Drew received mindspeech from Ry, he sent mindspeech out to Lissa and all her mates as he and Drake raced toward Roff's suite. Winkler, who was with Lissa, folded her to Roff's door. Lissa looked terrified to Drew as he and his brother arrived almost at the same moment.

"Where could he go?" Lissa moaned.

"Mom!" Tory shouted at the end of the hall. He broke into a lope, leaving Ry and Trik behind.

"Torevik Rath, if I find out you've upset him—we were waiting until the proper moment," Lissa wiped tears away. "I sent all the guards out looking, but nobody saw him leave the palace."

"There's no need to look, he's here." Roff opened the door to his suite, and Toff was beside him, held tightly against Roff's chest with a strong, well-muscled arm. A soft, leathery wingtip covered part of Toff's back. Toff had both arms around his father, and it looked as if he'd been crying.

"They're happy tears," Roff murmured and tightened his hold on his son.

"Thank the stars," Lissa muttered.

Chapter 14

Lissa's Journal

*L*issa's Journal

"He spent the last three nights in Roff's suite, but eventually decided to go back to his room with the other boys." I leaned against Winkler in bed. His hand was rubbing my belly—he'd already called for a croissant and some milk, which I'd eaten while he watched. He didn't want a repeat of the wastebasket scene. I didn't want a repeat of that either, but didn't voice my opinion aloud.

"At least he knows, now, and seems to be content with it," Winkler agreed. "And he's a teenager. They need their own space, no matter how well they get along with their parents."

"True," I agreed. "I still don't know whether to be mad at those boys for telling him, or to be grateful to them."

Blood Reunion

"I think it went better than any of us could have hoped," Winkler pointed out judiciously, a mischievous glint in his almost-black eyes. "Toff went straight to Roff when he found out. You can't hope for a better outcome than that."

"Roff is happy," I said. "Toff is happy. You're right, we can't hope for a better outcome than that."

"On another note, when are we taking Narissa to Evensun?" Winkler leaned back and kissed my nape, sending a shiver through me. Everybody (who wants one) ought to be gifted with an amorous werewolf in their bed at least once in their life. Just sayin'.

"In three days, and Aurelius and Thurlow are taking her. I don't want any part of that," I mumbled as Winkler kissed his way down my spine. Honestly, I think sex is mother nature's way of blocking unpleasant thoughts. Mine were certainly blocked in very little time.

* * *

"Look." Trik held out his arms as he grinned helplessly at Ry, Tory and Toff. He was standing for the first time in his life.

"Damn," Tory swore in amazement.

"Do you need someone to help you balance?" Toff thought to ask as Trik wavered slightly.

"Maybe," Trik chuckled. "But I'm standing!"

Toff reached Trik just in time—he might have fallen when the knock came on their shared door.

"Well, look at you," Queen Lissa walked in, followed by Uncles Drake, Drew and Winkler. Gavin wandered in only a moment later.

"See?" Trik was quite proud of himself.

Chapter 14

"I see," Lissa nodded. "That's outstanding. You'll be running in no time."

"I want to. I want to know what that feels like," Trik turned excited green eyes toward the Queen.

"I came to see you, Trik," a dimple appeared in Lissa's cheek as she smiled at him. "I've received messages from Shadow and Glendes Grey. They'll be performing the rite at Grey House to test the talent of two others in a week. They asked if you wanted to be included in this year's rite or if you wanted to wait until next year."

"They want to include me?" Trik's voice squeaked, causing him to flush.

"Of course they do. If that's what you want." The Queen smiled encouragingly.

"I do," Trik nodded enthusiastically. "Please tell them yes."

"You can tell Shadow yourself—he'll be here with Nissa in two days."

"Nissa's coming?" Toff squeaked this time.

"Yes," Lissa's smile brightened—she was looking forward to Nissa's visit, too. "On her off-day."

Toff's mind flew in all directions. He wanted to plan something special. He wanted to buy Nissa a gift. He wanted her to himself, just to sit and talk.

"I think we need a week for all that," Drake laughed after pulling the thoughts straight from Toff's mind.

"Yes," Toff lowered his chin, suddenly embarrassed.

"We want all those things, too, honey." Lissa stood before him, lifting his chin again and studying his face. "But we only get her here once in a while, so we have to be careful or we'll wear her out. This is her off-day, and she needs to rest a little."

Blood Reunion

"Can we go to the beach house?" Tory asked. "Trik needs some sun."

"You know, I think that's a good idea," Lissa agreed. "I'll just tell Shadow to bring Nissa there, and all of you can spend an hour or two on the beach."

"I'll see the ocean?" Toff was breathless with excitement.

"You'll see the ocean," Lissa hugged him tightly.

* * *

"I want you to go with Tandias," Zellar snapped at Gren. "He can slip past the barrier surrounding Le-Ath Veronis. It's quite lucky for us that Tandias was once of a race that holds power apart from that of the Ra'Ak. He gets past Le-Ath Veronis' barrier using that ability. Too bad Viregruz didn't send you after the bitch Queen when he had the chance," Zellar turned to Tandias.

"He had a schedule to keep, and I was kept busy elsewhere," Tandias turned a warning look on Zellar. "My master seldom asked me to deviate from my assignments, and he felt that the Queen's death might be achieved through other means. I intend to avenge his death. Do not question my master's choices again." Tandias turned away from Zellar.

"Yes, well," Zellar cleared his throat before focusing on Gren, "Once you're on Le-Ath Veronis, tap into the core again," Zellar continued. "We'll need your talent and you'll need the extra power when we attack the Queen's palace," Zellar blinked his remaining eye at Gren.

"We can't get you back to one of your original tapping sites, so you'll have to tap the core from another spot. Tandias and I believe this to be the best place." Zellar rapped the electronic map Tandias had procured for him on Gloesse.

Chapter 14

Gren studied the map, eventually working out the images presented. "That's an outcropping of rock in the Western Sea," he complained, raising his gaze to Zellar's face. He looked away quickly—he couldn't keep his eyes on Zellar's raw, left countenance for long; Zellar didn't like it and Gren found it uncomfortable anyway.

"It's perfect," Zellar declared. "They call it The Tooth for a reason—it's steep and pointed, plus the rock is extremely sharp. It's also ten clicks from the shoreline. Nobody goes there. Tandias will find a safe place for you to stand while you tap into the core beneath the water."

"We could tap another planet," Gren muttered, staring at his shoes. They were worn through the soles, but Zellar refused to find shoes or additional clothing for him. He was tired of sleeping on the floor, too, but Zellar had struck him once already for complaining.

"Tandias and I intend to exact the greatest amount of revenge against the Queen of Le-Ath Veronis. This," Zellar tapped the corner of his closed and useless eye, "she did this to me. She destroyed Tandias' brotherhood, too. We both want to destroy her and her planet. Tapping from multiple locations kills it faster."

Gren stared in shock—tapping the planet killed it? He wanted to moan in frustration. He had begun to regret his liaison with Zellar, and this only made it worse. His parents were on Le-Ath Veronis. They liked it there.

"Ah," Zeller nodded and turned away with a laugh. "You didn't know that, did you? Get used to it," Zellar turned again swiftly and slapped Gren hard across the face. "And don't let me hear your complaints again. You'll go with Tandias tomorrow, you'll take the power and then we'll make our plans."

Blood Reunion

"Just put your swimsuit and a change of clothing for dinner in your bag," Roff sat on Toff's bed while Toff dithered over what to take to the beach house. "We'll take extra clothing later and leave it there, so you'll have it if you need it."

"What about sunburn?" Toff turned to his father.

"Ry can provide a shield for everyone—it's a simple spell any warlock can manage. Nissa can probably do it as well, I've just never asked," Roff replied.

"Papu, I don't know why I never thought we were related before—our eyes are the same color. Our hair is the same color, too. Master Morwin is teaching me about genetics in my science lessons."

"You should have met your older sister," Roff sighed and stared at his hands. "Did you read her records, too? Members of our family either have black or light-brown hair. Your grandfather had light-brown hair. His parent had black hair."

"I read the records; my sister's name was Giff, but much of the information refers to her as him. Why is that?"

"Lissa can identify which comesuli will be male or female after the turn. Giff was destined to be a female Winged Vampire, which is quite uncommon. Her loss was a grievous one, child."

"Did I know her?" Toff looked troubled. Roff beckoned with a hand, so Toff went to sit beside his father.

"She watched you whenever I couldn't," Roff placed an arm around Toff. "Fed you, bathed you, did everything for you that she could. We both loved you, son, very much."

Chapter 14

Toff hung his head. He imagined that mentioning Griffin's visit when he'd first come to the palace would only upset his father, so he didn't say anything. More and more, though, he found himself disliking Lissa's father, and felt the strange man had many things to answer for.

"Come now, finish packing you bag and I'll fly you to Casino City. I imagine that a bauble might be found there for Nissa."

"Really? We can go shopping?" Toff beamed at his father.

"We really can," Roff grinned and tousled Toff's hair.

* * *

"We will form the circle in four days," Tiearan informed the village elders. "I hoped to do it sooner, but the illness that swept through our humanoid population has prevented it."

Tiearan wanted to vent his frustration, but as chief of the Green Fae, he couldn't. All those inside their boundary were affected in some way or another by the energy drain from the core's tapping. Peaceful inhabitants snapped at one another. Several fights had broken out within the humanoid population, and then the fever came, sweeping through those who were susceptible and leaving them weak afterward.

"I will be ready." Willow had come, but was anxious to return to his animals. He'd only come to hear the date and had no desire to be around the others longer than necessary.

Tiearan nodded as Willow walked toward the wide barn door. He'd chosen the barn where they crushed grapes for winemaking, because it was more than large enough to hold the elders without bringing them too closely together. Tiearan had seen firsthand what pushing them together might accomplish during this trying time; arguments often came, and he had no desire to act as peacemaker on this day.

"All of you, gather here in four days. The circle will convene and we will repair this blight. Go now and prepare. Charge your crystal and be ready." Tiearan dismissed them with a sigh.

* * *

"It doesn't hurt." Nissa smiled at Trik's words. For the first time in his life, Trik had walked with the others to the beach, closely watched by Roff.

Lissa and a few others had chosen to stay on the balcony overlooking the private stretch of sand attached to the beach house. It wasn't really a beach house, although that's what everyone called it. The structure was actually a smaller palace, suited to its location near the beach on the light half of the planet.

"What can you tell me about the rite?" Trik asked. He, Nissa, Roff, Ry and Tory were all sitting on the sand after playing in the surf for nearly an hour. Roff stood farther down, looking westward over the sea.

"Grampa Glendes usually does it," Nissa began. "He takes your head in his hands and everything goes dark. You won't remember anything past that until you wake up, but Daddy says that Grampa described it once. He said it's like looking at a star field at night, when Grampa looks into your mind. The more stars there are, the more powerful the wizard will be. Grampa will wake the wizard's talent with a little power of his own, and Daddy says that all the stars, which were only pinpoints of light before, will shine like the sun after that. You'll be able to tap your power after Grampa Glendes wakes it up."

"Nobody ever described it to me at Belancour Manor," Trik huffed. "They all said I didn't need to know."

"They were wrong to ignore or mistreat you," Toff muttered angrily. He could identify with Trik easily.

"I wish you were coming, too," Nissa nudged Toff's shoulder with her own. Toff made sure to sit beside her when they'd all flopped onto the wet sand.

"Me, too," Toff admitted. "I always wanted what the others around me had. Even the halves had a lot of power, but I didn't have anything."

"It's hard, growing up in that environment," Trik nodded. "They all flaunt what they have and there you sit, thinking you'll never have anything."

"Dude, you'll have it now," Ry grinned at Trik. "I think Dad might show you a trick or two, after you go through the rite."

"You think so?" Trik offered Ry a hopeful glance.

"Yeah," Ry replied with a shrug. "Dad knows all kinds of stuff."

"Grandfather was always jealous of the Karathian Warlocks. Said they hid their talents and wouldn't let anybody know how they did anything," Trik said.

"Dad's not like that. He showed Sissy how to cast illusions," Ry grinned at his sister.

"I can cast really good illusions after Uncle Erland showed me how. Daddy said I couldn't do it anymore inside Grey House, though," Nissa grumped.

"After you made the kitchen staff think they were getting attacked by a dragon," Tory snickered. "Because they were cooking liver for dinner."

"I was grounded for three weeks," Nissa mumbled, her face turning pink. "Uncle Erland taught me how to add sound to the illusion, and dinner sort of got ruined that night."

"How old were you?" Toff put an arm around Nissa.

"Eight," she said, leaning into his embrace.

Trik chuckled at Nissa's admission. "Some of Belancour's best wizards couldn't do that," he proclaimed.

* * *

Gren backed up against sharp, uncomfortable rock as he stared at the ocean far below. Tandias stood on a narrow ledge nearby, waiting for Gren to tap the core. Gren's feet barely had enough room; he'd felt ill when Tandias first placed him on the small shelf of rock. Any wrong movement might send him plunging into the waters below. Waves crashed and boomed against the dark base of The Tooth.

"Get on with it, whelp," Tandias growled. He didn't like the location any better than Gren. Gren breathed a shaky sigh and reached out with his power.

* * *

Lissa's Journal

"Here." Gavin handed a glass of pineapple juice to me. I'd chosen to sit on the western balcony of my beach house so I could easily keep an eye on the kids. Gavin settled on the wide chaise beside me after I accepted the drink he'd asked the kitchen staff to prepare.

"Thanks," I sipped the juice before leaning my head against his shoulder.

"They're still sitting in a circle on the sand," Gavin observed, lifting an eyebrow as he watched the young ones below us.

Chapter 14

"They're talking, and I think they did that to give Trik a rest. He can walk, now, but that doesn't mean he's up to a marathon." I leaned back and wrinkled my nose at Gavin.

"Cara mia, if we weren't babysitting," he growled, leaning in to rub my nose with his.

"We are babysitting," I reminded him. "There's always later," I added, wrinkling my nose again. "Besides, it's almost lunchtime. Did you ask Web to have towels ready? They'll be tracking in sand, too."

"Web informed me that all has been made ready," Gavin's mouth tugged upward at the corner. That always makes me want to melt in a puddle. I think he's figured that out, too.

"If I weren't pregnant, there would be some time bending right now," I whispered before leaning in to kiss Gavin. Just as his lips closed over mine, the beach house shook. And then continued shaking.

* * *

"What the hell?" Drake gripped the doorframe tightly with strong fingers—he and Drew had just finished blade practice with some of their elite troops and intended to shower inside the barracks before joining Lissa and the others at the beach house for lunch.

Another earthquake had taken them by surprise, and this one looked to be stronger than the last.

"Where?" Drew shouted over the noise of falling bricks and toppling furniture.

"To the west," Tony folded in, almost falling as his feet settled onto an unsteady floor. The tiles were threatening to buckle beneath them.

"But there's nothing but water to the west," Drake's voice wobbled as he replied.

"Fuck!" Drew shouted. "Sound the alarm. This will cause a tsunami, and those people in Sun City will be swept away!"

"Lissa's at the beach house," Drake turned frightened eyes to his brother.

"Let's go, there's no time to waste," Tony said. All three disappeared just as the ground seemed to be settling down.

* * *

Roff had taken to the sky as soon as he'd gathered Trik, Nissa and Toff in his arms. Tory had grabbed Ry's arm and skipped his brother to the beach house already. Flapping determinedly toward the second-floor balcony, Roff watched in horror as the ground beneath shook harder and trees toppled.

"The floors are cracking," Lissa pointed out as Roff landed on the balcony. Tory and Ry were already there and Gavin was prepared to fold everyone away. Lissa was correct—the marble beneath their feet was splitting and roof tiles were breaking and falling to the ground.

"I'll take Roff and the kids, Gavin, bring Lissa and the comesuli," Drew appeared on the balcony beside Roff. "Drake and Tony are sounding the alarm in Sun City, but Drake's sending mindspeech, saying the tourists and gamblers are just standing on the beach, staring at the receding water."

* * *

Lissa's Journal

Chapter 14

I'd never seen Drew looked so frightened, and I'd watched him stare down a fifty-foot Ra'Ak before. I'd never felt so helpless, either. Karzac warned me—scared me, even—about using any power during pregnancy. The rush of power through the body could easily kill an unborn child.

If I weren't pregnant, I could gather the entire population of Sun City inside my mist and haul them to higher ground. I'd already *Looked*—a huge wave was coming and it would drown everything in its path.

"Lissa, do not even contemplate this," Karzac appeared beside me, his green-gold eyes quite stern as he gazed at me. "I will carry you to safety, and Drew and Gavin will bring the others. If those fools in Sun City choose to ignore the sirens instead of running for their lives," he didn't finish his statement, he merely lifted me in his arms and we disappeared.

* * *

"Run for your lives," Tony place compulsion on a knot of tourists walking toward the beach instead of away from it. They turned immediately and ran.

Here it comes, Drake's mindspeech rang clearly in Tony's mind. *The epicenter was only a few miles out, and the crowd here is beginning to see the wave. Now they're running*, Drake added. *Get away or you'll be run down.*

Going now, Tony replied and folded space.

* * *

Drake stood apart and watched as screaming people ran away from the high wall of water descending upon them. The narrow strip of sand lying in front of Sun City's most expensive casinos and hotels would be engulfed—there was

279

no doubt of that. As a member of the Saa Thalarr, he was forbidden to interfere. Never had he regretted it so much. Waiting until the last moment, he folded away. Water roared through the streets and alleys of the city behind him, drowning out the cries for help.

* * *

Lissa's Journal

Three hundred seventeen people died. Three hundred seventeen, most of whom had been drawn to the beach out of curiosity instead of heeding the sirens blasting all over Sun City. Was I upset and depressed? Of course. I could have saved them. Instead, I chose to save my child.

"Lissa, please stop moping." Karzac pulled me against him. We were on the bed in my suite while comesuli and vampire work crews crawled through the palace, repairing cracks and breaks throughout.

News crews were hovering over the remains of Sun City, reporting on the deaths caused by the tsunami. In between, journalists were showing the last vid images recorded from casinos and hotels, depicting tourists who were flocking toward the danger instead of running away.

Sound recorded with the images clearly indicated that warning sirens were wailing throughout the city. Those who died had paid for their curiosity with their lives.

"It is not your duty to save everybody," Karzac whispered against my ear. "Perhaps a few might have died anyway, had they heeded the warning. The numbers would have been drastically reduced, however, had that happened. Do not accept the blame for this."

"I picked the worst possible time to be pregnant," I muttered, covering my eyes with a shaking hand. I had a headache, too, on top of everything else. I was just too tired and depressed to ask Karzac to heal it. An empty feeling lay at the pit of my stomach—one that threatened to bring on a bout of nausea.

"We will not stand for that," Karzac murmured gently as he touched my forehead first, taking away the headache. Then his hands wandered toward my belly and the nausea disappeared. "I have asked Drew to order something from the kitchen for you—you've barely eaten in the past two days."

Yes, it was two days since the tsunami and I still felt ill. Emergency stations had been set up in Casino City. Casino basements had turned into temporary morgues and a flock of vampires volunteered to arrange travel plans for those tourists affected by the disaster.

Others had signed up to contact families of the deceased and help get bodies shipped to their home worlds. Donations were pouring in from wealthy vampires, so no family was forced to pay to have their loved ones returned to them.

Aurelius and Bryan had approached me for an interview to send out to the Alliance the evening after the tsunami. I'd done the interview, although I felt like weeping the whole time. It was difficult to get through some of the information, before telling everyone about the emergency stations, where to go for help or information and that travel and shipping costs would be covered by donations from private citizens and the crown.

Kifirin was noticeably absent, and I was too weary and despondent to send mindspeech to him. I did receive communication from Ildevar Wyyld, however, and he'd sent a large amount from a personal account to help defray costs, along with condolences and a healthy dose of concern for me.

Somehow, I suppose through Norian, he'd learned of the pregnancy. Ra'Ak or not, Ildevar Wyyld was a very decent man.

"Lissa?" Connegar and Reemagar appeared inside my bedroom, followed by several other Larentii. Renegar and Pheligar were among the nine tall, blue Larentii now inside my suite.

I'd only met Graegar and Garegar of the Wise Ones before. Now, all five Wise Ones stood at the foot of my bed. I knew their names, and marveled that they'd arrived without their protectors. Who was I to question them, though? Hiragar, Meligar, Tenigar, Graegar and Garegar carefully examined me with lifted eyebrows as I extricated myself from Karzac's embrace.

"We have news," Graegar announced. Was it me, or did he sound sad?

"What we have to tell you will not be easy, and coming after such a tragic event," Garegar added.

"I am Tenigar, eldest of the Wise Ones," one of the others spoke. He was roughly the same height as Pheligar— eight and a half feet, and his blue eyes held the depth of countless millennia. I was guessing he might be as old as Ferrigar, who was three million years old. It made me want to sigh. He'd seen everything, most likely, during his long life.

"We have uncovered the source of these earthquakes," Tenigar said. "It is not natural, as you and the others may have assumed. You did not *Look* for their source, assuming they were such. That is not the case."

"What?" I snapped. Karzac attempted to grab me but I slid off the bed too quickly.

Chapter 14

"Tapping cores does not always result in earthquakes. It is only thus when an untried power attempts the tapping, and they fumble about while tearing into the power of the core. The young one who escaped from your dungeon is the one responsible for this, and we fear he did it at another's bidding."

"But Gren couldn't have caused this one," I stared at all five Wise Ones. He had. I could see it in their faces. "How did he return?" I whispered. Karzac caught me before I dropped to the floor in shock.

"Ra'Ak," Pheligar replied. "An unusual one, of a race we thought long dead. With that kind of power behind him, he will be difficult to detect and able to get through almost any shield." Pheligar and Ren had been waiting patiently beside Connegar and Reemagar, and hadn't spoken until now.

"I had to search diligently for the power signature, it is so muted." Pheligar continued. "As Liaison for so long for the Saa Thalarr, I have become quite sensitive to any activity from the Ra'Ak, and it was the tiny bit of that power which alerted me and pointed me in this one's direction. Because of what he was before he was turned Ra'Ak, it will be difficult for anyone to make note of this one. He has much experience in getting in and out without causing a stir."

"A Ra'Ak brought that murderous brat back, just to tap our core again? Oh my gosh, this means Le-Ath Veronis is dying." I struggled in Karzac's embrace. He ignored my struggles with stoicism, displaying a strength I didn't realize he had.

"We believe that the drain will not be extremely detrimental for the next five months, after which you will be able to make the repairs yourself," Tenigar took up the conversation again.

"But it will be detrimental," I said, giving up my silent battle with Karzac and settling against him.

"Yes. Any drain on a core's energy will be harmful. In our experience, crime will increase, deaths will increase, suicides will increase," he didn't finish, I held up a hand to stop him.

"In other words," I said, "Draining the core is like draining the heart out of people. And with a planet full of vampires, that can cause a big problem."

"Yes. If they decide to commit a crime or create havoc," Graegar agreed.

"Fucking lovely," I muttered.

"And since Le-Ath Veronis is a victim of multiple tappings," Tenigar began.

"The crime, deaths, suicides and other chaos will happen faster, is that what you're saying?" I lifted an eyebrow at him as I finished his statement.

"In a word, yes," he nodded.

"How many times did that little creep tap the core?"

"It's not the number of times, it's the number of locations that really matters," Renegar replied. "He tapped it from three locations."

"Fucking wonderful," I sighed. My headache was officially back. "Karzac, how quickly can I repair the core after the baby comes?" I turned in his arms and studied his face. His green-gold eyes were thoughtful as he contemplated my dilemma. Yes—it was my dilemma—the Larentii couldn't interfere, although they likely held the power to repair a planet's core. It also made me wonder about the race they'd mentioned—the one they'd assumed was dead.

"I would wait at least a month after the baby's birth, to get your strength back," Karzac admitted, lowering his eyes.

Chapter 14

"So, six months, then, before we can fix this." I wasn't happy about that, and it frightened me that Le-Ath Veronis would likely be thrown into chaos during that time. "What about the crimes and the depression and everything else?" I asked Pheligar. "How long will it take for all that to go away?"

"It will not disappear overnight," Graegar answered for his Larentii grandfather. "It could take months—or years, even—for all of it to subside."

"And in the meantime, we have to deal with the additional crime, mental illness, what have you," I moved away from Karzac and tossed up a hand in helpless resignation.

"We believe that all this is a concentrated effort to harm you and your planet," Garegar offered. "If you allow this to upset you, then your enemies are winning already."

There's nothing like stating the obvious. I already knew Zellar was involved with Gren and Gren's disappearance, now I knew the how. The Larentii hadn't told me what race this Ra'Ak had belonged to, and I wondered at that.

There was more to the story here, but they didn't want to tell it. We didn't know how old this Ra'Ak was, anyway. He could have been turned before his race died out, and he was the only one left. That was what I hoped for, anyway.

"Looks like I have two jobs waiting, then," I huffed. "First, to repair Le-Ath Veronis' core, and then to hunt down Zellar, an unusual Ra'Ak and Gren." I watched as all nine Larentii breathed a group sigh of relief—I hadn't asked them about the former race of this Ra'Ak and they seemed mighty happy that I hadn't.

* * *

Blood Reunion

"Lissa, this will be the perfect time to return to Grey House. Trik will be going through the rite, and I hear that Toff would love to come for a visit." Shadow was good at wheedling, I'll give him that. "Besides," he added, "it will take you away from your worries here."

Shadow had shown up, his dark hair cut and styled, dressed nicely in black and looking quite handsome. It was the arsenal he used in his attempt to lure me back to Grey House.

He knew, just as all the Inner Circle did—Le-Ath Veronis' core had been tapped, criminals were on the loose and there wasn't a damn thing I could do about any of it for at least six months. Those fool Larentii had gotten away without telling me who the baby's father was, too. Frankly, the question hadn't even entered my mind, I was so stunned at the other news they'd brought.

"Look, we'll have the monthly family dinner, just as we always do, and the rite comes after that. You didn't come for Nissa's rite. Trik needs as many familiar faces around him as he can get—being ousted from your family can be a trying experience, Karzac says so."

Shadow was still pleading his case, his gray eyes begging. He was doing a damn fine job, too, of making me feel guilty. Yes, I felt guilty because I hadn't been there for Nissa. I'd feel guilty again for not being there for Trik.

"Shadow, I've had a headache since the tsunami, did you know that?" I blinked into his gray gaze, my fingers gripping the end of my braid. We were inside my study; I sat on my sofa there and Shadow knelt at my feet. I'd come to my study to try to get work done, but Shadow had shown up shortly after. I had to make a decision quickly, too; the rite was scheduled for the following day.

Chapter 14

"Come on, baby. You can come. I'll be with you every second, and you can punch Grampa in the face if you want." Shadow's last statement was accompanied by a lopsided grin, so I knew he was teasing.

"I've considered punching him before, you know," I huffed.

"I know. I think Dad, Grampa and I all know that," he nodded and rose to slide onto the sofa beside me.

"Are they all going to talk and whisper when I come?" Yeah, the hormones were probably doing the talking, because I sure as hell felt paranoid about the whole thing.

"I'll turn them into toads." Shadow was grinning again.

"You will not," I attempted to brush away the arm he placed around my shoulders.

"I will," he ignored my attempts to push him away and leaned in for a kiss. "How many shall I tell them to expect?" He pulled away to smile gently at me.

"Trik, for sure," I sighed. "Tory, Ry, Toff, Roff. And me."

"Yes!" Shadow's answer said it all.

Chapter 15

"We're all going?" Toff's eyes were wide as he stared at his father.

"We're going. Lissa, too," Roff chuckled at Toff's excitement. "When we finish checking these bottles, I'll take you to Casino City to pick out something to wear. Family dinners at Grey House are formal."

Toff grinned at his father—Roff's honey-brown eyes gleamed with excitement—he wanted to go just as badly as Toff did. "Child, not many are invited to Grey House. Their offices are located on another planet, and that's where their clients come. Very few outsiders are allowed on Grey Planet—for any reason. Normally it's family only who get to witness the rite, too. This is an honor." Roff ruffled Toff's dark hair.

"Can we sit with Nissa?" Toff asked in a shy voice.

Blood Reunion

"I think your mother will insist on it," Roff laughed.

* * *

"Trik, it's not a big deal," Ry attempted to calm his adopted brother. "Grampa Wylend did mine, but there are several other warlocks who do it, too. Sissy's right—you don't remember it and it isn't painful. Dad was right there with me and says it's no big deal."

"No big deal? I've never heard that phrase before," Trik blinked worried green eyes at Ry.

"Mom has a ton of unusual phrases. Just wait till you hear her say holy crap."

"I've never heard of that being sacred," Trik giggled nervously.

"Are you boys dressed?" Queen Lissa swept into the room. Trik stared—she was dressed in a royal blue, jeweled gown that likely cost a fortune.

"I have to wear the colors of the jewelry makers, since Shadow is a Master Wizard in that Division," Lissa held out the long skirt of her dress. "And I have to sit at the Master Wizard's table at the front. Because I like being in a fishbowl," she added with a snort.

"We're dressed, Mom. See?" Ry held out his arms. He and Trik were clothed in dark gray suits with white, high-collared shirts.

"Mom, I can't get this button done," Tory walked in, fumbling with the top button on his shirt. He was dressed identically to Trik and Ry.

"Here, I'll do it," Lissa reached up to button Tory's shirt. "There. All done," she patted his shoulder and smiled at him. "I'm sorry you have to sit in the back, but Shadow says your

290 "

Chapter 15

High Demon talent for neutralizing power has to be kept away from the rite."

"That's okay. Ry, Sissy, Toff and Roff will be with me," Tory grinned. "And nobody will have to crane their necks to see over my head."

"Will Uncle Shadow take us?"

"Uncle Shadow is definitely taking you," Shadow walked in wearing a huge grin and a long, royal blue dress robe over a white shirt and black slacks.

"You'd think it was Christmas, the way you're gloating," Lissa swatted his arm.

"What's Christmas?" Trik asked, his curiosity overcoming his nervousness.

"One of Mom's holidays. Every year, she gives everybody gifts for no apparent reason," Tory said. "We get the best stuff."

"When is Christmas?" Trik couldn't help but ask.

"In five months," Lissa said. "Karzac tells me the baby is due around that time. Don't worry," she held up a hand when Ry started to say something. "You'll get your presents, just like always. Kyler and Cleo are prepared to get everything done for me, if the baby comes around that time."

"The gift wrap is always red and green," Ry whispered to Trik. "And there's a tree. With lights. We don't know why." Lissa heard and laughed.

"We're ready," Roff and Toff walked in, Both dressed in dark suits.

"Toff, you look so handsome," Lissa hugged him.

"Kyler and I are coming," Flavio walked in with Kyler. "Cleo is already there with Harvel, waiting for us."

* * *

Blood Reunion

Lissa's Journal

I wanted to hug Flavio. He didn't go to Grey House often with Kyler, although as one of her mates, he was welcome. As Glendes' Daughter, Kyler was required to attend the family dinners, but she usually took Rik or Pheran Tiger. Flavio's reason was understandable—he didn't appreciate the stares whenever he accompanied Kyler to Grey House. Yes, he was the handsomest male there when he went, but the attention from some of the female wizards was uncomfortable for him. He was going this time to show support for me. Sometimes, we vampires had to stick together.

The Grey family was huge, probably at least eight hundred members, and the cavernous dining hall used for the monthly family dinners held all of them. Thankfully, not all of them would attend the rite—Glendes limited that to immediate family and those closest to the children going through the rite—more than that terrified the child. Yes, the children were normally six years old and if they were like Nissa, they were already scared witless when Glendes put his hands on them. They didn't need a huge audience there, gawking.

"Trik, are you good to go?" I stood on tiptoe to kiss his forehead—he was as tall as Ry and looked ready to bolt if somebody said boo to him.

"I'm ready," he said, squaring his shoulders. I still saw the worry in his green eyes, however.

"It doesn't take long," Shadow came forward and patted Trik's shoulder. "And it doesn't hurt. It's just the waking of your power. I was scared witless when Grampa did it for me all those years ago, and when I woke afterward, I remember thinking that it wasn't an ordeal at all."

"Queen Lissa?" Trik said, his eyes meeting mine.

Chapter 15

"What, honey?" I asked. Something big was coming, I could tell by his expression.

"I never got to call Melida Mom. She wouldn't allow it," he muttered, dropping his eyes. "Morwin showed me copies of the adoption papers. It says you're my adoptive mother, and Shadow is my adoptive father."

"That's right," I nodded, not sure where this was going. "If you want to change that when you're older, we can talk about it. Right now, those papers say that Shadow and I will take care of you and treat you as our own." My heart hurt for him—I'd known all along that Melida was a nasty piece of work. I hoped she hadn't abused Trik after his birth. She certainly had when he was still in the womb.

"I like that part," he muttered. "Can I call you Mom and Dad?" His eyes darted from me to Shadow.

"Son, you can call us anything you want," Shadow pulled Trik into a hug. Right then, my opinion of my Grey House wizard went up quite a few notches. "It'll be all right," Shadow added. "Your mother and I will be right there with you." I realized I was crying as I watched Trik's arms go around Shadow's waist.

* * *

"You thought you could just sneak around without letting me know you were back?" Friesianna gave Narissa a hard stare. The former Elemaiyan Queen showed her age—gray streaked her brown hair, just as Narissa's auburn locks were threaded with silver. Friesianna no longer dressed in rich fabrics; nothing of the sort was available on Evensun. She gathered clothing from new arrivals, usually after their deaths at the hands of her servants.

Blood Reunion

"Shut up, bitch," Narissa snarled. "I know you don't have Le'meruh any longer, it was removed with the rest of your power. If these lapdogs of yours realized that, they'd leave you in half a blink."

Narissa struggled between two Elemaiyan guards—they'd led a hunting party when Narissa's appearance on Evensun was first reported. She hadn't been difficult to locate; Narissa hadn't bothered to hide her tracks. They'd dragged her to Friesianna's cave afterward. The cave was a wide, easily defensible space with plenty of room for Friesianna, her guards and her servants.

"Well, we don't intend to let you go, bitch," Friesianna's gaze was hard as she flung Narissa's insult back. "I know you're related to the whore who took our power and put us here. You'll pay for that, I promise."

Narissa's eyes grew wide and she struggled against the two who held her when she saw what approached from the back of Friesianna's cave.

* * *

Lissa's Journal

If one more Grey dipped their head or bowed while murmuring "Queen Lissa," I was going to hurl. Sure, they all wanted me to feel welcome, but honestly, the attention thing was getting old fast.

Steady, Shadow whispered in my mind. *We're here for Trik, remember?* He had my arm tucked tightly in his, leading me through the elite of Grey House wizards. Roff and the kids followed us, allowing Shadow and me to clear a path for them. There was a ritual for every Grey House family dinner; most of the family gathered inside the dining hall and when everything was ready, Glendes, Eldest of Grey

Chapter 15

House, led a procession of the Master Wizards and their mates inside to the main table.

Roff could take the kids in and get them seated, but I had to walk in later on Shadow's arm, while everybody stared. To top it all off, I was feeling queasy. Who says my life can't be fucked up in so many ways I can lose count? If I knew who'd fathered this child, I might strangle him. Maybe that's why the Larentii didn't tell me. I watched as someone came forward and escorted Roff, Trik and the others into the massive dining hall.

"Feeling all right?" Shadow let go of my arm and pulled me tight against him.

"Is my green color showing?" I looked up into his concerned face.

"Only a little. I asked the staff to bring juice and water to the table for you, not wine," he added, rubbing my back. "I know you have other children, but you didn't carry them. This will be a first for all of us." Shadow's sigh tickled my neck. "I'd like to rub your belly right now, but Grampa gets a little testy about overt displays of affection at family dinners."

"Overt displays?" I leaned back to look at his face again.

"Dad says Grampa hit him in the back of the head with a dinner roll once, when he decided to kiss Mom at the table."

"Did he throw it or use power to launch a bread attack?" The vision of Glendes throwing anything at his grown son's head made me snicker.

"I believe a bit of power was involved, yes," Shadow grinned.

"Do they call it the sourdough offensive, now?" I snorted when I laughed, and that brought everybody's attention straight to Shadow and me.

Blood Reunion

"Dad claims he has a scar," Shadow chuckled. If the anteroom filled with Master Wizards hadn't been aware of our conversation before, they were now. I heard whispers and giggles after Shadow's statement.

"Pay no attention to my son," Raffian announced to the crowd as he and Shannon made their way to Shadow's side. "We dropped him on his head when he was a baby."

"Raff, how hard was that roll Daddy hit you with?" Kyler snickered. I noticed that Flavio was suddenly studying the elaborate carvings on the ceiling.

"Come on, Flavio, you know you want to laugh," I called out. Had I ever heard that old vampire guffaw? Not until now. He was laughing helplessly while holding onto Kyler, who grinned mischievously. Cleo, who stood next to Kyler, began to giggle. Harvel, her Master Wizard mate, laughed.

"Well, this means one thing," I said.

"What's that?" Shadow asked, putting his arms around me again.

"That Glendes will never let me come back to Grey House."

"What's this?" Glendes, Eldest of Grey House and tyrant extraordinaire, appeared before Shadow and me. If he thought I was going to cower before him, he could think again.

"Lissa, you are a member of the family," Glendes said, reaching out to take my hand. And then he shocked the hell out of me by raising my fingers to his lips and kissing them. "You are always welcome here. Now, if the rest of you are ready," he turned and addressed the others, "we will march inside and behave with decorum. The occasional giggle will be ignored. Follow me." He walked away, adjusted his black robes, took Lira's arm and led us into the dining hall.

Chapter 15

* * *

Trik swallowed nervously. Two six-year-olds waited with him inside a small room. "What's your name?" The smallest of the two asked. He sat beside Trik, his brown eyes curious as he gazed up at the older boy.

"Trikleer," Trik answered. "But everybody calls me Trik. What's yours?"

"Lucas," he replied shyly, hunching his shoulders. "Me and Dane want to train with Master Raffian."

Trik blinked, only then realizing that Raffian was his adoptive grandfather. "Why do you want to train with Master Raffian?" Trik asked.

"Because everybody says he's the most powerful wizard in Grey House," Dane, the other boy, answered. Unlike Lucas, he was taller, chubbier and had blue eyes. Those blue eyes were now trained on Trik. "Sometimes he yells," Dane went on, "but they all do. We'll be working with Third-Tiers anyway, after we're assigned."

Shadow had already explained the levels of wizardry at Grey House to Trik. Apprentice was the lowest level, with Fifth-Tier wizard status coming after the apprentice could perform to those standards. Most apprentices gained Fifth-Tier level at the age of eighteen. When a wizard gained Third-Tier, he or she might be allowed to help train apprentices. Only a few gained Second or First-Tier status, and Master Wizards, who were at the highest level, were very rare.

"Who do you want to train with, Trikleer?" Lucas asked.

"It doesn't matter. I just feel lucky to be here," Trik replied.

Blood Reunion

"Lucas? It's time," a Third-Tier wizard poked her head inside the door. She was with the Art Division, as designated by her green robe.

"Coming, Aunt Milli," Lucas slid off his seat and wobbled toward his aunt.

"Someone will come for you when it's time," Milli reassured Dane and Trik before placing an arm around Lucas' shoulders and closing the door behind him.

Not long after, one of Dane's uncles arrived and escorted Dane from the small room, leaving Trik alone, wondering whom it might be that would come for him. "Trik?" Nissa walked through the door and held out her hand. A grin split Trik's face as he stood and grasped Nissa's fingers with his.

* * *

Tiearan studied the circles of Fae before him. It began with a small circle; the oldest and strongest in the village comprised that circle. Those next in power formed a circle outside that one, with the weaker ones forming four increasingly larger circles past that.

Children were in the last circle, and their energy would be used only as a last resort. The first and second circles held crystal, none of the others did. Tiearan believed those two circles would be the only ones involved.

Sighing, Tiearan stepped through gaps in each circle until he reached the center of the first and smallest circle. Nodding to Rain and Willow, who sat beside each other there, he settled himself at the center of all the circles and drew out the crystal orb he wore on a chain about his neck. All the Fae were silent as they watched Tiearan center his power.

Chapter 15

* * *

"You will not be harmed; this is only to awaken your power." Glendes Grey, gray-eyed and dark-haired, focused on Trik's face as Trik sat before him in a comfortable chair. *I know you're worried,* Glendes' voice filtered into Trik's mind. *Don't be. If you could see the two who went before you right now, you'd know they were in the kitchen, laughing and eating ice cream.*

"Now, let's see how we do," Glendes actually smiled at Trik as he placed his hands on Trik's forehead. Trik didn't remember what happened after that.

* * *

Multiple tappings on the core, Tiearan sent mindspeech to Rain. *We'll have to call on the outer circles.*

Agreed, Rain replied. *Tell me when you are ready to approach all the sites.*

I will, Tiearan assured her. *Going to the outer circles now, to gather power.*

* * *

Lissa's Journal

"He'll wake in a few minutes," Shadow rubbed my shoulders as I stared at Trik's limp body. Shadow had carried him into a nearby room and laid him on a sofa so Trik could wake on his own.

"He's got some power there," Glendes assured us as I knelt next to the sofa and stroked Trik's hair. "I'd say at least Second-Tier, if he applies himself."

"You can tell?" I turned to stare up at Glendes.

299

"I have a good batting average. Isn't that what you call it?" Glendes smiled.

"What did you say about my Nissa?" I asked. She, Roff and the others were waiting outside for us and couldn't hear.

"Nissa was off the scale." Shadow was the one to give me an answer. "That's why we were concerned when things weren't going so well." He ducked his head as he told me that bit of news. "It just turned out that she was taking orders too literally."

"Lissa, don't be angry with us, we were doing the best we could," Glendes sighed. "We've never had a female wizard with this much power. We're designing rules as we go along in Nissa's case."

"You could have treated her as a granddaughter and not one of your minions," I grumped.

"We know that. Now," Glendes raked a hand through his hair. Well, I now knew where Shadow got that gesture. "Lissa, please have patience with us. We're trying. And I promise that Trik will get the attention he needs and deserves. I'm placing him with Shadow and Raffian. They'll keep an eye on him and make sure he's cared for as he learns."

"He's only just started walking," I pointed out. "I hope you slave drivers remember that and give him plenty of rest breaks. I think he's going to miss Morwin, too. Morwin will certainly miss him. He says that he hasn't seen a student apply himself as well as Trik does in a very long time."

"What?" Trik blinked his eyes open.

"Honey, how are you feeling?" I brushed brown hair away from his face.

"I feel fine. Is there ice cream?" He grinned at me. That grin was worth a fortune.

Chapter 15

"Trikleer, we're placing you with Master Wizards Shadow and Raffian, in the Jewelry Division," Glendes said over my shoulder.

"Really? Where did Dane and Lucas go?"

"Dane went to Master Wizard Harvel, in the Armor Division; Lucas went to Master Wizard Killien, in the Art Division. You'll see them at mealtimes, if you want."

"Will I see Nissa at mealtimes, too?"

"Of course, and you and Nissa will be invited to have lunch with Lira, your great-grandmother, at least once a week."

I stared at Glendes. Was he finally becoming human?

"I'm going to miss you at home," I brushed Trik's cheek with the back of my hand.

"I'll come home with Nissa," he said. "Mom."

"I'll arrange to have most of his clothing brought in. You'll be wearing the white and royal blue vests of an apprentice in the Jewelry Division," Shadow helped Trik sit up. "And we'll all go to the kitchen for ice cream."

"I think there's a way to see to his education," Glendes walked beside me as we stepped toward the door. "Morwin can be brought here in the mornings, by one of my Second-Tier assistants. He can instruct these and any of the others he wants to teach here, if that's all right with both of you. He will be returned to Le-Ath Veronis to teach afternoon lessons for Rylend and Torevik. I know of Morwin's expertise—Nissa had better instruction from him than from any of my instructors, and she only studied with Morwin for a year before moving to Grey House."

"Connegar recommended Morwin," I studied Glendes' face for a moment. "If a Larentii recommends somebody, then you'd be foolish not to listen."

"Agreed," Glendes nodded. "Do you think Morwin will consent to come?"

"I think he'd be honored that you asked," I replied.

* * *

Rain was screaming. Tiearan heard it as if it were from a distance. He couldn't disengage, and his connection to the crystal had been lost. Somehow, the core was draining him and the others, and he couldn't stop it. It held all of them, now, sucking their power away. He could only hope that it would let them go once they lost consciousness.

* * *

Corent's thoughts were on Toff as his vision narrowed and darkened. Unlike Tiearan, he knew what was likely to happen. They'd placed their hand in the maw of a hungry dragon, and now the dragon was devouring the body connected to the hand. Was this Kifirin's judgment? Corent felt debilitating pain as power was stripped away from him at an accelerated rate. Redbird, sitting beside him in the second circle, was already unconscious. They were dying—all of them—and nothing could save them now, not even Queen Lissa. She was pregnant and couldn't bring her power to bear. A sigh escaped Corent as his consciousness fled.

* * *

Lissa's Journal
"Shadow, I think something is wrong." We sat in Grey House's kitchen, eating bowls of ice cream. Nissa sat between Toff and Trik, bumping shoulders with both of them and smiling. It was good to see all of them so happy, but my skin had begun to itch and my thoughts turned to Le-Ath Veronis.

Chapter 15

"What is it?" Roff turned to me, just as Shadow did.

"I don't know—but I need to go home," I mumbled. The itching had ramped up in the space of seconds.

"I'll take her," Shadow stood. "The rest of you finish your dessert." Shadow folded me home quickly. I found Belen inside my study when Shadow landed me there.

* * *

"We can send mindspeech to Mom," Ry whispered to Tory. He and the others had been taken to Glendes and Lira's private quarters after they'd finished their bowls of ice cream.

"I don't want to upset Sissy—I haven't seen her this happy in a long time," Tory whispered back. He and Ry sat in a corner of Lira's sitting room—it wasn't as stiff and formal as her receiving room. Ry glanced in Nissa's direction; she was chatting happily with Lira, Toff and Trik.

"I've received mindspeech from Shadow." Raffian Grey, Shadow's father, sat next to Ry. "I'll take all of you home after a while. A problem has cropped up on Le-Ath Veronis, but it's nothing for you to worry about."

"Is Mom okay?" Ry asked, watching Raffian's face closely for any clues.

"Your mother is fine. Shadow is with her, as are Gavin and the others. She is in no danger, young warlock." Raffian smiled at Ry before rising and walking toward Glendes, who stood near the door. Ry watched closely as Glendes bent his head to hear Raffian's whispers.

"That smile didn't reach his eyes," Ry muttered. "Something's going on."

"He wasn't lying when he said Mom was fine," Tory observed. "And he was truthful when he said that Uncle

Shadow, Uncle Gavin and the others were with her. He just left some stuff out," he added.

"Yeah. I get that idea, too," Ry nodded.

* * *

Lissa's Journal

Dead. All of them, with the exception of Corent, whom we found wandering outside the large barn, completely dazed. Corent sat before me now, inside the home he'd shared with Redbird.

"Willow is missing, I can't find him," Corent rambled, his hair turning a dark gray. I'd never seen it turn that color.

"We'll look for him," I promised. "Corent, tell me what happened. Take your time." While he sat there on a broad tree stump, hands dangling over his knees and in complete confusion, I sent mindspeech to Karzac.

Karzac appeared in a blink, asking me silent questions as he ran his hands over Corent. Belen, too, stood out of the way in a corner of Corent's main room. He had information to give me, but I wanted Corent's story first if I could get it.

"We tried to set it right," Corent's voice sounded better after Karzac held the half-Elemaiya's head in his hands for several moments. "The core. We tried to stop the drain and replace the power. It was too much for us, and once it held us in its grip, it wouldn't let go." Corent spoke as if from a distance. As if he felt separated from it at the moment.

I felt sorry for him, and had no idea how he'd come out of this alive, when bodies littered the floor in a nearby barn. Even the Fae children hadn't escaped. I wanted to weep at the sight of their lifeless forms lying beside their parents.

Rigo, Aryn, Drake and Drew were holding the humanoid population back from the site. They all wanted answers, just as I did. Some of them, too, had lost mates and Half-Fae children. We would have to deliver that news, too, and it was a sad and terrible business.

"I can place him in a healing sleep," Karzac offered, as I stared at Corent. Le-Ath Veronis, tapped by a renegade Half-Fae child, had exacted a terrible price against those attempting to repair the damage. The combined power of all the Green Fae hadn't satisfied even a fraction of that hunger.

Somehow, miraculously, after the Fae died, Le-Ath Veronis' core had been healed. Belen told me that the moment I'd landed in my study. He was waiting to tell me how that miracle happened as soon as we finished here.

"Bring Corent to the palace, then, I don't want any of the humanoids blaming him because he's still alive," I said. "He can stay as long as he wants, or we can move him to the beach house when the repairs are done."

Corent would likely prefer the sunlight there, but my beach house was still undergoing repairs after the tsunami swept through it. A wall of water almost as high as its third-story roof had washed through, nearly bringing the whole thing down. I didn't want to think about the lives lost then—I had to deal with the lives lost now.

"Corent, can you stand?" I reached out a hand.

"I'll fold him there," Karzac held me back. "Gavin, will you bring our girl?" Karzac glanced at Gavin, who stood behind me. "Have Anthony and Rigo explain what happened. I'll send for some of my colleagues if healing is required." Karzac took Corent's elbow and disappeared.

"Aryn, will you look for Willow?" I turned to him—he'd come with the others.

"Of course, love. Send mindspeech if you learn anything else from Corent that might be helpful."

Blood Reunion

I nodded to him before lowering my eyes. "Lissa," he came forward to take my face in his hand. "We will see you through this. I promise. Let us bear these burdens for you now. This is a weight you should not be forced to carry in your condition."

I love you, I whispered in his mind.

And I you, he replied. *Go with Gavin. I and the others will deal with this tragedy.*

"Cara mia, come," Gavin pulled me away, and we were gone.

* * *

"Did you know it would kill all of them?" Thurlow had gone hunting—for Kifirin.

"I knew it would kill anyone connected to the circles. I had no idea they would call in even the weak and the young."

"You said nothing," Thurlow accused.

"I have made the promise not to interfere."

"But these belonged to the Light."

"That matters not to me." A curl of smoke escaped Kifirin's nostrils. "I did not make the decisions that placed them in this danger. It is not my duty to counsel them, in any case. All these decisions were theirs to make."

"Wait, I am receiving mindspeech from Lissa," Thurlow turned away from Kifirin for a moment before turning back. "One survived, and another may still be alive. Corent lives and Willow's body was not found." Thurlow watched Kifirin's face and felt satisfaction when he saw the brief glimpse of confusion and disbelief settle there before it disappeared.

"You did not expect that, did you?" Thurlow accused.

"They weren't connected to the circle, then."

Chapter 15

"Lissa says they were. Corent rose and walked away after the others died, and Willow's body cannot be found."

"That should not be possible," Kifirin declared, breathing smoke.

"You wanted this, didn't you? The moment Toff was away from them, you allowed this."

"I have no care that they thought Toff would reach his majority at age eighteen."

"You did nothing to dispel that rumor, then. You never said when your judgment would fall, except that it would come when Toff reached adulthood. Theirs come to adulthood at age eighteen."

"I am not responsible for anyone's misconceptions." Kifirin's face turned dark. Thurlow knew the Thifilathi threatened.

"Did you repair Le-Ath Veronis' core afterward?" Thurlow asked his final question.

"It has been repaired?" Kifirin lifted an eyebrow in surprise. Thurlow stared at the dark god—he was just as shocked as Thurlow had been at that turn of events.

"It has been repaired. I can only imagine that any adverse effects will be neutralized quickly, since it has only been a short time after the initial tapping. Surely you know how unusual this is."

"I had nothing to do with it. Are you sure?" Kifirin's black gaze settled on Thurlow's face.

"I cannot lie—of course I am sure," Thurlow snapped. "I will leave you now." Thurlow turned to go before he made the Lord of the Dark Realm angrier than he already was.

* * *

Lissa's Journal

"I wasn't sure at first," Belen settled on a corner of my desk while Gavin pulled me onto his lap on my sofa. "The signature is there, for those of us who have been gifted with the knowledge to detect it."

"Kifirin?" I asked. He was the first I suspected of healing the core.

"Kifirin had nothing to do with healing the core. I have received a message from Thurlow, however, and he says Kifirin withheld information from the Fae on when Toff would come to adulthood. They thought it was when the child reached eighteen years."

I inhaled a shocked breath at Belen's statement. "Lissa, you must understand," Belen continued, "Kifirin is Lord of the Dark Realm. If he fails to behave accordingly in some things, at least, complete balance cannot be maintained."

I gaped at Belen. "You're not kidding, are you?" My voice was a whisper.

"No, beloved, I am not, as you put it, kidding."

"Then who healed the core? The Larentii? Did the Wise Ones do this?"

"The Wise Ones had nothing to do with this, although it did involve *Changing What Was*."

"Who else can do that, then? I thought they were the only ones." I was completely confused, now. The Mighty Hand had mentioned that ability to me once, as had Connegar, but it was relegated to the Wise Ones and generally was directed at individuals, not entire planets. This was *Changing What Was* on a much larger scale.

"We believe that the one who did this also is responsible for relocating Willow," Belen added. "He is currently on Morningsun. I think he will be acting as advisor to King Brandelin and his brother."

Chapter 15

"And the fact that he holds power won't go amiss, either," I muttered. "Is Willow all right?"

"He is confused, just as Corent is, but he will be a good fit where he is. Another of the Mighty is responsible for this, Lissa. Do you know what that means?" Belen's eyes are usually bright—sometimes so much so that it is difficult to gaze into their depths. His eyes were now dark and troubled. Both of us knew about one of the Mighty already. Belen was saying that another had come.

"What does it mean?" My breath hitched as I watched Belen's face.

"When all three appear, the god wars will come," Belen whispered. "That information cannot leave this room." I nodded, stunned at his words. The god wars.

Anyone who knew of the Mighty also knew of the impending god wars. Renegades belonging to all the echelons holding power would break away and wage war against those who would try to hold the universes together and steady against them.

The Mighty would be hidden when they were thrust into a humanoid existence, to keep the renegades from destroying them in their new bodies. Becoming corporeal was the only way the three would be allowed to interfere. Without them, everything could be destroyed.

It was at that moment, too, that the baby moved. My eyes widened and my hand went to my belly.

"The child is Gavin's son," Belen announced before disappearing abruptly.

Gavin rose with me in his arms. Carefully, he placed me on my feet before kneeling before me and wrapping his arms around my waist. Until that moment, I'd never seen Gavin weep. These were tears of joy.

Chapter 16

"Young ones," Master Morwin began, "Many things happened that night."

Toff was still struggling to understand any of it, and he, like Tory and Ry, hadn't been given the full tale. They realized this, too. Perhaps they would learn more from Morwin.

They missed Trik's presence. He was now at Grey House, learning from Shadow and Raffian. Master Morwin was spending his mornings at Grey House, so Toff's lessons had been moved to the afternoon with Tory and Ry, after working with his father most mornings at the winery.

Toff was still trying to grasp that all the Fae were dead except Corent and Father Willow. Queen Lissa referred to Corent and Willow's survival as a miracle and refused to talk about it.

Corent had been at the palace for two days before moving to the beach house, which was still undergoing repairs. Toff had visited with Corent while he was at the palace, but Corent still seemed confused by the ordeal and hadn't talked much.

"We know the core was tapped, and I had to beg Dad to tell me what that meant," Ry offered.

"It has been repaired and that is a great miracle, all of its own," Morwin nodded, his bushy eyebrows wriggling animatedly. "I hear that your Uncle Thurlow went to speak with Willow on Morningsun, but he is quite confused and remembers little of what happened. Corent, sadly is much the same."

"Do we know anything, Master Morwin?" Tory asked.

"Very little. Your mother is still searching for many answers. I have not the reason why these souls thought they were strong enough to do this deed. Perhaps a few Larentii might accomplish this, as they are the most powerful beings that I know. The Fae are many steps below the blue giants. This was a foolish attempt, and had they consulted the Queen, I'm sure she would have told them so."

"They felt responsible," Toff muttered, hanging his head. "I learned that from Corent. He didn't think the Queen knew that Gren tapped the core, and they wanted to make the repairs before she found out. Tiearan said they owed her a debt, and they wanted to pay it."

"Young one," Morwin came to stand before Toff's desk, "I beg you to never say that to the Queen. She will feel guilt over it, and that should not be. None of this is her fault. Surely you can see that."

Chapter 16

"I do," Toff nodded. "Papu says the same. I only say that here, because I know you will protect the information. And the Queen."

"I will protect the information. Do you agree?" Morwin turned to Tory and Ry.

"Dad says the same," Tory nodded. "He knows."

"My dad does, too," Ry said. "Mom won't hear it from us."

"Very good," Morwin's eyebrows danced. "Now, shall we turn to the geography of Wyyld? There are unexplored mountains and forests there, did you know?"

* * *

"I don't care that the core has been healed. When we attack, and we will soon, we will tap it again. It was probably those fool Larentii she has following her around like lapdogs," Zellar snapped at Tandias' report.

"I trust this one will not be as clumsy as he was before?" Tandias turned dark eyes on Gren, who cowered before the strange Ra'Ak. "I know you take pleasure in the deaths that resulted from this one's fumbling, but it also alerted the Queen to the fact that her planet had been tapped. Had it been done smoothly, we could have continued to drain the core without her knowledge." Tandias was angry and barely holding that anger back. If he didn't feed soon, these two might make a useful meal.

"Tandias, please feed, your testiness has not gone unnoticed," Zellar muttered. "I will discipline this one," he jerked his head in Gren's direction. Gren backed against a bare, stone wall, frightened immediately.

* * *

Blood Reunion

Lissa's Journal

"Lissa, I had second and third thoughts before bringing this one to you." Aurelius, golden-haired bear that he is, stood inside my office, a filthy, scruffily dressed Elemaiya gripped in one of his large hands. Aurelius had recently learned that he would be a grandfather. As Gavin's sire, he claimed that honor. "You asked me to let you know if Narissa met her end, and that is the news this one brings. He has another tale to tell, however." Aurelius shook the Elemaiya, who cringed in the tall vampire's grip.

"What tale is that?" I asked, staring at the Elemaiya. Once he'd been a Queen's guard for Friesianna—I knew that from *Looking*. At least my *Looking* skills and mindspeech didn't affect the child; I could use those talents whenever I wanted.

"I w-watched Friesianna die," Parlethis groveled before me. "After we killed Narissa, someone came. I cannot describe this person, they forbade it, and I cannot break that command. This person stood over Narissa's dismembered torso, and then gazed angrily at Queen Friesianna. 'A swift killing is one thing,' this one said. They were quite angry, we could tell. 'Torture is something I will not tolerate,' this one added. And then, Friesianna and all her guards except me disintegrated. I was left alive and ordered to explain to you that Friesianna and her bullies are no more. They—and your grandmother—are dead."

Parlethis giggled, then, and it was a crazed sound. I could see that he was terrified. Terrified that whoever had killed Friesianna would return for him. I had three guesses who'd done this, and two of them didn't count.

Only a Larentii or someone with a greater power could accomplish this kind of feat. The same one who'd healed the core had likely done this deed. I stared at the cowering Elemaiya and shook my head. If this member of the Mighty kept it up, he (or she) would draw the attention of our enemies very soon. I sighed and nodded to Aurelius, who folded the prisoner away.

"Cara mia?" Gavin stole inside my study.

"Honey?" I lifted an eyebrow at him.

"Aurelius sent mindspeech. He said you might need comfort."

"Your sire is worth the weight of Le-Ath Veronis in gold," I sighed. "Narissa's dead."

"He told me that, too," Gavin was beside me quickly, lifting me and settling me against him. "My love, tell me that she did not deserve death."

"She did," I nodded. "But she was tortured by Friesianna first. Friesianna has apparently met her demise because of it," I added.

"One of hers did this?" Gavin sounded puzzled, but he placed a kiss on my forehead anyway.

"No. Somebody else showed up. Gavin, this is beginning to worry me. If the Mighty tip their hand before all three are together, we could be destroyed."

"I know we cannot speak of this with any of the others, except perhaps Kiarra, Adam and Merrill. I have the idea that Belen has approached Kiarra at least, and now those three are worried, too. I have not the notion where this might end. Are they playing a longer game than we know?" I looked up into Gavin's dark eyes as he spoke—he was deeply troubled by this.

"I don't know." I buried my face against Gavin's shoulder.

Blood Reunion

"Love, do not worry so. We will face these troubles if they come. Meanwhile, we must trust that things will come out right in the end."

"Yeah. Can we go to the kitchen? I want ice cream." I didn't add that I also wanted to forget the whole, sorry mess. That likely wouldn't happen for a while.

* * *

"Narissa's dead." Griffin had asked to speak with Cleo and Kyler at Merrill's old manor in Kent. Griffin sat behind Merrill's desk in his study, recalling that Lissa's lessons from Merrill had occurred there. Merrill hadn't changed much inside his study over the years, and the letter opener, which resembled a Roman sword, still held a place of honor on Merrill's desk.

Cleo and Kyler sat in Merrill's guest chairs, staring at their grandfather. They resembled their now-deceased grandmother greatly, with long, auburn hair and nearly gold eyes.

"Em-pah, we knew it would come," Kyler admitted. "We just didn't know when, exactly."

"She is dead, as is Friesianna and her guards. Except one," Leather creaked as Griffin leaned back in Merrill's chair. "Friesianna had Narissa tortured and dismembered. Someone took offense at that act and separated Friesianna's particles. I was wondering if either of you had a hand in that."

"As a healer for the Saa Thalarr, I can't," Cleo pointed out.

"I was elsewhere when it happened, and wouldn't have interfered anyway," Kyler muttered. "I don't argue with

316

Chapter 16

Narissa's death, I just have a problem with how it was accomplished."

"Those responsible for it are dead." Griffin stood and turned to stare out the window behind the desk.

"Do we have any guesses who killed Friesianna?" Kyler asked.

"No. Kiarra may suspect and I hear that Belen has spoken with her, but as I am retired, I am no longer privy to that information."

"Maybe we'll find out someday," Cleo offered. "Did you talk to Conner about it, Em-pah?"

"Conner won't talk to me. Not since I fucked up with Toff and Trell."

Cleo and Kyler exchanged worried glances.

* * *

"When will we see Nissa and Trik again?" Toff asked. He, Ry and Tory were spending the day in the Queen's library, doing research for an assignment. Rain was falling on an off-day. They'd planned a trip to the light side for a picnic and some rock skipping on a pond, but the rain had spoiled their plans.

"Uncle Shadow said he'd bring them tomorrow—Trik needs more shoes, so we're going shopping. Sissy said he spilled some of the spelled resin they use to make the gray jewels on two pairs of boots," Ry said.

"I wish I had mindspeech," Toff grumped, tapping the end of a paragraph on his comp-vid with more emphasis than it deserved. He wanted to contact Nissa whenever he felt like it. Ry and Tory didn't realize what a gift they had.

"Maybe Mom can give it to you. After the baby comes," Tory responded with a grin.

"She can do that?" Toff asked, his eyes wide.

"Mom can do a lot of things," Ry snickered. "When she isn't pregnant."

* * *

"They didn't yell that much and I get new shoes," Trik gloated as he accepted a newly created protection jewel from Nissa.

"I'm glad it was enough to make three protection jewels. It was easy to pull the resin off your shoes, but that stuff discolors. Dad already saw that." Nissa's eyes danced mischievously.

"I just want you and Toff to have protection, and I wanted to replace my jewel, too," Nissa proclaimed as she pulled a second protection jewel necklace over her head. It would be keyed to Toff when she saw him the following day.

"You'll be able to protect yourself before long, but this will help until then." Nissa brushed back curly, light-brown hair and leaned against the wall with a happy sigh.

She and Trik had met inside Trik's new bedroom—Shadow had cleared a space for Trik inside his and Nissa's spacious suite. They'd settled on the floor at the far side of Trik's bed, in case Shadow walked in. Again, Nissa had made the protection jewels without her father's knowledge.

"I know what these are worth," Trik brushed fingers over the dark-gray, faceted jewel that Nissa had fashioned from spelled resin. "My grandfather was always angry about these," he added. "The Belancours couldn't do anything close to this kind of work."

"You'll learn how to do it yourself," Nissa vowed. "I think Daddy is more than happy with the power you have."

Chapter 16

"You think so?" Trik's eyes held a gleam of hope in them.

"Yeah. Daddy's happier than I've seen him in a while," Nissa nodded.

* * *

Lissa's Journal

"I can see you've already heard we're going shopping," I lifted an eyebrow at Ry and Tory, who were giving me expectant looks.

"But we haven't heard where," Ry wheedled. I swear, that child was going to be just as handsome as his father, and could wrap anyone around his nimble fingers already. Erland said that Ry had a future as an ambassador for Karathia—if that's what he wanted.

Wylend, my grandfather, was already hatching a plot to send him to a private school on Wyyld when he was eighteen. That school trained the children of Kings, Queens, presidents, prime ministers and anybody else in charge of anything. It also cost a fortune to attend, and Wylend was prepared to pay.

My only problem with that idea is that I knew Tory would want to go with his brother and Garde was holding back—he didn't want to send Tory if Tory couldn't turn Thifilathi.

Any position Tory might hold on Kifirin required that he be High Demon in most respects, and that included the ability to become Thifilathi. I assumed Garde also meant that Tory wouldn't be considered High Demon if he couldn't blow smoke whenever he got his underwear in a knot.

It made me angry every time I thought about it, and Garde and I had an argument when Garde first brought it up.

Blood Reunion

Most High Demon males turned by the age of twelve. Tory hadn't.

I accused my High Demon mate of being prejudiced against his son because he was only half High Demon; Garde hadn't defended himself very well against that charge and ended up blowing clouds of smoke before skipping away. It was still a sore spot between us.

"Where are we going, Mom?" Tory was now begging.

"If you must know, we're going to Hraede again. It's safe there and Rigo is going with us. Drake and Drew are folding us in and out, but they have training to do tomorrow so they can't stay with us." I moved forward to hug my High Demon child. He was so tall, I could only put my arms around his waist. "Shadow only gave us tomorrow afternoon to spend with Nissa and Trik, after their lessons in the morning."

"So we have to hurry to make the most of our day," Ry nodded as I pulled away from Tory.

"We'll have to hurry if we make more than two or three shops," I agreed. "If either of you need shoes or clothing, now is the time to make a list."

"I guess you haven't changed your mind on tattoos," Tory teased.

"Look," I poked him in the chest with a finger, "If you're twenty and can't seem to stop yourself, I won't stop you either. But if you want good ones, like Drake and Drew's, then you need to go to Falchan and take your uncles with you."

"All right," Tory high-fived Ry over my head. Rolling my eyes, I walked away from both my tattoo-crazed sons.

* * *

Chapter 16

"Do you think I depend upon you for all my information?" Tandias gazed angrily at Zellar. "I managed to place an obsession on one of the Queen's palace employees. She and her children will be visiting Hraede tomorrow, with only one vampire attending her. We will attack her there. It will be much simpler than taking you past the shield around Le-Ath Veronis. Once the Queen is dead, our goals will be accomplished, wouldn't you say?"

Zellar stared at Tandias. Now he understood why Viregruz had found this particular Ra'Ak so valuable. An obsession—that ability was extremely rare and difficult to perform. Only a few among Tandias' former race might have been able to accomplish such a feat. An obsession placed by one of that race could convince the most unwilling to tell all their secrets or happily commit murder.

Whereas compulsion would force the recipient to act as a vampire commanded, it was limited to specific commands. Obsession left the victim willing to volunteer their deeds if they thought the one placing the obsession might be pleased by their actions. Victims fawned over their new master and craved any encouragement. Zellar found himself wondering how many assassinations had been carried out by those closest to the victim, after an obsession had been placed.

Shaking himself to dispel those thoughts, Zellar turned back to Tandias. "I assume you have an itinerary?"

"I know where the Queen is likely to be. That should be enough." Tandias' pointed teeth gleamed as he laughed.

* * *

"You can keep the old one if you want," Nissa held out the new protection jewel to Toff, who seemed reluctant to remove the old necklace, although the jewel had been emptied when Gren attacked. "This one will key itself to you when you put it on."

Nissa smiled her encouragement to Toff, who shyly accepted the gift and slipped it over his head. The gray jewel was carefully hidden beneath his shirt, right beside the first one.

"I have something for you, too. Papu helped me pick it out," Toff's cheeks pinkened slightly as he pulled a small box from a pocket. "Then Uncle Drew made it the right size," Toff added as Nissa accepted the box and opened it. Nestled on a bed of satin lay a gold filigree ring.

Nissa stared at Toff. "This is so pretty," she fumbled with the ring, pulling it from the box. "I don't have any rings," she added. "I have necklaces and bracelets, but that's all." She slipped the ring on her finger—it fit.

"I know, that's why Papu suggested it," Toff grinned impishly. "It looks good on your hand."

"Thank you." Nissa hugged Toff enthusiastically. Toff wrapped his arms about her and hugged her back.

* * *

Lissa's Journal

We'd gone to a restaurant for lunch first, before venturing out to buy shoes and clothing for the kids. Tory ate two ox-roast sandwiches while Nissa smiled at her brother.

Rigo was at my elbow as we watched Trik try on several pairs of shoes and boots in a shoe shop later. Shadow demanded that sturdy shoes or boots be worn in his and Raffian's workshops—it was lucky that the two pairs of boots Trik ruined were thick leather—the spelled liquid resin usually burned whatever it hit. That stuff only became neutral after it hardened and accepted a protection spell.

Trik's boots had spared his feet, as Shadow had known they would.

"Honey, if you like those, we'll get them," I said as Trik attempted to choose half of the four pairs he'd set aside.

"I like all of those," Nissa nodded as Trik glanced her way. I didn't want to say anything, but my daughter already had two admirers—Toff and Trik. When she turned sixteen, I might have to sit down and have a talk with all of them. I think Shadow already knew to keep a watchful eye on our daughter.

"I just never had anything new before I came to Le-Ath Veronis," Trik mumbled, stacking boxes of shoes neatly. I wanted to cry at his admission, and then add happy tears for the fact that he was now using both hands.

He was walking very well, too, and Morwin kept me updated on his progress (and Nissa's) almost every day. I'd hugged Morwin when he reported that Trik and Nissa were happy. Nissa finally had someone to confide in at Grey House, and Trik was happy that he felt wanted and needed for the first time in his life.

"Mom always takes us to Barat's for clothes," Tory whispered to Trik as we walked into a shop that carried clothing. It also had a separate, very popular electronics store inside, which sold comp-vids and other supplies children might need for the classroom. As a result, Barat's was a chain that had shops on nearly every Alliance world.

"Can Tory and I look at mini comp-vids?" Ry pleaded as soon as they were inside the door. I wasn't surprised by his request—they loved that part of the store and it was often harder than finding teeth on a rooster to keep them away from it.

Blood Reunion

"All right, but don't wander away," I cautioned. Tory was so tall he would likely intimidate anyone who had nefarious thoughts and Ry was talented enough to blast someone through a wall if he wanted. He'd inherited all his father's gifts plus a few extras, I think, and Wylend predicted he'd be a First-Level warlock—the highest level attainable—when he was grown.

"We'll be back when you get to the jacket department," Ry promised as he and Tory walked swiftly away. Toff, who'd been content to stay beside Nissa, watched them go. He was torn, I could tell, because he probably wanted a new mini comp-vid just as Ry and Tory did. A new version had been released recently by Schuul Enterprises, and everybody wanted one.

Get a mini comp-vid for Toff, Nissa and Trik, too, I sent to Ry, who sent a *yippee* back.

* * *

"She'll scent us if we're not shielded properly," Zellar growled at Gren, who watched Toff from a distance. Gren and his companions stood in a dimly lit corner of the store, watching with eager malice as the Queen and a handful of others looked at clothing.

Zellar worked to shield Tandias, too, although Gren and the Ra'Ak failed to cooperate. The Ra'Ak, like Gren, was anxious to reach his target—Queen Lissa only had one vampire mate with her and he could be easily dispatched, once Tandias became Ra'Ak.

"We'll get there soon enough," Zellar hissed as he added another layer to an already thick shield, his hands weaving as he whispered the required spells.

* * *

Chapter 16

Rigo, I'm feeling itchy, I sent to my oldest vampire mate.

"Tiessa, what do you sense?" Rigo's mouth was near my ear as he whispered the words.

"I can't tell; it keeps appearing and then disappearing. This is really weird," I mumbled back. Nissa, Toff and Trik were going through a rack of shirts nearby and laughing at the slogans printed across the front. They couldn't hear us and I was thankful for that.

"Have you experienced anything such as this before?" Rigo asked softly.

"No, and it's really confusing," I replied. "It's like somebody is turning a tap on and off." I raised my eyes to Rigo's face—he was certainly concerned.

"Has anyone been able to hide anything from you before, love?" Rigo's worry was increasing, if the furrowing brow was any indication.

"Only that idiot Viregruz, and," I lifted a shaking hand to my mouth. "Oh. My. God. Rigo, we're in trouble," I gasped. We were already too late—the blast knocked out half the walls and plunged the store into darkness.

* * *

Zellar realized his mistake quickly—he couldn't see in darkness any better than Gren could. He wasn't sure about Tandias—Ra'Ak kept any weaknesses to themselves, just to prevent them from being exploited.

At least part of his plan had worked flawlessly; every humanoid shopper inside the store was now unconscious.

Blood Reunion

"I need light," Gren hissed. He'd kept his eyes on Toff—until the lights went out.

"Do it yourself, I'm busy holding the shields," Zellar snapped. "I have an outer shield on the whole store—she won't be able to send out mindspeech; it'll just bounce back. Tandias, can you see anything?"

No reply came from Tandias—he'd already turned to Ra'Ak and was slithering through the spacious department store. Gren, who caught a glint of light gleaming on copper scales, followed in Tandias' wake while Zellar cursed behind him and remained where he was.

* * *

Lissa's Journal

I sent hasty mindspeech to all my mates, but trouble was already in front of me and only Rigo and I could see it coming. My mindspeech echoed back to me in my mind; it hadn't gone out.

That meant one thing to me—Zellar was shielding everything inside the store. He'd blocked Viregruz's presence in the past after tapping a planet's core. He'd obviously learned how to do the same with mindspeech. Every humanoid inside the store had fallen, too; all of them rendered unconscious from one of Zellar's tricks, no doubt.

I felt terrified and queasy at the same time, and it was an effort to push those feeling aside. I hadn't felt this helpless since I'd been human.

"Kids, get behind me," I hissed as I watched the Ra'Ak slither his way toward us.

"Mom? What's going on?" Nissa fumbled her way toward me, Toff and Trik each gripping one of her hands tightly.

Chapter 16

"Come." Rigo pulled all three of them forward and gently placed them behind us. All that stood between us now was a few minutes and a vampire who had no experience fighting Ra'Ak.

* * *

"No big deal, bro," Ry whispered to Tory. "I can make light without thinking about it. I think Mom and the others are in trouble, though." Ry pointed a finger at the floor, creating the barest hint of light. He and Tory made their way toward the department where their mother had been when they'd last seen her, navigating their way through overturned shelves, racks, broken walls and unconscious shoppers.

* * *

Lissa's Journal

A decision lay before me. Sacrifice my unborn child to save the others, or hope that Rigo could delay a Ra'Ak, a power-mad warlock and an evil apprentice while the rest of us attempted to escape.

Yeah. Right. The odds of our escaping went into negative territory and Rigo would likely die. We'd all likely die, actually. Zellar had made his plans carefully; somehow, he'd discovered where I would be and had taken full advantage.

On Le-Ath Veronis, there were too many around me and I'd be better protected. Now, on what was reportedly the safest world in the Reth Alliance, I was under attack by one of the worst criminals the Alliance had ever seen.

* * *

"Holy crap," Ry muttered. The Ra'Ak either hadn't seen him and Tory, or he was ignoring them in favor of a better target—their mother.

"Somebody's walking behind the Ra'Ak," Tory hissed, turning his gaze on Ry.

"Wait, you can see?" Ry blinked at Tory in confusion.

"Yeah. Don't ask me how, but I've always been able to see better than you in the dark. I think it's that brat who almost killed Toff," Tory added, turning back to the Ra'Ak crawling through the store and the one who crept along behind the giant serpent.

"He's aiming for Mom, and she can't do anything," Ry hissed, slapping his taller brother on the back. "And that brat is aiming for Toff, I'd bet all the money on Karathia on that."

"Yeah."

Ry barely saw it in the dim light emanating from his finger, but a curl of smoke came from Tory's nostrils.

"Dude, he's about to kill Mom. And Sissy, too." Ry knew that the Thifilathi came whenever a High Demon became very angry. He had to fan Tory's anger quickly.

* * *

Trik, Mom can't use any of her power, it'll kill the baby, Nissa sent to Trik. She'd already attempted mindspeech with her father, but it had bounced back into her mind. Somehow, something was blocking any mindspeech sent outside the store. Mindspeech inside the store still seemed to work, however.

What can we do? I can barely see, Trik replied mentally.

See that little bit of light to our right? That's Ry, lighting his way through the store, Nissa sent. *Tory is probably with him. If we ever needed Tory's Thifilathi, it's now. Uncle Rigo might be able to slow a Ra'Ak down, but that's all he'll be able to do without some kind of power.*

What about our protection jewels? Trik asked.

They might slow a Ra'Ak down a little, but the Ra'Ak are really powerful. My protection jewels are aimed more at two-legged enemies.

* * *

Lissa's Journal

Tiessa, please stand behind me and begin to back the children away, Rigo whispered in my mind. My Hraedan vampire mate, Rigovarnus I, was prepared to give his life in order to protect mine and that of my children.

We're coming, Mom. Ry's voice came directly behind Rigo's.

Baby, run away, this is a Ra'Ak, I returned immediately. I couldn't keep the moan from my mental voice. At that moment, I wished for Erland, Garde, Gavin, the twins and anyone else who might be able to come.

My body trembled with dread as I watched the Ra'Ak approach, his scales scraping over debris from the initial blast. He was almost upon us. I watched in horror as his mouth opened, revealing the usual rows of lengthy, sharp teeth. This one was prepared to devour us.

* * *

"Tory, Mom's scared to death." Ry's words made Tory turn around. A cloud of smoke poured from his nostrils and his eyes were dark and feral instead of clear blue. "She's going to try to save Sissy and the others, and it'll kill the baby. Maybe her, too." Ry kept hammering away at Tory, praying the Thifilathi would come. Tory growled, and it was a sound Ry never expected to hear from his brother's throat.

* * *

Lissa's Journal
Tiessa, do no go to mist yet. Let me make my attempt first, Rigo had a hand behind his back, waving me away. I was doing the same for Nissa, Toff and Trik, begging Nissa in mindspeech to back Toff and Trik away. Telling her to run the moment the Ra'Ak moved again.

* * *

Gren's eyes had adjusted to the semi-darkness. His target—the baby-faced eunuch, was hiding behind the woman. And look, was he holding hands with a little girl? Gren wanted to laugh.

Finally, Toff the worm was going to die. He was responsible for Gren's parents' deaths. There was no other explanation. Gren intended to make Toff pay dearly—for all the deaths he'd caused in the Green Fae village.

Gren hadn't used any of the power he'd collected from Le-Ath Veronis' core. He was like the sun crystal he'd coveted so many years. He'd gathered power and now he'd use it to kill Toff and the other two who stood with him. Gren smiled and amassed power, preparing to launch it and commit murder.

* * *

"Nissa, that's Gren. He'll hurt you," Toff hissed. Toff hadn't failed to recognize Gren, even in such poor light. Toff pushed Nissa behind him.

Chapter 16

Toff, I'll throw a spell if he even thinks about it, Nissa replied mentally.

I'm with you, Toff, Trik offered, stepping up beside Toff and keeping Nissa where she was—behind both of them.

He's building power—his hands are glowing, Nissa's mental voice was terrified. She knew what a power spell looked like as it gathered strength. Gren, Toff's old enemy, was prepared to kill all three of them. *Please, let our protection jewels hold,* Nissa sent up a silent prayer as she peered at Gren through the narrow space between Toff and Trik's shoulders.

* * *

Lissa's Journal

Everything seemed to happen in slow motion from that point forward. The Ra'Ak leaned back, preparing to strike. Rigo's claws slid out and someone ran around the Ra'Ak, his hands up and light forming around them.

Gren. Gren was still bent on killing Toff.

"Run!" I screamed at all my children. Three bursts of very bright light, much like old flashbulbs popping in rapid succession came, the store lights blinked on in the building and my half High Demon son in Full Thifilathi, roared as he charged the Ra'Ak.

Chapter 17

Zellar stared in disbelief. Every rumor he'd heard in the past concerning this child bore out his own theories—that a half High Demon would never turn. This one had turned. No matter what he did, now, no matter how strong the spell, Zellar would have no recourse against this one.

He still held hope, however, since this was a young and untried High Demon and Tandias was an experienced fighter. Zellar resolved to hold the shields and watch—as long as the battle remained in Tandias' favor.

* * *

Lissa's Journal
I kept more screams from escaping as the Ra'Ak charged Tory. Rigo, acting faster than I could think, rushed Gren.

Blood Reunion

Three flashes of light—likely from protection jewels worn by Nissa, Toff and Trik—had blown the Half-Fae back.

Tory's Thifilathi was now close enough to neutralize Gren's power, but the young Fae wasn't giving up his quest to kill Toff. Gren had only been knocked back temporarily by Nissa's protection jewels, a testament to the power he'd stolen from my planet. Rising swiftly, he lifted a metal rod from a rack to strike at Toff, Nissa and Trik. Rigo wasn't about to let that happen.

The noise, too, was deafening, as the Ra'Ak attempted to sink long, poisonous teeth into my son's Thifilathi. Tory roared and slashed out with huge, clawed hands. "Back out of the way," a hand and a familiar voice was pulling me away from potential danger—the Ra'Ak's body and his lethal, poison-tipped scales were threatening to roll in my direction while I dumbly stood and watched the monster battle my son.

Gren's blood, too, now drenched Rigo's right hand—the decapitation hadn't taken a blink to accomplish. Gren had no battle experience and he'd only focused on Toff, Trik and Nissa, never thinking an attack might come from behind.

"Daddy?" I blinked tears away as I stared at the one who'd come—Griffin. His eyes, normally a deep, hazel well of knowledge and experience, now held a wealth of pain I couldn't define.

"I don't have much time; I need to help my grandson, there. He doesn't have experience fighting Ra'Ak. I do. I've come from the future. Somebody found me and told me I had to come. I would have come anyway, but I can't deny the order I was given."

With that, Griffin turned to his fighting animal, a huge, brown and gold Gryphon, who leapt at the Ra'Ak, his sharp beak biting deep into the Ra'Ak's neck as the giant serpent snapped at Tory. The Ra'Ak screamed and swept his tail behind him, knocking deep piles of debris aside.

"Ry, Nissa, help me move the people," I shouted, running forward. With that first sweep of the Ra'Ak's tail, unconscious bodies were being buried beneath heaps of wreckage. I prayed that none had come in contact with the Ra'Ak's scales—that was a swift and painful death for most humanoids, even with a healer from the Saa Thalarr present.

* * *

Zellar muttered an expletive as the giant, mythical creature attacked Tandias from behind. Only one race held the ability to become Gryphon now. The gryphons had died out long ago; the Copper Ra'Ak had deliberately destroyed them.

With a Gryphon and a High Demon fighting him, Tandias had no hope of winning his battle. Gren was already dead; Zellar had witnessed the swift beheading at the hands of the vampire.

Knowing his demise was only moments away, Zellar did what came naturally to him. He folded as far away as he could and hoped the Gryphon wouldn't come hunting him afterward.

* * *

Lissa's Journal

Nissa, Toff and Trik were behind me as I rushed forward, ducking another sweep of the poisoned tail while Griffin and Tory continued their attack. Ry and Nissa, pulling together, used their power in tandem to lift debris away and dump it in a vacant corner.

Blood Reunion

Only people were left behind, littering the floor like scattered and forgotten rag dolls. Rigo joined us, gathering bodies and delivering them swiftly to the vestibule. At least the store's square entry was still standing and mostly in one piece.

Toff and Trik were working together, too, each grabbing an arm of the nearest unconscious person and pulling them to safety as the Ra'Ak's tail made another sweep, barely missing my children.

Griffin squawked as the Ra'Ak, bleeding gouts of greenish-yellow goo, leapt forward to snap at him. Tory took that opportunity to grasp the thick neck with his claws and squeeze.

"Look out!" I shrieked. I knew what was coming, but couldn't do a damn thing about it. The Ra'Ak's tail struck the ceiling as he went into his death throes, bringing ceiling tile and more debris raining down.

Nissa screamed and ducked as a metal beam almost hit her and Ry. Toff and Trik, who'd just delivered another unconscious body to the vestibule, turned swiftly as Nissa screamed. Toff, unmindful of the danger, ran toward Nissa, who'd dropped to the floor beside Ry.

Then the inevitable came. The Ra'Ak dusted with a boom and a powerful blast, with chunks rocketing outward at hundreds of miles per hour. Rigo snatched Trik back and dropped to the floor, holding the teen beneath his body. Ry threw a protection shield up, which encompassed him, Nissa and me.

The only one who wasn't covered in some way was Toff, who was halfway between Ry's shield and Rigo's protection. A chunk of Ra'Ak, larger than Rigo's fist, hit Toff in the head. I screamed as the blood flew and Toff dropped like a stone.

Chapter 17

The last thing I remember is the floor coming toward me at an unusually accelerated rate.

* * *

"Stand aside, this is why I came." Griffin shoved Ry and Rigo aside to get to Toff. "I was sent to do this," he added, kneeling beside Toff's unconscious body. Trik held Nissa against him nearby as she wept—Toff had tried to help her and he'd been severely wounded in the attempt.

The teen comesula had been struck when the Ra'Ak dusted and now Toff was unconscious on the floor, his head bleeding profusely. Griffin and Rigo knew it was a killing blow the moment they saw Toff's wound.

"What happened?" Drake and Drew, followed by Gavin, Roff, Tony and Karzac, appeared nearby. Roff moaned in agony as he dropped to the floor beside his son.

"Karzac, I need you to keep Toff alive until I can give him blood," Griffin ordered, ripping back a sleeve and extending his arm to Rigo. Rigo sliced Griffin's wrist as Karzac knelt beside Toff and placed his body in stasis.

* * *

Lissa's Journal
"My blood is a gift to you, Toff." My father's voice was the first thing I heard when I regained consciousness.

"What?" I struggled to sit up. Something was holding me down.

"Lissa, just lie still until Karzac can come." My vision swam, but I would recognize Gavin's voice and scent anywhere.

"What happened?" I lifted a hand to rub my forehead, still feeling dizzy and confused.

Blood Reunion

"Cara, Toff was hit when the Ra'Ak dusted. Your father is saving him the only way he can now be saved. He is too young for the turn, you know this."

"Lissy, Zellar managed to get away," Tony knelt with a sigh on my other side. "Drake and Drew say he was hiding in a corner, likely holding the shields up while waiting for Gren and the Ra'Ak to do the deed for him. When things started going downhill, he skipped out, just like the coward he is."

"Mom, will Toff be okay?" Nissa's voice was tearful. She and Trik now stood beside Tony, who was still kneeling beside me. Tony pulled Nissa against him and hugged her close.

"Blood of the Saa Thalarr is a wondrous thing, young one," Karzac moved Gavin over so he could put his hands on me. "Toff has received your grandfather's blood. He is stable and sleeping, now. We will transport him and your mother to Le-Ath Veronis as soon as I make this examination."

"Karzac," I begged.

"Lara'Kayan, I will check the child first," he assured me, placing hands on my belly. He bent his head and closed his eyes.

"What? What's wrong?" I struggled in Gavin's grip.

"Love, the child is fine. I hear his heartbeat. It is quite strong. Perhaps he enjoys excitement already," Karzac offered a lovely smile.

"Thank goodness," I muttered, and that's the last thing I remembered for a while.

* * *

"Daddy, when will we know something about Toff?" Nissa fingered her ring as she leaned her head against

Chapter 17

Shadow's shoulder. Shadow bent his head to kiss Nissa's hair.

"Cleo tells me that under normal circumstances, the recipient of Saa Thalarr blood sleeps for twelve hours before waking, healed of all their hurts. She says that because of Toff's special circumstances, he may sleep longer than that."

"What special circumstances? Is he going to be all right?"

"She seems to think so, yes," Shadow nodded, his gray eyes offering an unspoken promise to his daughter. "Karzac says that your mother will be fine, too. She was scared that you and your brothers might get hurt. Toff was the only one hit because he was outside your brother's shield."

"Yeah. I was scared, too, Daddy. There was so much blood."

"I know, baby." Shadow brushed a tangle of Nissa's hair away from her face. "But Karzac says Toff won't remember much. I think that's a good thing."

"Yeah."

* * *

Lissa's Journal

"Rylend Davan Morphis, for having the presence of mind and wielding sufficient power to hold back Ra'Ak dust, I promote you to Fourth Level Warlock." My grandfather, Wylend Arden, smiled at my son as they stood at the foot of my bed. Wylend had agreed to make the confirmation in my bedroom, because Karzac was being a curmudgeon as usual and refused to let me up for long.

A chain of gold squares, worth enough to buy Ry a house somewhere, was laid around his neck. Erland, who sat on the bed beside me, looked ready to pop buttons off his shirt, he was so proud. We both clapped loudly when Ry turned and grinned at us.

Nissa, too, was scheduled to receive a promotion to Fifth-Tier from Glendes, and that would come as soon as I was allowed out of bed. Roff was keeping me updated on Toff, who seemed to be going through some sort of change, although he and Karzac refused to tell me anything. They promised that I'd see for myself soon enough and I contented myself with that.

Trik, well, Shadow was proud of him, too, and planned to hand a certificate citing his bravery and a gold cuff holding a protection jewel he'd made himself to our adopted son on the same day Nissa received her promotion.

Garde had something planned for Tory, but everybody else except High Demons had been excluded. I resolved not to kick Garde's ass over it, no matter how much I wanted to.

* * *

"Torevik Rath, for bravery and selflessness, I award the King's favor and a grant of land on the Southern Continent," King Jayd placed a thick chain of gold about Tory's neck. "And as King of Kifirin, I proclaim you High Demon before Kifirin and all the Dark Worlds lying within his realm. You are bound to uphold Kifirin's laws that he has set forth, and defend them against any who come against him or his realm. What say you, High Demon Torevik Rath?"

"I solemnly swear to uphold the laws as written by Kifirin, Lord of the Dark Realm. I Pledge fealty to you, King Jaydevik, who rules under Kifirin, for all my life."

Tory knelt before Jayd in Jayd's throne room, where the likeness of several Kings, carved in black marble, stood behind the throne. Gardevik Rath, Jayd's Prime Minister, stood beside his brother's throne, smiling at his son.

I wish Mom were here, Dad, Tory whispered mindspeech to his father.

Son, this is a private ceremony. Only High Demons are ever invited, Garde replied. *You can show her your chain when I take you home.*

You and Uncle Jayd are invited for the ceremony at the next Council meeting, Tory pointed out.

Son, we'll discuss this later, Garde replied, ending the conversation.

* * *

Lissa's Journal

"Lissa, I wanted to tell you and Roff about Toff before he wakes." Griffin sat in my study, on one of my guest chairs. Roff had pulled another chair around my desk and now sat next to me. I could see he had mixed feelings about this meeting with Griffin, but neither of us could deny that Griffin had saved Toff's life.

The well of sadness was still in Griffin's eyes, too, and I was at a loss to explain it. This was still a Griffin from the future, and I wasn't sure how to deal with that, either. He'd appeared to me once before from the future, and I'd died not long after. Only with help from the Mighty Hand was I brought back at all.

"It was at the command of one of the Mighty that I came," Griffin muttered, lowering his eyes and staring at his hands. "Not the one you're familiar with, either," he looked up, then, hazel eyes studying my face to gauge my reaction. "Nobody ignores a direct command from one of them, although I would have come anyway. I owe Toff. And Roff," Griffin nodded in Roff's direction.

"The other things, well, the debt I owe to Trell has been paid—at least in part."

"Do you want to talk about that?" I asked.

"No. Please don't ask." Griffin wiped wetness from his cheeks. "And I ask you, if you see me in the here and now, that you say nothing to me. Sometimes, it really is better if you don't know. If you can't see it coming."

"I won't say anything," I promised.

"I will remain silent," Roff agreed.

"Thank you." Griffin whispered. "What I have to tell you about Toff is this; I was commanded to come and give him blood. I was also commanded to give him something else. It was a gift I carried that I never used. Your child," Griffin turned his eyes to Roff, "always wished for power like the Elemaiya had. Not only will he wake as an eighteen-year-old adult vampire, complete with genitalia and the wings guaranteed by his heritage, but he will also wake with the power I was born with, as King Wylend's half Karathian son. I believe Toff will be quite powerful when Glendes rouses that gift. I urge you to have Glendes perform the rite soon, before my father discovers this. He may demand that Toff be delivered to him so he can train the gift. Toff loves Nissa, and it will be a terrible shame if they are separated." Griffin rose.

"I am sorry. For many, many things," he nodded to Roff and me before he disappeared.

"Holy crap," I stared at Roff in shock.

* * *

Chapter 17

"Look, there's Mom." Nissa bumped Trik's elbow and he turned to stare. Ry and Tory, sitting next to Trik at the dinner table, turned as well.

"At least she's feeling better," Ry sighed as Queen Lissa entered the dining hall, closely followed by Roff. Someone else was with them.

"Oh, my gosh." Nissa scooted her chair back hastily.

"Nissa?"

He was beautiful. At least as handsome as his father, if not more so. Tall, too, with wings pulled tightly against his back. Toff's dark hair was brushed back from his forehead and his face split in a wide grin as he caught sight of Nissa. In seconds, she was running toward him, shouting his name. He caught her up and whirled her in a circle, making her laugh with joy.

"Well, I'll be filled with damnation," Ry exclaimed. "Do we know why this happened? Do we know how this happened?" Ry turned and stared at Tory and Trik.

"No idea, bro," Tory grinned.

"It's wonderful," Trik breathed. "Absolutely amazing."

"Your mother says Nissa may not date until she's fifteen, and will only be allowed to go on supervised dates until she's seventeen," Erland Morphis sat beside his son. "And if I know young people at all, everyone involved will immediately find a way around all that."

"I heard Zellar got away," Tory said, changing the subject.

"You heard correctly. But I have information that even your mother doesn't have yet," Erland added. "I'll tell her later. She's not the only one who saw Griffin before he left."

"What did he say?" Tory asked, curiosity getting the better of him.

Blood Reunion

"That Zellar is not her problem. That someone else will come who will make Zellar a target. Lissa has to put chasing Zellar out of her mind."

"Mom probably won't like that," Ry observed.

"Well, I have to convince her. To me, at least, it all makes a weird sort of sense. Look—Nissa's playing with Toff's wings."

Ry, Tory and Trik turned in their seats to see Toff's smile as Nissa carefully lifted a wing away from his body.

* * *

Lissa's Journal

Once Erland presented his case, I agreed with him. If Trik ever learned who his father was, it wouldn't be a good idea if I were the one who handed Zellar his death. I heard through some of Erland's less than savory contacts on Campiaa that Zellar had given up his idea of revenge against me and disappeared from everybody's radar.

I suppose that after he'd witnessed Gren and the Ra'Ak's deaths, he wanted no part of me anymore. Norian was still tracking him, but the trail had gone cold. I pushed the thought of it away as my pregnancy progressed.

I failed to understand, too, how Gavin still found me attractive after I was eight-and-a-half months along and waddling like a duck. Some of the others were disappointed when they learned who the father was, but I had a long life before me. They all had a chance, I think.

When my due date came and went, and then Christmas came and went, I started to worry.

"The child will come, have no fear," Karzac announced one morning. He was checking on me every day, which annoyed me no end.

"Gavin gets to carry the next one," I muttered.

"Lissa, the next one could be someone else's. That's a long list of mates you have," Karzac pointed out with a wicked grin.

"You know, you may be getting that sense of humor anyway," I tapped his chest. "Uh-oh."

"What is it?"

"Hey, you're the doctor here. I think I just wet the bed."

"Lissa, your water broke. We may have a baby before the day's out."

"Crap. And I wanted pancakes for breakfast."

* * *

Seven hours later, Gavril Tybus Montegue made his way into the world. I may have threatened Gavin several times while I was in labor, but he ignored my offer to remove certain parts of his body when a contraction hit.

I screamed and grunted and pushed, although Karzac only requested the pushing part. Karzac just shook his head at my yelling—apparently, he'd heard similar statements for more than fifteen thousand years.

I slept after holding my son for a little while, until someone touched my cheek.

"Hi," he said.

"Hi."

"How's the baby?"

"Fine. Has a good set of lungs, not unlike his father. Looks like when they want to yell, that's exactly what happens."

"Knowing Gavin, I am not surprised."

"Me either, actually."

"I heard that another one showed up." He changed the subject abruptly. I wasn't surprised about that, either.

"Yeah. That's what Belen says, anyway."

"No way to tell who?"

"Don't even know the sex," I sighed, struggling to sit up. He and I were connected, all right. Had always been connected. I lifted an eyebrow at my great-uncle. "You mean you don't know either?" I stared at him.

"We aren't supposed to know." He raked fingers through light-brown hair. "We're supposed to find one another, though, when the time comes."

"Well, I guess the time hasn't come yet," I pointed out. "Griffin did say that he was sent from the future, so this one could have bent time to get here. Come on, you know we're not prepared right now. And the third one hasn't shown up, yet."

"I guess you're right," he grinned.

I just want to go on record, too, and say that when one of the Mighty grins, it's like turning on the sun during a really dark day. Who knew, too, that at the end, I'd not only know one of the Mighty, I'd be related to him, too—at least in a corporeal sense. I grinned right back at him.

The End